Praise for *Rek*
the first book
FOUNTAIN CREEK (

D0453976

Alexander has written a charming historical romance that features
well-drawn characters and smooth, compelling storytelling that will
have readers anxiously awaiting the second installment of the
FOUNTAIN CREEK CHRONICLES. Highly recommended. . . .

—Tamara Butler, *Library Journal*
(Starred Review)

It's a pleasure to read this debut book. Rich prose, a realistic setting
and characters, and a compassionate story of love will keep you
turning the pages long into the night. . . .

—*Romantic Times* TOP PICK (4½ stars)

[A] tenderhearted story of redemption. . . . Rarely does a debut novel
combine such a masterful blend of captivating story and technical
excellence. Alexander has introduced a delightful cast of winsome
characters, and there's a promise of more stories yet to be told.

—Kristine Wilson, *Aspiring Retail*

Tamera Alexander has penned an *outstanding* debut lyrically rich in
life's lessons and faith in God's love, featuring two very likeable pro-
tagonists. It is generously peopled with memorable secondary characters this reader will be anxious to see in the future books of this
series. This is a novel that should easily find its way into your hearts
and onto your keeper shelves!

—*InspirationalRomanceWriters.com*

A beautifully written and anything-but-old-school inspirational
romance. *Rekindled* . . . is an examination of faith. Not only leaps
of spiritual fidelity, but also the faith in self individuals choose when
challenged to live their love, as well as their beliefs.

—Michelle Buonfiglio, Romance:
B(u)y the Book, *WNBC.com/romance*

Books by

Tamera Alexander

FROM BETHANY HOUSE PUBLISHERS

FOUNTAIN CREEK CHRONICLES

Rekindled

Revealed

Remembered

Fountain Creek Chronicles (3 in 1)

TIMBER RIDGE REFLECTIONS

From a Distance

Beyond This Moment

Within My Heart

TAMERA ALEXANDER

✦ FOUNTAIN CREEK CHRONICLES | BOOK TWO ✦

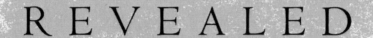

REVEALED

BETHANY HOUSE PUBLISHERS

Minneapolis, Minnesota

Published by Bethany House Publishers
11400 Hampshire Avenue South
Bloomington, Minnesota 55438

Bethany House Publishers is a division of
Baker Publishing Group, Grand Rapids, Michigan.

Printed in the United States of America

Library of Congress Cataloging-in-Publication Data

Alexander, Tamera.
    Revealed / Tamera Alexander.
        p.   cm. — (Fountain Creek chronicles ; 2)
    ISBN-13: 978-0-7642-0109-7 (pbk.)
    ISBN-10: 0-7642-0109-3 (pbk.)
    1. Ex-prostitutes—Fiction. 2. Widows—Fiction. 3. Fugitives from justice—Fiction. 4. Voyages and travels—Fiction. 5. Frontier and pioneer life—West (U.S.)—Fiction. I. Title.
    PS3601.L3563R48   2006
    813'.6—dc22
                                             2006019415

Then Jesus told this story to some who had great self-confidence and scorned everyone else: "Two men went to the Temple to pray. One was a Pharisee, and the other was a dishonest tax collector. The proud Pharisee stood by himself and prayed this prayer: 'I thank you, God, that I am not a sinner like everyone else, especially like that tax collector over there! For I never cheat, I don't sin, I don't commit adultery, I fast twice a week, and I give you a tenth of my income.'

"But the tax collector stood at a distance and dared not even lift his eyes to heaven as he prayed. Instead, he beat his chest in sorrow, saying, 'O God, be merciful to me, for I am a sinner.' I tell you, this sinner, not the Pharisee, returned home justified before God. For the proud will be humbled, but the humble will be honored."

LUKE 18:9–14 NLT

Colorado Territory, May 14, 1870
In the shadow of the Rockies

ANNABELLE GRAYSON MCCUTCHENS stared at the dying man beside her and wished, as she had the day she married him, that she loved her husband more. Loved him with the same desire he felt for her. Given all the men she'd known in her past, how was it that now, after meeting a truly good man who loved her despite what she had done and been, her whole heart wouldn't open fully to him? No matter how she tried.

Jonathan tried to pull in a deep breath. Sitting beside him, Annabelle cringed as she heard the air thread its way down his throat, barely lifting his barrel chest. The shallow movement of air rattled dull against the fluid in his lungs.

An ache started deep inside her. How could this solid mountain of a man have been brought low so swiftly? The chest pains had started without warning. But the fatigue and coughing fits Jonathan had experienced in recent weeks had taken on a deeper, more ominous meaning in past days. How could the heart of a man beat so strong and steady in one sense and yet be fading so quickly in another?

A breeze whipped the wagon canopy and drew Annabelle's focus upward toward a languid summer sun, hanging half masked behind the highest Rocky Mountain peaks. A burnt-orange glow bathed the vast eastern plains in promise of the coming twilight. The group they'd set out with from Denver nearly a week ago had waited with them a day, as was the agreement from the outset in such circumstances, in order to see if Jonathan would gain strength. But when Jonathan's pain worsened and the prospect of recovery dimmed of all hope, Jack Brennan reluctantly explained the group had to push on. They needed to make up for a late departure due to unaccustomed spring rains in order to reach the Idaho Territory before the first snowfall.

After several minutes Jonathan's breathing evened. His eyes were closed, and Annabelle wondered if he'd slipped back into sleep.

"You're as pretty as I've ever imagined a woman could be, Annabelle." His voice came gentle. He lifted a hand and brushed his fingers across her brow and down her cheek.

She gave a bleak laugh and shook her head at his foolishness. "Yes, I'm quite the catch. I'm glad you got me when you did, 'cause I had others waiting in line, you know." Seeing his mouth tip on one side, Annabelle smiled.

She'd been pretty when younger, but beauty was a trait that time—and choices she'd made—had erased from her features, and she knew it. A thin, puckered scar marred the top of her right cheekbone, etching its jagged flesh-colored path up her temple and into her hairline. She'd lived with it for the past fifteen years, and it served as a tangible memory of her first lesson in what some men who had visited the brothel termed pleasure.

"What do you think you're doin', Annie girl?"

Only then did Annabelle become aware of how she was tugging her hair down on that side of her face. Quickly dropping her hand, she laughed in hopes of covering her self-consciousness. The sound came out flat and unconvincing. "I'm just thinking about how you must find scars attractive, Jonathan McCutchens."

With accustomed gentleness, he caressed her cheek. "I find *you* attractive, Mrs. McCutchens. Only you."

His tenderness silenced the ready quip on her tongue, and the ache inside her rose to a steady thrum. She cared more for this man than she had any person in her life, so why couldn't she coerce her feelings to mirror his? For as far back as she could remember, she'd known that feelings in themselves couldn't be trusted. Emotions lived for a moment, then faded, and they even turned traitorous, given time. So she'd learned not to give them much heed. She'd simply expected things to be different between them as husband and wife.

She'd asked God many times to increase her desire for Jonathan. But apparently God didn't listen to prayers of that sort. Or maybe He just didn't listen to hers.

"Thank you for havin' me as your husband, Annie. I had such plans for us . . . for our child." He moved his hand, and she guided it to rest over the place where their son or daughter was nestled deep inside. Jonathan softly caressed her flat belly as though trying to comfort the tiny babe within.

His hand moved in slow circles over their child, and she shut her eyes tight as an unwelcome memory fought its way to the surface. She sat there, defenseless and mute, as years-old guilt and shame crept over her again. Pregnancies in brothels were common, but so were aloes and cathartic powders to terminate them, often leaving the girls who took them damaged beyond repair.

That she was carrying Jonathan's child was a blessing. That she was pregnant again . . . was a miracle.

"I'm so sorry to be leavin' you like this, Annie. It's not—" His deep voice broke with emotion. "It's not turning out like I planned. I'm sorry. . . ."

She shook her head and leaned close, bringing her face to within inches of his. "Don't you dare say that to me, Jonathan McCutchens," she whispered, laying a cool hand to his forehead. A sigh left him at her touch. "It's me who needs to be saying it to you. I . . ." Her mouth moved but the words wouldn't come. Knowing the path her life had taken, most people wouldn't understand, but intimacy of this nature still felt so foreign. "I'm sorry for not being the kind of woman you deserved. You're the—" She pushed the words past the uncomfortable knot in her throat. "You're the finest man I've ever known, Jonathan. And I thank you for . . . for taking me as your wife."

He sighed again, his gaze moving over her face slowly, as though seeing her for the first time. Or maybe the last. Then with a shaky hand, he motioned behind his head, toward the front of the wagon.

"There's something in my pack there. Something I wrote this mornin'."

Annabelle glanced over her shoulder, then back at him. Without asking, she guessed what it was. She gave him a knowing smile, attempting to draw out the truth.

Jonathan's focus remained steady.

His desire to provide for her was noble, but the loathing in his younger brother's eyes the last time they'd seen him in Willow Springs remained vivid in her memory. Eight long years had passed since the two brothers had last seen one another before that ill-fated reunion last fall. And Matthew Taylor's reaction that October night seven months ago made her certain that what Jonathan's letter likely proposed would prove impossible.

Remembering how the two men had argued, and having been the cause, Annabelle still felt the sting of it. Born of the same woman but to different fathers, the brothers bore little resemblance in stature or mannerisms. Or, it would seem, in disposition.

Matthew didn't know she carried his older brother's child, but that wouldn't change his feelings about her, or what she had been—what she would always be in his eyes.

With a small sigh, she shifted in the cramped quarters to retrieve the letter from Jonathan's pack. She didn't open the letter but laid it on her lap, then took Jonathan's hand and leaned close to whisper, "You know I can't do this, Jonathan. Even if we knew where he was, I couldn't ask Matthew for—"

His feeble grip tightened. "It's not for Matthew. The letter's . . . for the pastor." A fit of coughing ripped through his body, and he fought for breath, clutching his chest until it passed. "I wrote it all down—everything. The pastor will know what to do . . . how to help you."

Annabelle smoothed her hand over his, wondering how much time they had left together. One of the women in their group familiar with heart ailments had told her he would only live a day or two at the most.

Annabelle looked into her husband's face and glimpsed again what she'd seen that afternoon last summer when they first met in the front parlor of the pastor's home. Jonathan McCutchens was the most honest man she'd ever known. Not that she'd known many honest men in her life. Kind, with a gentleness that belied his solid six-foot-two-inch frame, and loyal no matter the cost, he'd made his own share of mistakes and was wise to the ways of the world, and to what she had been. He claimed to have loved her from the moment he saw her, and though she didn't understand how that could be, she cherished the notion that it might be true.

Studying him in the gathering shadows of the wagon, Annabelle wished she could see herself, just once, as Jonathan saw her. But she knew herself too well to ever imagine seeing anything other than a sullied and tainted woman when she looked in the mirror.

Something flickered behind Jonathan's eyes, and she coaxed her tone to resemble more of a statement than the question lingering in her mind. "So the letter's for Pastor Carlson, then."

He gave a slow nod. "I listed out everything. The ranch land waiting for you in Idaho, the bank where our money is."

Annabelle smiled. She'd brought nothing of material value into this marriage, yet he always referred to it as *our* money.

"There should be enough left for you to live on, after the pastor hires a guide to get you there. The ranch is still young, Annie, but it should do well. Carlson can—" His breath caught, and he choked.

Annabelle could hear the sickness filling his lungs as he coughed. She rolled another blanket and stuffed it beneath his head and shoulders in hopes of helping him breathe. "Shhh . . . I'll be okay, Jonathan. Don't you worry about me. I'll find my way," she assured him, wanting to believe it herself.

Jonathan's breathing came raspy and labored. His look grew determined. "Carlson can hire a trustworthy man to help you meet up with another group headin' north. The pastor'll take care of you. I'm sure of it."

His tongue flicked over chapped lips, and Annabelle moistened them again with a damp cloth. Though Jonathan harbored no ill feelings toward his brother— forgiving others seemed the same as drawing breath to him—she knew the wound from the broken relationship had left a scar. She wondered if Matthew realized how deeply Jonathan loved him, and therefore how deeply the rift had hurt him.

"I want you to have all that's mine, Annie. All that I wanted to share with you. Just take Pastor Carlson the letter . . . please."

Dabbing his fevered brow, she finally nodded.

She could tell he wasn't convinced. She'd never tried to deceive him—except for that once. But when he'd looked into her eyes that night, he'd known.

With effort, Jonathan raised his head. "Annabelle, give me your word you'll go back to Willow Springs and do as I've asked."

After all you've done for me, Jonathan. After all you've sacrificed . . . She managed a smile. "I give you my word, Jonathan."

He eased back onto the pallet, the strain in his features lessening.

"Would you like more broth? Or more toddy for your cough? I left it warming on the fire."

He nodded without indicating a choice. She knew which would help more and rose to get it. Climbing back into the wagon, Annabelle settled herself beside him and lifted spoonfuls of the warm honey-and-whiskey mixture to his lips. He raised a hand after several swallows, and she put the toddy aside.

Not a minute later, his eyes were closed. He was resting. For now.

She let her gaze move over his brow and temple, then along his bearded jaw. By outward standards, he was a plain man, not one who would turn a woman's head as he walked down the street. But thinking back on the more handsome men she'd known in her life, she realized that none of them matched the goodness of the man with her now.

She took his large work-roughened hand in hers. He didn't stir. *How I wish I desired you the way a wife should desire her husband, Jonathan McCutchens.* On their wedding night Jonathan had loved her as though she were a fresh young girl, untried and unspoiled. She'd sought to give him what she thought he wanted, fast and sure like she'd been taught, but she hadn't counted on his patience or his earnestness in seeking her pleasure. Never had she counted on that. And there, too, she'd disappointed him.

Though she'd only meant to spare him hurt, that was the first—and last—time she'd ever tried to deceive him.

She slowly let out the breath she'd been holding.

His hand tightened around her fingers, and only then did

Annabelle realize he'd been watching her. The depth of his obvious devotion, so thoroughly undeserved, sliced through her heart.

"Will you lie down beside me, Annie?"

A soft breeze flapped the wagon canvas. "Are you cold? Do you want another blanket?" She half rose to get it from a crate near the front.

He gently held her wrist and urged her down beside him. "No. . . . I just want to feel my wife beside me, for you to be with me for a while."

For a while.

The naked supplication of his simple request only deepened the thrumming inside her. *Until the end, is what you mean.* She lifted the cotton blanket and tucked herself against him. Careful not to put her weight on his chest, Annabelle pressed close, aware that he wanted to feel her body next to his. She strained to hear the beat of his heart, to memorize its rhythm.

"I need to say some things to you, Annie, and I—" Pausing midsentence, he held his right arm against his chest for a moment, taking in shallow breaths, before finally relaxing again. "And I know you're not keen on this kind of talk." His voice came gentle in the encroaching darkness, resonating through the wall of his chest in her ear. "My brother's young. He didn't have the best of chances when he was a boy, like I told you before. The hurt he took on then, bein' so young, stayed with him and went deep. I was older, so I think I bore it better than he did. He still has a lot to learn, but he will. You and me, Annie, we—" He gave an unexpected chuckle, and Annabelle remembered her reaction the first time she'd ever heard him laugh. Like a sudden rain shower on a dusty summer day, the sound shimmered through her and eased the burden of the moment. "You and me, we got an advantage over Matthew in a way. At least that's how I see it."

"Advantage?" She huffed a laugh. "Oh yes, I can see what an advantage a man like you and a wh—" His arm tightened around her. Annabelle caught herself and pressed her lips together. So often Jonathan could quiet a sharp reply with the slightest look or touch.

Jonathan was no saint and neither was she, but Matthew Taylor struck her as being an upstanding citizen, well liked and respected—despite his opinion of her. The few times she'd seen

Matthew when he was helping Kathryn Jennings, he'd been out-wardly cordial, but she'd read the truth in his eyes, reminding her of how far she'd fallen. What advantage they had over a man like him, she couldn't imagine.

As though reading her thoughts, Jonathan cradled her head with his hand. "We've both been forgiven so much, and we know it. We've seen who we are without Jesus, what we look like with all our stains coverin' us. Until a person realizes that, I don't think they can be near as grateful as they should be. They can't give other people the mercy they need because they haven't seen their own need yet."

Nestling into his embrace, she let the truth of his words seep into her. The pastor's wife back in Willow Springs had said much the same thing to her the morning Larson and Kathryn Jennings remarried a year and a half ago. Annabelle could still remember the chill of snow stinging her cheeks the day of their wedding, after Larson Jennings had, in essence, returned to his wife from the grave.

"Someone who has been forgiven much, loves much." Wisdom shown in Hannah Carlson's eyes as they watched the happy couple. "Take Larson there. He was so filled with jealousy and distrust that it nearly blinded him a second time to the woman God had chosen for him. But now his love for her is greater than it ever was because he's seen his own weaknesses, as well as Kathryn's. They love each other in spite of those weaknesses. Actually more, because of them—if that makes any sense." Hannah's gaze had moved to settle on her husband. "A couple can't really love each other like they're called to until they truly know each other, and a love like that takes a while to happen. Most times it takes a lifetime, coming slowly. Then at other times, the swift power of it can take your breath away."

Annabelle envied the love shared by Larson and Kathryn Jennings—the couple who first started her down this new road leading away from who she'd been to who she was now.

Someone who has been forgiven much loves much.

Hannah had eventually shown her the passage of Scripture where that thought came from, and Annabelle had tucked a hair ribbon between the pages to mark the spot. It was still there. She considered getting up to retrieve her Bible, but she didn't want to leave Jonathan's side. She remained quiet beside him, carefully tracking the slow rise and fall of his chest.

She reached up and fingered the thick brown hair at his temples, brushing it back with soft strokes. He turned his head into her touch, and she marveled again at the depth of his feeling for her. "You redeemed me, Jonathan," she whispered, not knowing if he could hear her or not. "You saw past what I was, who I've been." *Who you'll always be,* came a familiar whisper. But as Hannah had taught her, Annabelle pushed it aside. "You ransomed me in a way, Jonathan. I would've died in that brothel without you."

Then it struck her, and the irony of the moment crowded the silence of the wagon bed. Here they were, abandoned and alone on the prairie. She, finally ransomed and free of her old life, and Jonathan—the one who'd paid the price for her freedom—facing death. Life simply wasn't fair.

"I didn't ransom you, Annie girl. Jesus had already done that." He brushed her cheeks with roughened fingers. "All I did was love you, and that was the easy part."

As he cradled her clenched jaw in his palm, Annabelle fought the emotion rising like a vast tide from somewhere deep inside her. Tears were foreign to her. Traitorous in a way. She'd spent so many years hiding her emotions, masking what she felt in order to survive. But now the tears forced their way out, as if there were no more room inside to contain the pain. Or perhaps no reason left to hide them.

"You were exactly what I wanted, Annie, no matter that you might see me in a different way. You were honest with me from the start. I knew how you felt about me. But you see . . . a person can't give what they haven't got." His voice went low, his tone harboring not a trace of bitterness. "A person can't love someone else until they've learned to love themselves first. God dug that truth deep into me a long time ago. You have the seed to love inside you, Annie. It just needs some time to take root, is all. Guess I figured that"—he gave a slight shrug—" 'til that time came, I loved enough for the both of us."

Annabelle closed her eyes for a moment and let his words wash over her. Grateful for the kindness in them, she also felt a quickening inside her and couldn't explain the ache in her chest. Nor could she deny that part of what he implied might be true.

That she didn't know how to love . . .

"A person can't give what they haven't got." That's what he'd said, and how she wished she could change that, especially in light of how undemanding, patient, and giving he had been. Her relationship with him was so different from her experiences with other men.

As she tried to sift through his meaning, something buried deep inside her began to unfurl—like a wood shaving tossed into the flame, seconds before it's consumed. The response was unexpected, and unnerving. Knowing she might not get another chance to say it, she slowly rose on one elbow and looked into his face, hoping she could put into words what was inside her. "I've never done anything in my life that would warrant your affection, Jonathan." She rested a trembling hand on his chest and watched his eyes narrow ever so slightly. "But if I could, I want you to know . . . I'd spend the rest of it learning to love you the way I wish I could right now in this moment."

She blinked and a tear slipped down her cheek.

Jonathan's expression clouded. He stared at her, and then gradually the lines of his forehead smoothed, and he smiled. "There it is, Annie girl." He brushed away the tear, laughing softly. "I can see the start of it now . . . in your eyes."

Wishing that could be true, Annabelle leaned down and kissed his mouth, tasting the lingering honeyed whiskey on his lips. Despite her former profession, this kind of intimacy was foreign to her as well. She brushed her lips against her husband's again, seeing how much it meant to him, and silently conceding that he was probably right. About one thing anyway—she did have a lot to learn about love. How did one go about learning to love themselves? Especially someone like her. And didn't a person have to be worthy *first*, before they could be loved?

She tucked herself back against him, and for a while neither of them spoke. Then Jonathan sighed slow and long. The effort seemed to come from somewhere so deep within that Annabelle rose slightly to make sure he was still with her. Death was a familiar stranger. She knew the works of his hands, and though she'd never seen his face close up, she sensed his coming.

Twilight descended, and on its heels came darkness, but she could tell Jonathan was watching her.

"I love you, Annabelle McCutchens, and where I'm going . . . I'll go on lovin' you."

Rising up for a second time, she leaned close and placed a feather-soft kiss on his brow, her throat threatening to close. "I love you too, Jonathan." And she did, in her own way. "I'm grateful you made me your wife, and I'm privileged to be carrying your child. Be assured I'll make certain our baby knows what a fine man his father was."

Jonathan took a quick breath. "Or *her* father. I'd've been happy with either."

She smiled, then hesitated, sensing him drifting from her in a way she couldn't explain. An old fear rose up inside. "Are you afraid at all?" she whispered.

He looked over at her, his brow knit together. "Of dyin'?"

She gave a slow nod.

He answered after a minute, shaking his head. "No. But bein' this close to it makes me wish I'd lived more of my days with this particular one in mind." He grimaced, then let out a breath and grew relaxed once again. "I think maybe I would've done a better job at life that way."

They both fell silent.

Wishing she could do more for him, Annabelle lay back down and stared out the back of the wagon into the night sky. Stars like tiny pinpricks sprinkled the heavens, and the softest whisper of wind blew across their bodies. Though Jonathan *had* redeemed her in so many ways, her salvation wasn't found in the arms of the man who held her now, or in his love, however much that had rescued her. It was in another man, a man she'd never really met—not face-to-face, anyway—but she knew He was real.

She huddled closer to Jonathan and his arm tightened around her.

"You cold?"

She shrugged slightly. "Only a bit." Even now, he thought of her. What she wanted from Jonathan, what she needed before he died, was not the warmth from his body but the flame that flickered within him steady and strong. That made a man like him look twice at a woman like her. That made her want to be a better person just by being with him.

Annabelle awakened sometime later in the night with a feeling she couldn't quite place. A cool May wind whipped the wagon's arched canopy in the darkness and she lay still for a while, listening to the steady patter of raindrops pelting the canopy overhead.

She reached up to check on Jonathan. And then she knew.

Just as quietly as he'd come into her life, Jonathan McCutchens had slipped away.

Through the night, Annabelle lay fully awake, silent and unmoving, but with her body no longer touching Jonathan's. As the faintest purple haze of dawn hovered over the Colorado plains, she pulled the blanket up closer around her and curled onto her side away from him, unable to drive away the chill.

Night rains scented the cool morning air with an unaccustomed sweetness, yet it couldn't stave off the loneliness crouching in the world that waited beyond the confines of the wagon.

With the rhythmic beating of Jonathan's heart now silenced, she shamefully wished she could join him in death. At the same time, she could almost hear him telling her to press on, to not give up. But the imagined voice paled against the fear swelling inside her.

Closing her eyes, she forced herself to focus on what lay beyond the cocooned silence of the wagon, to the wakening life outside— the skittering of some small animal rustling in the sparse prairie grass, a gentle breeze flapping the tented covering, and the distant lowing of their milk cow, followed by a dissonant clang of the bell looped around the animal's neck. She had tethered the milk cow to the wagon late yesterday afternoon, but the animal's stubborn persistence had apparently won out. Again. Jonathan had been right— her square knot did need some practice.

Thinking of how he'd often poked fun with her on that point, Annabelle slowly drew herself to a sitting position and turned. With a most tentative touch she smoothed a hand over her husband's stilled chest, not allowing her hand to linger overlong.

She rose slightly to peer into his face. Peaceful, serene. And gone.

Her voice came out a whisper. "What will I do without you in this new world, Jonathan? How will I find my way?"

Truth was, she didn't want to. Not without him to guide her.

A dull ache running the length of her spine spurred her to shift positions, and she heard something crinkle.

The letter.

Holding the folded sheet of paper up to the early morning light, she made out the barest trace of Jonathan's script showing through the page. She could almost read the words. . .

It wasn't sealed. No envelope.

She squinted for a second, then slowly looked away from the page. She lowered the letter, folded the piece of paper yet again, and tucked it inside her shirtwaist. Along with the spoken promise to deliver the missive addressed to Pastor Carlson, she'd made an unspoken one of trust as well, and that vow to her husband was as binding in death as it had been in life.

ANNABELLE PUSHED HARD ON the southern route back to Pikes Peak, stopping in Denver only long enough to have Jonathan's body prepared for burial. She reached the edge of Willow Springs shortly before sundown on the seventh day after Jonathan's passing. Relief, mingled with sadness, settled in her chest upon seeing the familiar town again. She thought she'd left this place for good. The sight nudged her memory, and she recalled something Jonathan had said to her as they prepared to make their move to Denver last fall.

"You're a new woman now, Annabelle McCutchens. The people in Denver don't know us." He always spoke as though she'd been his equal, something she'd never gotten used to. "They'll assume you are what you look like on the outside, and they'll be right." He ran his hand lightly over her dark hair washed clean of the fraudulent scarlet dye and cradled her face, her blue eyes absent of smudged kohl. "They'll see what I see . . . a lady. A beautiful young wife comin' to town with her handsome catch of a husband."

Annabelle warmed at the memory and the playful wink he'd given her. In his final hours, Jonathan had made it clear that he wanted to be laid to rest here in Willow Springs. Driving on through town, toward the pastor's home, she couldn't help but think of how they'd met, courted, and married here near the banks of Fountain Creek. She was glad to bring her husband back to their first home, after all he'd done for her. But in her heart, she knew with certainty that Jonathan McCutchens was already Home.

She pictured the fine pinewood dresser he had fashioned as a wedding present now sitting abandoned on the plains, along with other items they'd been forced to leave behind. The afternoon Jonathan's chest pains had worsened, only days out of Denver, men from Jack Brennan's group had helped remove the piece of furniture from the cramped wagon so he could rest inside, sheltered from the heat of the day. With the load of provisions they carried, there still had barely been enough room for Jonathan. If he were here, he would tell her not to worry about the furniture, that it was foolishness to dwell on what she couldn't change. On what wouldn't last. And he would be right, of course. And yet . . .

She guided the wagon down a side street and, while still some distance away, spotted Pastor Carlson. He was chopping wood by the side of the white-framed house.

He turned and briefly glanced in her direction before refocusing on his task. Then he went absolutely still. His head came back around a second time. The ax in his hand slipped to the earth.

He met her at the wagon and helped her down, his expression mirroring question and concern. Patrick Carlson looked past her toward the wagon bed. Annabelle watched his face as the shock over hearing about Jonathan's death mingled with disbelief, then gradually gave way to grieved acceptance.

He took the letter from her hand, and as he read, his shoulders took on an invisible weight. "When did Jonathan write this?"

"The day he died. He made me promise to bring it back here to you." Accepting help, especially from men, had never been easy for Annabelle. Not that the pastor was any threat in that regard, but seeing the earnestness in his eyes, she almost wished she'd read the letter before giving it to him. "I hope Jonathan's request doesn't put a hardship on you, Pastor. Whatever he's asking, I'm sure he never meant it to be that."

"So you haven't read this?"

She shook her head and looked down at her hands clenched at her waist. "Jonathan never said I couldn't read it . . . exactly. He only said that he wrote it for you, so I figured I'd better not. . . ." At the touch on her arm, she lifted her chin.

"All this letter says, Annabelle, is that Jonathan loved you very much, and that he wanted to provide for you—"a soft question lit his eyes, followed by the faintest sparkle—"and for his unborn child."

Annabelle acknowledged the silent question with a nod. "We found out just before we left Denver. He was real happy over it."

"Hannah will be heartbroken to hear about Jonathan but will warm to sharing your news, Annabelle." He motioned toward the footpath leading to the house. "Are you . . . *faring* well?"

She walked beside him, hearing his unspoken question. "For the most part. I'd hardly know anything was different but for the tiredness and the queasy spells that have come in the past couple of weeks."

"Hannah will commiserate with that, no doubt. And she'll have far more advice than I'm able to offer on the subject." His tone grew somber. "I'm assuming Jack Brennan and his group moved on north?"

"After they waited a day with us. Jack Brennan's a fine man, and they did all they could." She told him about her trip back through Denver and how the undertaker had prepared Jonathan's body for burial, fashioning a coffin for him. "We can't wait much longer to bury him."

Patrick glanced back at the wagon. "I'm willing to take care of the details, if you're in agreement." At her nod, he took her arm and guided her up the porch stairs, then called out Hannah's name. He turned to her. "I'm sorry about Jonathan, Annabelle. Before either you or Jonathan knew of his fate, God's heart broke for you both. I hope you understand that."

Though she didn't, Annabelle nodded, hoping her lack of understanding didn't cancel out what little trust she did have. Until recently, she and God had never really been on good speaking terms, and even now, it felt as though she were the only one doing any talking these days.

The hinges on the front door squeaked, and she turned.

Hannah walked from the house, and the smile lighting her face gave Annabelle an unexpected sense of coming home. When Annabelle whispered the reason for her return, Hannah's arms came around her in a rush, drawing her close.

The safety of another woman's embrace—the wordless language it spoke—comforted Annabelle so deeply that the façade of strength she'd carefully constructed since Jonathan's death swiftly gave way.

Late that night under cover of dark, Annabelle left the Carlsons' house and skirted down the familiar back alleys of Willow Springs to the opposite side of town. When she rounded the corner and the brothel came into view, she paused. Seeing it again, especially at night, hearing the raucous laughter and tinny notes being pounded out on the parlor piano, gave her a strange sense of being out of place and time. The red-curtained windows spaced at even intervals along the second floor were dimly lit, but she knew the rooms weren't empty.

Not at this time of night.

Her gaze trailed to the third window from the back and she waited, watching. How many nights since leaving Willow Springs had she lain awake and worried about Sadie—the young girl whose past too closely resembled her own. Jonathan had purposed to buy Sadie from the brothel too, after Annabelle had asked him, but the madam wouldn't negotiate with Jonathan on that one. Fifteen years old, with waist-length jet black hair, smooth brown skin, and dark almond eyes, Sadie's youth and exotic beauty made her one of the most requested girls in the house. Annabelle didn't think she would ever understand the nature of some men and why they desired one so young.

The same gnawing ache that she experienced each time she pictured Sadie still trapped there started knotting her stomach, then slowly clawed its way to her chest. How could she have ever left that child behind? She'd protected Sadie—or tried to—since the girl arrived at the brothel almost four years ago.

Annabelle headed for the darkened back porch, determined not to make the same mistake again. The door wasn't locked.

Memories crouching just inside sprang full force when Annabelle stepped into the kitchen. Stale cigar smoke and the stench of soured whiskey seemed to ooze from the wood-planked floor and walls. An overly sweet bouquet of lilac, reminiscent of perfume the girls wore, hung in the stagnant air, but it couldn't quench the mingled scent of days-old sweat and humanity.

The place looked different to her—shabbier, older, more dismal than she remembered. Yet a quickening inside told her it wasn't the building that had changed.

"Betsy will be mighty glad to see you again. And mighty angry."

Recognizing the familiar voice, Annabelle turned to see Flora lounging in a kitchen chair, lace-stockinged legs propped on the edge of the table, cigarette in hand. The harsh-looking blonde smiled, but the smile held no welcome.

"Hello, Flora. Has Betsy missed me that much?"

Flora blew out a thin trail of smoke. Her eyes narrowed. "So where did you take her? Betsy had Gillam check every parlor house between here and Denver."

Annabelle frowned, not following.

Flora laughed as she stood, snubbing out her cigarette. "You always were a good liar, Annie. I'll give you that. Betsy cussed a blue streak when she found out she was gone."

"Found out who was gone?"

"Drop the act, Annabelle. We all know you did it with the help of that man you left with." She raised a brow. "We just couldn't figure out how you did it or where you hid her."

Uneasiness crept through Annabelle. She glanced toward the door leading up to the rooms. "What are you talking about, Flora?"

The suspicion weighing Flora's expression lessened. She pinned Annabelle with a look, then cursed softly. "You really don't know what I'm talking about, do you?" The hardness in her face melted away. "Sadie disappeared nearly four months ago. We all woke up one morning last January and found . . ." She hesitated, firming her lips. "We found blood on her pillow, Annabelle. Sadie was gone."

CHAPTER TWO

T HE NEXT DAY, WITH Hannah Carlson on her left and Kathryn Jennings close on her right, Annabelle stared at the fresh mound of dirt marking her husband's grave and felt a double sense of loss. First Jonathan, and now Sadie. She'd awakened during the night, regretting having ever left Sadie behind, wondering where the girl was now, if she was still alive. Odds were against it.

Thinking of Jonathan and what he'd done for her, what he'd tried to do for Sadie, Annabelle felt an invisible cord binding her to the place where she stood. *How could a man like you have chosen to love a woman like me, Jonathan?*

She tried to listen as Patrick paid tribute to her husband's life, but the sleeplessness of recent nights kept flanking his words with random thoughts. They crowded one atop the other like voices competing for her attention, blurring Patrick's testimony and dragging her back.

One man's voice, distant yet distinct, jarred her concentration more than all the others.

"She doesn't love you, Johnny. She's only using you, doing what she knows best. You know that, right?"

Annabelle hadn't been able to see Jonathan's face that night, but as she peered through the spacing of the roughhewn plank door she had glimpsed Matthew's, and the rage in his features only sharpened at the calm in his brother's response.

"I know Annabelle doesn't love me, Matthew. Not yet anyway, not like that. But she will, given time. I'm trustin' she'll learn to love me."

While Matthew's insults cut deep, the truth Jonathan spoke with such tenderness, about her lack of wifely love for him, knifed through her heart.

Matthew's dark eyes went near black, and his fists clenched at his sides. Annabelle stood in the shadows of the tiny back room, feeling every bit the whore Matthew Taylor claimed she was. How quickly the sins that had supposedly been washed clean in Fountain Creek so often crawled back over those muddy banks to slather her again.

That was the last time Jonathan and Matthew had spoken to one another, and what they'd said, the sound of their voices, was ingrained in her memory.

". . . and Lord, we commend the soul of Jonathan Wesley McCutchens to you today. You created the first man, Adam, from the dust of the earth, and our earthy bodies are like his, unable to live forever. But your Word promises that after a believer dies, you will give him a new body, a heavenly one, like Christ's. And holding to that, Lord, we trust that Jonathan is now clothed in that new body and that he's standing in your presence even now."

Silence followed, and Annabelle looked up to find Pastor Carlson watching her. He motioned, and she stepped forward with a clutch of purple and white columbine, nearly crushed from having been clenched tight in her hands. She laid them at the foot of the rough-fashioned wooden cross that bore Jonathan's full name.

Stepping back, she caught Larson Jennings focusing on something that lay just beyond her. She followed his line of vision to a grave not far from where they gathered. She knew the spot well for having visited there several times with Kathryn not so long ago. Larson knew it well too, for at one time the grave had been his.

Annabelle turned back to find Larson's gaze on her. Though fire had ravaged his face beyond recognition as the man he'd once been, his eyes still held the bluest hue she'd ever seen. Such a piercing, vibrant blue that it gave the impression he could see right into a person. Kathryn had once said as much. But the awareness in

Larson's stare didn't bother Annabelle in the least because Annabelle had seen into him the very same way.

He directed a crooked smile at her, and the unlikely kinship she shared with this man, who was as close as a brother might have been, swept through her.

After a moment, Kathryn leaned close. "We'll stay with you as long as you like, Annabelle. Take your time."

Annabelle squeezed Hannah's and Kathryn's hands in hers. "Thank you, friends."

She stared across the narrow valley bordered by mountains on the west to the clear bubbling waters thrashing between the banks of Fountain Creek. She let out a sigh. "Jonathan would've liked this spot." They had walked these banks together countless times. Birthed somewhere deep inside the Rockies, the stream, famous for its hot-spring pools, forged a path through miles of underground channels, braving twisting canyons and rocky plunges on its long trek to Willow Springs.

If only she possessed a smidgen of that river's fortitude.

There were thorns in her heart that nobody else knew about, but somehow Jonathan had known. He had seen. They'd torn at her flesh until her tears had finally flowed. Tears had fallen in her heart most all her life, but it wasn't until she'd seen them fall from Jonathan's eyes that Annabelle finally began to suspect that she was worth far more than the dark, craven whisper had once convinced her was true. Somehow this man had begun to piece together the jagged shards of a young girl's shattered life.

Though her life had just started over in some ways, a part of it was ending almost before it had begun. Yet standing here between these two women, sheltered by the memory of Jonathan's love that seemed to reach beyond the grave, Annabelle found she wasn't quite so frightened.

At the same time, she knew she couldn't stay here in Willow Springs. Jonathan had known that too, and in his kindness, in his dying hours, he had prepared a way for her and their child. Annabelle didn't know how she would get there, but she fully intended to finish the journey she and Jonathan had set out on together.

May 30, 1870

WHEN MATTHEW TAYLOR REACHED the outskirts of Willow Springs, he coaxed the tan gelding back to a canter, veered northwest, and urged the mount up a steep embankment. Despite the many miles put behind them in the last month, the horse made the rocky ascent with seemingly little effort.

Once they crested the ridge Matthew reined in and leaned down to stroke the animal's lathered coat. "Well done, fella," he whispered. "We're almost there." The gelding tossed its head and whinnied in response. Matthew's hopeful anticipation at seeing his brother again lessened when he thought of how he and Johnny had parted ways last fall. Prior to meeting up that night, if memory served, it had been eight years since he had last seen Johnny, and six years of silence had stretched between them since their last correspondence. Yet remembering all they'd been through together helped to ease the knot in Matthew's stomach. With a soft click of his tongue, he prompted the horse onward to their destination.

Newly leafed aspen flanked the seldom traveled back road leading to Willow Springs. Though Fountain Creek was masked from view by moss-grown boulders and clumps of willow trees, the familiar sound of the mountain-fed stream cascading over smooth rock bore strange resemblance in Matthew's mind to a deep murmured whisper of *Welcome home.*

In a way, he wished he'd never left this place and that Willow Springs *was* still his home. Just like he wished he could erase his decisions of the past year and start over again. At the same time, he felt a bitter tug inside him knowing that if any other choice had been left to him, he would never have returned here—not when considering why he left in the first place nearly eighteen months ago. His sole reason for coming back was to find Johnny.

He wanted to see him. *Needed* to see him again. Especially now.

Matthew heard a rustle in the brush behind him and pulled up short. He turned in the saddle and glanced behind him while pulling his rifle from its sheath. He waited, watched. When a small ground squirrel scampered from behind a rock, he shook his head at his own skittishness and continued down the path.

Thankful for every mile distancing him from the Texas border, he assured himself that he was still days ahead of whoever was following, *if* they were following. He had no doubt that his former associates in San Antonio would have carried through on their threat if given the chance.

His only question now was how far they would go to do it.

When the shack came into view, he reined in. The weathered structure looked much the same as it had the last time he'd seen it. Huddled against a rocky foothill and partially hidden behind overgrown brush, it sagged beneath the weight of too many harsh Colorado winters. The place appeared deserted. Matthew dismounted and scanned the surroundings, watching for signs of inhabitants. If someone were here, they would have heard his approach.

Staring at the partially open door, his thoughts drifted back to that October night last fall when he'd stood in this very same spot, his heart thudding. Same as it was now. A letter he had received from Johnny had prompted that visit. And as it turned out, the contents of that same letter were what compelled him back here today.

Johnny had been in Denver last summer buying cattle, and Willow Springs being the last place he knew regarding Matthew's whereabouts, he'd come looking for him. But Matthew was already gone by then. His brother got word from the livery owner in town that Matthew had headed south, toward San Antonio, so Johnny chanced writing him there.

Matthew still remembered his astonishment at recognizing Johnny's handwriting on the envelope.

Johnny wrote that he had sold the family farm in Missouri—four years earlier—and had purchased ranch land in Idaho.

Idaho . . . Matthew wondered again what had persuaded Johnny to do such a thing.

In the letter, Johnny had explained that since he'd used the proceeds from the family homestead to purchase the land in Idaho, half the land rightfully belonged to Matthew. Jonathan was inviting his brother to join him. But Matthew had very much doubted that the "ranch" Johnny had started in Idaho was anything to speak of. As far back as he could remember, his brother had always possessed a knack for stretching the truth. Besides, when leaving home at the age of fifteen, Matthew had knowingly relinquished any ownership to his birthright. And had done it gladly, without a backward glance.

Filled with painful memories, the homeplace hadn't been worth much anyway, and Matthew would have paid any price to be out from under Haymen Taylor's harsh hand. Which should have made what Johnny had penned next seem like a godsend.

Your father is gone now, Matthew. You can come home.

As though it were yesterday, Matthew recalled reading those words for the first time and remembered the oppressive weight being lifted from his shoulders. But the freedom that accompanied hearing that news had also been laced with regret. It wasn't right somehow . . . a son not mourning his father's passing.

The memory faded, and Matthew gave the partially-opened door a nudge. It squealed on rusted hinges. He scanned the inside. Empty. A scene flashed in his mind, and through a haze of memory, he pictured his brother standing there just beyond the doorway last October.

Johnny's face had reflected obvious surprise as he glanced from his new bride to his younger brother, his introduction still hanging between them. Johnny must have sensed something, because doubt flickered across his face. "Have you two already met somewhere?"

Hesitating, her eyes wide, watchful, knowing, Annabelle

Grayson finally stepped forward. She recognized him—there was no doubt in Matthew's mind. "I look forward to getting to know you, Matthew. I've heard wonderful things about you from Jonathan."

He'd known her instantly. Her blue eyes appeared less pronounced without the smudged kohl, and her hair was much darker than he remembered. She'd traded a tawdry gown for simple homespun, but it couldn't change what she was. Did Johnny really not know? Had the woman not told him?

Wordless, Matthew stared at her until her brow, formally heightened in greeting, slowly disappeared behind a mask of carefully guarded emotion. She truly expected him to act as if he didn't remember who she was?

Something skittered in the cobwebbed corner of the now-abandoned shack, and Matthew shook his head to clear the memory. Surely by now Johnny had come to realize what a mistake he had made by marrying a woman like Annabelle Grayson and had put her aside. If not, Matthew planned on making sure he did, for Johnny's sake as well as his own. Thankfully their mother, God rest her soul, wasn't alive to know just how low her eldest had sunk.

Decent women were scarce in the western territories. But even with all his faults, his older brother deserved better than a woman like her. Annabelle Grayson had tried to take advantage of Kathryn Jennings' friendship a while back, no doubt seeking money or whatever else she could get. Concerned about Kathryn's reputation, Matthew had done his best to discourage her befriending the fallen woman. People always tried to take advantage of Johnny's kindness too, but Matthew wasn't about to stand by and watch it happen to his brother with this conniving little whore. Not when it could end up costing him his own birthright. A birthright he ended up needing now, however paltry.

Without a backward glance, Matthew closed the door to the shack. Considering what to do next, he gathered the reins and led the way to a place in the creek where the watercourse curved and the stream ran smoother and deeper. Letting the animal drink, he laid his hat aside and slaked his own thirst, then cupped handfuls and poured the icy water over his face and throat, freeing a layer of dust and dirt from the day's ride. Maybe Johnny had thought to leave word for him in town. It was worth a try. After all, he'd come this far.

A half hour later, Matthew witnessed for himself that the seamier side of trade in Willow Springs hadn't wasted any time expanding its boundaries. He passed two new saloons and another two-story wood-planked building that resembled the brothel one street over. Iron bars guarded the bottom floor windows, and red curtains shaded the top. Three women lazed against the porch railing. They leaned over invitingly and called out to him as he rode past.

Before Matthew could catch himself, his gaze lingered, which only emboldened their efforts. Immediately, he looked away. And as he did, words rose to his mind that helped drown out their impudent invitations.

"Remove thy way far from her, and come not nigh the door of her house: Lest thou give thine honour unto others . . . lest strangers be filled with thy wealth."

At the remembered warning in Scripture, Matthew thought again of Johnny. He prayed he could talk some sense into his brother this time. Before *that woman* saw to Johnny's complete ruin.

Two men working together outside the Willow Springs Hose Company No. 1 looked up as Matthew passed. They waved, then went back to polishing the red-painted wheels of the hose cart. Commercial buildings crafted of wood frame and stone false fronts flanked the street, and at the corner stood the Baird & Smith Hotel. The hub of Willow Springs's business district had changed little in his absence.

Matthew stopped at the livery to board his horse, guarding his side of the conversation with Jake Sampson, the livery owner. Sampson knew more about the people of Willow Springs than anyone had a right to, and he shared what he knew with little prompting. Which might just prove advantageous today.

Sure enough, with casual mention of the couple's last name, Matthew had all the information he needed, or wanted, about the husband and wife he'd worked for when he last lived there. The man, his former boss, had been a good friend. Or so Matthew had once thought.

At midmorning the main thoroughfare in Willow Springs bustled with activity, and Matthew welcomed the anonymity of a crowd. The boardwalk swelled with people. Wagons lined the streets, workers loaded and unloaded freight. Women wrestled baskets in one hand and children in the other. Matthew opted to take the dirt-packed street instead and moved to descend the stairs. He knew where he needed to go next and headed in that direction, welcoming the chance to sort his thoughts.

He'd said things in anger to Johnny the last time they'd seen each other, most of which hadn't even been true. Matthew had simply been giving vent to his disappointment in his brother—and in himself. He had so much he wanted to say to Johnny now, and one thing stood out above the rest. He needed Johnny to know how much he appreciated all he'd done for him, especially when they were younger. Haymen Taylor's harsh discipline would have broken Matthew physically, just as the man's words had crippled his spirit. But Johnny had stood in the gap for him, time after time, and Matthew intended on making it up to him somehow.

Being six years older, a good three inches taller, and with a barrel chest that made him look even more imposing, Johnny had always been a bit of a hero to Matthew, despite their differences. Matthew admired his brother in many ways, yet he'd never told him that outright. Their mother had remarried after Johnny's father died, and according to Johnny, her second marriage had been a hasty one. Soon after, their mother became pregnant with a second child—with him. Laura McCutchens Taylor hoped this new man in their lives would offer the financial stability she couldn't provide and that he would be a good father to her two sons.

Both of her wishes had been met with disappointment.

Spotting the post office ahead, Matthew stepped up to the edge of the boardwalk and waited for the foot traffic to pass. Then he entered and closed the door behind him, amazed at the sudden quietness without the outside noise. He took a place in line and spotted an announcement board on the wall a couple of feet away. One advertisement in particular caught his eye. Two words written in capital letters across the top immediately drew his attention.

He stared, letting them sink in. He read the next few lines, then reached over and yanked the handwritten slip from the billboard.

Stepping back into the queue, he read the notice again and weighed his options.

The advertised job would pay well and offered guaranteed wages. A third on hire, the rest upon reaching the destination. The amount listed wasn't enough to erase what he owed, but it would certainly bring him a good sight closer. And the job would keep him moving in the right direction—north, and as far away from Texas as he could get.

A month had passed since he managed to disappear one moonless night from the town of San Antonio. Pushing north, he hadn't lingered in any one place more than a night or two, skirting the larger towns and staying only long enough to chop firewood or repair fencing at an outlying homestead in exchange for a meal. But no matter how many miles he put behind himself or how many excuses he piled in his favor, he couldn't outrun his guilt.

He'd made poor choices since leaving Willow Springs, and he knew it. He simply needed more time to get together the money he owed. Time the men in San Antonio hadn't been willing to give.

Matthew heard the post office door open behind him, and a tingle of awareness prickled up the back of his neck. In a move that was becoming disturbingly familiar, he slowly turned toward the two women who had just entered, one of them holding a small girl in her arms, then to the man now filling the doorway.

The stranger locked eyes with him, and Matthew's mouth went dry.

If the guy was wearing a badge, his black duster hid it from view. But his solemn stare was enough to prod Matthew's guilt until Matthew felt certain his expression alone would give him away. He forced himself to hold the man's gaze for a few seconds, then slowly faced forward again. He spied a second exit behind the mail counter, roughly twelve feet away. He'd have to clear the tall counter, but that was doable, given the alternative. Wishing he knew what was happening behind him, he listened for the man's approach. Then the woman directly in front of him turned and gave a sudden gasp.

Matthew tensed, fisting his hands in readiness.

"James . . ." The woman took a step toward the door. "I thought we were supposed to meet at Myrtle's. I'm not quite done here yet."

A long pause. "I got done early and thought I might catch you here," the man finally answered.

Slowly, Matthew let out the breath he'd been holding. His eyes closed briefly as tension ebbed from his body. Hundreds of miles stretched between him and San Antonio, but still he couldn't shake his sense of being followed. Moving forward in the queue, he chided himself for being so jumpy. He suddenly noticed a cluttered board that ran half the length of the post office wall, and the voice of reprieve inside him fell silent.

Pinned along the top and sides of the board, in no apparent order, were charcoal-drawn likenesses of men. They stared back at him, their hollow eyes silent in pronounced guilt of the crimes written beneath their names. Matthew slowly scanned each likeness, grateful when he didn't see a single familiar face among them. Swallowing with effort, he suppressed an unmanly shudder.

Behind him, a woman softly cleared her throat. Matthew looked up and realized the queue had advanced in front of him yet again. He moved forward.

He shifted his weight, weary from weeks of riding and bothered by the reminder of why he'd originally left Willow Springs a year and a half ago. At the livery that morning, casual inquiry to Jake Sampson had provided the answer to some of his lingering questions.

Apparently Larson Jennings' once-failed ranch was going to succeed, and Larson and Kathryn were expecting their second child come fall. Hearing the news stirred mixed emotions inside him. He once considered Jennings to be his friend, but the bitterness of betrayal tinged any thought of his former boss now. Matthew bowed his head.

"Can I help you, sir?"

A feminine voice drew him back. Matthew stepped to the vacant window. With any luck, the woman behind the counter would provide him with the information he sought. "Yes, ma'am. Would you please check and see if you're holding any letters for a Mr. Matthew Taylor?"

The clerk held his gaze briefly, repeating his name, before leafing through the drawer of mail beneath her counter. "I'm sorry, but we have nothing under that name, sir. Were you expecting something important?"

Matthew nodded and pushed up the brim of his hat in order to see her better. "It might've been sent a few months ago. I've been away for a while. Or it could've been mailed from here to San Antonio and then returned. Is there anywhere else you could check . . . in case it was put aside?"

A slow smile curved the corners of her mouth, and gradually Matthew became aware of her interest. She gave a slow nod in answer to his question. A dark wayward curl brushed against her cheek, and he responded to the twinkle in her eyes. She was attractive, and he'd wager from her manner that she was a lady on every count.

As though she could read the thread of his thoughts, a rosy blush deepened her cheeks. "I'd be happy to look in the back for you, Mr. Taylor. If . . . you have a minute."

"I do," he answered, smiling. "And thank you. I'd appreciate that." He watched her go, absently fingering the advertisement in his hand. He glanced at it again, and as if the slip of paper could offer an opinion on the subject, it seemed to confirm the fact that he'd be moving on again, soon. And though tempted to pursue this lady's wordless invitation, Matthew knew better. He stuffed the paper into his shirt pocket for safekeeping.

She returned minutes later, empty-handed, offering an apologetic shrug. "I'm sorry, but there's nothing there either."

He hesitated. Maybe there was a different way to go about this. "Could you tell me if you have a forwarding address for a Mr. Jonathan McCutchens? He had a place here up 'til a few months ago." Although Matthew would hardly call the two-room shack where his brother and that . . . *woman* . . . had lived a real dwelling.

The clerk was already reaching for a long slender box. "Let me see . . ."

Matthew waited as she thumbed through the pieces of paper. Johnny had always been the more impulsive one. Some people might have labeled him foolhardy, but Matthew actually admired Johnny's sense of fearlessness and had come to believe that sometimes his brother, though good-intentioned, simply didn't think things through well enough before acting. Most of the time it ended up working for him somehow.

Growing up in the wake of Johnny's missteps, Matthew had determined to live more cautiously, not to make the same mistakes, and he'd managed to carefully maneuver the pitfalls that Johnny had fallen prey to. Namely, with women. Even as a young man, Matthew realized that God had given him an extra measure of restraint. And for that, he was grateful. Not that he didn't struggle with natural desires. He did.

There were many times when the thought of taking a wife, of sharing that union with her, would consume nearly every waking thought. The desire within him was strong, yet he knew God intended for that desire to be met in marriage. And he'd determined long ago to wait—despite the struggle and despite Johnny's merciless ridicule about it when they were younger.

Besides, it wasn't like he had anything to offer a woman right now. Especially one who appeared as good and kind and deserving as the young lady staring back at him from behind the counter.

She shrugged her slender shoulders. Her smile dimmed, but not her sparkle. "I'm sorry, but if you'll check back with me tomorrow . . . maybe something will have come. . . ."

"Thanks just the same, ma'am," Matthew said, suddenly eager to leave. "I appreciate your help." He tipped his hat and didn't look her in the eye again.

He stepped outside to the boardwalk only to see Hudson's Haberdashery across the street—the shop where Kathryn Jennings had once worked. He turned and strode in the opposite direction. As he rounded the corner, the scent of baking bread and roasting meat taunted his appetite, and hunger gnawed his belly—just as the failure of recent months gnawed his bruised pride.

Pulling the piece of paper from his pocket, he moved off to a side alley to read it again. The name on the advertisement seemed familiar to him for some reason, but he couldn't quite place it. He'd always believed in signs, and though it had been a while since he'd felt that inner prompting, surely this was God paving a new path for him, giving him a second chance.

Matthew removed his hat, frowning at the road dust now coating it. He tunneled callused fingers through his hair. It was too long for his own taste, and a month's growth of beard gave him an untamed look he doubted would be of much assurance to the person who had placed this ad. Counting the last few coins in his pocket, he watched his list of options narrow with a pang of clarity.

Two hours later, in his last change of clean clothes, he stepped from the barbershop. He ran a hand over his smooth jawline and inhaled the scent of bay rum. Shaven, shorn, and bathed, Matthew made his way back across town to the address listed on the advertisement. With no money left to satisfy his hunger, he stopped by Fountain Creek and drank deeply of the cool waters until the pangs in his belly eased.

His luck was about to change. He could feel it. After all, how difficult could it be to escort one widow woman to the Idaho Territory?

CHAPTER FOUR

T HE PLAYFUL INTIMACY OF the scene made Annabelle feel as though she should get up from the breakfast table and leave, yet she couldn't. It was like a compelling story she couldn't put down. She watched Patrick, then Hannah, to see what would happen next.

"But it'll only take a few minutes, Hannah, and I'd really like your thoughts." Bracing his long arms on either side of his wife from behind, Patrick tossed Annabelle a smile as he cornered Hannah against the washtub in the kitchen. He leaned close. "Please, it's a difficult subject to broach and it'll only take a few minutes."

Hannah swished her fingers in the soapy water and flicked it over her shoulder into his face. "I'm busy with the dishes, Patrick. I can't listen to it right now. Maybe later."

He nuzzled her neck. "Come on . . . my sermons are so much better with your input. As a woman, you have insights I don't have."

Annabelle watched, mesmerized. Hannah didn't stiffen at Patrick's touch, nor was there the least sense of her having to endure his hands on her body. Quite the opposite was true. Even Hannah's protests seemed like an invitation.

Hannah's mild objections finally dissolved into giggles as she turned to face him. Her arms encircled his waist as he pulled her close. "And what's the *difficult* topic for this week, Pastor Carlson? How to live with a pesky preacher?"

Apparently thinking he'd won the standoff, Patrick reached for the stack of papers on the kitchen table. But when he did, Hannah scooted out of reach.

With the table as a safe barrier between them, she winked at Annabelle. "I pose my question again, Pastor Carlson." Her voice turned playfully formal. "What's the topic that I, being of the female persuasion, have such incredible insight into?"

Patrick gave her a wicked grin. "The deceptive nature of sin."

Hannah's jaw dropped open in teasing shock just before her laughter erupted.

Annabelle couldn't help but join them both, giggling. She marveled at their ease with each other and the way Hannah looked at Patrick. The love between them was almost tangible, and the intensity of it caught Annabelle off guard.

Her throat tightened in response, her smile faded. Would she ever look on a man the way that Hannah looked at Patrick, or so strongly desire a man to touch her like that? To caress her like Patrick surely did Hannah when they were alone? And why hadn't she felt that with Jonathan? Just pondering the thought felt traitorous to his memory, and Annabelle bowed her head in response.

Then she noticed the silence in the room and slowly looked up.

Hannah's eyes brimmed with unshed tears. "Oh, Annabelle, we're sorry." Her voice wavered.

Sick regret lined Patrick's expression. He came to kneel beside her. "Please forgive us for joking like that. On my honor, I never intended to hurt you—neither of us did. Women are no more prone to sin than men are. I was only teasing Hannah because she wouldn't listen to my—"

Annabelle raised her hand, realizing the misunderstanding. "No." She shook her head. "That's not it at all. Nothing either of you said hurt me." She managed a smile at Patrick, then included Hannah. "It's just that . . . what the two of you have . . ." She swallowed, hoping to loosen the knot in her throat. "I've never . . . I've never known that before." Annabelle hesitated, not wishing to dishonor Jonathan's memory in any way. "Jonathan and I . . . It simply wasn't like that between us." She took a quick breath. "I feel selfish

even *thinking* these things much less speaking them aloud, but . . .
I guess I'm wondering if I'll ever . . ."

Hannah came and put an arm around her shoulders. "Annabelle,
it's not selfish at all to want to be loved. And of course you'll
experience this. You would have had this with Jonathan. I'm sure
of it. The love between you two just didn't have time to grow—
that's all."

Patrick quickly agreed, but Annabelle couldn't help but wonder.
What she and Jonathan had lacked in their marriage went far
deeper than the simple passage of time or a husband and wife
becoming more familiar with each other.

With deepening clarity the same truth that gripped her heart the
night Jonathan passed away suddenly tightened into an awful fist.
Physically tensing, she realized, without any doubt, that the fault of
what had been lacking in their relationship—though Jonathan had
never once cast blame—lay with *her*, rather than with them as a
couple, as she'd once thought. Would the life she had once lived
render her forever incapable of truly loving a man that way? Or of
allowing herself to be loved?

Or could what Jonathan had said be true. *"A person can't love
someone else . . . until they've learned to love themselves first."* Fragile
hope stirred inside her at that one key word. Jonathan had known
she wasn't capable of loving him like that even before she had. And
still, he'd married her. But didn't a pupil need a teacher in order to
learn?

A dull ache started in her stomach, constricting to a spasm
that had become more familiar in recent days. She stood, a hand
cradling her waistline. "Patrick, I'd be happy to listen to your
sermon . . . later, if you want me to." Her body flushed hot, then
cold. An unsettling sensation quivered her stomach. She moved
toward the back door, shooting Hannah a look. "But first I need to
take a quick walk out back."

Hannah nodded, understanding softening her gaze.

A knock sounded from the front porch.

Their collective attention flickered in that direction. Hannah
gently pushed a dishcloth into Annabelle's hand, motioning for her
to go on. "I'll get that, and one of us will be out to check on you in
a bit."

Annabelle let the screen door slam behind her, but above its clatter she heard the insistent, repeated knocking coming from the front door. Whoever was waiting on the other side . . . patience certainly wasn't one of their virtues.

A while later, aided by the fence post at the furthermost edge of the Carlsons' garden, Annabelle stood slowly, thankful the nausea had passed. She held a hand to her forehead a moment longer until the dizziness lessened, then blew out a breath. Inspired by spring rains, wild flowers flourished in the field behind the Carlsons' home, and Annabelle feasted her senses, turning her face into the warm breeze.

If the past week was any indication, her pregnancy was going to be a rocky one. But she would never wish away this baby, this lasting thread tying her to Jonathan. If the baby was a boy, he would carry on Jonathan's family name. Annabelle placed her hand over the smooth front of her skirt. Whether boy or girl, with God's help, the child would be taught Jonathan's faith. She would make certain of that.

She couldn't imagine adding to her present nausea the constant jostling and bumping of a wagon over the nearly one-thousand-mile trip to Idaho. Yet she waited every day for an answer to the ad Patrick had penned for a hired guide to accompany her. If someone didn't answer soon—

"Mind if I join you, ma'am?"

Lost in another world, Annabelle startled at the deep voice behind her. She turned and couldn't keep from smiling at the comical expression masking Patrick's face.

"I'd be much obliged, ma'am, if you'd let me keep company awhile with you. Seein' as my horse done died on me and I walked the last twenty miles barefoot."

Her smile widened to a grin. Patrick's imitation of a languid cowboy, made complete by the tipping of his invisible hat, coaxed a laugh from her—and a confused squint.

He grinned and shrugged his shoulders as if to say he didn't know why he was doing it either, then glanced back to the house. His look turned sheepish. "Mrs. Cranchet just stopped by for a visit."

"Ah ..." Annabelle nodded, remembering the elderly widow who often dropped by unannounced with "divine inspiration" for Patrick's sermons. She'd overheard the woman on two occasions while in the Carlsons' home, and from what Annabelle gathered, the topics were never things that Mrs. Cranchet struggled with herself. Mainly they came in the form of veiled gossip. *"Fred Grandby was seen going into the saloon last Friday, so you might want to teach on the evils of liquor,"* or *"Martha Triddle has been sporting too many new dresses of late, highly fashionable ones at that, so a lesson on vanity would be most timely, Pastor Carlson."*

Annabelle worked to lend sincerity to her tone, while trying to hide her smile. "But Patrick, I thought Mrs. Cranchet normally came to see *you.*"

A faint blush accompanied his wince, and Patrick shrugged again. "The honest truth?" He arched a single brow.

"That's the best kind."

"I'm just not up to listening to her sermon suggestions today. Not with tomorrow's sermon still at loose ends."

Annabelle noted the papers in his hand. "I see. So Hannah bailed you out again, huh?"

He nodded. "I'm married to a saint. The most wonderful woman a man could have."

"That she is, my friend. And she did pretty well for herself too."

Patrick smiled a wordless thanks. "You feeling better?"

"Much. For now, at least." They chatted for a moment, and then Annabelle took the opportunity to ask him about the advertisement.

"Still haven't heard anything, but I'm sure we'll get a response soon."

If only she shared his certainty. "It's the end of May. If I can't hire a guide in the next few days and leave soon, it'll be nearly impossible to catch up with Brennan's group. Besides, I hear we need to allow enough time to get there and get settled before the first snowfall." The option of traveling alone with a man she didn't even know for the entire trip to Idaho Territory was out of the question in her mind. She knew, better than most women, the basic nature of a man. What was more, she knew Jonathan would have been against it.

"I checked around town yesterday." Patrick ran a hand along the rough pine fence railing. "There's not another group scheduled to leave from Denver for the Idaho Territory 'til next spring."

Upon hearing that, Annabelle's determination to make this journey took deeper root. After all, she had promised Jonathan, and this had been his last wish for her and their child.

A stinging reminder of the reason she needed to leave Willow Springs rose in her memory, further deepening her resolve. The cool looks she'd drawn from people in town the other day, followed by their not-so-hidden whispers, hurt far more without the invisible protective wall she'd spent years building. For an instant, she'd been tempted to tell the people what hypocrites they were, especially two of the men she remembered entertaining at the brothel. But in the end, she couldn't do it.

She wouldn't reconstruct that wall of isolation, not when hands of love and friendship had worked so hard to tear it down, brick by stubborn brick. Not when she remembered Jonathan and the grace he'd introduced into her life. Still, it baffled her how folks could read the same book and come to such different conclusions. Funny how the Bible seemed to soften some while toughening others.

"I understand what you're saying, Patrick, but Willow Springs can never be my home again. I can't stay here—not even if it's only until next spring."

Looking as though he wished he could change her mind, or perhaps the circumstances, he finally nodded. "But if we don't get a response soon, you might have no choice. Traveling alone with a guide until you catch up with Brennan's group is one thing, but traveling alone with a man you don't know for three months or more is another. I don't think that would be wise, Annabelle." He paused. "If I might be so bold, you're an attractive woman, and though it's not plain to see yet, you're carrying your husband's child. I feel honor bound to Jonathan to make sure you're both safe."

The intensity in Patrick's eyes caused Annabelle's own to sting. "Thank you," she whispered. "That's one of the kindest things anyone's ever said to me."

"Jonathan loved you very much. He was right to put conditions on who he wanted to escort you there."

She frowned. "What do you mean?"

"In his letter." Patrick's brow wrinkled. "You haven't read it yet?"

At the shake of her head, he motioned for her to stay there. He returned minutes later and held out the letter. "I apologize for not sharing this with you earlier. Forgive me."

Patrick's expression was pure kindness and seemed to see straight into her heart. She wondered if this was how Jesus might've looked at people.

"Jonathan McCutchens was right to have loved you as he did, Annabelle. I'm sure he wouldn't mind if you read this."

She took the letter.

"Patrick! Annabelle!"

They both turned to see Hannah hurrying toward them from the house, a spark of urgency speeding her step. "There's someone here to see you, Patrick. And no, it's not Mrs. Cranchet." She took a second to catch her breath, then grabbed Annabelle's hands in hers. "It's a man. And he says he's answering your ad!"

H E's WAITING ON THE front porch." Hannah's tone conveyed her hopefulness about the prospect, but Annabelle's stomach somersaulted at the news.

A mixture of excitement and alarm raced through her. She hadn't considered what she would ask about a man's experiences or references, or how she would gauge whether he was qualified.

Patrick pressed his sermon notes into Hannah's hand, then turned to Annabelle. "With your permission, I'll interview him first, just to get a feel for how he might work out." He waited, his expression holding a question.

Relieved, Annabelle nodded.

Patrick glanced at Jonathan's letter still in her grip and that expression of kindness moved into his eyes again. "I'll see if he meets Jonathan's criteria."

Eager to read the letter, she agreed. "I'd appreciate that. Then, if you think he does, I'd like to speak with him before we hire him."

As Annabelle watched Patrick and Hannah walk back to the house, she couldn't help marveling at how she had reacted to Patrick's suggestion that he interview the man first. She once would have balked at such an offer. Annabelle *Grayson* had spent the majority of her life shunning men's help, doing everything within her power to avoid being dependent on anyone— especially a man.

Yet in the past year, Annabelle *McCutchens* had learned to open her heart. Granted, those old defenses oftentimes rose up without warning, but the past months of knowing Jonathan, of learning—in gradual increments—to trust, and finding that trust confirmed, had softened her. She liked the change.

———

As soon as Matthew spotted him through the screen door, he realized why the name on the slip of paper had sounded so familiar. He took a step back as the pastor pushed open the screen door. "Pastor Carlson, I appreciate you meeting with me, sir." He extended his hand and introduced himself.

"Mr. Taylor, good to meet you." Carlson had a solid grip and a smile that encouraged trust. "My wife tells me you're answering the advertisement. I appreciate your interest in the job." He motioned toward one end of the porch.

Matthew opted for a chair by the porch swing, preferring something stationary. His nerves were jumpy enough from thinking about the interview on the way over. This job was an answer to prayer—he could feel it. He had the necessary experience, and if he could just make it past this initial interview with Pastor Carlson, he felt certain he could win the widow's favor and the job would be his.

He perched his hat on the porch railing and leaned back in the chair, not wanting to appear overeager. "I'm definitely interested in hearing more about it, seeing if it'll be a good fit for me. I think the timing could be right, and I've had experience on the trail—that's for sure."

"You look familiar to me, Mr. Taylor. Have we met before?"

"Call me Matthew, please. And both yes and no to that question. I visited your church before, a while back, but we've not formally met."

"Ah . . . thought so. I rarely forget a face, especially those of people who've fallen asleep during my sermons."

Appreciating Carlson's matter-of-fact delivery, Matthew also caught the subtle gleam in his eyes. "I only slept through the boring parts that morning, Pastor. I promise." Then he smiled. "Had me a right good nap though."

Carlson feigned being stabbed in the heart, then sat up straight again. "You've been talking to my wife, Matthew. Sounds like something she would say."

They both laughed, then exchanged pleasantries before finally turning to the business at hand.

The pastor leaned forward in his chair. "Let me take a few minutes to tell you about the situation. I'm meeting with you first, Matthew, as a courtesy to the widow on whose behalf I placed the ad. She's been through a very difficult time, and I offered to help her by speaking with all interested parties first, asking them some general questions, making sure they had the experience the job requires."

Matthew nodded, attentive to the phrase *all interested parties.* How many other men was he up against?

"So why don't you tell me a little bit about yourself? Where you're from, what jobs you've had . . ."

"I'm originally from Missouri," Matthew started. "Left there back in '52 and have lived out West ever since. I've traveled throughout the western territories, been to California and Washington too." He summarized his travels, skimming over his time in Colorado, knowing that if Carlson asked where he'd worked in Willow Springs, Larson Jennings would likely not give him a favorable recommendation. Not after what had happened with his wife, however innocent the circumstances had been. "I know the Colorado Territory like the back of my hand, and the land up north through the Wyoming and Montana Territories."

"I hear that's pretty country up there."

"Mighty pretty, with lots of space for a man to breathe." Matthew raised a brow, remembering the bitterest December he'd ever experienced while he was in Montana. "But it gets cold in the winter, with some powerful north winds . . . snowdrifts that'll cover a cabin in no time." He glanced past the porch to some horses grazing in the side field.

"Do you get home often?"

Matthew turned back at the question. "Home?"

"Back to Missouri?"

"Ah . . . no, I don't. Not nearly as often as I'd like," he added, knowing the answer was a far stretch. "Most recently I've been down in Texas, but I'd like to make my way up north again."

"Well, this job would certainly take you in the right direction. I'm assuming you're not married, Matthew?"

"No, sir. Haven't had that pleasure yet."

"But you hope to one day?"

Hesitating at the unexpected question, Matthew finally gave a shrug. "One day, I guess. Sure. When I meet the right woman."

Carlson's gaze grew intent, and Matthew got the impression that the pastor was watching his reactions just as closely as he was listening to his answers. Matthew didn't shy away from the scrutiny.

"Do you hold the Bible and Jesus's teachings in high regard?"

It suddenly sounded like Patrick Carlson was interviewing him more for would-be suitor rather than trail guide. But Matthew chalked it up to the man being a minister. Men of the cloth were a breed unto themselves. He'd learned that at an early age.

"Yes, sir, I do. Have since I was young."

Carlson leaned forward in his chair and rested his forearms on his knees. "I appreciate that, Matthew." He paused, obviously choosing his next words with care. "The advertisement stated that the woman you would be accompanying is a widow. What it didn't say is that she's very recently widowed. Barely two weeks ago, in fact. She and her husband were on their way north when he took sick. He died on the trail, from a failing heart is what the coroner in Denver said after she described her husband's symptoms to him. She brought his body back here for burial."

"So they were originally from here, then?"

"They met and courted here. Willow Springs is as close to a home as either of them had since they married. I think that's what made coming back here the right thing for her to do in this situation, at least for the time being." Carlson looked away momentarily. "Her husband was a fine man. He loved his wife very much and cared for her with a great deal of gentleness and thought. In a final letter penned to me, he was very specific about the kind of man he wanted assisting his wife on this journey. First in joining their wagon train, then in escorting her on to Idaho. It's going to take time for her to work through her grief at his passing—it being so unexpected and them being newly married."

Newly married. Matthew's attention honed in on that. He'd

naturally assumed from the term *widow* that it would be an elderly woman he'd be escorting. In light of this information, Carlson's more personal questions took on new meaning. Especially if the woman was nearer to his own age.

Carlson's wife appeared at the screen door with a tray of drinks in her hands. Matthew stood immediately and went to open the door for her.

"Why, thank you, Mr. Taylor." She set the tray down on a table beneath the front window and handed them each a glass of tea, then held out a plate of cookies.

Matthew's mouth watered at the sight of them. Not wanting to appear greedy, he resisted the urge to take more than two. Biting into the first, he remembered how hungry he was.

Both cookies were gone within a minute. "Those were the best oatmeal cookies I've ever had. Thank you, ma'am."

She offered him more, playfully nudging the plate forward when he hesitated. He gladly took two more and thanked her again. Mrs. Carlson was a pretty woman, dark-haired and with eyes so kind they made you look twice just to be certain the kindness in them was real. It sure seemed to be.

Matthew polished off another cookie and took a long drink of tea. Mrs. Carlson sat in the porch swing, her expression bright with curiosity. He hoped he wasn't going to have to answer another passel of questions to win her over as well. But from the look on her face, that hope was slim.

"So have the two of you been getting to know each other?"

Realizing she'd directed the question at him, Matthew swallowed and cleared his throat. "Yes, ma'am, we have." He quickly searched for something to comment on, hoping it might redirect the conversation. He spotted the pots of flowers set out along the steps leading up to the porch. "You've made a real nice home here, Mrs. Carlson. Something a man would appreciate coming home to."

"Why, thank you again, Mr. Taylor. That's very kind of you to say."

"Mr. Taylor's been telling me about his travels," Carlson told his wife. "What groups he's guided and where he's been. He's got a lot of experience."

Taking the cue, Matthew washed down the last of his fourth cookie with a quick swallow of tea. Though he'd never exactly guided a group before and hadn't told the pastor he had, he knew that the way he'd presented the information to Carlson moments before had left that point open for interpretation. He didn't intend on lying to this couple, but he'd braved more mountain passes than he could count, along with crisscrossing the arid plains east of the Rockies, and he could do this job. He knew he could. And he needed it. He only had to convince Carlson—both Carlsons, it would seem—that he was qualified.

He set his glass beside him on the floor and straightened in his chair, then turned his attention to Mrs. Carlson. "Like I was telling your husband, I've traveled a great deal. In the past several years, I've ridden trail from here up to Washington and Oregon, then back down through California. I've been from here to Wyoming and Texas and—"

"Wait . . . have you lived here in Willow Springs before?" Hannah Carlson's eyes went round.

Matthew made a conscious effort not to wince when Carlson's wife leaned forward. Two thoughts ricocheted through his mind at that moment. One, that the pastor would ask why he hadn't seen him in church more often once discovering how long he'd lived here. That could be answered easily. A second, and far more dangerous question, was that Carlson might inquire—no, definitely *would* inquire by the way he looked at that moment—as to where Matthew had worked while living here. Actually, it was surprising that he'd been able to evade the question so far.

Matthew took another swig of tea, his mind working. "Yes, ma'am, I did live here briefly." No, that was a lie. "Actually, I lived here for six years . . . before going to Texas, where I've been involved in—"

"Really?" Mrs. Carlson held out the plate of cookies to him again. "Then I'm sure we know some of the same people."

His appetite soured, he shook his head at her offer . . . and at her question. "I doubt it, ma'am. I worked at a ranch a ways south of here. Remote place in the foothills."

The look the couple exchanged was not comforting.

Carlson's gaze turned appraising. "You know a lot about ranching, then?"

Matthew nodded, forcing a smile. "Been ranching all my life. I grew up on a ranch and it just seems to keep following me." Though the dream of owning his own spread had dimmed considerably in recent months.

"Who did you work for while you were here? We've lived in Willow Springs for years and know a lot of the folks."

Larson Jennings had never gone to church as far as he knew and had always been open in his disdain at the idea. Kathryn, on the other hand . . . The ranch had been too far from town for her to go, but she had probably visited once she'd moved into Willow Springs after her husband had disappeared.

Answering the question, he felt the job slipping away. "I worked for a man by the name of Larson Jennings."

Mrs. Carlson's smile went slack. Her brow rose. "You worked at the Jennings' ranch?"

Matthew's stomach churned. "Yes, ma'am. I was Mr. Jennings' foreman."

The pastor's surprised expression mirrored his wife's.

Matthew worked to keep defensiveness from his tone. "If you'd like to contact him for a reference, I can tell you where they live. But they typically don't come into town but two, maybe three, times a year."

Patrick Carlson gave a laugh. "As you probably guessed by now, Matthew, Hannah and I know the Jennings. Know them very well, in fact." His look sobered. "But if you've been gone for a while, you may not be aware of what's happened to Larson and Kathryn."

Matthew knew the story all too well, but he listened anyway, nodding at the right times and still failing to understand the reasoning behind what Jennings had done.

Despite the months of separation, Matthew still held a grudge against Larson Jennings. Jennings had allowed him to make a fool of himself with his wife, watching it all from a distance. Matthew had pursued Kathryn's affections after Jennings had disappeared— had even offered to marry her after her husband had "died," and he would've too. If she'd said yes. Matthew was thankful now that she hadn't.

Though his feelings for Kathryn had been genuine and honorable at the time, his hurt over the situation had healed quickly. Too quickly for the kind of love a man should hold for his wife.

He could honestly say he wished Larson and Kathryn Jennings well in their life together, but it still bothered him how Jennings had deceived them. Especially Kathryn being with child. And part of him, a part buried inside him that Matthew preferred not to explore in depth, still had trouble accepting that Kathryn had chosen such a broken shell of a man over him.

Something Mrs. Carlson said jolted him back to the moment. And about caused his heart to stop. Matthew fought to remain seated. "I beg your pardon, ma'am?"

"I said the Jennings should be dropping by here shortly. They're coming into town today. At least that was their plan about a month ago."

When Carlson rose, Matthew followed his lead, fighting the urge to bolt from the front porch and never look back.

Annabelle stared at the folded letter in her hand. A quiver wove its way through her. Not one of fear or even dread but of knowing that she was about to turn the final page in a brief, cherished chapter of her life. These were the last words she would ever *hear* from her husband. Once she read this letter, everything about Jonathan McCutchens would become a memory. There would be nothing left to discover about the man he'd been.

For that reason part of her wanted to stash the letter away and save it for a later time. But the greater part of her was curious, hungry for any last morsel that might mention her or their child. Regret riffled through her again. Jonathan had deserved a better woman, a woman who could've been not only his companion but his closest partner in every way.

Then another thought struck her—one that had first occurred to her when Jonathan had told her about the letter that afternoon in the wagon. The question had been lurking just beneath the surface of her mind, masked by layers of grief. Now it rose with defensiveness.

What if Jonathan *had* included something about Matthew in this final missive? A last message for his brother, perhaps?

Annabelle turned the letter in her hands and slowly lifted one creased flap. How would she react if Jonathan asked her to give Matthew a message? She doubted whether she could locate Matthew even if she wanted to, but that wasn't what really bothered her. What wore on her most was the surprising resentment rising inside her against him for the hurt he'd caused his brother. And that she had been the underlying cause didn't help any.

She seated herself on a wooden bench in the garden and took a deep breath. Spreading the letter in her lap, she skimmed the page for a second, taking in the uniform flow of Jonathan's handwriting. That was another thing that had first surprised her about him. Jonathan's hands—thick-fingered, scarred, and callused from years of ranching—didn't fit with his smooth flowing script.

Dear Pastor,

If you're reading this it means that I'm gone and my Annie is going to need your help. I'm writing you during what I think will be the last sunrise I see on this side of eternity. You live what you preach, and that accounts for why I'm penning this letter to you. That and I know you'll go to God for what to do next. Annabelle trusts you and your wife. She'll accept your help where she might not from someone else.

That land in Idaho is waiting for us, like you and I talked about. It's paid for free and clear, and I want Annabelle to live there. Her and our child. I'm sending them back to you, but we both know she can't stay in Willow Springs. She'll never have the chance at the new life she deserves while living in the shadow of her old one.

Let this letter serve as authority for you to draw funds on an account in my name from the Bank of Idaho. Get enough to hire a guide to take Annabelle to meet up with Brennan's group and then see her safe to our land in Idaho.

Annabelle's eyes widened at the amount Jonathan had noted in the margin. She'd never known anything about his financial standing. She'd never asked. But surely this amount would empty his account completely.

As she read the next paragraph, an ache started somewhere near the center of her chest.

> The guide you hire must be an honorable man, Pastor. A man who won't try to take advantage of my wife in any way and who will be mindful of her condition. The trip will be hard enough, but Annie being with child will make it even harder, and I don't want anyone adding to her burden. I don't reckon to understand how you'll settle on the right man for the job, but I trust you will. And that you'll have a knowing inside you when you do.
>
> I'm watching Annie sleep right now, and she's so pretty it hurts to have to look away. How is it that when she takes a breath, I feel my own chest rise and fall? I confess that anger wells inside me at God taking me so soon. I know the Almighty doesn't need me to keep Annabelle and our child safe, but I sure had looked forward to lending Him my help for a few years. I imagine Annie will take my body back there with her. Wherever she decides to bury me will do, but I'm awful partial to being beside Fountain Creek. She and I spent many an afternoon there as we courted. Again, I'm obliged to you for your help with that.
>
> I always thought I was a real forgiving man, and I guess I was in recent years, but as I look back over my life now, I wish I'd done more of it faster and with less begrudging. Why do we learn some things so late in life, Pastor? I wish I was asking you this face to face because I know you'd have an answer. And it'd be a good one for sure.

The smooth flow of script halted.

A dark blotch of ink circled and bled through the paper as though Jonathan had hesitated, considering what to write next. Annabelle's chest tightened further as she read his last words. She heard his voice clear in her mind, as though he were right beside her.

> All of us die eventually, and only what we do for God will last—I know that now. Our lives are like water spilled out on the ground. It can't be gathered up again. I think that's why God tries to bring us back when we've been separated from Him. He

doesn't sweep away the lives of those He cares about, and neither should we.

I'm grateful for your trust in this and am asking God to repay your kindness one hundred fold.

Jonathan Wesley McCutchens

The words on the page blurred in Annabelle's vision until they were a jumble of dark, muted streaks. She wiped her tears before they blotted the paper, smudging the ink. Jonathan made no mention of Matthew, and secretly she was relieved. The last wishes of her husband were undeniably clear, and besides, Matthew didn't deserve even the smallest portion of Jonathan's benevolence or his land—not after the hurtful things Matthew had said to him and the way he'd treated him.

Unexpected heat spiraled from her chest up into her neck at that last thought, and her conscience gave swift censure to the attitude behind it. Jonathan had forgiven Matthew so fully, without ever being asked. So how could she do any less if ever forced to make that choice. A tiny smile lifted one side of her mouth. The chances of their ever meeting again made that a pretty safe bet on her part.

Annabelle stared at the letter in her hands, then at the folds that Jonathan had creased in the pages. She trailed a fingertip along those edges. He had been a plainspoken man, not given to flowery speech or long-winded conversation, but he'd had a way with the pen, with stringing words together on paper.

She didn't think Jonathan had ever seen her there, hidden in the shadows watching him, long after she should have been asleep, but she'd watched night after night as he'd filled pages with words, writing until the oil lamp gave off a purple plume. At first it struck her as odd that he spent so much time writing when he never made mention of it.

Then one morning not long after they were married and situated in Denver, she discovered the charred remnants of a letter half hidden in the cool embers. She carefully slid the quarter sheet of paper from the curled ashes. It was burned around the edges, crackly to the touch yet still legible in parts. A letter written to Matthew . . . asking forgiveness for Jonathan's part in their argument that night while offering it without measure, and inviting Matthew to come and share Jonathan's land in Idaho.

In all Jonathan's midnight scripting, how many letters had he written to his younger brother in hopes of reconciliation, only to have them end up in the fire? Had he ever mailed any of them? Wouldn't Jonathan have told her if he had?

Annabelle sighed and lifted her face to the sunshine and breeze. If it had fallen to her alone to pay the price for Jonathan marrying her, she could have borne that and done so gladly. But the price that Jonathan paid in losing his only brother in the process had been too high. Being six years older, Jonathan had considered himself more of a father to Matthew than a brother.

Turning back to the letter, her attention returned to a phrase: *only what we do for God will last.*

That one thought summed up the Jonathan Wesley McCutchens she'd known.

Our lives are like water spilled out on the ground. It can't be gathered up again. . . .

He hadn't swept away her discarded life as so many had done, but he'd chosen to bring life to her by purchasing her—literally— from the brothel. Annabelle focused on the hard-packed dirt beneath her feet. So much of her life had been spilled on the ground like water. Wasted and irretrievable.

But not anymore.

She exhaled a breath and drew another in, taking it deep and full into her lungs until she could hold no more, and then she blew it out again. Before Jonathan died, she'd lain beside him in the wagon wishing for the same flame of faith to flicker within her as it had glowed within him. She knew the Source of the flame. What she hadn't known then—what she couldn't imagine even now—was what the cost of having that same flame burn within her would be.

Would the faith she longed for, a faith like Jonathan's, end up costing her more than she'd bargained for?

In the hush of the moment a breeze stirred the leaves of the cottonwood tree overhead. Within its gentle swooshing rhythm Annabelle heard the faintest susurration, the reminiscence of a voice.

Only what we do for God will last.

Her breath caught and slowly, silently, she acknowledged it.

Mostly fearful of the pledge she made in her heart, Annabelle couldn't ignore the strange sense of release, of freedom, that accompanied it. No matter where she went from this moment on, one thing was certain—she determined to live her life in a way that would last.

———

Sheer will, and desperation at having nowhere else to turn, kept Matthew's feet planted on the porch. His mind raced. Facing Kathryn Jennings again would be hard enough, but seeing Jennings himself . . . The last time he'd seen his former boss had been at a distance, and Jennings' loathing had been palpable from where he'd stood.

"You must stay and see them, Matthew, if you have time." Carlson's expression brightened with anticipation. "And join us for dinner as well. I'm sure they'd love to see you again after all this time."

He nodded, imagining how that scene might unfold. Getting caught naked in a Montana snowstorm held more appeal at the moment.

Hannah stood and gathered the empty glasses. "Oh yes, please stay for dinner. We have plenty, and that would give us a chance to get to know you better." She walked inside, catching the screen door with her booted heel before it slammed closed.

A trickle of sweat inched down the back of Matthew's neck. He reached for his hat. Part of him still wanted to run, but another part of him was so tired of running, of constantly looking over his shoulder, that he couldn't imagine leaving this house without having secured this job. How else would he get north to find Johnny? He had no money. No other real friends to speak of. No family. And it wasn't as if homesteads where he could pick up odd jobs every few days dotted the eastern plains for miles on end.

Until that moment, he hadn't realized how much of his hope he'd pinned on the pastor hiring him.

"Pastor, about this ad . . ." He pulled the piece of paper from his pocket and held it out as though doing so would help make his point. "I want you to know I can do this job. I guarantee you I can. I've got the experience, and I can leave as soon as I get supplies inventoried and make sure the woman's wagon and team are travel worthy."

Carlson motioned for Matthew to follow him down the porch steps. "Let's take a walk around back. There's someone I'd like to introduce you to. I've got to tell you . . . you sure seem to have the credentials we're hoping for, Matthew, especially with your expertise in ranching."

Glad that Carlson seemed pleased with his credentials, he didn't quite follow the man's last comment. "I'm not sure what you mean about my expertise in ranching. The ad says you need a trail guide."

"The widow I placed this ad for is bound for Idaho to ranchland her husband purchased some years back. I'm not sure what condition the ranch is in now, how far along it is, but I'm guessing she'll need an experienced hand once she gets there—someone she can trust, if you're interested. She knows nothing about ranching, and I understand there's a lot of land."

"Speaking of the woman, Pastor . . . If you don't mind, can you tell me a bit about her?"

Carlson turned and gave his shoulder a friendly squeeze. "I'll do you one better than that, Matthew. I'll introduce you to her right now."

The casual gesture of Carlson's hand on his shoulder brought Matthew up short, reminding him of the way Johnny used to grab hold of the back of his neck when they were kids. Never enough to really hurt—just being boys. Johnny would always wear that smile too. It surprised Matthew how much he wanted to see his older brother right at that moment.

Though he'd been only four at the time, he had a distinct memory of Johnny coming into their bedroom late one night, putting an arm around his shoulders—something he didn't normally do— and whispering that their mother had died. Johnny explained that it was because of a sickness in her heart. The doc said her heart had a peculiar weakness to it and it just plain gave out on her. But even at that young age, Matthew knew different.

His mother's heart hadn't just stopped—it had been broken by Haymen Taylor.

As he followed Carlson's path around the side of the house, Matthew thought again of the things he'd said to Johnny the last time he'd seen him, *how* he'd said them. A streak of remorse flashed through him. Johnny had been in the wrong, but still . . . he could've handled things better than he did. He had to find a way to get up north, to find his brother again and make amends.

Which meant he had to get this job.

Looking beyond the pastor, he spotted a woman leaning against the fence railing that bordered the meadow. Something in her posture made him slow his steps, something that told him she was shouldering a heavy burden. Maybe it was the way her head was inclined as though listening for something on the wind, or maybe it was the manner in which she stared out across the field as though focusing on something in the distance.

Whatever it was, it gave him pause. What would it be like to travel hundreds of miles with a woman who was steeped in such grief?

He'd not had much experience around women—having had no sisters, and a mother who died before he'd gotten the chance to really ask about the gentler sex. But then again, how hard could it be to get along with her? Women were simpler creatures at heart, he figured, and had always taken a shine to him right off. Hopefully, this lady would be no different.

The woman turned. Her gaze went to Carlson first, then shifted to him.

Recognition landed a swift kick to Matthew's gut.

Hers too, judging by the sudden widening of her eyes.

Matthew heard the pastor speaking, but the sound came to him as through a long tunnel, over the rush of a freight train roaring in his head. He fought to breathe, to maintain his footing. He looked down at the advertisement still in his hand, and all he could picture was his brother.

Memories flashed at random intervals, faster than he could take them in—the way Johnny ducked his tall frame when passing through a doorway, his uncanny accuracy at reading the night sky and knowing tomorrow's weather, and how years ago he'd gently won over that neglected half-starved filly until she responded to Johnny's slightest whistle.

He winced at the searing glut of pain lodged in his throat, and at the next memory of his brother. Not so much an image, really, as it was a muffled sound—the familiar crack of leather meeting flesh.

Matthew bowed his head as something inside him gave way. And with a sickening realization, he knew he'd never see his brother again.

ANNABELLE GROPED FOR THE fence at her back and stared at the last man she'd ever expected to see again, much less to answer her ad. Their eyes met, and she read everything in his expression.

She imagined every thought and emotion flashing through his mind as the pieces jarred painfully into place, and she knew the exact moment Matthew Taylor realized that Jonathan was dead.

His tanned face grew pale. His fists trembled. He looked from her to the piece of paper now crumpled in his grip and staggered back a half step. He let out a breath as part of him seemed to cave in on himself. Then a wounded look moved over him. He closed his eyes.

In that instant Annabelle felt the same stabbing loss as when she'd awakened in the wagon to discover Jonathan dead beside her.

Surprisingly, even after Matthew had hurt Jonathan so deeply, after he'd treated her with such contempt, Annabelle still wished she could comfort him somehow. Perhaps because she knew so keenly what he was feeling at that moment.

But when his gaze met hers again, the bold absurdity of that impulse hit her hard.

Matthew's dark brown eyes turned near black with intensity, and in them welled up anger and judgment—swift, deep, and complete.

She told herself to look away, but she couldn't. As surely as the older brother had loved her—had promised to keep on loving her—it seemed the younger was determined to hate her. How was it that in one brother's eyes she'd always seen what she might be, whereas in the other's she would always be reminded of what she'd once been?

"Mr. Taylor, I'd like to present Mrs. Jonathan McCutchens. She's the widow I was telling—" Patrick must've noticed Matthew's expression because his own clouded. "Is something wrong?"

Patrick looked at Annabelle for explanation, but she was unable to find the words.

Matthew cleared his throat and put his hat back on. "Seems I'm not the man for this job after all, Pastor. Sorry to have wasted your time." His deep voice sounded strained, betraying emotion Annabelle knew he would have preferred to keep hidden from her. "Please give Mrs. Carlson my best. Good day to you, sir."

Not looking at Annabelle again, he walked away.

Patrick started after him. "Matthew, wait—"

"Patrick, don't." Annabelle took hold of his arm, her voice barely above a whisper. "You don't understand. Please, just let him go."

Annabelle watched Matthew disappear around the corner of the house, his bearing stiff and proud—a pride she'd first glimpsed two years ago, the night Kathryn Jennings had introduced them and Matthew delivered the news of a man's body, presumably Kathryn's husband's, being discovered. Long ago Annabelle had grown accustomed to people shunning her. But this was something more.

Matthew's disdain for her ran deeper than merely passing her over or calling out an insult on a town street. When she looked into Matthew Taylor's eyes, she knew that no matter what she did, she would never be able to sway his opinion of her. Whatever scale he used for measuring a person's worth, she would always weigh in somewhere right alongside dung.

"What don't I understand, Annabelle? He didn't even get a chance to meet you. How could he just—" Patrick's mouth fell open slightly. "Did you know him before? From the brothel?"

Annabelle shook her head, taking no offense at the question. It was a fair one. "No, it's nothing like that, I promise you."

"What is it then? What just happened here?" For the first time, Annabelle heard frustration in his voice. "He seemed perfect for the job. He has experience, and more than that, I think he's the type of man Jonathan would've wanted to accompany you on a long journey like this." His voice grew quiet. "The kind of man he was writing about in his letter, a man who would safeguard your honor."

Annabelle fought back a bitter laugh at the thought of her *honor* ever being in peril with Matthew Taylor. "On that count you're absolutely right, Patrick. My honor, fragile as it may be, would indeed be safe with Mr. Taylor no matter how long the journey, I assure you." A dull ache started in her left temple and she reached up to massage it. The events of recent weeks, paired with her pregnancy, were taking a toll.

"He's the only man who's answered the ad, Annabelle. You might not get another chance to leave this spring." When she didn't offer further explanation, he stepped closer. "Please help me understand what just happened here. I spent the last hour interviewing this man, who seemed perfect for the job, I might add. Then I bring him around here to introduce him to you, and he acts like he's seen a ghost."

The loss shadowing Matthew's eyes still haunted Annabelle. She'd seen that look only one other time in her life, and that man had also been mourning the loss of his brother.

"In a way, I guess he did see a ghost, Patrick. The ghost of my late husband. You see, the man you just interviewed"—she raised a brow—"the one you think would be perfect for the job . . . is Jonathan's younger brother."

Matthew didn't stop until he reached the banks of Fountain Creek near the edge of town. He slumped down in the shade of a large cottonwood tree and dropped his hat beside him. He fought to gain his breath. His gut ached, and he leaned back against the rough bark for support, hoping the pain would pass.

Johnny . . . gone. He couldn't believe it.

Yet when he'd looked into that woman's eyes a few minutes ago, having already heard the story from the Pastor, he'd known it was true.

Oh, God . . .

Matthew's stomach suddenly rebelled, and he made it to the bushes before emptying its meager contents. After the nausea passed, he crawled to the creek's edge and drank sparingly, then lay down on the sloping bank. Wiping his eyes, he let out a ragged breath. He squinted against the slivers of sunlight edging through the canopy of willows above him. A warm breeze rustled the branches.

He turned and fixed his gaze on the runoff swelling the creek's muddy banks, the water surging and tumbling down from higher climes as winter snowpack succumbed to warming spring temperatures. How could Johnny be dead? How could he have still been with that harlot after all this time? And why? Matthew had been so sure his brother would come to his senses and cast her off. But Johnny always was too gullible, and look where it had gotten him.

Sitting up, forearms on his knees, Matthew rested his head in his hands until the throbbing that came with being ill lessened to a sluggish ache. He blew out a breath and rubbed his face, wiping the unfamiliar dampness from his cheeks. Exhausted, having nowhere else to go, and lonely in a way he couldn't remember being, he gave in and lay back down, listening to the icy stream tumble and swirl past him as events of the day replayed in his mind.

Nothing had turned out as he'd thought it would. He was on the run, had no money, no job, no prospects for either . . . and he'd lost Johnny. Even if he had all the money he'd dreamed of making down in Texas, if things had worked out differently for him somehow, he would trade it all just to have his brother back.

When he awakened later, the afternoon sun was well on its daily trek toward the rocky peaks in the west. His stomach still ached, but it was more from emptiness now than from being upset. The earlier conversation with the pastor returned to him—what Carlson had said about "the couple."

All he'd mentioned about the man's death was that he'd died from a failing heart. Knowing what kind of woman Annabelle Grayson was—deceitful, manipulative—Matthew couldn't help but wonder if she'd had anything to do with it. Since learning about their marriage, he'd known she had only wedded his brother to escape the brothel and get whatever she could from him. Johnny had all but admitted as much. And now Johnny was gone and Annabelle Grayson was left with everything. Including the ranchland in Idaho, which should've rightfully gone to him. After all, Johnny had used the money from the sale of their family farm in Missouri, at least in part, to purchase the land up north, and he'd originally offered Matthew half when he asked him to come and work it with him last fall.

A recurring sense of loneliness stole through Matthew as he considered his lost opportunities. Both with the land and with his brother. Never mind that he'd snubbed Johnny's offer at the time— that didn't change the fact that the land should go to him.

He stood and reached for his hat. So what should he do now? Where should he go? Even if he still wanted the job, which he didn't—no way was he helping that scheming, loose-moraled woman—he didn't stand a chance once Larson Jennings and the pastor compared notes. Besides, Annabelle Grayson would paint him in the worst light possible.

No, the only thing left for him was to find a job here, for the time being, until he could get enough money to move on again. Though he didn't know where he would go.

Heading back to the livery for his horse, a thought struck him and Matthew changed his course. He approached his new destination with caution, wanting to make certain no one else was around. It didn't take him long to locate the spot.

The recently shoveled dirt mounding the plot had settled but wasn't yet the hard-packed ground it soon would be in this dry climate. The patch of earth the pastor had chosen to bury Johnny pleased Matthew. Near Fountain Creek, in the shadow of the Rocky Mountains, it was peaceful and a place Johnny would've liked.

Reading his brother's name carved across the top of the simple wooden cross, Matthew removed his hat and stood for several moments in the quiet, the rush of the creek the only sound filtering through the silence. He figured Carlson had spoken at the burial, and he wished he'd been around to hear. Matthew hoped he had said fine things about his brother, personal things. A man shouldn't be laid to rest without words particular to him being spoken, words about his life, about how he'd lived and what contributions he'd—

"Taylor?"

Surprised, Matthew looked up. Seeing who it was, his eyes narrowed. He knew the man standing in front of him, or had at one time. But it still felt as though he were staring at a stranger.

"I figured you might stop by here before leaving town again, and I wanted to see you." Furrows of scarred flesh lined Larson Jennings' face and neck, and the skin on the right side of his face had healed at an awkward angle, sloping his eye. He took a step toward Matthew, then stopped. Jennings looked like he'd aged twenty years in two. "I'd like to talk to you about what happened between you . . . and my wife."

Matthew detected accusation in Jennings' tone, and his defenses rose. He already had a good idea of what Jennings would like to say to him and wasn't eager to hear it. "I've got some things I've been wanting to say to you too."

Jennings nodded. "I'm sure you do." Then he said nothing, as if giving Matthew the opportunity to go first.

"You were wrong not to reveal who you were from the start, Jennings. To let us go on thinking you were gone. How could you do that to her? Letting her think you were dead all that time?"

His former employer looked as though he might offer a reply, then apparently thought better of it. At least he knew when he was wrong.

One particular night stood out in Matthew's memory, when he'd waited for Kathryn outside of Myrtle's Cookery and had walked her home. He'd tried to kiss her that evening. Heat poured through him wondering if Jennings might've been there in the shadows, watching that too. "Do you know what Kathryn went through all those months? Waiting for you, wondering if you were dead or alive? Trying to hold on to the ranch? Then the afternoon they found that body . . ."

Matthew shook his head, recalling the day he'd escorted Kathryn to the coroner's office to view the remains of what they thought was her husband. Part of him had been thankful Jennings' body had finally been found. He hated seeing Kathryn in so much pain, and yet he also hated not being able to be with her, to take care of her like he had wanted to do at the time.

"You should've seen what she went through, Jennings. How

could you do that to her? And her carrying your child."

Jennings took in a slow breath. "That's just it, Matthew. I didn't know she was carrying my child. I thought . . ." He glanced away as though ashamed to look at Matthew. "I thought the child belonged to someone else." His raspy voice grew even softer. "For a while I . . . I thought the child was yours."

Matthew knew some folks had assumed that, but for Jennings to have actually believed it? "How could you think that of Kathryn? Don't you even know your own wife?"

His pained expression eased. "I do now," he answered slowly. "Thank God, I do now."

The fire had altered Jennings' appearance, but the look in his eyes seemed to have changed too—in a way Matthew couldn't quite describe or account for. Jennings closed the distance between them, and though Matthew outweighed him, Matthew braced himself.

Jennings held up a hand. "I'm not here to fight you, Taylor. Though God knows I wanted to at one time." A crooked smile turned the edges of his mouth. "You must admit, it could tend to rile a man to discover he's not hardly cold in the grave yet and a friend he's trusted for years is setting sights on his wife." He sighed and shook his head. "But that's not what I'm here for, Taylor. That's all behind us now.

"What I'm trying to do is apologize to you. What I did was wrong. I had my reasons at the time, but they still don't make it right. I'm sorry my actions caused you pain, and I'm here to ask for your forgiveness." Jennings shifted his weight, glancing away, then back again. "Kathryn told me about your kindness to her, how you helped her after I didn't return, what you did to try and save our ranch, our land." His gaze grew intent. "I thank you for that. I was wrong not to reveal myself after I returned but . . . well, let's just say I had some learning to do. About myself and about my wife. And a lot about my Lord."

Matthew stood numb in the face of Jennings' admission.

Over the years of working for Jennings, he'd grown to admire the man. Jennings could be hard at times and had a trigger temper, but he'd always been fair with him. Jennings possessed a natural business sense that Matthew respected, even envied. Yet Matthew would never have described the man standing before him as benevolent and could never recall Larson Jennings ever having admitted he was wrong, much less sorry.

That was something he would've remembered.

Unsure of what to say or how to act, and not wanting to lessen Jennings' responsibility in the matter, he simply accepted the confession. "I appreciate your apology, Jennings. Kathryn is a fine woman. You're lucky to have her."

"That I am, friend." Jennings stared at him for a moment longer, then looked past him to the grave. "I'm sorry about your brother. I only met Jonathan a couple of times, so I didn't know him well, but Pastor Carlson sure spoke highly of him. Said he was a good man."

The compassion in Jennings' voice, in his manner, caused Matthew's chest to tighten. "Yes, he was." Then it hit them that he'd never told Jennings he had a brother. Neither had he told Carlson. That left only one explanation—Annabelle Grayson. Of course she'd told them, and no telling what else she'd said about him. Turning them against him, making up all sorts of lies, as she did to trap his brother.

"I was by the pastor's house earlier, and he asked me some questions about you having worked for me." Jennings' expression grew somber. "I want you to know I answered his questions honestly."

The back of Matthew's neck heated as he imagined how that conversation must have gone and what Pastor and Mrs. Carlson must think of him now. Eager to end this conversation, he silently acknowledged Jennings' candor with a tilt of his head and turned to go.

"I told Carlson you were one of the finest ranch hands I've worked with and the best foreman I've ever had."

Matthew slowly turned back, not sure he'd heard right. But Jennings' expression confirmed that he had. "You told him that. About me?" It didn't make sense. Why would he do such a thing? Especially when he could have had his revenge and paid Matthew back tenfold. "Why?"

"Because it's the truth. You're a good man, Taylor. Not perfect, mind you," he added, wit underlying his tone, "but good."

In view of Jennings' unexpected charity, Matthew's jaw went rigid with emotion. It still didn't make sense to him. "But the other stuff with Kathryn, that was true too."

Jennings held his gaze for a moment, then nodded. "Fair enough. But the way I figure it, a man sometimes gets to choose what path he takes and sometimes he doesn't. Then other times, God sends someone along who gets to help him make that choice. He's done that through certain people in my life, and I'm a better man for it." Again, that wry smile. "Once I choked down enough pride to be able to accept their help, that is. Which has never been an easy thing for me."

Jennings looked away briefly, then slowly extended his hand.

Taking a deep breath, Matthew considered the man before him, wondering why he would give him this second chance, especially when Matthew knew it was unlikely he would have done the same had the roles been reversed.

Still not understanding, but wishing he somehow could, Matthew accepted Jennings' outstretched hand.

When they parted ways, Matthew headed back to town and toward the livery. Best to get his horse and move on. But to where? And with what? With pockets empty and a stomach to match, he didn't even have money for a meal, much less the few coins he needed to pay Jake Sampson at the livery. A sense of loss and the longing for justice wrestled inside him, vying for control. If granted one wish in that moment, hands down it would be to have Johnny back. Over all else.

But if granted a second, it would be to make Annabelle Grayson pay.

CHAPTER SEVEN

THE NEXT MORNING, Annabelle stared at the sheaf of bills stuffing the envelope that Patrick handed her. It wasn't that she'd never seen that much money before—she had. It had simply never belonged to her. After the madam at the brothel took her cut, in addition to room and board, clothes, cosmetics, and perfume, it left scarce little for the girls in the end—the madam's intent, no doubt.

Annabelle counted the bills again as Patrick climbed into the wagon beside her. "Jonathan never said anything to me about money while he was alive, and I never questioned him. But I never dreamed he'd put this much aside. So is everything settled? Does this close his account at the bank in Idaho?"

Patrick remained quiet for a moment, then gave her a sideways glance. "Everything's settled. That's the amount Jonathan wrote in his letter to withdraw for you, remember?" He gave a little smile, flicked the reins, and worked his way around the wagons parked at the mercantile and feed store. "Money enough to get you safely to Idaho, along with plenty to pay an experienced trail guide."

"Yes, I know, but . . ." Annabelle barely noticed the crowded boardwalk bustling with people, feeling in her gut that there was something Patrick wasn't telling her. She allowed the silence to swell between them, giving him opportunity, while watching him from the corner of her eye.

His attention remained on the road.

Perhaps he was trying to think of a way to bring up the subject of Matthew Taylor again. She'd known last night that all of Patrick's and Hannah's questions about her relationship with Matthew—if one could call it that—hadn't been answered. Certainly Matthew had already left Willow Springs, or soon would, if his reaction to seeing her the previous afternoon was any indication. She couldn't deny the fact that part of her, after the initial shock of seeing him standing there yesterday, had welcomed the sight of him. After all, to her knowledge, he was Jonathan's only living kin, and Matthew had probably known her husband better than anyone. Matthew represented a last tie to Jonathan, however threadbare.

It seemed odd to her now when she thought back on the times Jonathan had spoken of his "little brother," recalling tales of their childhood days. The picture her imagination had formed of that "little boy grown up" bore little resemblance to the man she knew as Matthew Taylor.

With a last glance at Patrick, she decided to let whatever was on his mind simmer for the time being. "I just think it's odd that Jonathan never mentioned the money before is all."

"Your Jonathan was a humble man, Annabelle."

Her Jonathan. Now that was a phrase she hadn't heard anyone use before. How did a woman like her merit that distinction with a man like Jonathan McCutchens? She missed him, and already their conversations were becoming fuzzy in her memory. So much of him was slipping away from her, and so soon. Being the last day of May, seventeen days had passed since Jonathan had died. Yet it seemed like much longer.

"I went ahead and signed all the necessary papers since Jonathan named me executor in his letter. All the documents have been finalized here and will be mailed to the Bank of Idaho. You'll need to visit there once you arrive and they'll help you with the rest." He pulled a stack of papers from his pocket and handed them to her, along with Jonathan's letter, which he'd taken with him as proof of Jonathan's last testament. "Keep this somewhere safe, and then show it all to the bank there. They know to expect you either sometime this fall or next, depending on how things work out."

Annabelle skimmed the document pages, not comprehending

all the legal jargon but vowing to read through it later. She put it, along with Jonathan's letter, into her reticule. "I appreciate all you've done for me, Patrick. So would Jonathan."

He shrugged off her thanks. "I'm glad to do it. I handle details like this all the time for people. Have I mentioned my fee yet?"

His teasing smirk coaxed one from her. "No, but if your fee involves enough to build a new church, I'm going to get suspicious." She huffed a laugh as the mental image took shape in her mind. "Can you imagine, a church building paid for by a lady of the evening?" The irony struck her as funny.

"*Former* lady of the evening. Now a lady in the truest sense," Patrick corrected, lightness in his tone. He squinted. "Hmm . . . a church building paid for by a sinner who was offered a second chance and decided to take it. I think it'd work." He tossed her a smile.

"And I don't think many of the good people of Willow Springs would darken its doors if they knew."

"The good people . . ." He shook his head, sighing. "Sadly, Annabelle, I'm afraid you might be right on that count. There are an awful lot of *good* people walking around this town who need healing. But, unfortunately, they don't even know they're sick. A person can't come to grips with God's forgiveness until they realize they're not worthy of it in the first place."

Warmth spread through her at hearing those words—and remembering back to that last night in the wagon. "Jonathan said very much the same thing to me the night he died. He said that he and I had an advantage over Ma—" She caught herself before saying Matthew's name. No need to give Patrick an open door to bring up the subject of him again. "Over . . . many people because we'd seen who we really are without Jesus. And until someone does that, they can't be near as grateful as they should be. Or as kind to others." Her laugh came out clipped. "I guess that should make me one of the most grateful people around, huh? And one of the kindest, to boot?"

"And that's exactly what you are," he said gently.

Surprised at his response, she savored it.

He guided their wagon down a side street, and her focus was drawn to a hunched-over figure not too far up ahead. "Patrick, would you mind stopping for a second. Please?" When he brought the wagon to a standstill, she climbed down using the wheel hub for a foothold.

The old peddler Kathryn Jennings had introduced her to pulled his rickety cart behind him on the side of the street, speaking to those he passed, whether they acknowledged him or not. When Annabelle caught his attention, a smile creased the sun-furrowed lines of Callum Roberts' bearded face.

He plunked down his old cart. "Miss Grayson, why I'll be. Don't you look mighty pretty today."

Annabelle didn't bother correcting him, on either point, and gently touched the tarnished brooch she'd pinned on her shawl that morning as an afterthought, so glad now that she'd worn it. Callum Roberts' eyes lit when he saw it. The brooch was a purchase she'd made from Mr. Roberts when she and Kathryn Jennings had been in town together one day last spring. The jewelry served to remind her not only of the ancient hawker but of a lesson in kindness she'd learned from Kathryn.

She and Kathryn had been talking at the time, and Annabelle would've passed by the old peddler without notice. But not Kathryn.

Kathryn stopped and talked to him, looking him in the eye, fawning over his wares, and purchasing two items Annabelle knew she had no need of. Then Kathryn had hugged the man—actually hugged him! Despite his smell. A tear had trickled down the old man's cheek, making Annabelle wonder how long it had been since someone had touched him, much less shown him such affection.

She leaned over and peered into the man's cart. "What sorts of things do you have today, Mr. Roberts?" She assumed that this collection of odds and ends contained many of the same items Kathryn had sorted through a year ago.

"Well, what are you hopin' to find?"

"Oh, no telling what might strike my fancy. How has business been?" He looked as though he might not have eaten a good meal in several days. Or weeks.

Knowing the temptation might be there for him, she studied his face for signs of being into the bottle. But his eyes were clear and bright, no tremors in his hands. No smell on his breath either, other than staleness and rotten teeth.

"Not too bad. Seems like more and more people are wantin' to go to that fancy store down the way there. Don't know why they would though, when I got what they need right here. For a bargain," he added, leaning down to rub his right leg.

Annabelle thought she'd noticed him favoring that same leg when she first spotted him walking down the street. "I couldn't agree with you more, Mr. Roberts." She finally settled on a worn, thinning volume no larger than the palm of her hand. The tiny book appeared to still contain all of its pages, but from the stains browning the edges, she wondered if the verses within would even be legible. The author's name on the cover wasn't familiar to her, but the title was captivating enough —*The Tell-Tale Heart.*

She also picked up a handheld mirror that must have been painted gold several lifetimes ago. The mirror's face was cracked in two places, and the ornate handle was marred by three hollow indentions that might once have boasted pieces of colored cut glass. Annabelle held it up to see her reflection, and she immediately noticed its obvious imperfections.

Her own, not the mirror's.

At the angle in which she held the mirror, one of the jagged cracks in the glass matched almost perfectly the scar edging down her right temple. She slowly lowered the mirror and managed to find her smile again.

"I can't thank you enough for these items, Mr. Roberts. I've been looking for a book to read and will put this mirror to good use. These will do nicely, thank you." She pressed some bills into his hand.

"Well, I hope you enjoy 'em. I shined that mirror myself just yesterday. Can't read much though, so don't know if that book is worth its weight or not. It's one of them stagecoach books, they tell me. It'll fit right in your pocket while you travel." Callum Roberts glanced down at the money in his palm, then back at Annabelle, who managed some quick backward steps toward the wagon. "Oh no, ma'am. This is too much. Way too much."

She climbed back up to the buckboard, a funny sensation flitting through her—like the sun was rising for a second time that morning, only this time . . . inside of her. She couldn't keep from smiling. "Nonsense, Mr. Roberts. These items are well worth it to me. Now you take some of that and go see Doc Hadley about that leg. Get yourself a new coat for winter, and some gloves too. Then head on over to Myrtle's and treat yourself to some of her fried chicken and bread pudding."

Through the thick growth of his unkempt beard, his lips quivered. "Thank you, ma'am. You're a good woman, you are."

Before emotion got the best of her, Annabelle indicated to Patrick with a nod that she was ready to pull away. When they'd gone some distance down the road, she chanced a look back.

Callum Roberts stood exactly where she'd left him, one hand resting on his cart, the other raised in a half wave. She offered the same in return.

When they reached the corner, Patrick glanced down at the items in her lap. "You just never know the value of some things, do you?"

Annabelle didn't answer. She didn't need to. As Patrick maneuvered their rig around a buggy in the street, she just kept thanking God for this marvelous, undeserved grace she'd somehow stumbled into.

Patrick pulled the wagon behind the house minutes later, hopped down, and came around to her side. Annabelle accepted his assistance as he helped her down. Then their eyes met. Something flickered behind his expression. That same *something* she thought she'd glimpsed in town earlier.

She smiled. "Okay, whatever it is . . . go ahead and say it."

"Go ahead and say what?" He turned away, but not before she saw a sheepish grin inching his mouth upward.

"You're not a good liar, Patrick. But it's a shortcoming that serves you well."

He turned back. "I was just wondering if there's any way I could still reach Matthew Taylor if he's in town, maybe talk to him about taking the job. You need to leave Willow Springs, Annabelle. Have a chance to start over again." As though sensing her disapproval, he continued without a pause. "When Larson and I spoke yesterday, he said that Matthew would make an excellent guide. I'm pretty good at reasoning with people, and I think I could—"

She held up a hand. "We discussed this last night, Patrick. Matthew is long gone by now." She started toward the house and

Patrick followed. "He wants nothing to do with me, I assure you. And for you and Hannah to hope otherwise . . ." She turned when she reached the back stairs, intentionally softening her tone. "Or for me to hope otherwise, is plain foolish. I'll leave for Denver this week. I'll get a room at a boardinghouse I know of there, wait until next spring, and then join up with the first wagon train that's heading north. I'll be fine, Patrick. I'll get a job—a respectable one, I promise." She winked. "And the months will pass in no time."

She laid a hand on her midsection, thankful for this lasting connection with Jonathan, and willed the look on her face to match the lightness of her tone. "Besides, traveling a thousand miles with this baby jostling inside me wasn't something I looked forward to anyway."

Annabelle hoped her smile looked more convincing than it felt. She'd spent most all of her life pretending, and she was good at it too.

Or at least she used to be.

CHAPTER EIGHT

LATER THAT SAME AFTERNOON Annabelle helped Hannah and her young daughter, Lilly, hang laundry in the backyard. Hannah seemed especially quiet, and Annabelle could easily guess why.

"You know, Hannah, Denver's not that far from Willow Springs. Maybe we could meet again before I leave next spring."

Eleven-year-old Lilly, with dark hair and violet eyes so much like Hannah's, beamed with excitement. "We could make a trip and see Aunt Annabelle before she leaves!"

Hannah finished hanging the sheet in her hands with a smile that Annabelle recognized as forced. "Lilly, would you please run inside and check on your brother for me? Bobby should be through with his snack by now." She waited until the girl was out of earshot. "I just wish you could stay here until then, Annabelle. I don't like the idea of you being in Denver all by yourself, especially being with child. If you don't want to stay here with us, I'm sure we could find you a place to live with someone from church. Someone who would be understanding about your situation and who has some extra room, maybe lives a ways out of town."

Doing her best not to laugh, Annabelle snapped her fingers. "I know just the person! Mrs. Cranchet! I could live with her, and that way she and I could knit together and come up with ideas for

Patrick's sermons." Hannah's droll expression only encouraged her. "Let's see, we could entitle the first sermon . . . 'The Virtues of Chastity.'"

Hannah's eyes widened. "Annabelle McCutchens, you ought not joke about such things. It's not proper." She pursed her lips.

Her tone sounded serious enough, and for a moment, Annabelle wondered if her joking had crossed the line. Again. But when Hannah lifted a hand to cover her grin, Annabelle giggled along with her.

Hannah leaned closer. "Can you imagine what Mrs. Cranchet would do if we asked if you could live with her?"

Annabelle cocked a brow. "Well, Patrick wouldn't have to worry about her giving him any more advice—that's for sure. She'd just keel over dead right there."

Though she had never attended church with Patrick and Hannah, Annabelle often wondered what it would be like to actually walk through the doors of a *real* church building, white steeple and all. Far-away memories, locked away since childhood, nudged the surface of her mind, yet they provided only the dimmest of recollections before fading. While living in Denver, she and Jonathan had spent Sunday mornings with a small group in someone's parlor, with the men taking turns reading Scripture. Nice as that had been, the thought of meeting in a "house of God" still held such appeal.

Patrick and Hannah had asked her to attend with them, many times, but she'd always declined, certain of the reception she'd get from Mrs. Cranchet, among others. Plus she didn't want the Carlsons paying for her mistakes—any more than they already had for taking her in to stay with them. So as much as she hoped to one day experience that type of gathering, the only sermons she recollected hearing were ones Patrick and Hannah, and a handful of others, lived out every day. As well as those Jonathan had lovingly delivered by example.

Somehow she couldn't bring herself to feel the least bit slighted.

Hannah shook out a damp shirt and hung it on the line. "What are you going to do in Denver for the next year? How will you get by?"

"Most importantly, I'm going to have this baby, and I'll manage fine. Don't you worry about me. With careful spending and getting a job either ironing or cleaning, I should still have enough come next May. Jonathan laid aside ample for us, Hannah. More than I expected."

Working together, they hung the rest of the laundry. The comforting aromas of soap and sunshine scented the warm air as the damp sheets made a soft fluttering noise in the breeze. Annabelle had never minded doing laundry; the act of scrubbing something clean had always felt good to her.

"Can I ask you a question?" Hannah picked up the empty basket and propped it on her hip.

Annabelle waited, sensing from Hannah's change in tone something was coming.

"About Matthew Taylor and what happened here yesterday . . ." Hannah looked at her for a moment as though testing the waters, then apparently decided it was safe to tread. "You told us last night that he was Jonathan's younger brother, but then you said something about Matthew having known that you worked at the brothel here in town and how he held that against you." Hannah bit her lower lip. "What doesn't make sense to me is the timing of all that. You left that life when you married Jonathan last September. Matthew visited you both last October, *after* you were already married. So how did he know about that part of your life?"

Knowing this answer wouldn't be a quick one, Annabelle motioned to a split-log bench situated at the meadow's edge. She sat down and Hannah joined her. "I first met Matthew Taylor about two years ago, through Kathryn Jennings. I'm not sure what you know about events that happened around then."

Hannah made a cautioning motion with her hand. "And I'm not asking you to tell me anything that would compromise you or Kathryn, or Matthew for that matter." She offered a weak smile. "But I must admit, what happened here yesterday afternoon did pique my curiosity."

"I certainly never expected to see Matthew Taylor again, much less for him to show up here." Leaning forward, Annabelle plucked a long piece of field grass and rested her elbows on her knees. "Like I said, Kathryn introduced us. Matthew Taylor took one look at me that night and . . . I could see it all in his eyes. The contempt . . ." She shook her head, remembering. "But it wasn't just that he didn't approve of what I did, of who I was. I was used to seeing that. It was the *way* he looked at me . . . Slowly, up and down, and not the way a man sometimes looks at a woman, mind you."

Hannah's expression turned thoughtful. "Like he thought he was better than you?"

Annabelle sifted the question in her mind. "No. More like he was glad that he *wasn't* me. That he was thankful he hadn't done the things I'd done or lived the way I'd lived."

"Did he say anything to you that night, once Kathryn introduced you?"

Annabelle nodded. "But I think it just about choked him." She managed a tiny laugh to ease the tension, but the sting from the memory still felt surprisingly fresh. "I remember what he said, word for word. 'It's nice that you have such a good friend in Mrs. Jennings.' So polite, so pleasant on the surface. But I knew what he was really thinking."

"And why do I think you said something that put him in his place? Some witty reply, perhaps?" Hannah's raised brow said that she was imagining what caustic comment might have left Annabelle's lips that night.

Annabelle shook her head. "That's just it. I saw what he was thinking, and . . . I couldn't say a word. I just stood there. I had no witty reply, Hannah, because . . . because I knew that all the things he was thinking about me . . . were true. I probably *had* done all the things he was imagining. And worse." She bit down on her lower lip. When she tried to swallow, the tightness in her throat wouldn't allow it. She dared not lift her eyes when she spoke next. "I have sinned so much in my life," she whispered. "Not a day goes by that I don't wish I could turn back time. That I could undo so much of what I've done."

She felt Hannah's arm come around her shoulder and didn't resist when she scooted closer.

"But all of that has been forgiven, Annabelle. All the bad you've done, that I've done—whatever it was. You know that."

Annabelle nodded. Moments passed, and she wondered how much more of what was in her heart she should share. She already trusted Hannah; that wasn't the issue. But she needed her friend's assurance as well, and her guidance. "What I'm going to say next, Hannah, will you promise not to take any of it as a discredit to

Jonathan as a man, or to his memory?"

Hannah tightened her hold on Annabelle's shoulder. "I promise."

"I'd already seen Matthew before Kathryn introduced us that particular night. I'd been waiting for her to come home. Matthew came to her door, knocked, and then left when she didn't answer. He never saw me." Using her fingernails, Annabelle made a small slit at the top of the blade of grass and carefully peeled down until she'd torn it into two identical strips. "This is going to sound odd—it does even to me—but there was something about the man I saw that night that . . . drew me. And that's not something that had ever happened to me before." She shrugged, feeling awkward and exposed. "I know you think that sounds strange, coming from someone like me, who's been with a lot of men."

"No, actually that doesn't sound strange at all, Annabelle. It makes a lot of sense." A sparrow landed on a fencepost nearby, and they both watched in silence until it flitted away again. "So what was it about Matthew Taylor that attracted you to him that night?"

The transparency of Hannah's question brought to the surface what Annabelle had only hinted at before. What *had* drawn her to Matthew that night? "The man I saw that night had a certain . . . confidence about him. Not mean-like or intimidating. It was more in the way he carried himself. I told Kathryn it was like he knew something the rest of the world didn't."

"Matthew Taylor is a very handsome man," Hannah said matter-of-factly. "That's something I noticed right off. Don't tell Patrick I said that though." She playfully nudged Annabelle in the side. "Preacher's wives aren't supposed to notice those things."

Annabelle smiled, recalling the details of Matthew's face, and those eyes . . . like warm whiskey on a winter night. She picked up another blade of grass and tore it as she had the other. "The second time I was introduced to Matthew Taylor was even worse. It made our first meeting seem downright friendly." She told Hannah about the meeting in the shack and how Jonathan and Matthew had fought afterward.

Hannah gave a sad sigh. "Before seeing Matthew again that particular night, had you discovered that he was Jonathan's brother?"

Annabelle hesitated before answering, wishing again that she could go back and handle things differently. "Yes, I put two and two together not long after Jonathan and I were married." In a way, she was actually indebted to Matthew. After Jonathan bought cattle in Denver last summer, he'd sent the herd north with his ranch hands, then came down to Willow Springs in hopes of finding his brother. Without Jonathan's search for Matthew, chances were good they would never have met and married. "One night after we were in bed, Jonathan began talking about his younger brother, about growing up together in Missouri, and about their mother. Then he mentioned his brother's name . . . and I knew."

"Did you tell Jonathan then?"

Annabelle slowly exhaled. "No. But once Matthew showed up at the shack, I wished I had. I just honestly never thought they'd see each other again—not with having lost track of each other all those years."

"How could you have ever known he'd just show up like that?"

Annabelle winced slightly. "Well, turns out Jonathan had learned of Matthew's whereabouts from Jake Sampson at the livery. After what happened with Kathryn and Larson, Matthew headed south to Texas. I don't remember where exactly. But I can't say that I blame him. He was probably as anxious to leave then as I am now. What I didn't know at the time was that Jonathan had written Matthew and had asked him to join him in Idaho." She looked out across the fields. "Had I known about that letter . . . believe me, Hannah, I would have handled things very differently. Maybe then some of this could have been avoided. Especially with how things were left between them."

Hannah exhaled slowly, as though taking it all in. "The two brothers certainly didn't favor each other much, did they? Not only in their coloring but in temperament it would seem." She gave Annabelle a knowing look.

Annabelle acknowledged it, then glanced toward the spot where Matthew had stood yesterday.

Physically, Jonathan had been tall and plain, built solid and broad, but was kinder and gentler than any man of that stature had a right to be. While Matthew's height and weight didn't rival his older brother's, his physique was lean and well-muscled, his dark hair unruly, but in a roguish way that made his brown eyes even more striking. Annabelle felt a check in her spirit. How strange it was that the better you got to know some people, the more—or sometimes less—attractive they could become.

"They had different fathers, so that would account for the difference in their appearance," Annabelle answered. But what about their temperament? What would make two brothers so different from one another? "From what Jonathan told me, his mother remarried when Jonathan was still young, and Matthew's father turned out to have a mean streak, especially when he drank. Jonathan had scars across his shoulders and arms from the man's whippings."

Hannah didn't answer for a moment. "I can't imagine someone who would beat a child. Or who would treat a woman that way either, Annabelle."

Absentmindedly Annabelle touched the scar that ran along her right temple and cheek, and the thread of memory tying her to her old self pulled taut once again. She'd come to think of her life at the brothel not in terms of years but as a separate life, so different from the life she was living now. For so long she'd been certain that she would die in that place. Had no doubt. But Jonathan had proven her wrong. He'd purchased her at a price and had then shown her the even greater price that had been paid to ransom her so long ago.

Seeing Hannah looking west, Annabelle traced her line of vision. The sun's golden rays bathed the range of snow-covered peaks in a luster of light, making it appear as though the mountains were glowing from the inside out.

When Annabelle looked back, Hannah's eyes brimmed with unshed tears. One finally fell and traced a path down her cheek. Hannah gave her a wordless hug, then stood and walked back to the house alone. Annabelle watched her go. Hannah reminded her of Kathryn Jennings in many ways. They were both so innocent, so naïve to the cruelty people were capable of.

Annabelle looked down at the shredded bits and pieces of prairie grass littering the dirt. It wasn't the meanness in people that surprised her anymore. It was the good in them that she found so unexpected.

CHAPTER NINE

M ATTHEW'S RESENTMENT TOWARD HER mounted as he walked through town toward the pastor's home. He'd wasted the last couple of nights stewing over it. Then he finally decided—why should he be made to feel like a beggar by the likes of a woman such as Annabelle Grayson? And for something that rightfully belonged to him in the first place?

He'd lain awake most of last night, turning the situation over in his mind.

That land had belonged to Johnny. As boys, they'd dreamed of one day owning a spread out west somewhere, of working the land together and leaving Haymen Taylor far behind. Haymen Taylor was gone now, so under the circumstances, even if the childhood dream had faded in Matthew's memory through the years, the property should rightfully be passed to Johnny's closest and only blood kin.

The thought of spending any length of time in that woman's company made Matthew's stomach churn. But considering the ranchland in Idaho and Johnny's original offer to share the land with him—Johnny's *desire* that they share it—Matthew kept moving forward. Besides, anyone who knew what Annabelle Grayson was and understood the truth about why she had married his brother to begin with would agree.

"Good day to you, sir."

Matthew slowed on hearing the voice.

"Care to look at my wares? I've got some nice things. You might find a little somethin' for your wife . . . or maybe a sweetheart."

Matthew turned and eyed the old codger approaching him. The man's clothing, dirty and stained, hung loose on his thin frame, and when he smiled, a scruffy beard parted to expose yellowed teeth. It was about that time the smell reached him. Matthew took a step back. The man was pulling a wooden handcart behind him, and Matthew peered inside, glancing at the contents, highly doubtful they were anything he would want, or anything of worth for that matter.

"I have some nice combs here." The peddler held out something. "Or maybe a perfume bottle she could put to good use."

Matthew thought of a good use for the perfume right now, if there'd been any left. "Sorry. Not interested." Even if he had a few coins to spare, which he didn't, Matthew feared that whatever he might give this man would end up in the saloon's cash drawer sooner or later. And, from the looks of things, he would guess sooner rather than later.

"Sorry, sir. I can't help you." Not waiting for a response, Matthew crossed the street, fully expecting the man to call after him, badgering him to buy something.

"That's okay, son. Maybe next time. Thanks for lookin', and God bless you today."

Hearing the voice behind him, Matthew slowed his steps and turned. The sight created a lasting picture in his mind. The aged hawker's feeble hand raised in a parting wave, baggy clothes hanging from his frail body, both reeking from having gone too long unwashed.

Yet the man wore a smile, and with so little in his possession.

Matthew shook his head, sensing a smile of his own coming on. In a parting gesture, he touched the rim of his hat and watched the man's face light up. Somehow knowing that the old codger wouldn't want to be the first to look away, Matthew continued on down the street, feeling oddly beholden to the man.

When the pastor's house came into view, Matthew's determination to regain his lost opportunity deepened. This job was his only means of getting north to claim the land, and he felt certain that with some explaining to Carlson, it could be his. Even if he had to swallow a chunk of his pride in the process.

Climbing the front porch stairs in twos, he removed his hat and rapped lightly on the screen door. He stepped back, wiping his sweaty palm on his jeans.

It felt good to have his hunger satisfied. He'd earned yesterday's dinner and that morning's breakfast by mucking out stalls. It had taken him well past dark last night to finish, and then he'd bedded down in the bunkhouse with the other ranch hands for a short night of little rest. When the rancher asked him earlier that morning if he could stay on for a while longer, Matthew declined. He had something better waiting for him.

When no one answered, he knocked again, harder this time.

A moment later the door opened.

"Why . . . Mr. Taylor, good morning." Unmistakable surprise registered in Mrs. Carlson's expression. She smiled, her brow wrinkling slightly.

"Good morning, ma'am. Is your husband in? I've come back to see him about the job."

She opened her mouth as if to say something, then nodded and indicated for him to come inside. "Yes, of course. Patrick's in the kitchen. He's . . . speaking with someone."

Just then Matthew heard Carlson's voice. A man's response followed, then a woman's soft laughter. They must be entertaining another couple for breakfast. He hesitated. "I'm interrupting something. I can come back later if this isn't a good—"

"Not at all." Mrs. Carlson's smile came more easily this time, and she waved him inside. "Now is fine. Please, make yourself comfortable here in the parlor. I'll tell Patrick you're here."

"Thank you, ma'am."

Preferring to stand, Matthew scanned the small front room. When he'd spoken with Patrick Carlson on Monday, he'd not been inside the house. A sofa and chair took up most of the space, the bare plank floor was neatly swept, the furnishings were simple but tasteful. He'd eaten earlier, but still the aroma of what he guessed to be pancakes and sausage made his mouth water.

He fingered the rim of his hat as he waited. At the sound of footsteps, he turned.

"Matthew, this is a surprise."

He accepted Carlson's outstretched hand, at the same time reading caution in his eyes. The pastor's grip seemed firmer than he remembered.

"I wasn't expecting to see you again. How are you?" Carlson sat on the sofa and motioned for Matthew to take the chair opposite him.

"I'm fine, and no, sir, I guess you weren't expecting me again, under the circumstances." Since leaving here two days ago, Matthew had wondered what Annabelle Grayson had told the pastor and his wife about him. Certainly they knew that he and Jonathan were brothers. But what else had she told them?

"I want you to know how sorry I am about your brother, Matthew." Carlson leaned forward. He laid a hand to Matthew's forearm, a gesture Matthew would've considered awkward coming from any other man, but it seemed second nature coming from Patrick Carlson. "Jonathan was a fine man and a good friend to both me and my family. Obviously I had no idea when we were talking earlier this week that he was your brother or I would have handled things differently, I assure you."

Matthew nodded, swallowing against the sudden tightening in his throat. "I appreciate that, sir. I'll admit, it was hard finding out that way . . . to take it in all at once. We hadn't seen each other much in recent years, and we didn't part on the best of terms either." He shook his head. "I figured I'd get another chance to make things right between us before—"

Matthew caught himself. He'd shared far more than he'd intended. Carlson had an openness about him that put a man at ease. For the first time, he imagined Johnny and Carlson being friends. Johnny would've liked him, just as he was growing to do.

Matthew sat up a bit straighter. "Sir, I guess your wife told you I'm here to talk to you about the job." At Carlson's nod, he forged ahead. "I told you about my work experience a couple of days ago, and I understand that Larson Jennings provided a favorable recommendation for me." He waited for a reaction. The silence, coupled with Carlson's steady stare, told him he had plenty of ground to regain. "My behavior on Monday must've seemed abrupt to you, and I'd appreciate a chance to explain that."

Again, that patient stare.

Needlessly, Matthew cleared his throat. "Well, when I saw Miss Grayson standing there, when I realized the gravity of the situation and what it meant, I was completely—"

"Mrs. McCutchens, you mean," Carlson said softly.

"I'm sorry?"

"You mistakenly referred to her as Miss Grayson. Her name is now Mrs. McCutchens." Patrick Carlson's tone remained friendly, but his demeanor stiffened ever so slightly.

Matthew sensed a tension in the room that hadn't been there a moment before. Heat shot up the back of his neck. Whatever Annabelle Grayson had done to entangle Johnny's affections, apparently she'd spun the same web that now held her in the Carlsons' good favor.

"Yes, of course." He forced a smile, everything within him rebelling at having to refer to her as Johnny's wife, even if it was true in the legal sense. In that same instant, a vision of the ranchland in Idaho sprang to mind.

Wide meadows lush with spring grasses bordered by a stream like Fountain Creek, birthed from the heart of the mountains towering over it. Envisioning what it would be like to have a place of permanence again helped Matthew to set aside his frustration. For the moment, anyway. Permanence was something he hadn't had in far too long. Constantly being on the move had grown wearisome, as had looking over his shoulder in every new town.

Concentrating on that thought, his response came more naturally the second time. "When I saw . . . Mrs. McCutchens standing there and I realized she was the widow you'd been telling me about, well, naturally I was shocked. I didn't know what to say, how to react, so I just left." He glanced away as the half-truth hung in the air.

"Understandable," Carlson said.

The man's tone held no malice, and yet Matthew felt a warning land silently at his feet. He stared at the plank floor, wondering what to say next.

A pause, not altogether uncomfortable, passed between them.

"I take it you weren't pleased with Jonathan's choice in a wife."

Matthew looked up at the question, feeling exposed and judged at the same time. Yet Carlson's expression suggested neither. While part of Matthew admired the pastor's directness, this wasn't going to be as easy as he'd first thought. He held Carlson's gaze as he answered. "Sir, I don't know what Miss Gray—what Mrs. McCutchens has shared with you about me, but I promise you I can do this job. I can get her safely to Idaho."

"Your credentials are not in question, Matthew. That's not what this is about. And as I said when we first met, your ranching experience is actually an advantage in this situation, if you decided to stay in Idaho, of course." Carlson hesitated, then glanced toward the hallway. "Another man has indicated interest in the job. He came by first thing this morning. I'll be honest with you, he has more experience in guiding and comes with several recommendations. And, frankly, I'm wondering if he and Mrs. McCutchens might not be better suited in this situation than the two of you would be, under the circumstances."

Matthew felt like he'd had the wind kicked out of him. "So you've already made your decision, then?"

"No . . . no. Nothing's final yet. We've all been discussing it in the kitchen. Why don't you join us?" He stood and indicated for Matthew to follow him.

Before Matthew could think of a polite way to decline the offer, Carlson had ushered him into the next room. If he'd felt judged moments before, now he felt as though he'd been summoned before a jury.

CHAPTER TEN

C ONVERSATION FELL SILENT as Carlson led him into the
kitchen. All eyes shifted to him.

Matthew's fingers tightened around his Stetson, and he
had to make a conscious effort not to crush the rim.

"I'd like to introduce Mr. Matthew Taylor." Patrick motioned
toward Hannah. "Mr. Taylor, you already know my wife." Hannah
Carlson was seated at the far end of the oblong kitchen table. To
her left sat an impressive-looking older man—silvered dark hair,
full-bearded, and rugged. "And this is Mr. Bertram Colby." The
deep lines of the man's tanned face, weathered by years in the sun,
bore silent testimony to countless miles on the trail. He could've
been fifty years old, or sixty. Matthew had no way of telling.

But one thing he intuitively knew—this man by the name of
Bertram Colby not only knew every pebble of every trail and rut
between here and Idaho, he'd probably helped blaze most of them.
The vivid image of the Idaho ranchland began to grow hazy in
Matthew's mind.

On Colby's left sat Miss Annabelle Grayson—that's who she still
was to him, regardless of what name he might use in deference to
the Carlsons—with her hands folded primly on the table before her.
Staring directly at Matthew, she gave an almost imperceptible nod
and weak smile. Matthew could muster neither and was the first to
look away.

He took the vacant chair beside Patrick and nodded when Hannah offered him coffee. "Thank you, Mrs. Carlson." As she filled his cup, he caught something in her expression. Not exactly what he would term judgmental—more along the lines of apprehensive. But he felt certain that Mrs. Carlson knew a great deal about Annabelle's side of the story, and that whatever she knew . . . it wouldn't end up working in his favor.

"Mr. Colby, you were telling us about a group you once led from Missouri?"

"That I was, Mrs. McCutchens. I remember a run we made back in '59 from Independence up to Oregon." Bertram Colby's deep rumble of a laugh reverberated in the small kitchen. "There were nigh onto sixty wagons in that group. We only managed about ten miles per day, and I tell ya, there was this one fella from Boston . . . He was the greenest thing I've ever seen."

Bertram Colby regaled them with stories from his past, and laughter filled the kitchen. As Matthew listened, it occurred to him that this man was not sharing his experiences in an effort to gain the job. These experiences were the whole of his life. He could no more cease telling them than he could cease breathing.

"Mr. Taylor," Annabelle said, laughter still lilting her voice. "I would imagine you have a story or two of your own to share."

Not looking at her, Matthew smiled, hoping the discomfort brewing inside him wasn't written plainly on his face. "But none as entertaining as what Mr. Colby has shared, I guarantee you."

Patrick shifted in his chair. "I'm certain both of you gentlemen know the territories well enough to guide Mrs. McCutchens there, and while it's not imperative that she meets up with Jack Brennan's group to accomplish that goal, I would personally feel more comfortable knowing she was traveling with a larger number of wagons, and people." He paused. "I think we'd all agree on the wisdom of there being safety in numbers."

Matthew didn't know if Colby got the pastor's drift, but he sure did. And he could assure Patrick Carlson that this woman's honor—however tarnished—was completely safe with him. Alone on the prairie or not.

"Matthew, in your estimation," Patrick said, "how long do you think it'll take to catch up with Jack Brennan's group?"

Matthew did some quick calculating, factoring in when Patrick had told him the wagon train originally left Denver. "With the size of Brennan's group, they're probably averaging eleven, maybe twelve miles a day. A single wagon, traveling light and with no herd to prod, can move faster than that, for sure. We could probably make upwards of eighteen, twenty miles on flat, open trail." He scanned the faces around the table, strangely heartened when he saw Colby's affirming nod. He sat up a bit straighter. "It being the first day of June, if we were to set a good pace, rising early and pushing into the night, I think Mrs. McCutchens could expect to join the group sometime around the first week of July—middle of the month at the latest—if fair weather holds."

Bertram Colby leaned forward, his forearms resting on the table. "I agree with young Taylor here." He turned to his left and looked at Annabelle. "Do you still have the set of papers Jack Brennan gave your husband before you set out from Denver?"

"I haven't seen them, but I know what you're talking about. I'm sure they're in our trunk."

"I've traveled with Brennan before," Colby continued. "It was a few years back now, but he usually gives his people a good idea of what towns they'll hit along the way, and when. Those papers should tell us what their scheduled supply stops are, depending on how the weather has affected their travels, of course. We can check as we pass through those places and see how long it's been since Brennan was there. That'll give us an idea of their progress."

Matthew watched Annabelle nod attentively, and he wished he'd thought to include all that. It definitely gave Colby an edge in the way of experience.

"Thank you, Mr. Colby, for addressing that issue and for being so thorough in your answer."

Whether intended or not, Matthew felt a subtle backhand in her compliment and smarted at the insult. Miss Grayson used her hands when she spoke, and it struck him as he watched her just how small they were. Delicate.

Then he noticed it for the first time. The thin band of gold encircling her left ring finger.

He stared at the wedding ring, only half listening.

A swift stab of pain knifed through him when he pictured

Johnny's body buried not far from there, and along with it, any opportunity to tell his brother he was sorry for what he'd said, what he'd done. And that he'd do things differently if he could. A vast hollowness rose within, and Matthew fought it back down, clenching his jaw. He should've come back here sooner. Should've tried harder to talk some sense into Johnny when he had the chance.

A sudden rush of anger filled the void inside him. If Johnny had never met this woman, maybe he would still be alive. Matthew recalled Carlson telling him how Johnny had died—a similar circumstance to their mother's death, it would seem. Though it didn't sound as though Annabelle Grayson could have done anything to change that outcome, how could he be certain she had even told them the truth about Johnny's death to begin with? The mounting doubt inside him only nurtured his dislike for the woman sitting across from him.

"Mr. Taylor?"

Matthew refocused, just now noticing that her left hand had disappeared from sight beneath the table.

"Mr. Taylor?" she asked again.

He blinked to clear his vision and forced himself to look at her. Annabelle Grayson's question suddenly processed with him, and he cleared his throat to answer, reminding himself again that no matter how he felt about her, he needed to win her favor. He needed this job to get to Idaho and to reclaim Johnny's land. *His* land.

"We could be ready to leave Willow Springs three days from now, ma'am. Bright and early Saturday morning." Her eyes were a lighter shade of blue than he'd put to memory, and far more discerning. While she wasn't wholly unattractive, looking at her wasn't pleasant for him. All he saw was Johnny. He redirected his answer and attention to Carlson instead. "There're a lot of tasks to be done, sir, as I'm sure you're aware. You and I talked about those things the other day, so I won't go back over those details now. But I'm confident that either Mr. Colby or I could get the job done and be ready to leave by the weekend."

"What exactly are some of those tasks that need to be done . . . Mr. Taylor?" Subtle challenge wrapped itself around Annabelle Grayson's soft voice, and Matthew dragged his focus back to her.

"I'd appreciate your going into some detail, for my sake. If you don't mind."

The muscles in his neck and shoulders tensed. He tried to decipher the intent behind her question but saw only a smooth mask of indifference, as if she hadn't anything better to do than to wait on him. Didn't take him long to figure out where she'd perfected that trait.

What he wasn't sure of was whether she'd asked him the question out of sincere interest or if she was testing him. Considering her former profession, he assumed the latter. He leaned forward, rested an arm on the table's edge, and aimed his comments at her, trying for a halfway sincere tone. "The first thing to be checked is your wagon and team . . . Mrs. McCutchens. Do you have horses or oxen?"

She stared a few seconds before answering. "Horses."

Matthew nodded once. He would've preferred oxen, but since they wanted to make good time—and the less time spent with this woman, the better—horses would do.

"Is that a problem, Mr. Taylor?"

"No, ma'am, no problem. How many?"

"Six. They're the grays out back."

"As I'm sure you're aware," he said, knowing she probably wasn't, "a wagon can travel faster with horses, but horses aren't as sturdy as oxen across the plains. They succumb to the heat faster. We'll need to make sure the grays are all in good health, that they're fit to travel. When's the last time you had them shod? And your wagon? Is it trail worthy to your knowledge?"

Patrick sat forward. "Taylor, I'm sure those are all things that—"

Annabelle shot the pastor a brief smile, then swung her attention back. "I assume, Mr. Taylor, that the grays are all still in good health. They were when they were purchased a month ago. I don't know when they were last shod, and to be honest, I'm not sure about the wagon. As I recall, the right rear wheel has a fissure along the outer rim." Her eyes narrowed slightly. "But I'll leave all that to either you or Mr. Colby to determine." She paused, a slow smile punctuating the authority underlying her words. "Depending on what I decide this morning."

Matthew caught her meaning and gave a curt nod, silently

reevaluating her. The woman could obviously hold her own, and she had a bent for communicating what she truly thought, regardless of what she said. Both traits he greatly admired . . . in a man. "Your current supplies will need to be inventoried. I realize you were already stocked to be on the trail a good long time, but I'd want to double check your provisions. Whatever's lacking will need to be ordered and picked up at the mercantile, feed store, and livery. I'd think most of what we need should be in stock this time of year. 'Course all of this will have to be paid for up front, Mrs. McCutchens." He tilted his head. "And I'm afraid your personal credit won't be any good to the vendors in this town."

Something flickered across her face, and Matthew knew she'd gotten his meaning.

She smiled pleasantly. "No need for credit, Mr. Taylor. I'll be paying for everything in cash."

Matthew stiffened at the thought, knowing she'd be using Johnny's money. And *his*. Annoyed at her confidence, he couldn't say that her answer had surprised him. With the generous wage she advertised to pay a trail guide, he figured she had money. Johnny had told him last fall that the ranch in Idaho was doing well. Remembering how Johnny used to exaggerate when younger, Matthew hadn't really believed him. Now he wondered.

"I'll provide the trail guide with the necessary cash so he can purchase the items we need," Annabelle continued. "Now . . . are there other more pressing issues you can think of, Mr. Taylor, that we need to discuss along these lines?"

Feeling dismissed and resenting it, Matthew nodded. "There's cooking that needs to be done before we can leave. But I'm afraid that'll have to be your responsibility." He kept his tone light and tipped one side of his mouth up. "I won't be much help in that area."

Bertram Colby let out a guffaw. "I'm not much of a cook either, Taylor, so she's outta luck on that with both of us."

Guessing his aim on this would be accurate, Matthew raised a brow and tried for an innocent look. "So let's just hope domesticity happens to be among your list of many talents, Mrs. McCutchens." A twinge of satisfaction registered with him at seeing the subtle wrinkle of her brow. "You'll need to salt down some pork. Dry some fruit, too, if you're of a mind to have that while on the trail. You might also consider—"

"Thank you, Mr. Taylor, for those suggestions." This time, her smile did not warm the blue of her eyes. "You're right in assuming that I'm not too familiar with this type of planning, but Mrs. Carlson has been kind enough to help me. And I think . . . if you were to be given the opportunity," she added, sounding as if he most likely would not, "you might be surprised to discover that I'm a pretty quick learner when it comes to some things."

Matthew hesitated only a second, his desire to put her in her place temporarily overshadowing his logic. "Actually that wouldn't surprise me a bit, ma'am. I was pretty much certain of that fact the moment we met."

He had expected a coolness to frost her expression, but instead it looked as though a candle had been snuffed out behind Annabelle Grayson's eyes. Immediately, Matthew wished he could take back his last remark, regardless of how good it had felt. Not because he was afraid of hurting the woman—though at the moment, her pained look wasn't giving him the pleasure he'd anticipated—but because he knew without a doubt that his careless remark had just cost him this job.

F OR THE NEXT HOUR, they sat around the kitchen table. More questions were asked and answered, though Matthew saw little point in it. Annabelle Grayson had already made her decision, and he'd made it easy for her. The subtle looks exchanged between Patrick and Hannah had been impossible to miss. No doubt they would encourage her to hire Colby.

He caught Annabelle staring at him twice and couldn't help wondering what she was thinking. Every time he looked at her he thought of Johnny. And every time he thought of Johnny, his dislike for her deepened.

"Your wagon tarp could probably stand another oiling too, ma'am," Bertram Colby continued. "In case of rain. You'll need to identify everything you plan on takin' with you, then we'll work to see if it'll all fit in." Colby shot a fast grin at Matthew and Patrick. "Sometimes womenfolk tend to think a farm wagon is as big as a house."

That drew some laughs, and as Mrs. Carlson refilled each of their cups with hot coffee, Bertram Colby told them of furniture and crates of fancy dishes being strewn all the way across Kansas and the Wyoming Territory. "It's like a regular mercantile in some parts. 'Ceptin' it's all free. Problem is, you can't pick the stuff up 'cause there's nowhere to put it. You just have to ponder it, shake your head, and move on. Either that or use it for firewood, which I've done many a time. I remember this fancy table and chairs we came across once . . ."

Matthew stole a glance across the table. As Colby prattled on about the items he'd seen people dump along the way, Annabelle stared into her coffee. A look of melancholy settled over her features. She moved the spoon methodically from side to side, as though lost in thought.

He recalled exactly how she'd been dressed, what she'd looked like, the first time he'd met her. Her dark hair had been coerced to an unnatural shade of red, and the features of her face had seemed harsher with all that color. And her dress, what little there had been of it, bespoke a woman who could be bought, and clearly had been, at a price. What had his brother ever seen in her? What had she offered him—other than the obvious—that would have possibly persuaded Johnny to take her as his wife?

As Matthew sat trying not to stare at her, he realized what gnawed at him most. If someone were to meet Annabelle Grayson for the first time today, or if they were to see her walking down the street dressed as she was now, wearing that blue print dress buttoned clear up to her chin, with white lace circling her wrists and neck, they would assume her to be a lady of character. They wouldn't see beneath the surface—to the prostitute who had enticed and manipulated her way into a good man's life in order to take what didn't belong to her. Though outwardly she might appear to be virtuous, with her misdeeds all carefully tucked away and hidden, beneath it all she was really just a cheap imitation of—

Annabelle stopped stirring her coffee and looked directly at him.

The dialogue in Matthew's head jerked to a halt.

Her expression gave nothing away as she openly searched his face. For some reason, he couldn't turn away. It would have felt too much like hoisting a white flag. As the seconds crept by, he grew steadily uncomfortable under her scrutiny, certain that Annabelle Grayson was privy to the turn his thoughts had taken just a moment before. He shifted in his chair, willing his expression to be as blank as hers.

He'd made his share of mistakes in life. That was undeniable.

And he was working to right them. But it was nothing compared to what she had done. He hadn't made a conscious choice to live as she had lived, to do the vile things she'd chosen to do.

Phrases came to mind, bits and pieces of well-ingrained warnings from a voice now silenced but still remembered. *"The lips of an immoral woman are as sweet as honey, and her mouth is smoother than oil. She'll seduce you with pretty speech. But the man who follows her is like an ox going to the slaughter or like a bird flying into a snare, little knowing it will cost him his life."*

How many times had he heard that from the pulpit? Then again at home. Those thoughts rooted in Scripture were just and true and to be heeded. No matter that the father who had restated them was not.

Matthew blinked and turned away from her.

Patrick leaned forward in his chair. "So gentlemen, is there anything else you'd like to say in closing before Mrs. McCutchens makes her decision?"

No surprise to Matthew, Bertram Colby nodded and answered in customary detail.

When it came his time to respond, Matthew worked to regroup his thoughts, still unable to account for the discomfort inside him. He pushed away his empty cup and tried to sound authoritative, knowing full well it would make little difference. "I agree with Mr. Colby. The journey to meet up with Brennan's group will be harder with just two people, but it can be done. If given the opportunity to partner with another wagon along the way, I'd do that for safety." He considered something that Colby had said. "I've had some dealings with Indians before too. While I know there've been skirmishes with the Arapaho and Kiowa in this area lately, the Cheyenne and Utes seem peaceable enough, and I don't foresee that being an issue where Mrs. McCutchens is headed."

Patrick stood and thanked both him and Colby for their interest in the job. "No doubt you're both qualified, and we appreciate your time this morning." His attention shifted to Annabelle.

She rose slowly. "I too appreciate your time, gentlemen, and your willingness to help me see this journey through." She looked Bertram Colby full in the face, then at Matthew only briefly. "If you don't mind, I'd like to speak with Pastor Carlson privately for a moment."

Colby stepped forward. "My condolences again on the loss of your husband, ma'am. I admire you for seeing this through to the end. Most women might stay put right here, where it's safe and familiar. I think your man would be real proud of what you're doing."

"Thank you, Mr. Colby. The thought that my husband would be proud of me pleases me more than you know."

The unexpected sincerity softening her voice drew Matthew's attention. He noted the sadness around her eyes and, had he not known better, might have believed it to be sincere.

Hannah Carlson led Bertram Colby to the front porch while Matthew hesitated, standing there, knowing he needed to say something. Yet unable to. The tension in the kitchen swelled. He'd never known silence could be so pressing.

He glanced across the table at Annabelle. Chin down, her hands were clasped over her midsection. She was going to make this as hard on him as she could. She'd already made her decision. That much was clear an hour ago. So why not just tell him now and get it over with?

He steeled himself, unsure which bothered him more—purposefully placing himself in the position of asking for anything of this woman, or facing the certainty that she would reject him just as surely as he'd once done her.

———

Annabelle watched Matthew as he shook Patrick's hand. His dislike for her was unmistakable. Gradually, he turned toward her. From his strained expression, it appeared as though the pride he'd swallowed in coming back here today wasn't going down too well. And she felt partly responsible.

She had intentionally baited him earlier by asking him to go into more detail about the tasks that needed to be done for the journey, and he'd walked right into it. But he'd almost forced her hand on it because he wouldn't look at her. He would start out talking to her, then quickly shift his focus to someone else, speaking to them instead. Then when he had asked how she planned on paying for the supplies, she had also anticipated his reaction at her response.

She suspected Matthew assumed she was after Jonathan's money, and knew he'd never believe how surprised she was to learn how much there had been. From his dark expression at hearing that she'd pay for everything in cash, Annabelle knew she'd guessed correctly. Hopefully Matthew Taylor wouldn't ever be fool enough to try his hand at gambling. It wouldn't serve him well.

As he had the first time she'd met him two years ago, he acted cordial enough today, but she sensed the truth of his dislike brewing just beneath the surface. And it hadn't escaped Patrick and Hannah's notice either.

She glanced at Matthew's hand resting on the back of the kitchen chair. His hands were nothing like Jonathan's. Nothing about Matthew Taylor reminded her physically of Jonathan at all. So why was it that every time she looked at him all she could see was her deceased husband?

Matthew Taylor was playing a part to get this job. Nothing more. Annabelle knew it, and from the coolness in his expression at the moment, he didn't seem to mind her knowing. Realizing that, she reminded herself that this man had just lost his brother, and that they hadn't parted on good terms last fall. She remembered the stories Jonathan had shared with her. They all led her to believe that these two men were—or at least had been at one time—very close, and trusting of one another. Until she'd come on the scene. . . .

"Thank you for your consideration for the job, Mrs. McCutchens."

Matthew ground out the words, and Annabelle was surprised he didn't choke on them.

"You're welcome, Mr. Taylor." She tried the tiniest smile again, a peace offering of sorts. He returned it, with all the feeling of a man sentenced to the gallows. What would it be like to travel with him all the way to Idaho? Many of those weeks unaccompanied?

Lonely was the first thought that came to mind. *Challenging* was the second. Neither of which were strangers to her.

"How are you?" she asked. The simple question came without forethought, surprising her.

Similar surprise registered in Matthew's expression. "I'm fine."

He looked down and away when he said it, which told her that he wasn't. Was the frown on his face due to pain at the loss of Jonathan or because of her presence again in his life? Or was it, perhaps, both?

She glanced toward the hallway where Hannah had disappeared with Mr. Colby, then back at Matthew. "If you'll excuse us for a moment, Mr. Taylor, I'd like to speak with Pastor Carlson alone, please."

She figured Matthew wouldn't like her dismissing him like that, and sure enough, before he left the room, his features darkened.

"What was that look for?" Patrick asked once they were alone.

Annabelle shook her head. "I don't think I've ever been so thoroughly unacceptable to anyone in my life." She attempted a laugh to ease the concern lining Patrick's face. "And that's saying a lot, believe me."

"I think God has made your decision much easier than I thought it would be, Annabelle. Much easier."

Silently considering the letter Jonathan had written in the last hours of his life—*Only what we do for God will last*—Annabelle felt a stirring inside her, and she slowly nodded. "I couldn't agree more."

"Bertram Colby is clearly the more experienced man as far as tracking goes, and he's been guiding wagons since before you were born."

"He may be a bit too quiet for me though," she said in mock seriousness. "I like a man who enjoys a little conversation." She arched a brow.

"He does like to talk—that's for sure. But I feel good about him, Annabelle, about his ability to get you there safely. He seems respectful too, someone Jonathan would've approved of. I sense Colby's a man who'll uphold your honor. After all, you'll be traveling together, alone, for at least a month, if not more."

Nodding again, Annabelle walked to the open kitchen window and looked out over the meadow. "I think I'd be safe on that count with both men." But undoubtedly safer with Matthew Taylor. He'd remain celibate for the rest of his life before touching the likes of her.

A warm June breeze stirred Hannah's lace curtains and filled the kitchen with the sweet blend of honeysuckle and lavender.

Only what we do for God will last.

Annabelle breathed in the mingled scents and sighed, letting the remembered phrase settle deeper within. She wanted to live the rest of her life with that thought as a sieve, a threshing floor of sorts in making decisions, in knowing what to do. How did she know if what her heart was telling her to do was right or not? She'd spent the last hour pondering that very question. Did a certain prayer exist that, once prayed, would bring immediate confirmation?

Jonathan had prayed about his decisions, sometimes aloud, sometimes to himself. She only wished she'd paid more attention to them now. He'd often prayed after they'd gone to bed, and she would fall asleep to the sound of his gravelly voice resonating in the darkness in the bed beside her. What she wouldn't trade to sleep beneath that blanket of prayer once more.

"Would you like for me to tell them?"

She turned at the sound of Patrick's voice and shook her head. "No. I think I should do it."

She detected a glimmer of respect as he waited for her to precede him to the front porch.

She pushed open the screen door and spotted Hannah and Mr. Colby sitting together talking. Or rather, Mr. Colby was doing the talking, regaling Hannah with another story from his many travels. Annabelle caught Hannah's eye and winked. Hannah's gaze flicked back to Mr. Colby and she nodded, focusing on her guest. Annabelle watched as Hannah's mouth slowly curved, and though her friend's stare remained fixed on Mr. Colby, somehow Annabelle knew the smile was meant for her.

Matthew Taylor stood beside them, but in every way besides his physical presence, he had separated himself. Hands stuffed into his jeans pockets, shoulders set, attention fixed on the mountain peaks to the west. He seemed to have erected an invisible wall around him. He hadn't even moved at the creaking of the door hinge.

"Gentlemen." Annabelle paused for a moment, staring at Matthew's broad back, wondering again if she was making the right choice, and if Jonathan would have desired something different. She waited until Mr. Colby rose from the swing and Matthew turned.

Matthew pulled his hands from his pockets, his expression

guarded. His eyes darted to hers, away again, then back. And in doing so, betrayed his earnestness. Aided by Jonathan's stories about their childhood, the sudden image of him as a little boy flooded her mind, and she glimpsed the remnant of the neglected child in the man before her. Unexpectedly, her heart softened toward him.

Matthew seemed to want this job so badly, and it made no sense. Certainly he felt no loyalty to her, even if she was his brother's widow. Perhaps he was doing it for the money? With his hands fisted at his sides, jaw clenched tight, she admitted that he did have a desperate look about him.

"Again, to you both," she continued, gathering her thoughts, "I want to say how much I appreciate you applying for the position. I'm impressed with your experience and have no doubt that either of you could guarantee my safety and well-being on this journey."

She took a step toward Bertram Colby and, in turn, saw Matthew slowly bow his head. She couldn't help but watch him from the periphery of her vision as he retreated a half step. "Mr. Colby, your stories are enchanting and make me want to see my new home in Idaho more than ever. Thank you again for your willingness to accompany me, but . . . I've decided to hire Mr. Taylor for this journey."

Annabelle saw Matthew's head come up. In turn, Patrick's eyes went wide and Hannah gave the tiniest smile.

"Not a problem, ma'am. Taylor here will do you a fine job, I'm sure." The genuineness of Mr. Colby's tone rang true, easing Annabelle's hesitance at declining him. A deep laugh rumbled up from his chest. "But I'll miss tellin' you all my stories around the fire at night, that's for sure. I've got lots of 'em too."

"I don't doubt that for a minute, and I'll miss hearing them." She hoped her gratitude was apparent to him. "And thank you again, Mr. Colby, for what you said earlier about my husband being proud of me for making this journey. You couldn't have paid me a higher compliment, sir."

Colby took her hand and brought it to his lips, then gently placed a kiss there. No man, not even Jonathan, had ever done that to her. Annabelle stared, wordless. What was it about a man lightly touching his lips to the crown of her hand that made her feel so feminine, so honored? Whether she was worthy or not.

Giving her fingertips a gentle squeeze, Mr. Colby released her. His gray eyes were keen, and Annabelle thought again that Bertram Colby possessed the friendliest countenance she'd ever seen.

"I'm of the mind, ma'am, that those who go on 'afore us can look back and see what's happenin' to their loved ones here. I've been told I'm wrong, that those in the hereafter aren't bothered with the goings on of now. But I've always been partial to the notion that they're gathered together, cheerin' us on somehow when we've fallen or had a hard time of it. And if that's so, I figure that's exactly what your husband's doin' right now, ma'am. He's cheerin' you on. You, and your little one that's on the way."

A quick intake of breath sounded from Matthew beside her, and cool reality doused what momentary warmth she'd felt at Mr. Colby's kindness. Matthew had been dealt a tough hand recently—learning of Jonathan's death the way he had . . . and now about Jonathan's child in a similar fashion. Though the topic hadn't come up again once Matthew had joined them this morning, she hadn't intentionally kept the news from him. But neither had she looked forward to his reaction upon hearing it.

With Mr. Colby's departure, it felt as though the front porch shrank to half the size.

No one said a word.

Still watching Mr. Colby as he walked back toward town, Annabelle knew Patrick and Hannah were waiting. She took a deep breath.

As well as she had been able to read Matthew up until then, Annabelle searched his expression and came up with nothing. His eyes were now dark, indecipherable, intimidating. So unlike Jonathan's trusting, honest gaze.

Vowing not to be the first to flinch, Annabelle reached into her past for lessons learned at a tender age. Intimidation was something a woman in her former profession quickly learned to deal with or she didn't last long.

Her pulse might be racing, but she had the practiced look of indifference down to an art, and she knew it masked the hurt clenching her chest. "Before Mr. Colby is completely out of sight,

Mr. Taylor, perhaps I should ask you again whether you're still interested in taking this job."

Varying emotions played across Matthew's face, but she could tell from his stance that he wanted to say something. He shot a quick look at Patrick and Hannah as though just remembering they were present, then back to her.

His jaw muscles flexed as he deliberated. "How do you know the baby is his?"

Annabelle's first instinct was to react. Then she thought about it from his perspective and nodded. "That's a fair question, under the circumstances. I know the baby I carry is Jonathan's because I have not been with any other man since June of last year."

Matthew nodded slowly, his entire countenance calling her a liar.

"I'm assuming, Mr. Taylor, that you can work your numbers?"

"Oh, I can work my numbers all right, ma'am. I also know how women like you work, and that's why this whole situation just doesn't add up to me. Why would a man like my brother choose to have a child with a woman like you? Tell me that."

Patrick stepped forward. "Hold it right there, Taylor. I won't stand by any longer and allow you to—"

"No, Patrick." Annabelle put her hand out. "It's fine. I want Mr. Taylor to be able to speak his mind."

Matthew leveled his gaze. "Ma'am, if I were to truly speak my mind, I'd have to ask Mrs. Carlson to leave first."

Annabelle didn't blink, silently admiring his swift reply but daring not to show it. This man had more spine than she'd credited him with. She stared up at him, her eyes never leaving his. "Patrick, Hannah, would you excuse us, please?"

Patrick protested, but Annabelle took him by the arm. "Please, Patrick."

His mouth slowly closed and they went inside. The screen door slammed closed, and then, to both the Carlsons' credit, Annabelle heard the inner door close as well.

"All right, Mr. Taylor. Hannah's gone. No other *ladies* are present to hear your opinions," she said, giving voice to his earlier insinuation. "Feel free to speak your mind. And please, don't hold back on my account."

F ROM HIS SURPRISED EXPRESSION, Matthew apparently hadn't expected her to call his bluff. Secretly, Annabelle doubted he had the courage to go through with it.

"Are you certain . . . Miss Grayson, that you want me to speak my mind?" The calm in his voice contrasted the edge in his stare.

She raised a brow at the sudden change in name. "If you and I are going to be traveling together for the next three months, Mr. Taylor, I'd rather you got it off your chest right now. And you can be sure that whatever you have to say, I've heard it all before."

He gave her a look that said he doubted that, then focused on some point beyond the front porch, as though weighing the cost of being completely honest. Annabelle couldn't help but wonder how it was that one brother got the more handsome features while the other got all the kindness. Or so it would seem.

Matthew's gaze briefly wandered over her face. "I can see why Johnny took a liking to you, Miss Grayson. In a way." His voice was soft, yet there was not a trace of tenderness in his features. "You have a spark about you, and you don't back down easy. My brother would've liked that about you right off. And you're quick-witted too, something he always admired."

Instinctively, for reasons she couldn't explain, Annabelle's guard rose.

"He was a good man, and he had a tender spot in him for lost things. When we were younger, Johnny was always bringing home something. He'd come in cradling a bird that had left the nest too soon or some pup with a broken leg. Mostly things that someone else had dumped along the side of the road. He wasn't too good at seeing things like they really were. He tended to see things . . . and people, like he wished they would be." He crossed his arms. "But I see what kind of person you are. You deceived Kathryn Jennings, and you apparently have the Carlsons fooled. Just like you did my brother. You know how to use people to get what you want. You wormed your way into Kathryn Jennings' life a while back, probably hoping she'd give you money from her land."

A flush of defensiveness heated her. "I never took one penny from Kathryn Jennings. Ask her yourself if you don't believe—"

"And then you saw an easy mark in my brother and won his favor. No doubt in order to lay claim to whatever he had that you could take." Anger flashed in his eyes and his arms went stiff at his sides. "I don't know how you managed it, but you talked him into buying you out of that brothel. You let him do it, all the while knowing you didn't care one whit for him. He knew it too. Or didn't you overhear that part? That night in the shack? Johnny told me then that you didn't love him, so please, don't stand here and pretend like you felt any different about him. Even he knew the truth!"

A good deal taller than her, Matthew Taylor had an imposing presence, especially when angered. His fists clenched and unclenched at his sides. Annabelle doubted he was even aware of doing it, yet it wasn't his fists she feared. She already figured he wasn't the hitting type, and she would know.

A number of thoughts flashed through her mind.

Confronted with his condemnation, she felt the familiar urge to retaliate. With a well-aimed glare, she had withered men whose expressions bore similar contempt, and she had taken pleasure in doing so. It typically came afterward, when the men had gotten what they'd come for and were putting their clothes back on, along with the convenient respectability they'd dumped at her door. Or when she saw them later in town, when loathing had replaced the former lust, and it seemed as though they blamed *her* for what they had chosen to do.

Jonathan would've said the person she once had been was now dead and buried, washed away in the swift current of Fountain Creek last summer. But as she stood there confronted by Matthew's accusations and tasting the bittersweet retaliation on the tip of her tongue, suddenly she wasn't so certain.

Knifed by Matthew's disapproval, she wanted nothing more than to turn that finely honed blade back on him. She knew how to do it too. Matthew wanted to talk about the truth? She would happily oblige.

"I overheard plenty of things in the shack that night, Mr. Taylor. Some of which were of a more . . . *personal* nature than others." She enjoyed watching those honey brown eyes of his lose a shade of confidence. "Things I'm sure you'd rather I hadn't learned."

His jaw hardened. His head tipped in silent challenge.

"I find it funny how a man like you—apparently one who knows so much about people and specifically women like me, as you phrased it—can somehow have managed to . . ."

The words caught in her throat. Something Bertram Colby had said earlier replayed in her mind, and the intentioned cruelty of what she'd been about to say jarred her. It shamed her to imagine that Jonathan might be witnessing her actions now, or that he could read her thoughts and know what she had been about to do. Especially in light of how kind Jonathan had been to her and how much he'd cared about his younger brother.

Matthew shifted his weight, pulling her attention back. "Feel free to speak your mind, Miss Grayson." In a gesture that was quickly becoming familiar, he cocked a single brow and gave her that half smile. "And please, don't hold back on my account."

In another situation, she would have enjoyed his clever wit as he parroted back what she'd said to him moments before. But not this time.

She scrambled to think of another response, one that would satisfy the dare in his tone. "I was going to say, Mr. Taylor, that . . . I find it funny how a man who thinks he has such insight into people, who understands their motives, can manage to have missed the mark so badly on his own brother." Jonathan's face filled her mind as she watched Matthew's smile fade. A place deep inside her opened, and the next words left her tongue of their own accord. "You stand here acting as though you cared so deeply for your brother, while I saw firsthand how you purposely shut Jonathan out of your life. How you said those hurtful things to him and then just left, after so many years of being separated, and without even saying good-bye. I wonder . . . do you have any idea how much you hurt your brother? How disappointed he was?"

Her body trembling, she closed her mouth and wondered where all that had come from. It hadn't been her intention, the last part especially, but remembering the hurt in Jonathan's face after Matthew walked out last fall had unleashed a well of resentment. And from the guilt lining Matthew's face that moment, it appeared she'd accidentally wandered onto a tender topic. For them both.

He was the first to look away.

Seconds passed. Neither of them spoke.

Just moments before, she'd been so certain about hiring Matthew for this job. She would've sworn she'd felt some kind of confirmation inside her. But now . . .

Annabelle was thankful for the muted sounds that filled the uneasy silence between them—the whinny of the grays in the field, the high-pitched squeals of six-year-old Bobby and his sister, Lilly, as they played out back, and the faraway rumblings of a passing wagon on the main road.

Matthew slipped off his hat, then shoved a hand through his hair, resignation lining his face. "Let's be honest with each other, Miss Grayson. At least about one thing." His deep voice grew soft again. "We both know you married my brother in order to get something you couldn't get on your own. Tell me that's not true."

Knowing he wasn't completely in the right, Annabelle wished she could deny what truth there was in his statement. "Part of what you're saying is true, Mr. Taylor. I never would've been able to leave my old life without your brother's help. But I did care for Jonathan. Very much. He was the kindest person I've ever known."

Matthew closed his eyes for a second, then nodded. "Thank you for being honest, Miss Grayson. About that, at least." He stared past her for a few seconds. "Johnny always was too trusting. He gave people the benefit of the doubt when they didn't deserve it. And for whatever reason, he couldn't see through you. I guess he was too . . . captivated by whatever it is that you do. But you need to know that I see who and *what* you are. And you don't appeal to me in the least."

His gaze swept the length of her—slowly down, then back up again—and true to his word, she detected nothing from him even remotely similar to desire. What Annabelle did see, with painful clarity, was the memory of her own flawed face in the splintered reflection of the hand mirror. Suddenly aware of the sharp rise and fall of her chest, she blinked to clear the unwelcome image.

He opened his mouth to say something else, then apparently thought better of it. He shook his head, clearly struggling with what to say next.

But Annabelle knew what was coming. He would tell her that she wasn't worthy to draw the same breath as him, much less take up space in this life. That people like her were rubbish and ought to be treated as such. She'd heard it all before.

Matthew looked down at his boots and sighed. A weariness seemed to move over him. "Miss Grayson, there's a list of things in my mind that I've been wanting to say to you for the last few months, since I found out about Johnny having married you. And for the past couple of days, since learning about my brother's death, that list has only grown longer." A frown crossed his forehead briefly. "But now that I'm here, standing face-to-face in front of you, with the chance to say all those things . . ." A slow sigh left him. He gave a halfhearted shrug. "Seems I'm not able to do it."

"On the contrary, Mr. Taylor, you've been doing quite well. Why stop now?" The words came out more softly than Annabelle would have liked, especially knowing that if she ended up hiring Matthew Taylor, he would feel a need to say these things to her eventually. Better to get it over with now. He needed a bit of goading . . . fine. She knew just what to do.

"You're not having second thoughts about there being a lady present after all, are you, Mr. Taylor?"

A faint smile ghosted his mouth before vanishing. "No, Miss Grayson, that's not what concerns me," he said softly, sincerity replacing cynicism. "I'm afraid the lady in you went missing a long time ago."

Unable to respond, Annabelle knew in that moment—call it a feeling, an instinct, some kind of intuition—that whatever else Matthew Taylor had to say wasn't something she had heard before. Nor was it something she would welcome.

"You probably won't believe me, and to be honest, I guess it doesn't really matter to me that you do, but . . . I was coming back here to Willow Springs hoping to find my brother and make amends. I'd never make Johnny out to be a saint. You knew him, so I'm assuming you found that out real quick. Underneath it all, though, he was a good man. A decent man." He glanced down, then back up at her, his expression pained. "You were honest with me a minute ago, so I'll be honest with you.

"I still hold the same opinion that I voiced that night in the shack. I think Johnny made a mistake in marrying you. I think you married him to get out of that brothel, to get his money, his land, and whatever else you could. And while I don't find any pleasure in saying this to you right now . . ." He gave a soft laugh without humor. "Not like I thought I would when I pictured it in my mind so many times, my brother, God rest his soul, deserved better than some sullied . . . tainted . . . used-up woman like you."

His last words came out slowly, softly, and with deliberate fore-thought. And each one found a weakness in her armor and struck to the heart.

Annabelle tried to draw a breath but the air felt trapped at the base of her throat. How often had she used those very same words when thinking about herself. But never had she heard them spoken back to her with such pained gentleness.

"And I still don't buy your line about the child being his either. If there even is a child. Convenient plan though—I'll give you that." He hesitated for a moment. "You asked me a question earlier. Now I guess I need to ask you the same one. Have *your* feelings changed? Are you sure you still want me for this job?"

Watching Matthew Taylor stand before her, patiently waiting for her answer, it was clear that he had no clue how much he'd just wounded her. Did she still want to hire him? Or would she rather have Bertram Colby? Bertram Colby would never *think* of address-ing her in the way Matthew Taylor just had. Of course, Bertram

Colby didn't know her past, and she hadn't just buried his only brother.

Only what we do for God will last.

In her mind's eye, Annabelle saw Jonathan's flowing script and the words he'd written, and something flickered inside her, akin to a flame, growing steadier and stronger. She slowly shook her head. "No, Mr. Taylor. I'm not sure that I do still want to hire you."

He let out the breath he'd apparently been holding. Again a look of resignation shadowed his handsome face.

"And I may well regret it one day. Soon," she added. "But the job is still yours."

He gave a brief, sharp laugh as if to say he thought she was jesting.

To prove that she wasn't, and knowing he wouldn't like it, she found pleasure in her next words. "We leave at sunrise on Saturday. That gives us three days. Do you think you can have everything ready by then?" Barely waiting for his nod, she continued. "The wagon's out back with the supplies—you can check the horses too. Prepare a list of items you think we'll need, and then let me look over it so I can add anything that might be missing. Purchase whatever else you think is required. See that the trunks and crates in the barn are loaded and that the team is hitched and ready."

Remembering, she reached into her pocket. "Here's money for the supplies as well as a third of your pay up front, as was advertised. If you need more, let me know. And just so our understanding is clear, Mr. Taylor, you'll get the rest once—"

"Once I get you to Idaho." He took the wad of bills from her hand without touching her and held her gaze for a beat longer than necessary. "I'm real clear on our understanding." He pocketed the cash. "I'll see to the horses first thing in the morning, and I'll have everything loaded and ready to go on Saturday." He nodded once. "At sunrise, like you asked. Mind you, I don't know what you're used to, but I aim to meet up with Brennan's group as soon as possible, Miss Grayson. We'll each have our duties on the trail too. Everybody has to pull their own weight. We'll keep a steady pace, movin' with the sun and resting come nightfall."

"I'll match whatever pace you set, Mr. Taylor."

He stared at her for a moment, then gave a slow nod. "Miss

Grayson, I do believe we have ourselves a deal."

"Very well." She turned to go, then paused. "By the way, I'd appreciate your addressing me by my married name. Like it or not, I *was* your brother's wife." She smiled and tasted a hint of arsenic in the gesture. "And for the record, I'll ask you to kindly remember who's done the hiring here."

She walked into the house, quietly closed the door behind her, and leaned against it for support. A tremble stole through her. What had just happened to her out there? She was supposed to be a new creature in Christ, refashioned in the likeness of His image, and yet she'd enjoyed every single second of putting Matthew Taylor in his place. How would she survive weeks on the trail with someone who brought out the absolute worst in her, and with so little effort?

Perhaps it wasn't too late to change her mind. She turned and peeked through a slit in the curtain.

Matthew stood poised at the edge of the porch steps, his profile testimony to his pensive mood. Perhaps he was sharing a thought similar to hers. She took the chance to observe him, feeling much like a child succumbing to the lure of the cookie jar. Handsome didn't aptly describe the man, no matter his shortcomings. Not with that languid air of confidence he wore so casually. But she knew better. That kind of appeal was only surface deep. If given the choice, she would choose the older brother again. Without hesitation.

Matthew suddenly turned and looked back at the door.

Annabelle dropped the curtain and pressed up against the wall, her pulse racing.

Not until she heard his boot heels on the porch stairs did her heart consider returning to a normal rhythm. She leaned her head back and sighed. Sizing people up had always been a gift, but she had definitely underestimated Matthew Taylor. Not only in the depth of his resolve but most assuredly in his devotion to his brother.

L IKE A TAP ON THE SHOULDER, instinct prompted Matthew to turn.

He did, slowly, and spotted the man standing in the open doors of the livery. Early morning light filtered gray through the cracks of the aging wooden structure, barely illuminating the interior. Heart pounding, Matthew noiselessly stepped back into the empty stall behind him, pretty sure the man hadn't seen him yet.

Jake Sampson took the reins of the stranger's horse and led the animal directly toward Matthew. Telling himself he was jumping to conclusions, Matthew couldn't ignore the warning bells going off in his head. He pressed up against the side of the stall and hoped Sampson would figure he was in the back with the grays he'd brought in that morning.

Sampson chose the empty stall next to his, and Matthew breathed easier.

"You gonna be in town long, mister?"

"Long enough. A day or two at most. I need directions to Sheriff Parker's office."

The voice wasn't familiar, but the accent bled of Texas drawl, and Matthew's jaw tightened hearing it. He'd definitely never seen the man before, but that didn't ease his discomfort.

"Sheriff Parker left Willow Springs a few months back. Man by the name of Joshua Garvin took his place. But I doubt he's in yet," Sampson said, closing the door to the stall. "That'll be two dollars down, and we'll settle the rest when you come back for him." There was silence for a few seconds and Matthew could picture Sampson pocketing the bills. "This being Thursday, Sheriff Garvin's over at Myrtle's about now havin' steak and eggs. You could prob'ly catch him over there. Got some business with him, do you?"

Matthew clenched his teeth at the way Jake Sampson was carrying on. He'd give any woman a run for her money.

"Just need to pass some names and faces by him. I'd be obliged if you'd look through them too, when you have time."

"Be happy to. Lots of people come through my place here, and I get to know all of 'em."

"Let me know if any of them ring a bell," the stranger said as the two men walked toward the front. "Any tips and I'll make it worth your while. I'll stop back by after breakfast and pick them up."

When Matthew finally heard the steady rhythm of Sampson's mallet on the anvil, he stepped from the shadows. Waiting until the man turned his back, Matthew quickly crossed to the back of the livery and made his approach from that direction.

Sampson looked up, smiling. "I about forgot you were here, Taylor. I'll get to them grays later this afternoon. They'll be ready by morning—don't you worry." He gave the lever on the side of the forge a few pumps, feeding the flames in the pit, then bent back over his work.

"No problem. I appreciate you seeing to them." Matthew spotted a stack of papers on Sampson's workbench a few feet away.

"You said you were leaving in a couple of days. Where you headed this time?"

Matthew studied Sampson for a minute, silently debating. "I feel like trying my luck in California."

"California . . ." Sampson let out a low whistle. "Now that's a place I promised myself I'd get to some day. Never have, though. Guess all that gold layin' around for the taking is gone by now, huh? You travelin' alone?"

"Mornin', Jake. Can you take a quick look at something for me?"

In unison, both Matthew and Sampson turned at the question.

Matthew recognized the man standing in the doorway from having seen him around town, but he didn't know his name.

"Sure thing, Wilson!" Sampson said, laying his hammer aside. "I'll be right with you. Just let me finish up in here." He wiped his hands on his apron. "It's gonna be a busy one, Taylor."

Grateful for the reprieve from the older man's questions, Matthew sighed. "That's okay, I need to be going anyway. Thanks again for seeing to those grays, Jake. I'll be back for them tomorrow."

As soon as Sampson disappeared out the front, Matthew crossed to the workbench and picked up the stack of parchments. He estimated fifteen or twenty sheets and leafed through the first ten, glancing up at the door every few seconds.

Eleven, twelve. Gradually, his unease lessened.

Hearing Sampson's laughter coming from outside, he kept flipping the pages, sometimes reading the name first, other times scanning the charcoal likeness. On one page, the reward amount at the top drew his attention, and he studied the rendering of the man below. Not really familiar looking but something about the face made him linger.

He read the name again. Nothing.

A noise sounded behind him. Matthew dropped the stack back onto the workbench and turned. Finding no one, he chided himself on being so jumpy and flipped through the remaining pages.

On the next to the last sheet, he froze.

His thumb and forefinger tightened on the parchment. An icy finger of dread trailed up his spine. He shot a quick look at the door, then back down again.

"I don't know. I may have that part inside, let's see if . . ."

Matthew creased the page and crammed it inside his shirt. Thinking again, he picked two more from the stack at random and did the same. Better not to draw attention to the one page that was missing. A crooked trail was harder to follow than a straight one.

"Find any you like, Taylor?"

Heart pounding, Matthew ran his hand over the harness he was now holding. "I like them all. You do real good work, Jake."

"Thank you, sir. I'll make you a deal on one too."

"I appreciate that. I'll think about it and let you know in the morning."

Matthew was halfway back to the Carlsons' before he realized he hadn't stopped at the mercantile. He retraced his steps and left the list with the woman behind the counter, managing to be friendly without encouraging conversation. Leaving the store, he made his way back to the Carlsons' home using less traveled alleyways and being sure to stay far away from Myrtle's.

"That was a delicious dinner, Mrs. Carlson. Thank you for inviting me to stay." When Hannah reached for his empty plate, Matthew handed it to her, rising from his seat. She motioned for him to sit back down, and he did so, reluctantly. He enjoyed the Carlson family, but the parchment he'd tucked into his saddlebag earlier was wearing a hole in his conscience, plus he was tired and sore from working on the wagon all afternoon.

"You're welcome, Mr. Taylor. I'm glad you could join us. You're invited to take the rest of your meals with us over the next couple of days too, if you'd like."

"Thank you, ma'am." He felt a tug on his sleeve.

"Are you staying for dessert, Mr. Taylor?" Lilly smiled up from the seat beside him. The eleven-year-old was a younger version of her mother, with thick dark hair and violet eyes—and a fondness for jabbering, as he'd discovered over the past hour.

"Of course he's staying, Lilly." Patrick scooted his chair back from the table and assisted Bobby up to his lap. "He wouldn't want to miss your mother's cherry pie. Now help with the dishes, please."

Matthew settled in for a few more minutes.

"Matthew, you're also welcome to bed out in the barn, if you like. That way you could work as late you want, and you'd be close in case Mrs. McCutchens needs something, or if the two of you need to discuss anything about your trip."

Knowing what Carlson was up to, he nodded, then looked across the table at Annabelle. She stared at Lilly, then back at him. He read something in her eyes and got the distinct impression that if they were alone she would tell him what she was thinking—which made him glad they weren't. Her gaze wove a trail to the base of his chair, and he suddenly became aware of a soft thumping noise on the floor . . . and then realized it was his own boot.

She smiled at the sudden silence.

He still couldn't believe she'd agreed to hire him after all he'd said to her yesterday. Even more, he couldn't believe all that he'd risked by saying it to her. Yet he would've felt like a coward had he not stood up to her, especially after the way she challenged him. The satisfaction he'd anticipated at telling her what he truly thought about her hadn't come, and he couldn't shake the memory of the look on her face. For the briefest time, she had appeared genuinely wounded, as though no one had ever told her what she was to her face before.

His thoughts went to the child she claimed was Johnny's. Who was to say she hadn't simply invented the story to further ensnare his brother? To keep Johnny from putting her aside? And even if she was in the family way, she couldn't prove it was his brother's baby.

He turned back to Carlson. "I appreciate your offer, Pastor. That would be handy, thank you." Staying in their barn would keep him from having to go back and forth through town too—something he wanted to avoid. He wished they could leave sooner, but there was too much left to do. "And actually, Mrs. McCutchens and I spoke yesterday. I think we got things pretty well laid out. Wouldn't you say, ma'am?"

Annabelle wore a pleasant countenance, no matter how quiet she'd been during dinner. Not that he was complaining.

"Yes, I believe we have a very clear understanding, Mr. Taylor." She rose and gathered the rest of the plates, then peered down at his right boot as she walked by.

Matthew pressed his boot hard to the floor. Silently appreciating her subtlety, he didn't show it. Even when she wasn't talking, the woman spoke too much.

After eating, in record time, the best cherry pie he could remember, he seized the opportunity and said good-night.

———

With her skirt covering her legs, Annabelle let them dangle off the front porch, swinging them back and forth. She breathed in the cool night air. "I think I'll miss the Colorado nights most of all." At least the ones she'd experienced since leaving the brothel.

Patrick sat next to Hannah on the porch swing a few feet away, his arm around her shoulders. The gentle creak of their swaying was the only sound in the darkness surrounding them.

"Hannah and I were wondering . . . did you and Jonathan talk much about Idaho? About your home there and what it would be like?"

"Some. He couldn't wait for us to get there so he could show it to me. He said it was the most beautiful land he'd ever seen, and that's saying a lot, because he loved it here. He actually said Idaho reminded him a lot of Colorado. But whatever kind of place it is doesn't matter—it'll be special to me because it was special to him."

She reached for her tea, and her wedding ring tinked against the glass. Being here again, talking on the porch late at night, reminded her of when Jonathan had courted her. They'd spent many an evening out here visiting with the Carlsons.

"I was thinking again today about Jonathan's letter," Hannah said. "I never realized he was so gifted with words."

"Neither did I." Annabelle smiled to herself. "Until I read it. I just knew he used to write some after I'd gone to bed."

Night sounds filled the quiet. Crickets, nestled safe in Hannah's flower beds, chirruped their lullaby. The aspen leaves quaked in the wind and the sound of a thousand tiny bells carried on the breeze. Annabelle closed her eyes, listening.

The snap of a twig brought her eyes open.

It sounded again, just around the corner, to the side of the house. Probably some curious coon foraging for a late-night dinner, but still . . . She searched the darkness, not frightened . . . just no longer convinced they were alone. Perhaps Matthew had decided to accept Patrick's invitation to join them after all. He'd seemed on edge at dinner tonight—jumpy. It could stem from his eagerness to start the journey, but she doubted it.

"Have you learned anything else about Sadie and where she might be?"

Hearing Hannah's soft question, a pressing weight filled Annabelle's chest. "No. I checked at the saloon yesterday, then went back to the brothel to talk to some of the other girls. I asked everyone I knew, but none of them could tell me anything." She listened for the sound on the side of the house again but heard nothing.

"Whoever has Sadie is long gone—I'm sure of it. With her looks, she stands out too much for them to keep her nearby." Which was part of the girl's appeal, and curse. "But maybe, in a way, that's a good thing. If she's in one of the towns we pass through on our way north, or has been recently, I should be able to track her down."

"What will you do when you find her?"

She appreciated Patrick's use of *when* rather than *if.* "I'll buy her, if they'll let me."

"And if they won't?"

Lifting her shoulders, she sighed. "I don't know. But I won't leave her behind. Not again. Every day I live free of that life, I think of that poor child still trapped in it."

She heard a deep exhale. The creak of the swing went silent.

"I don't know quite how to ask this, Annabelle."

She looked over at Patrick in the darkness. His head was bowed, his forearms resting on his thighs. "You can ask me anything, Patrick. Same for you, Hannah. You both know that."

"We don't want to pry, Annabelle." The darkness couldn't mask the tenderness in Hannah's voice. "We just want to try and understand. . . ."

"Understand what?" she asked after a long pause.

Patrick's words came softly. "Understand what you've been through. You told Hannah and me that you'd spent sixteen years . . . working. . . . I don't mean any offense by this question, but . . ." He paused, as though unable to force out the words.

"How could so many years go by without me finding some way to escape?" Annabelle said, finishing the question for him.

"Did you ever think of just running away? Maybe leaving during the night?"

Patrick's hesitance touched her, as did his naiveté. "First off, I'm afraid there's little left that would offend me, and I can't imagine any of it ever coming from either of you two." Annabelle gently rubbed her wrist, feeling the knot on the underside. "I did run away, lots of times at first. But the beatings got worse each time they brought us back."

"Got worse?" Hannah asked.

"The madams I've worked for employed men too. There was always one, at least. He made sure the customers stayed in line, that they didn't get too rough with the girls. He'd break up fights and handle any business the madam might have with the law. He also made sure the girls were 'safe.' At least that's what they called it." Gallagher, Betsy's man, came to mind. Annabelle shuddered thinking about what he'd done to her and the other girls, making sure they knew their boundaries.

"If a girl ever disappeared, the madam would send him to bring her back, on account of what the girl owed. Half of everything we made went to the madam right off the top, and then we also had to pay for room and board and clothes. A girl can't get credit on her own—none of the merchants would lend to us." She thought of Matthew and how he'd not so delicately made that point the other morning. "So we had to borrow the money, from the madam."

"Which always just got you further into debt." Patrick's voice deepened in understanding.

"You'd end up owing her more and more. Sometimes she'd offer to forgive what a girl owed in exchange for signing a new contract. I did that the first couple of times, thinking I could earn my way out." She huffed. "Never worked. She only worked you harder—longer hours and more customers per night."

"I had no idea." His voice came out a whisper. "I'm so sorry."

Hannah's soft sob in the darkness echoed his apology.

"After trying to run away and being brought back so many times, each time a little more broken than the last, some of the girls I knew were just so tired they got out the only way they could. They'd overdose on morphine or laudanum . . . but I never could do that." Not that she hadn't considered it.

Fighting an old fear, Annabelle firmed her lips together as Sadie came to mind again. Oh, God, what had happened to that child? Where was she? Annabelle searched the darkened fields to the side of the house. The thick tufts of spring grasses, now calf-high, shone gray in the moonlight spreading out across it. "I was too afraid." Her laugh came out brittle as a slivered memory skirted beneath the veil separating her old life from the new. "I felt trapped. I didn't want to live anymore, but I was even more afraid to die."

"We're so sorry, Annabelle," Patrick repeated again, his voice a rough whisper.

The silence stretched between them.

She turned and looked back at them. Patrick's head was bowed—Hannah's too. He was such a good man, a godly man, as she'd learned to think of him, and he wasn't completely naïve to ways different from his. And Hannah was as good as she could imagine a woman being. The three of them hadn't spoken much about her life in the brothel before, but when they had, she'd always been honest. She wondered now if she'd been too honest in her answers tonight.

"I'm sorry for what all those men have done to you, Annabelle."

So unexpected was Patrick's response, the soft compassion in his voice, that she didn't know what to say. It sounded as though he were offering an apology *on behalf* of all those men. How many there had been, she couldn't remember. And didn't want to. Though she couldn't erase them from her memory, she could live from this day forward as if she had. And that's what she determined to do.

CHAPTER | FOURTEEN

FRIDAY MORNING MATTHEW ARRIVED at the livery before
dawn. His sullen mood only darkened upon discovering he
wasn't the first customer in line. The man already waiting
wasn't familiar to him, but he seemed harmless enough. Matthew
glanced up and down the street, thankful that most of the town
wasn't yet stirring and that the short stocky man beside him wasn't
bent on conversation.

Surprise shone on Jake Sampson's face as he pushed open the
oversized plank-wood doors. "Why, you're both up awful early this
mornin'." He looked down the darkened street. "Beatin' the crowd,
eh?" He laughed as though he'd told a good one.

They followed Jake inside.

"You here for that wagon, Duncan? It's ready, and if I might
say"—he winked, offering that crooked smile he so often wore—
"it's a fine piece of work. I stayed up last night makin' sure it's all
just like you . . ."

As Jake prattled on, Matthew assessed the wagon near the back
of the building, then considered the man beside him. Duncan
appeared hard-pressed to look directly at Jake, and he was giving
the hat in his hands a fairly good workout.

"Jake." Duncan interrupted him and shot a look at Matthew
before briefly lowering his head. "I don't know how to tell you this

but . . . I'm not gonna be able to take the wagon. I still need it, mind you, and I plan on doin' right by you. . . . I just don't have the cash right now."

The smile slipped from Jake's face. "Is it Ellen again?"

Duncan nodded, not answering for a moment. He cleared his throat. "Doc Hadley's been doin' all he can, but she's just not gettin' much better. And our son's come down with it too, so works kinda piling up for me." His expression grew earnest. "But I brought what I could today." He dug into his front pocket. "Take it as a pledge on my part, that I'll—"

Jake shook his head and waved the money away. "I'm not gonna do that, Duncan."

The man held out the bills again. "It's not much when weighed against what I owe, but I need you to take it. I won't feel right about things if you don't."

Matthew watched, wordless, curious to see Jake's reaction. Jake was right—the wagon was a fine piece of work. Sturdy and solid, built for heavy loads over long miles, and no doubt it bore Sampson's customary excellence in craftsmanship. However foolish the man might be otherwise. Plus the cost of materials alone must have set him back a fair amount.

Jake laid a hand on Duncan's shoulder, and in that moment, Matthew watched a depth of understanding move into Sampson's expression that he would never have expected possible. "Duncan, I want you to go back home, get those two dappled mares, and come back and get this wagon. It's yours. I know you're good for it, and frankly, it's better for you 'n me both if you keep that farm goin'." He clapped the man's shoulder. "That way we both come out ahead in the long run."

Duncan finally nodded. "I don't know how to thank you, Jake." He held out the money again, his expression insistent.

Jake took the bills. "Tell you what. Does your Ellen still have some of them preserves put up?"

"You know she does. She makes the best around."

"You bring me back a couple of jars of her strawberry and we'll call it even for now. Deal?"

Matthew watched as the two men shook hands, still marveling at the brief transformation in Sampson.

Once Duncan left, Sampson's usual crooked grin was back in place. "You're here for those grays, right, Taylor? Them's some fine animals."

Matthew considered the man before him. The old Jake Sampson was back. For now. "Yes, they're fine enough." He nodded in the direction Duncan had headed, unwilling to let go of what he'd witnessed. "That was a nice thing you did just now."

Jake shrugged it off. "Weren't no more than other people have done for me when I needed it." Jake held his gaze for a second. "You ever been down on your luck, Taylor?"

The question, coupled with Sampson's close scrutiny, jolted him.

"I have," Jake continued, heading back toward the grays. He motioned for Matthew to follow. "Been down on my luck, I mean. It's a hard thing for a man not to be able to make it on his own, but when he's got a family to take care of . . ." He shook his head. "Not bein' able to protect the ones you love can just about do a man in. That, and losin' his dignity."

Sampson paused by a stall. "A man's gotta know that his word is worth somethin'. When he gets up in the mornin', he may see someone in the mirror that ain't done real well by the world's yardstick, but he'll be able to hold his head high if he knows he's done what he could and that he kept his word." He patted the pocket that held Duncan's meager payment. "Take away a man's dignity, and you take away the very thing he needs to keep pushin' ahead in this world."

Matthew nodded, unable to think of a response to such unexpected counsel while also grappling with the disturbing feeling that Jake Sampson knew the truth about him. But that was impossible. The old man hadn't had time enough to go through that whole stack of parchments yesterday . . . had he?

In silence, they worked together to harness the grays. Matthew paid Sampson what he owed and climbed up to the buckboard. "Thanks again for doing this so quickly for me."

"That's my job. Take care of yourself, Taylor. And pick up some of that gold out there in California for me, ya hear?"

Matthew managed a smile. Wasting no time, he headed to the mercantile, where he pulled the wagon around to the back and loaded the supplies. Shortly past eight o'clock, he arrived back at the Carlsons', his suspicions about Sampson knowing his secret having lessened considerably. He breathed easier knowing he wouldn't have to make another trip into town before leaving tomorrow morning.

Then he saw it. The note tacked to the barn door.

Without reading it, he knew who it was from. She was starting early today. Shaking his head, he climbed down from the wagon and strode past the note into the barn.

He spent the next hour unloading crates of additional supplies and other items from the wagon. He carried them into the barn, then sorted them into stacks so he could inventory and repack them for the long journey. Hefting a fifty-pound sack of flour from his shoulder to the workbench—a request Miss Grayson left on a note last night, her fourth note in the past two days—he heard the back door to the house slam shut.

Stepping into the shadows of the barn, he watched her as she crossed the yard to the clothes hanging on the line. Annabelle looked in the direction of the barn, and he wondered if he only imagined the quick shake of her head. Then he glanced at the note still posted on the doorframe and smiled.

One more reason to get on the trail—where *he* would be in charge.

He walked to the well out back and sent the bucket plunging into the darkness. Listening for the splash, he waited a few seconds, then hauled the bucket up. After drinking his fill, he poured the rest over his face and neck. The morning air was crisp and customarily dry, so he'd barely broken a sweat, but the water still felt good against his skin.

He needed to get out of this town. No—revise that—he needed to repay his debt. But realizing that wasn't possible anytime soon, the former option was the only one available to him.

Back inside the barn, he tossed a quick look over his shoulder at the house and scanned the yard. Empty. He hesitated, then withdrew the pieces of folded parchment from the bottom of his saddlebag. He sat down on a stool, pulled the bottom page out, and moved it to the top.

It still didn't seem real to him, sitting here, staring at his own likeness. His face was thinner now and shaven of the beard depicted in the drawing. But the name printed in bold capital letters across the top made the crude depiction of his features needless.

He ran a forefinger across his Christian name, the name given to him by his mother, and was glad she wasn't alive to see this. He'd said something similar to Johnny in anger the last time he'd seen him, and that comment loomed in the background of his thoughts, but Matthew stuffed the memory back down, unwilling to deal with it at the moment.

He had only one personal recollection of his mother, and it wasn't even a memory, really. He couldn't remember the exact color of her eyes or how she had fashioned her hair, or what she used to wear. But tucked away in his memory of her was the scent of dew-laden honey-suckle and sunshine. That's all he had left. Laura McCutchens Taylor died when he was only four, so he'd had to depend on Johnny to fill in the holes in his memory, creating pictures of her in Matthew's young mind that he still clung to as a grown man.

Strange how deeply he could miss his mother's presence in his life when he couldn't even remember having known her.

He moved his finger across the page to his last name. He stared at it, feeling a remnant of the relief—mixed with guilt and resent-ment—that he'd experienced when first learning his father was finally gone. A son shouldn't be relieved to hear that his father had died. It wasn't right. Then again, Haymen Taylor had never been much of a father to either of his sons.

Matthew took a deep breath and slowly exhaled. The stranger he saw yesterday at the livery was most likely a bounty hunter. It made sense that the men searching for him would choose that route. His debts weren't exactly of a legal nature, after all. The stranger yesterday hadn't looked like a Texas Ranger, despite the telling drawl. But he couldn't be sure.

He stared at the reward amount. Sobering thing for a man to see his life measured in a sum, and not even a very large sum at that. For just a moment he imagined that his former employer in San Antonio would let him pay the reward money and call it even. But Señor Antonio Sedillos didn't work on payment plans, and he never negotiated. Matthew had learned that firsthand.

He bowed his head and heard the thumping of his own heartbeat.

Nauseating heat filled his stomach, then quickly subsided, leaving a cold seed of fear in its place. How had he sunk this—

"Mornin', Mr. Taylor."

He nearly jumped out of his skin. "Lilly . . ." Her name came out in a rush. The Carlsons' daughter stood just inside the barn, her hands behind her back. "What brings you out here, little one?"

He shoved the parchments back inside his bag and cinched the leather tie tight. He needed to burn them, but there'd not been time for that at the livery yesterday morning. And he couldn't risk leaving anything that might be discovered in the livery forge.

"I'm not that little, Mr. Taylor. I'll be twelve next month."

He smoothed his sweaty palms on his jeans, noting the stubborn tilt of the girl's chin. "Oh really? That old?" Dressed and ready for school, she rocked back and forth from the balls of her feet to her heels.

She stopped rocking. "Are you angry at me?"

"No, not at all. Why would you think that?" Seems Lilly had inherited her father's directness as well as her mother's beauty. "You look very pretty today, Lilly."

"Thank you." She beamed at the compliment, fingering her ankle-length skirt. "Mama says for you to come get some breakfast. She made biscuits and gravy." Her eyes lit as she ran her tongue over her lips. "We all ate earlier, but I'm keeping your plate warm on the stove."

She fell into step right beside him, and though she did well in compensating, Matthew noticed her slight limp. He wondered if she'd been born with some problem or if it had happened through an accident. He held the back door open for her and heard noises coming from the kitchen. Maybe Annabelle would already have eaten by now; he didn't welcome another spar with her. He could only hope.

"Good morning, Mr. Taylor. Did you see my note?"

Sometimes hope was a shallow thing. "Morning, Mrs. McCutchens." He took a seat at the far end of the table. Lilly deposited a plate before him, all smiles. "Yes, ma'am. I saw it. Thank you, Lilly," he added in a whisper. It surprised him when she claimed the chair next to his. He took a bite of biscuit smothered in sausage gravy. "Mmm, you were right, little one. This is delicious."

Lilly's eyes widened. "I told you, Mr. Taylor, I'm going to be—"

"Twelve years old next month." He nodded. "That's right, I remember now. You're practically all grown up."

She rewarded him with another smile. *Sweet kid.*

Matthew felt Annabelle watching him, waiting. He savored another bite, feeling the satisfying effects of having food in his stomach.

"And, Mr. Taylor?" Annabelle's voice gained a tone, one he'd heard before.

He took his time looking up, remembering her parting words two days ago on the porch. *"Kindly remember who's done the hiring here."* He grimaced as he pictured again the smirk she'd worn. Never had a woman spoken to him so bluntly before, and with such challenge. It wasn't becoming.

"And . . . what, ma'am?" he finally said.

"What's your answer?"

"Actually, I haven't had time to read your note yet."

Her sigh mirrored his own irritation. "Mr. Taylor, I wrote telling you that I think we need to delay our departure by a day because—"

"No. That's impossible." He plunked down his fork and rose. The kitchen chair scraped across the wooden floor. "We leave tomorrow morning at sunrise, as planned."

Lilly reappeared at his side holding the coffee kettle. He hadn't noticed she'd left. "More coffee, Mr. Taylor?"

Annabelle shrugged. "Well, I don't see how waiting one more day is going to make that much difference. Hannah is planning to go to visit a friend of hers a ways from town today. The woman's ailing, and I'd like to go along to meet her, especially since I won't be back here . . . at least not for a long time."

As though the matter were settled, she presented her back to him.

Matthew bristled, sorely wanting to cross the room and wring her little neck. "Mrs. McCutchens, first off, I'd appreciate you not turning your back on me when we're having a discussion. Some might see that as rude."

Ever so slowly, she faced him again, one dark brow arched.

"And secondly, I suggest, ma'am, that you enjoy your visit this morning and then come home and finish packing. Because that wagon is leaving tomorrow morning as planned."

"Mr. Taylor, would you like some more coffee?"

Matthew worked to keep his tone even with the girl. "Yes, Lilly, that's fine. Thank you." When she didn't move to pour, he noticed her fading smile. Not knowing what he'd done wrong, he added another quick "Thank you, Lilly" in hopes of making it right.

She filled his half-empty cup to the brim and returned the pot to the stove, her shoulders still slumped. "I'd best be off to school now."

Not knowing why, he somehow felt responsible for Lilly's sudden change in mood, and he was at a loss to know how to right it.

She stood at the doorway, her eyes doleful. "Bye, Mr. Taylor. I'll see you this afternoon. You'll still be here, right?"

Matthew nodded as she closed the door. His breakfast was not nearly as appealing now. Not with what this woman had just sprung on him. A charcoal image sprang into his mind. He had to win this argument, plain and simple.

"Mrs. McCutchens . . ." Using her married name now that they were alone rankled him, but it was a concession he was willing to make. Especially under the circumstances. "You hired me to get you back with Brennan's group, then on to Idaho before the first snowfall. That means we have a schedule to keep." He raced to think of reasons one day would make such a difference. Other than the obvious one, which he couldn't tell her.

"Be careful with her, Mr. Taylor."

He squinted, then glanced behind him. "Be careful with who? What are you talking about?"

Annabelle shook her head and gave him a pitying stare. "You have absolutely no clue, do you?"

"No clue about what?"

"About that sweet young girl who just left here."

He glanced in the direction Lilly had gone. The woman had lost her frail mind.

"She's smitten with you, Mr. Taylor." A single brow slowly rose. "For whatever reason," she added just loud enough for him to hear.

He scoffed. "You don't know what you're talking about. Which brings me back to your original question. No, we're not delaying one day. We leave here tomorrow as planned. They say rain is supposed to be moving in soon, and I want to be on our way before it does."

"Who's saying that?" She peered out the kitchen window. "Doesn't look like rain to me."

"I won't take the chance of being delayed, Mrs. McCutchens. Not when I've given my word to Pastor Carlson that I'll get you to Brennan's group no later than mid-July." He watched her expression, trying to gauge the effectiveness of his arguments. But whatever this woman was thinking, she managed to keep it hidden. As much as he'd been dreading being alone with her on the trail, he would take that over the certainty of the fate that awaited him here. "We'll need every day we have to catch up. Unexpected things happen on the trail and could end up costing us a day or two, or more. Time out there is precious, especially when you consider limited provisions, water supply, unpredictable weather," he said, ticking the items off on one hand. "You hired me to do a job, ma'am. Now I suggest you let me do it."

Her eyes narrowed for a brief instant, and he prepared for opposition.

"All right, Mr. Taylor. We'll do it your way . . ." *This time,* is what he heard in her pause. "I'll be ready to leave in the morning as planned."

It took him a few seconds to process that she'd given in to him. "Well . . . all right, then." He managed what he hoped was an authoritative nod and finished his biscuits and gravy, suddenly not minding that they'd grown cold.

He'd just won the second round.

F OLLOWING BREAKFAST AND THE run-in with Annabelle Grayson, Matthew welcomed the solitude of the barn. He finished sorting the last of the provisions and repacked them in boxes and crates that would best use the wagon's limited space. Then he inspected the repair he'd done on the wheels and checked the underside of the wagon's carriage for a second time, to make sure it was sound.

"Taylor?"

Matthew turned at the masculine voice, unprepared to see the couple standing a few feet from him. Or the little boy hanging on to his father's hand.

"I'm sorry if we're interrupting you, Matthew." Larson Jennings smiled, then nodded toward his wife beside him. "But Kathryn wanted to see you before you left. And so did I."

Seeing Kathryn Jennings pulled Matthew back in time. Standing here before him now, she looked very much as she had two years ago. His attention went involuntarily to her midsection, and when he realized he was staring, he jerked his focus upward.

A slow smile curved Kathryn's mouth, and she gave a tiny nod.

Matthew immediately looked at Jennings, knowing the man would've decked him for even glancing at his wife in past years. All the ranch hands had been smart enough to keep their distance from

Kathryn Jennings. Well, at least while Jennings was watching.

Not a hint of retaliation showed in his expression. "I was glad to hear from Carlson that you got the job."

Matthew briefly ducked his head. "I was glad when I heard it too." When the couple both laughed, Matthew joined them. "Thank you again, Jennings, for . . . what you said to Pastor Carlson."

"I only told him the truth." Jennings wore an easy smile. "Every man needs help from time to time. I was glad to do it." His wife leaned in to him, resting a hand on his chest. He put an arm around her waist, and Matthew couldn't help but notice how right the scene before him seemed. "I think little William and I will head on into town. We'll be back to pick you up later this afternoon." Jennings bent down and hoisted the toddling dark-headed boy, then lifted him so Kathryn could give him a hug. "Come on, partner. We've got some horses to go look at."

With his son in his arms, Jennings extended his hand to Matthew. "We're staying in town tonight. I've got some business in the morning, but we'll be here bright and early to help with the final loading and to see you off."

"Thank you. I appreciate that." Matthew found Jennings' grip firm and strong, same as earlier that week, regardless of the injuries the man had sustained two years ago. He looked at the little boy; the resemblance to Jennings was striking. Same coloring as his father, same blue eyes. Bits of Kathryn shone around his chin and nose, but no way could Jennings ever deny this boy was his son.

"How've you been, Matthew?" Kathryn asked after Larson and young William were gone.

He shrugged. "Fine."

"You're looking well, if that says anything about how life's been treating you."

Thinking of what was stashed in his saddlebag a few feet away, he was glad she didn't know how his life was truly going. "I can say the same for you too. You look beautiful, Kathryn. Just the same as the last time I saw you." He thought again about how much he'd once cared for her and how glad he was now that things had worked out the way they had between them.

Her expression softened. "For a long time now, Matthew, I've wanted to thank you for being such a strength to me . . . when I went through that time. I'm grateful for everything you did for me. For us."

"I was glad to do it," he answered, reminded that Jennings had just told him the same thing.

"I was sorry to hear about your brother. Larson and I didn't know Jonathan well and, of course, never knew the two of you were brothers. We were present at his and Annabelle's wedding, and your brother seemed like a very kind and thoughtful man. He certainly seemed to care deeply for Annabelle."

She paused, as though waiting for him to say something, but then continued. "Annabelle is a very special woman, Matthew. She's become a dear friend to me, and I . . . I realize you don't know her well, so you might be tempted to think like some here in town do— that she hasn't changed all that much. But I want to assure you she has. She's a very different woman now than when you first met her." A tentative look moved into her eyes. "You'll be traveling together for several weeks, and I hope you'll try and find some common ground between you. Give her a chance to show you who she's become. Try not to make up your mind too quickly." She gave him a hopeful smile. "People *can* change, you know."

He wanted to disagree, but the earnest quality in Kathryn's voice wouldn't let him.

"Sometimes, Matthew, old expectations can cause us to miss seeing changes in people. No matter how well you may think you know a person, sometimes things simply aren't as they appear."

"Isn't that the truth," he whispered, gradually smiling along with her.

"I don't mean to overstep my bounds here, but have you imagined what it must be like for her? To try and become someone new in a place where everyone knows what you used to be, knows every mistake you've ever made—even the secret things? And they remind you of it at every opportunity."

The intensity in her eyes was so piercing that he wondered for a second if she knew the truth about *him*. About what he'd done. Shame burned within him at that possibility, but further scrutiny laid his fears to rest. Her expression held no accusation—only concern.

Then it hit him. He did share common ground with Annabelle

Grayson. They both had pasts they would prefer to keep hidden. Only he had the upper hand in this case—she didn't know about his. He would've thought discovering that advantage would bring satisfaction. Instead it brought an unexpected sense of hollowness.

"I give you my word, Kathryn. Because you've asked, I'll work to keep an open mind about her." Though it wouldn't be easy for him. Nor was it likely that Annabelle Grayson McCutchens would make it so.

———

Annabelle stood by the wagon and watched as Kathryn and Hannah took turns giving the older woman a hug. Their sentences spilled out on top of one another.

"Miss Maudie, it's been too long." "It's so good to see you again." "Are you feeling better?" "We brought you some vegetable soup and those oatmeal muffins you bragged on last time."

Holding their hands, Miss Maudelaine backed up a step, drew in a breath, and beamed. "Oh, my dears, too long it's been. And yes, I'm feelin' much better these days. Especially now."

Annabelle smiled. True to Kathryn's word, the Irish lilt in the woman's voice made everything she said sound pretty. The woman's white hair glistened like morning frost in the sun, and she possessed a regal air that invited attention.

"Seein' you ladies again is like water to a thirsty soul. Hannah, lovely as ever you are, dear. And my favorite man of the Word, how is he farin' these days?"

"Patrick's doing fine, Miss Maudie, as are the children. They all send their love."

"And I return it to them, to be sure. And Kathryn . . ." Miss Maudie made a *tsk*ing sound. "Just look at you, darlin'. All beamin' with that mother glow again. You'll soon be bringin' another sweet babe into the world. And how is that dear husband of yours? I'd love to see Jac—" She caught herself, starting to call Larson the name he'd once gone by, and gave her head a shake. "To see Larson is what I meant. I'm afraid your husband might always be Jacob first to me."

"He's doing well and sends his love too."

"I wish you could've brought that precious William with you. I bet he's grown a foot since I've last seen him."

Annabelle saw Miss Maudie's eyes flick in her direction, and she felt the warmth of the woman's smile all the way to her toes.

"Yes, William has grown," Kathryn said. "And he's into everything too, which is why I left him in town with Larson this morning. Besides, I wanted this to be a ladies' day. We brought a special friend with us, Miss Maudie." Kathryn gently drew Annabelle forward. "Annabelle, I'd like to introduce Miss Maudelaine. She oversees the main house here at Casaroja. And Miss Maudie, this is Mrs. Jonathan McCutchens, a very dear friend of both Hannah's and mine. Annabelle leaves tomorrow for the Idaho Territory. We wanted to spend her last day together, and both Hannah and I wanted the two of you to meet . . . so we just decided to tear ourselves away from packing and bring her with us."

Miss Maudie clasped Annabelle's hands. "It's a pleasure to meet you, Mrs. McCutchens. May I call you Annabelle?"

"Of course."

"And I prefer Miss Maudie, if it pleases you." She winked. "*Miss Maudelaine* makes me feel so old."

As they sat in the front parlor, Annabelle sipped her spiced tea, admiring the delicate china cup and saucer. And the house! All the beautiful furnishings and plush carpets. Kathryn hadn't done Casaroja justice in her description of it, or the surrounding property. But of course, Kathryn wouldn't think any place grander than the cabin Larson had built for her on their ranch up in the mountains, along Fountain Creek.

"Thank you for bringin' me the soup, dears, and the muffins. My favorite, by far."

Annabelle felt a cool touch on her arm. Miss Maudie was leaning forward and smiling in her direction.

"Now, Annabelle dear, tell me a bit about yourself. Both Kathryn and Hannah claim you as a dear friend, so I know God must've cut the three of you from the same cloth. Did you get to know one another at church? Or through the quilting circle in Willow Springs, perhaps?"

Hearing the woman's assumptions, Annabelle nearly choked on her tea. She carefully placed the saucer and cup on the table and cleared her throat, then shot a hasty look at Hannah and Kathryn.

She gathered from their expressions that neither of them had told Miss Maudie about her past.

Annabelle cleared her throat. "I actually met Kathryn a couple of years ago when . . . a mutual friend introduced us one night. And then Hannah and I met at Kathryn and Larson's wedding December before last."

She'd kept her answer within the confines of the truth, but somehow it still felt deceptive. The conclusions this good woman would no doubt draw would paint her in a light she had no right in which to be painted. She tried to catch Kathryn's attention, and Hannah's, but without success.

Miss Maudie's countenance sparkled. "Isn't it a wonder how God weaves friendships into our lives? Little do we know what He's doin' at the time. But then, reflectin' back on things"—she waved her hand—"that's when you're able to see His hand workin', for sure. I think it's wonderful He's brought together three such fine women."

The longer Miss Maudie spoke, the more Annabelle's discomfort increased. When she and Jonathan lived in Denver, and again when they were part of Brennan's group, the people there hadn't known about her past. But that seemed different somehow. Those people had never attributed her with the goodness that Miss Maudie obviously was.

"Excuse me, Miss Maudie." She paused, wondering how to phrase her confession. "But I'm afraid you're mistaken about something. I'm not at all the—"

"I completely agree, Annabelle," Kathryn interrupted, sitting forward.

Relieved that her friend had come to her rescue, Annabelle felt a twinge of disappointment that she'd had to.

"You're most definitely mistaken about something, Miss Maudie," Kathryn said. "You used the phrase *three fine women.*" She emphasized the words, her expression tender as she briefly glanced at Annabelle. "You miscounted. I believe I see *four* women of such distinction sitting in this room."

The look Kathryn gave her said they would discuss it later.

And later that afternoon, when they were nearly back to Hannah's home, Annabelle could stand it no longer. She stood and hunched over the back of the buckboard, peering at Kathryn and Hannah. "Why did you do that?"

Still watching the road, Kathryn turned her head slightly. "Do what?"

"Give that good woman the impression that I'm like you two. *'Three such fine women,'*" she said, doing her best to imitate Miss Maudie's accent.

Hannah laughed. "You *are* a fine woman, Annabelle McCutchens."

Annabelle made a face. "You know what I mean. Regardless of how both of you may see me, there's a difference between us because of the things I've done. And to present me as a . . . a lady to someone like Miss Maudie just feels deceitful to me somehow."

Kathryn pulled the wagon to a stop behind the Carlsons' home and set the brake. "I think I know what you're referring to, and I have an answer."

"I never doubted that you would," Annabelle said, winking. "Either that or you'd make one up real quick." She easily avoided Kathryn's playful swat.

Kathryn's expression grew thoughtful. "Even though we've been forgiven, we don't have the ability to forget. We carry around inside us the memory of poor choices we've made, and also of wrongs done to us, not of our choosing." She gave Annabelle's hand a gentle squeeze. "As you move on with your life and away from Willow Springs, you're going to meet scores of people who will never know about the life you lived here. And most of them will never need to know. But I'm sure, somewhere along the way, God will prompt you to share your story with someone." She shrugged. "Either to give them hope or to show them what a difference forgiveness can make in a person's life. And when that time comes, there may be a cost to your sharing about your past, but there'll also be a blessing in your taking that risk and being obedient to God's prompting."

"Kathryn's right, Annabelle, you'll know the time and the place. Just listen for His voice."

Annabelle nodded, certain she'd never find two women who she would love more than these. From the corner of her eye, she spotted Matthew working just inside the barn.

When he noticed them, he immediately stopped his work. "Here, let me help you ladies."

He went to Kathryn's side first, Annabelle noticed. Watching him, she wondered if he still harbored feelings for her as he had at one time. If he did, it didn't show. He held Kathryn's hand and steadied her as she climbed down, then hurried to the other side to do the same for Hannah. Meanwhile, Annabelle climbed from the back of the wagon on her own accord.

Her feet had barely touched the ground when a wave of nausea swept through her. She clutched her midsection and gripped the side of the wagon for support.

Hannah was quickly at her side. "Annabelle, are you all right? Matthew, could you help her, please?"

Matthew came alongside, but Annabelle waved him away, knowing he was only there at Hannah's request. "I'm fine. I don't need any help." A dull pain, similar to her monthly ache but much worse, spasmed in her lower abdomen. She doubled over, taking short breaths through clenched teeth.

Kathryn's arm came around her shoulders. "We need to get you into the house. Matthew, would you carry her inside, please?"

Annabelle felt his arm come around her from behind. She put out a hand. "No . . . just . . . give me a minute to catch my breath."

Kneeling down, Kathryn gently brushed the hair from her face. "Have you had pains like this before?"

Annabelle shook her head. She shot a quick look at Matthew, reading uncertainty—and doubt—in his eyes. She lowered her voice to a whisper. "I've had some cramping recently . . . but nothing like this."

Kathryn stood. "Matthew, would you help Annabelle back into the wagon, please. I'm taking her to Dr. Hadley's."

→ C H A P T E R | S I X T E E N

H ERE, LET ME HELP YOU."
The doctor offered his hand, and with his assistance, Annabelle sat up.

"I'll give you a few minutes to dress, and then we'll talk." He closed the door behind him.

Annabelle got dressed and smoothed the front of her skirt, trying to ease her concern by telling herself that she'd simply been overdoing it lately. She needed more rest. Her hand lingered on her abdomen, and she remembered another time, years ago. . . . She'd told herself many times since then that what had happened had all turned out for the best. After all, what kind of mother would she have made? Yet the same question still haunted her now.

A knock sounded on the door.

"Come in."

Doc Hadley opened the door and motioned for her to join him on the bench beneath the curtained window. "Why don't we have a seat over here? Let me say again how nice it is to see you after all this time, Mrs. McCutchens." His smile was gentle. "I still like the sound of that. And let me assure you right off that everything seems to be fine with your baby. There are no problems that I can tell."

Annabelle let out a sigh, briefly closing her eyes. "Thank you, Doc Hadley."

"My guess is that this was your body's way of telling you to slow down and get some extra rest. And a mother-to-be needs to pay close attention to those signs."

She nodded. What fondness she held for this man. He'd doctored the girls from the brothel for years and had always treated them with tender concern—never harshly or with disdain.

He reached over and covered her hand. "You have my condolences on your husband's passing. Did he suffer long?"

Annabelle stared at his hand atop hers on the bench, then told him the details.

He nodded every few minutes, listening. "So you're alone now?"

"Yes. And no. I've hired someone to take me to Idaho. We leave in the morning." She leaned forward, laying a hand to his arm. "Unless you think I shouldn't be traveling that far."

"No, no. You're still early on in your pregnancy, Mrs. McCutchens. No more than two months, I'd say, give or take a couple of weeks based on what you've told me. And like I said a moment ago, everything appears to be fine. It's normal for your body to experience some changes during this time. But if you start cramping again, or certainly if you have any bleeding, you need to seek a doctor's care right away. Bleeding isn't wholly uncommon during a pregnancy, but most often it's your body's way of alerting you to a problem. So I advise that you get ample rest and listen to what your body is telling you." Gray eyebrows arched, he waited for her affirming nod and then patted her hand and stood.

He hesitated. "Might I ask you about a young woman I treated at the brothel once?" At her consent, he continued. "She was very young, had long dark hair, and—"

"That would be Sadie."

"Yes, I believe that was her name. Whatever happened to that child? I haven't seen her for quite a while."

"I'd like to know the same thing. I went by to see her when I got back into town recently and she was gone. They told me she just disappeared." Annabelle felt a rush of protectiveness, and accountability. Her jaw clenched in response. "The girls woke up one morning and found her room empty. Someone took her, but they don't know who." She looked down at her hands. "There was blood on her pillow."

"Well, that explains it, then." Doc Hadley shook his head. "I've found myself thinking of that child at the oddest times in recent months, for no apparent reason. And every time I've given her over to God's care again, not knowing what to ask for, really—just feeling the nudge to pray."

Annabelle felt a blush of hope at his words. "I'm determined to find her, even if I have to check every brothel, gaming hall, and saloon along the way."

"And I think you'll do it too. Be careful, Annabelle, and God be with you in your search." He cocked his eyebrow again. "And also with whoever has her once you find them."

Later that night, Annabelle summoned her courage and picked her way across the dark yard, coffee cups in hand. She walked into the barn, armed and ready, somehow knowing that Jonathan would have wanted her to try.

The faint orange glow from the oil lamp told her where she would find him. She spotted Matthew in the far corner, leaning against a barrel, head down, intent on the paper in his hand. Nearing his side, she waited for him to look up. He didn't. He *would* make her be the first to speak. The man was so stubborn sometimes, so sure of himself, she was tempted to—

Quelling the response that came naturally, she readied a smile and took a step closer. "Thought I'd drop in and see how you're doing."

He jumped and spun around. She took a quick step back, hot coffee sloshing over the sides of the cups.

"What are you doing here?" Irritation darkened Matthew's face as he moved the piece of parchment behind his back.

"Good evening to you too, Mr. Taylor." Wincing at the momentary sting, she quickly reminded herself why she'd come. Remembering helped curb her sarcasm. "I'm sorry. I didn't mean to scare you. I thought you heard me walk up just now."

"You didn't scare me. You just . . ." He shook his head, then strode to his saddlebag and stuffed the parchment inside.

The action drew her attention, and she wondered what it was that'd had him so engrossed. She liked to read, and it tickled her curiosity to guess what his favorite type of stories might be.

Personally she liked the ones with intrigue, those that left you guessing about the villain and where the stolen treasure lay hidden.

He motioned to stacks of crates and boxes near where they stood. "I already picked everything up from the mercantile and will go through it tonight, make sure the order's all accounted for."

"That's not what I'm here about, but thank you." Determined to see this through, she held out a cup of coffee.

He glanced at it, then back at her.

His tentative expression coaxed a laugh. "It's safe, I promise you. I've already paid you a third of your salary, Mr. Taylor. It wouldn't do for me to try and poison you now." She nudged the cup a few inches closer to him. "I'd wait and do that once we're closer to Idaho. Makes more sense, don't you think?"

That earned her a slight *humph* but not the half grin she'd hoped for. He took the coffee but didn't drink it.

He stared at her for a second—then understanding registered in his features. He reached into his vest pocket and pulled out a wad of bills. "This is what's left over after buying the supplies. I was going to give it to you tomorrow morning." His tone grew defensive. "There's almost seven dollars left. You can count it."

The visit wasn't going as she'd planned. "I appreciate that, Mr. Taylor, but you can keep the money. No doubt we'll need something else along the way."

"Just want you to know how much is left."

"I trust you, Mr. Taylor." The words were out before she had fully processed them. And their untruth weighted the silence.

His stare turned appraising.

Her wish in bringing him coffee was that they might arrive at some sort of unspoken truce before leaving in the morning. But maybe that was too much to hope for, and too soon.

He stuffed the money back into his vest pocket, then shifted his weight.

She sensed he wanted her to leave. Which made her even more determined to stay. At the same time, she thought of their run-in two days earlier on the porch and silently asked for God to put a guard over her mouth. She didn't know if there was a place in the Bible with that specific thought but knew there ought to be. If only for her.

She helped herself to a seat on a stool by the wall and sipped her coffee. "So . . . are you ready to leave Willow Springs?"

His eyes narrowed. "Why do you ask?"

Defensive again. "No particular reason, just trying to make conversation."

He gave her that slow half smile. "Hobnobbing with the hired help, huh?"

It was a start. "Something like that." She glanced at his untouched coffee. "Would you like me to taste it first? Show you it's safe?" A gleam lit his eyes, and she could well imagine the sharp replies running through his mind about drinking from the same cup as a woman like her.

He took a sip, the gesture answering for him.

"I'm flattered. Seems you trust me too, Mr. Taylor."

"Not hardly, ma'am. I just figure you need me. For now, anyway."

She lifted a brow.

"Like you said, you've already paid me. I'm thinking I can enjoy coffee at least until we're—" he tilted his head as though in deep thought—"across Wyoming."

"And then what?"

"Then I might have to start brewing my own."

Sarcasm shaded his smirk, but still there was a genuineness about it. He didn't trust her, but at least he was honest in his distrust. Watching him, Annabelle tried not to analyze why his smile seemed to lift her spirits so. "I thought you said you couldn't cook. Have you been holding out on me?"

"Nope. But given that or death, I might try my hand at it."

He looked at her then, and a frown crossed his face, as though he just remembered who he was talking to. He took another swig of coffee, watching her over the rim, then dumped the remains in the dirt. "I think I've had enough for one night, ma'am."

Annabelle studied him for a beat, then rose. He was dismissing her, and she let him. She'd gotten what she'd come for.

CHAPTER SEVENTEEN

S O YOU STILL HAVE NO LEAD as to where Sadie might be?"
Kathryn packed the last of the coffee in the wooden box and
tamped the lid shut with a hammer.

"None at all," Annabelle said, surveying the last remaining items
on the kitchen table. She relayed to Kathryn what she'd told Patrick
and Hannah on Thursday night.

The entire house had awakened early—all but the children. Darkness still cloaked the world beyond the warm glow of the Carlsons'
kitchen. Annabelle had hardly shut her eyes last night for the anticipation of the journey, and she was already feeling the effects from
lack of sleep. She took a deep breath and waited for the discomfort in
her lower back to pass, careful not to reveal it in her expression.

Larson walked into the kitchen and looked around. "What goes
next, ladies?"

Patrick followed behind him. "Load us up."

Annabelle pointed to the box Kathryn just finished, then to two
others on the table. "Thanks, fellas. We're almost done in here."

Both men gave her a silent salute, shouldered their loads, and
disappeared out the door.

Now that it was time to leave Willow Springs, her feelings were
in a jumble. She'd visited the cemetery last evening and laid fresh
flowers on Jonathan's grave. Oddly, that hadn't bothered her as

much as she'd thought it would. He was no more in that hole than she was. He had started his new life, somewhere, wherever heaven existed, and she was starting a new life too. One that waited for her far away from here.

What bothered her most was leaving these friends behind. She looked across the kitchen at Kathryn and Hannah, busy chatting as they packed the last few items. Annabelle wished she could inscribe every detail about them on her memory so that once she was far away and lonely for the familiar, she would be able to recall with clarity the contrast in their hair color—the way Kathryn had her long blond tresses swept up while Hannah's dark curls spilled down her back—the warm bubble of their laughter, and most of all, what it felt like to be accepted by them.

Would she make friends where she was going? Movement beyond the kitchen window caught her attention, and a shadowed figure emerged from the barn. Matthew's confident stride was easily recognizable. Remembering the unspoken truce they'd reached last night, Annabelle wondered if she might make a friend on this journey after all.

At the touch on her shoulder, she turned.

Kathryn's expression held reassurance. "We'll get word to you if we hear something about Sadie, okay?"

Annabelle nodded, knowing in her heart that they wouldn't. Whoever had Sadie was long gone. When she turned back to the task at hand, she caught Hannah raising the lid of a box they'd already sealed shut. Annabelle wouldn't have thought anything about it but for the guilty look on her friend's face. Hannah slipped something inside, then closed the lid again. Bless that woman's heart, she couldn't lie to save her life.

Annabelle walked over beside her. "What are you doing?"

"What?" Hannah straightened and brushed her skirt. "Nothing. Just . . . finishing up packing."

Annabelle lifted the lid and let out a sigh. "Oh, Hannah, no. These are two of your best napkins, and you only have four to begin with."

Hannah's feigned look of surprise melted into a smile. "Maybe it'll bring some civility to the long trip. Use them on occasion and think of us."

"No, I can't. . . ."

"Don't try arguing with her, Annabelle." Kathryn's tone smacked of conspiracy. "What they say about pastors' wives is true. Sweet on the outside, tough as nails within."

Knowing the comparison was accurate, Annabelle looked at the embroidered treasures and felt tears rising in her throat. "Thank you, Hannah," she whispered and ran a finger over the elaborate *C* encircled with delicate flowers.

"You be sure and take Matthew with you when you go into those towns looking for Sadie, all right?" Hannah laid a hand on her arm. "You don't need to visit those places alone. Especially at night. It won't be safe."

Annabelle offered something resembling an affirming nod and hoped her friends would take it as such. "Don't forget, I'm used to dealing with those places, and those people. It'll be fine."

Kathryn stopped folding the towel in her hand. "Annabelle McCutchens, that was not a yes."

"And we're waiting for a yes." Hannah stood, feet planted, hands on hips.

Annabelle had to smile at seeing the less-than-intimidating sight before her. "I'm not afraid to go by myself. I know how things work. I'll be careful. I give you my word."

"I know a little bit about how those things work too, and I'd feel much better knowing Matthew was with you." Kathryn tried to look stern, but Annabelle didn't buy it. "You are the most stubborn woman I've ever met, Mrs. McCutchens."

Hannah tossed Kathryn a look. "Oh I don't know about that, Mrs. Jennings. You could give her a run for her money."

Kathryn's mouth fell open. "And just whose side do you think you're on, Mrs. Carlson?"

Annabelle enjoyed the way they playfully went after each other. Oh how she would miss these women. Struck with an idea, she cleared her throat. "I don't claim to be knowin' whose side anyone is on, my dears," she said, surprising them with her best Miss Maudie imitation, "but I'm for sure knowin' that God must've cut us *three such fine women* from the same cloth, don'tcha know."

She was certain their laughter could be heard halfway to town.

"It's the relationship between you that concerns me most, Matthew. That's what I'm unsure about."

Matthew and Pastor Carlson strode from the wagon into the barn. Matthew tugged his gloves into place, then hefted two of the remaining boxes. A few more trips and they would have everything. He hadn't slept well last night, unable to shake the feeling that something bad was about to happen.

Not wanting to leave things with Pastor Carlson on a bad note, Matthew worked to keep the irritation from his voice. "What do you mean, Pastor, when you say, 'the relationship'?"

"I mean the two of you heading out together like this, barely able to talk to each other." Carlson grabbed two boxes and fell in step behind him.

"That's not true, Pastor. We talk." When she left him no choice.

Carlson huffed. "Yes, when you have to, and then it's with clipped answers. And there seems to be this . . . undercurrent running between you two, like the creek when it swells with the spring thaw. There's always the potential for danger."

Stalling for a response to that last comment, Matthew set his load down by the wagon and went back to the barn. He wasn't partial to conversation this early in the day—especially one that struck such a deep nerve. At least Jennings wasn't present to hear this. He was helping the women inside.

Undercurrent . . . Matthew sighed. That was a good way to describe what he felt when he was with Annabelle. Something hidden passing between them that he couldn't see, and didn't care for. And even worse, couldn't predict. They'd be talking about one thing when he'd suddenly get the feeling she meant another. He'd made a pledge to Kathryn Jennings to try and view her "dear friend" differently, but that was one promise he'd be hard-pressed to keep. As far as he was concerned, Annabelle Grayson was still the woman who had tricked his older brother and stolen his own birthright. Selfishness, plain and simple, was why he'd taken this job. He needed to leave Willow Springs, and she was his ticket out. Plus she had something that belonged to him, and he aimed to get it back.

He stacked one box atop another. "We're civil to each other, Pastor."

"That's just it, Matthew. You're civil—sometimes you're even polite. But you don't really mean it." Carlson shook his head, his expression heavy with concern. "At least you don't seem to from where I stand."

Matthew suppressed a sigh. A twofold band of pain stretched from the back of his neck around to both temples. Its steady drum kicked up a notch as he lifted two boxes and retraced his steps to the wagon, with Carlson behind him.

He hadn't seen Annabelle yet that morning but had heard her laughter coming from the kitchen moments ago—him along with half the townsfolk she'd probably awakened. She tended to laugh a lot when she was with Hannah and Kathryn, and something about overhearing their laughter earlier had sparked a jealousy inside him, one he couldn't explain and didn't welcome.

He looked back at the house, almost hoping she wouldn't be ready on time. He would enjoy seeing the look on her face when he reminded her that she'd wanted to leave right at sunrise. Just thinking about it lightened his mood.

Carlson dumped his load beside the wagon and let out a sigh. Matthew sincerely wished he could say whatever it was the man wanted to hear.

"Pastor, I get what you're trying to say—I think I do, anyway. And I understand your concern. I'll admit there're moments I even share it. I wonder if I'm doing the right thing, headin' across the plains with that woman. But she hired me, I accepted the job, and we're leaving within the hour." He hesitated, bowing his head. None of that had come out right. "Sir, it's like you're asking me to change how I feel down deep, and I can't. Not just like that. Every time I look at her, I see my brother, and I'm reminded that . . ." Emotion tightened his throat. Matthew looked away, gauging how much to share. Bringing up the issue of the land would only further muddy the waters, as would mentioning Annabelle's partial admission of why she'd married Johnny in the first place. Best to stick to the more general truth. "I'm reminded that Johnny's not coming back. And I can't help but wonder if things might've been different if he'd never met her. If she was still in that brothel."

Carlson took a minute to answer. "So you blame Annabelle for Jonathan's death?"

Matthew thought of his mother. Was it possible that Johnny had died the same way? From the same thing? He couldn't be sure and knew he'd never be able to prove it one way or the other. With effort, he finally managed to shake his head in answer to Carlson's question, but mainly because it was the response the pastor wanted. He still held Annabelle Grayson partially responsible.

Carlson stared for a moment, gray twilight masking his expression. From the set of his shoulders as he walked back into the barn, Matthew could tell he hadn't believed him.

Matthew slid a few of the boxes into the wagon and started to climb in. He paused and looked west, wishing he could tuck the view before him inside his pocket. The mountains he loved rose to their lofty height, their jagged peaks etched purple-black and barely discernable against a dark mantle of sky. The meadows beside the Carlsons' house were still and quiet. So peaceful. If only he had that same peace inside him.

Estimating a half hour at best before the sun crested the horizon, he climbed into the tarp-covered wagon. Shadows steeped the interior. He secured a rope around a group of crates and pulled it taut.

"Where do you want this?"

Matthew looked up to see Carlson balancing a fifty-pound sack of flour on his shoulder. "Over here." He hoisted the sack, wedged it between a trunk and another crate in the center of the wagon, and draped it with an oiled cloth to guard against moisture.

"You'll be on the trail for a long time, Matthew. Alone. Just the two of you. At night."

Matthew's head came up. Up to that point, he'd admired Carlson's straightforwardness. Now he found it grating. "If you're worried about something happening between us, Pastor, don't be. I give you my word, sir." He gave a quick laugh. "I won't touch her."

"It's not so much her virtue that concerns me with you, Matthew. It's her well-being."

Thinking it was a mite late to be worrying about the woman's virtue, Matthew stood as tall as he could in the cramped quarters and looked down. He tried to gauge where Carlson was heading. That patient look of his revealed nothing. The pastor would've made quite the gambler had he ever been inclined. Matthew's pockets felt lighter just thinking about it. Clamping a tight lid on that thought before it went any further, he jumped down from the wagon bed.

The pounding in his temples rose to a steady thrum. He needed coffee.

"I've agreed to get Mrs. McCutchens safely to the Idaho Territory, and that's exactly what I'll do. I've got experience on the trail. I know what to expect and what to watch for. . . ." When Carlson didn't respond, Matthew rubbed the muscles cording the left side of his neck and blew out a weary breath. "I already gave you my word, sir. What else do you want?"

"I want the tone of your voice to match the seriousness of the pledge you've made, Mr. Taylor. That's what I want."

Wordless in the face of such harsh honesty, Matthew could only stare. He liked Patrick Carlson, had quickly grown to respect him, and it stung to think that if the pastor had made the decision of which man to hire, Bertram Colby would probably be standing by the wagon this morning. His guess was that Carlson had counseled Annabelle against hiring him too. That realization was sobering. Once again he had failed to live up to someone's expectations.

They shouldered the last load from the barn in silence.

Carlson set his boxes on the ground beside Matthew's. "Before you leave this morning, Matthew"—his tone softened—"I'd like one assurance."

Matthew nodded.

"Promise me you'll take proper care of Jonathan McCutchens' wife. Regardless of what you think of her, Jonathan chose Annabelle. He loved her. And I feel a keen sense of obligation to Jonathan in that regard, and a responsibility to see that Jonathan's last wishes are seen to."

When Matthew heard the word *obligation* coupled with his brother's name, every thought was swept from his mind, save one. The appreciation that he'd returned to show Johnny didn't have to go altogether undone, no matter his feelings. He'd get Annabelle Grayson safely to Idaho. Not for her sake, but for Johnny's.

He looked Carlson straight in the eye. "These past few days haven't been easy ones for me, sir. Or for her, I realize. I've been abrupt and short with you at times, and I apologize. I'll gladly tell the same to Mrs. McCutchens when I see her this morning." If that would help matters any. "I've had a lot thrown at me since comin' back here, but I've got a job to do and I aim to do it well. So, in answer to your question . . . yes, sir. I give you my word. I'll take proper care of Annabelle McCutchens, and I'll see her safely to Idaho."

Carlson stared through the dark, then finally laid a hand on Matthew's shoulder and nodded once.

"Here you are, gentlemen." Hannah appeared from around the corner of the wagon holding two cups brimming with steaming coffee. "We're almost done inside—just finishing up." She handed each of them a mug and walked back to the house.

Carlson leaned against the back of the wagon and took a long, slow sip. Matthew joined him. The coffee washed down the back of his throat, and he savored the rich smoothness. "Your wife sure makes a good cup of coffee. I'll miss that on the trail."

"You shouldn't have to miss it much. Annabelle made the coffee this morning." As though anticipating Matthew's disbelief, Carlson nodded. "Hannah taught her how to cook before she and Jonathan moved to Denver. It took a while, but Annabelle finally caught on. She makes the lightest baking powder biscuits you've ever tasted. They were Jonathan's favorites." He winked. "They're every bit as good as Hannah's, but don't tell Hannah I said that."

Thankful for the lighter turn in conversation, Matthew remained quiet and let Carlson set the pace, never doubting that he would.

"Jonathan and Annabelle first met here, in our home. Did you know that?"

"You're jokin' me, right?"

Carlson chuckled. "I'm not, and frankly I'm surprised you never asked me about it. Guess I thought you already knew. They met right here . . . in the *preacher's* house," he said with emphasis.

"Hmph. I figured he'd met her at . . . work." Matthew immediately regretted the voiced thought. Johnny had visited brothels in his younger days, and though Matthew didn't condone it, somehow it seemed different for a man to go there once or twice, or even a few times, than for a woman to choose to make a living at it. "What I meant to say is that I thought maybe Johnny had—"

"You don't have to make excuses for your brother, Matthew. I know Jonathan was a good man. I also know he wasn't perfect, by a long shot. I'm not a man who normally blushes . . ." He gave his head a slight tilt. "But your brother's past, well, it had some color to it."

Thinking of the antics Johnny had pulled in their younger days, Matthew felt a smile crook one corner of his mouth. "That's for sure," he said quietly, his feelings at the moment running bitter-sweet.

Carlson set his mug on the wagon bed. "Part of what made being around Jonathan so enjoyable was that he didn't try to cover up the mistakes he'd made. Don't get me wrong—he wasn't proud of them. He just never tried to be someone he wasn't. Jonathan had this way of making others feel at ease around him . . . no matter who they were."

In a way, it felt good to talk about his brother, but it also threatened to open a rush of emotions that he preferred to keep bridled.

"I joined your brother and Annabelle in marriage not far from here." Carlson nodded toward the banks of Fountain Creek. "Their marriage was legally binding in every sense. As far as the law is concerned . . . and in the eyes of God."

It dawned on him what Carlson was saying. "Pastor, I never doubted they were legally married. My only question to Johnny was why."

"Did he tell you?"

"Not an answer that satisfied."

"Are you sure you just weren't listening closely enough?"

"I was listening. I just don't understand why any man would ever choose a woman like that."

Carlson surprised him by smiling. "A woman like that . . ." His expression took on that patient look again, as though waiting for Matthew to say more.

Matthew didn't and felt relief when Carlson finally got up and walked back into the house.

Drinking the last of his coffee—no grounds in the bottom of his cup, he noticed—he set his mug aside and walked to the front of the wagon, where four grays stood hitched and ready. The other two were tethered to the back, alongside the milk cow. He would switch two horses out at a time as they traveled, to give the animals a break from pulling. The team should fare the thousand-mile distance just fine in his estimation—Johnny had chosen well.

The tan gelding also tied to the back pranced and whinnied as though vying for Matthew's attention. Matthew walked over and gently rubbed the white tuft between Manasseh's eyes. "We're almost ready, boy," he whispered softly. The horse seemed as eager as he was to be on the move again.

"So, Mr. Taylor, are you ready?"

Annabelle stood waiting by the buckboard, carpetbag in hand. Steeling himself, he walked over to her. "Yes, I am, Mrs. McCutchens. But first, I . . ." His throat constricted. Thinking back to what he'd said to the pastor helped loosen it, but not much. "I need to offer you an apology, ma'am." Ignoring the rise of her brow, he looked down and briefly focused on the hard-packed dirt beneath his boots. This was more difficult than he'd thought it would be. "I've been abrupt with you in the past few days, and . . ." He forced his gaze up. "And I apologize."

She studied him, her expression guarded. Then she looked past his shoulder. Matthew turned to see Patrick Carlson standing with his family by the house, waiting, along with the Jennings family.

"Need," she whispered, barely loud enough for him to hear, "or want, Mr. Taylor?"

"Beg your pardon, ma'am?"

"Do you need to offer me an apology, Mr. Taylor? Or do you want to?"

He slowly gained her meaning. Did the woman never take anything at face value? "An apology's been laid on the table, ma'am. Regardless of its motivation." No way was he giving her anything further. She could take it or leave it.

"Oh, but it's the motivation behind an apology that makes it honest . . . or not."

His jaw went rigid. She was a fine one to be talking about honesty. He detected the faintest smile starting, not on her mouth but in those blue eyes of hers. This was the kind of charm that would've worked on Johnny, that would've attracted him. But it had the exact opposite effect on Matthew. "My apology stands, Mrs. McCutchens. Do with it as you see fit."

She pursed her lips for a moment as though considering a deal. "I guess I'll just have to trust that your motivation is sincere." She threw a believable smile over his shoulder, presumably to their audience. "I accept your apology, Mr. Taylor," she said more loudly, "and I appreciate your kind words."

He huffed softly, watching the mirth deepen in her eyes. It wasn't lost on him what she was doing. She'd guessed right about his insincerity, and they both knew it. But she apparently wanted things to appear as if they'd patched up their differences before heading out on the trail. The hypocritical little—

But hadn't he done the very same thing just moments ago with Carlson? And wasn't that why he agreed to offer an apology in the first place?

Irritated by the discovery, Matthew reached for his hat on the buckboard, ready to be gone from this town. He only wished he were leaving Annabelle Grayson behind with it.

ANNABELLE WORKED QUICKLY IN the encroaching darkness. She gathered clumps of dried prairie grass for tinder and arranged a sparse stack of kindling from the supply they'd brought with them in the wagon. The distance she and Matthew had covered since leaving Willow Springs early that morning left her feeling drained, and strangely at odds with herself.

She scooted close to the pile of kindling and reached for the flint and steel, then spotted him from the corner of her eye. As he untied the horses, she couldn't help but watch him.

Where Jonathan had been burly and powerfully built, Matthew's leaner physique enabled him to move with a fluid grace she felt certain he wasn't aware of. She'd known plenty of men overly assured in their own charm and looks, and while no doubt Matthew Taylor had to be aware of his effect on women, his confidence—the quiet sense of confidence that he wore as comfortably as his weathered leather vest—didn't strike her as being rooted in self-conceit.

She blinked, realizing he'd caught her staring.

By the question in his stance, he was awaiting an answer.

Her stomach knotted. "I'm sorry, I didn't hear what you asked."

"Do you want me to take the water bucket or not?" Irritation flattened his tone.

It took her a second, but she nodded, feeling a bit foolish at being so moved by his simple offer. "Yes, I would appreciate that. Thank you."

He retrieved it from the wagon, not looking at her as he passed, then headed toward the stream they'd spotted earlier over the slope.

Filling the water bucket was something Jonathan would've done for her without prompting, and she wouldn't have given it a second thought. But Matthew Taylor was not her husband, and she couldn't expect the same courtesies from him that she'd received from Jonathan. He was a hired hand. She remembered the day on the porch when she'd reminded him of just that. The expression on his face . . . If a glare could kill a woman, she would've been dead a hundred times over by now.

They had quickly fallen into a rhythm with each other during their first hours on the trail. Basically one of not speaking. She'd ridden in the back of the wagon, mainly because that's where he'd led her and she hadn't wanted to argue in front of the others before leaving. His forced apology from earlier that morning replayed again in her mind, and she shook her head. The way he'd looked at her . . .

Regardless of how Matthew addressed her, his eyes told the truth about the kind of woman he thought she still was.

She blew out a breath and forced her attention back on getting a fire started. With renewed fervor, she gripped the flint and steel over the dry stack of weeds and grass. She positioned the tools in her grip the way she remembered Jonathan doing it—the C-shaped piece of steel in her left hand, close to the kindling, and the flint in her right.

She struck the flint downward on the face of the steel. Once, twice. Again.

Nothing. Not the tiniest spark.

She tried again, consoled in remembering that it sometimes took Jonathan seven or eight tries before he got a healthy spark. She decided to keep count. *Four, five, six . . .*

On the trail, Jonathan had always built the fire first thing when they stopped. Then he went about his chores while she readied supper. Apparently Matthew considered building the fire women's work, which was fine by her. She could do this.

Ten, eleven, twelve . . .

She was eager to prove her independence to him, and to herself. She'd even been cautious of him seeing her tears that morning as she had said her good-byes to the Carlsons and Jennings, along with their children. Matthew didn't look at all comfortable with the scene, and she suspected good-byes weren't his strong suit, especially since knowing how the parting with Jonathan had gone.

Kathryn and Larson drew her into an embrace, but hearing Matthew's tentative voice behind her, she'd strained to hear the exchange.

". . . and I appreciate your kindness to me, Pastor. You and your family's. Who knows, I might even come to miss our talks."

Patrick laughed. "I know I will, Matthew."

Twenty-one, twenty-two, twenty-three . . .

Annabelle repeatedly struck the flint and steel, with no success. Her throat tightened as she remembered what else Matthew had said that morning, and done. It had endeared him to her in a way she wouldn't have imagined possible.

"Lilly, your birthday is coming up soon. Next month, I think. I picked up a little something for you while I was in town yesterday. It's not much, but . . ." Matthew reached into his pocket and pulled out a length of lavender hair ribbon. He let it curl slowly into the girl's upturned palm. "The color reminded me of your eyes. I thought it might look pretty in your hair."

Lilly's arms came around him in a hug.

Matthew looked at Patrick as though seeking direction on what to do next. Patrick tilted his head in Lilly's direction, and Matthew gently patted her back. After a moment, he stepped back and turned his attention to young Bobby. "Your turn, boy." He dropped a piece of saltwater taffy into the boy's palm.

Bobby's grin had been thanks enough.

Annabelle couldn't remember the exact words Patrick Carlson had prayed over them following that, but she did remember the peace that came with hearing them. Now if only she could somehow tuck that feeling away for coming days.

Thirty-three, thirty-four, thirty-five.

She stopped and stretched, then brushed back a strand of hair from her forehead. Her stomach was empty, her body fatigued, and again, she felt a sense of unrest inside her. Crouching back over the kindling, her back aching, she struck the flint against the steel again and again.

On her forty-seventh try, her hold slipped and the flint's edge bit into her thumb. Heat flooded her, and she clamped her mouth tight against the word burning the tip of her tongue. She closed her eyes as the wound began to throb. She brought the place to her mouth and tasted blood.

"Don't you know how to start a fire?"

Matthew was standing a few feet behind her. Hearing the disbelief in his voice, seeing the attitude in his stance, she found that the air of unspoken confidence she'd been admiring about him only moments earlier suddenly became a lightning rod for her frustration.

"Don't you know how to start a fire?"

His innocent question sparked a less-than-appropriate response, and Annabelle clenched her jaw in order to keep it contained. Oh, she knew *all* about starting fires. . . .

She chanced a closer look at him. For all of his self-importance and know-how, Matthew Taylor appeared completely oblivious to the subtle undertone of his question. How easy it would be to take him down a notch or two, especially when remembering what she'd overheard during his conversation with Jonathan in the shack last fall. While Matthew's innocence was refreshing, the smug look on his face wasn't.

He shifted his weight and stared down. "So, can you do it?"

Her jaw aching with restraint, Annabelle felt the unspoken "or not" of his statement hanging in the air, poised above her head like an ax ready to fall. She would light this confounded campfire if it took her all night. "Yes, I can do it."

He bent down beside her. "Because if you need help, Mrs. McCutchens"—condescension thickened his tone—"all you have to do is ask."

If he thought she was going to ask him for anything. . . . "No thank you, Mr. Taylor." Her cheeks hurt, her smile was so wide. "We each have to pull our own weight, remember?"

A twinkle lit his eyes, and not a friendly one. "I think I do recall saying something along those lines."

She turned back to her task.

The sound of his muffled departure brought a sense of relief, and loneliness.

It had been dusk when he'd finally stopped to make camp. Though Annabelle had wanted to stop at least an hour earlier, she hadn't said a word. Nausea had accompanied her most of the morning from the steady jolt of the wagon, so she'd gotten out and walked often during the day. But she'd told Matthew she could match whatever pace he set, and she was determined to do just that, no matter the soreness, and without complaint. As long as it didn't endanger her child. Doc Hadley's instructions were never far from her mind, and she hadn't overexerted today. She was only tired and hungry, and needed to rest.

She gripped the flint and steel again. On her sixty-fifth try, a spark glinted off the flint. And quickly died. On her seventy-fourth try, she managed to direct a stubborn spark toward the dry tinder and gently breathed life into the fledgling flame. Adding bits of dry grass, she watched the fire grow and was so pleased with herself she actually chuckled. She'd have their dinner of biscuits left over from breakfast and salted pork warmed and ready in no time.

Turning to glance behind her, her joy faded.

Another campfire, already burning, stronger than hers, flamed on the other side of the wagon, a good fifteen yards from where she knelt. Matthew lay stretched out before it on his bedroll, saddle beneath his head, hat over his face.

Annabelle couldn't decide whether she wanted to laugh or cry. He'd no doubt watched her struggle to build her fire, then had accomplished the task with such ease. She hadn't thought much about where each of them would sleep, but for some reason she hadn't envisioned separate fires, and so far apart.

For too long she'd been untouchable, like the leper she'd read about the other night, the one Jesus so willingly placed His hands on when all others shunned him and ran the other way. Then one morning, Kathryn Jennings had appeared in her life and that sense of isolation had begun to ebb. Kathryn had touched her life first. Followed by Larson, and more recently, Hannah and Patrick, and then Jonathan. *Her* Jonathan, as Patrick had described him.

These people had all accepted her, loved her. So why did she feel such emptiness inside?

She retrieved the items she needed from the wagon, placed the biscuits and ham in the cast-iron Dutch oven, and hung the pot from an iron tripod she had straddled over the flame. Then she searched the dark, empty miles of prairie around her. Her gaze finally settled on the fading orange glow backlighting the highest snowcapped peaks to the west. It was then that the answer came to her silent question from moments before. . . .

Because she was alone again—that's why this emptiness. She'd left all of those people who loved her—and who she loved—behind.

Minutes passed. Using a cloth, she lifted the lid from the Dutch oven and took out two of the three biscuits and a good portion of the ham. Matthew didn't look up when she approached his fire, but she knew by the tensing of his jaw that he was aware of her.

"I thought you might be hungry." She spotted a slice of half-eaten jerky beside him on his bedroll.

"Thank you, but I've already eaten." He didn't move. His hat hid most of his face.

Unwilling to be put off so easily, she stooped to lay the tin beside him. As she did, a spasm of pain shot through her lower back and abdomen. Her breath caught. She put a hand out to steady herself and accidentally brushed against his leg.

Matthew pushed himself up, backing away in the process.

As swiftly as it came, the pain subsided. Annabelle took a steadying breath.

Matthew's eyes were wide, his expression wary.

It slowly dawned on her. . . . He thought her move had been intentional. And from the alarm in his expression, that thought scared the living daylights out of the man. Either that or it disgusted him beyond words.

Carefully, she rose and took a step back, trying for a pleasant smile. "I'm sorry, I just . . . lost my balance there for a second. Too much riding today, I guess."

He looked at the tin plate, then gave her a cursory glance. "I said I've already eaten. I'm not hungry." He nodded toward her fire. "You best turn in. We leave with sunup in the morning and have a long two days of travel ahead of us if we want to reach Denver by nightfall on Monday."

At the mention of Denver, she realized she hadn't told him yet.

"I've got some business there that night, so I'll head into town right after we make camp."

"Business?" he asked, his suspicion evident.

"Yes, that's right. It shouldn't take me long." Despite Hannah's and Kathryn's concern, this was something she needed to do on her own. She also knew that where she was going was no place for a man like Matthew Taylor. Besides, no matter how honorable her intentions, the last thing she wanted was for him to see her in a brothel or in a saloon. "Good night, Mr. Taylor," she said quietly.

"What sort of business takes a woman into town after nightfall?"

She paused and looked back, giving him a dry smile. "Why . . . I'm touched. Are you worried about my safety?"

"I've given Carlson my word to get you safely to Idaho. And that's what I aim to do."

She laughed softly, raising a brow. "What do you know . . . Chivalry's alive and well on the western plains."

He apparently did not share her humor.

She finally managed to subdue hers. "I promise you, Mr. Taylor, I won't delay our progress." She thought of her task in Denver two nights hence and prayed that, if Sadie was there, somewhere, God would see fit to guide her steps so she could find the girl. "On the contrary, if my trip is successful, we'll need to leave as soon as we're able."

A S ANNABELLE APPROACHED THE gaming hall, she wondered again how this town had ever gotten its nickname. The city of Denver resembled anything but a sparkling jewel on the bosom of the desert—this part of it anyway. Thankfully, for her, the businesses she needed to visit were located within close distance of each other, and were on the east edge of town, near where they'd made camp.

She'd covered the short distance into Denver in about ten minutes' time. Matthew hadn't plied her with questions on the intent of her visit before she'd left earlier that evening—not like she thought he might. His lack of inquiry spoke volumes about his lack of interest. She was a job to him, a means to an end, and nothing more. And yet she realized that wasn't quite true. Not completely anyway. Matthew's intense dislike of her, whether he realized it or not, actually gave her hope, however slight, that he might one day change his mind about her. After all, she'd learned long ago that wherever strong emotions existed, change was still possible. It was apathy, not hatred, that rendered hope impotent.

The boardwalk outside the gaming hall was littered with empty bottles and crumpled trash. Tinny piano music drifted through the open doors and a telltale waft of alcohol floated toward her from the saloon next door. Annabelle looked back down the street in the direction from which she'd just come.

Sadie hadn't been at that brothel, but a girl Annabelle had known years ago was. After Patrice got over her initial surprise, she'd been guardedly friendly toward Annabelle, especially considering how the two of them had fought at one time.

"I haven't seen any girl that fits that description, and I'd remember her for sure. Men would go crazy for that around here, which wouldn't do me any good, now would it?" Patrice's eyes swept the length of Annabelle. "You've held up well . . . considering how long it's been."

"You look good too." Annabelle smiled, sorry for the lie.

In truth, Patrice Bellington was still one of the most beautiful women she'd ever seen. Her long blond hair and creamy complexion had always enticed the men, and the fancy nightgown she wore hugged her body, accentuating the merchandise. But there was a hardness to the woman's face, in the set of her mouth, that made Annabelle ache for her.

"You got out."

Annabelle nodded. "About a year ago."

"Did you buy your own way?"

"A man I met. He paid Betsy's asking price."

Patrice's brow arched and she whistled low. "You must've impressed him."

She gave a quick laugh. "Actually, he bought me sight unseen, so to speak."

Disbelief shone in Patrice's painted eyes. Then she frowned, and Annabelle saw another emotion surface, crowding out the doubt. *Longing.* She recognized it only because she'd felt that same keen hunger in her own life, for so many years. And still did.

Patrice nodded slowly, as though just now understanding what Annabelle had said. "So he takes his pleasure in other ways." It wasn't a question, and Annabelle knew exactly what she meant.

"No, he didn't beat me. Jonathan never laid a harsh hand to me."

"Didn't?" Patrice huffed. "He's already left you?"

Annabelle told her about Jonathan and watched tenderness soften the woman's features. Until tonight, Patrice Bellington hadn't crossed her mind in years, and Annabelle couldn't help but wonder how many other people she'd known, some of them well, yet had forgotten along the way.

Sounds coming from the gaming hall snapped Annabelle back to the moment. The place was crowded this time of night. Business was good. Visiting the local brothels had turned up nothing, so this place was her last hope until the next town. She climbed the stairs to the boardwalk. Working to keep her hope alive, she walked inside.

––––––––

From a darkened alleyway, Matthew watched her enter the building and then slowly bowed his head. This was exactly what he had suspected would happen. Though a small part of him—a part he'd not even realized existed until that moment—had hoped she'd prove him wrong. Pastor Carlson, Kathryn Jennings, everyone . . . had done their best to convince him that Annabelle Grayson was a changed woman.

Seems he was the only one who hadn't been played the fool.

Manasseh whinnied behind him. Matthew walked over to where he'd tethered the tan gelding. Stroking the tuft of white between the horse's eyes, he looked back at the gaming hall. Still thinking about the brothels Annabelle had visited over the past couple of hours, he debated whether to wait for her. But for what purpose? If she was thinking of entering that life again, there was nothing he could do to stop her.

At the same time, his brother had paid a high price for that woman's freedom—and not just in money. It angered him to think she would so hastily cast aside the sacrifices Johnny had made for her.

He waited, irritation building inside him as an imaginary clock ticked off the minutes in his head. Just when he'd decided to ride on back to camp, she walked out. And she wasn't alone. The man with her leaned closer and said something. Annabelle shook her head. The fella's laughter drifted toward him. Matthew could hear them speaking but couldn't make out their conversation.

His stomach twisted tight watching her, thinking about what she'd most likely been doing for the past few minutes. More than a hand of friendly poker went on in a place like that. Johnny's face came to mind, and the tightening in Matthew's gut hardened to an ache. How could a woman be so devoid of feeling and morals? And supposedly when she was with child? Which he still wasn't convinced of, especially seeing this.

Matthew was already to the edge of the street when he caught himself and stopped short. What was he going to do? Walk over there and accuse her of something when he had no solid proof? He knew her well enough to know she'd lie. At the drop of a hat she'd be spinning another web of deceit. No, he would have to catch her in the act, where she would have no excuse. How could Johnny have ever cared for a woman like her?

He strode to his horse, then rode the long way around town back to camp.

———

Annabelle snuck a glimpse at Matthew beside her on the buckboard but didn't attempt to draw him into conversation. Not after having failed twice already that morning. She'd been pleased to find him still awake last night when she'd arrived back at camp and had hoped for the chance to talk with him, maybe begin to smooth things over between them. But the cold, stony silence he had presented told her, yet again, that this was going to be a long journey to Idaho.

Last night's venture into Denver had turned up nothing. No one admitted to having seen Sadie or to having heard anything about a girl matching her description. Annabelle had, however, run into an old "friend" in the gaming hall. He'd followed her outside, interested in something more. When she told him she'd left that life, he'd laughed. As though she'd been joking. Remembering his response deepened her appreciation, yet again, for Jonathan McCutchens, as well as for the man sitting beside her now.

If not for Matthew Taylor, she might never have met Jonathan. Smiling, she snuck another look beside her and toyed with the idea of sharing that tidbit of truth. Yet she very much doubted that Matthew would find that poignancy of fate very amusing at the moment.

They stopped at midday to rest and to water and tend the animals. Matthew prepared to change out the lead horses while she went about preparing their lunch. Cold biscuits and salted pork. No time to build a fire; that would wait until evening. As she filled his plate and set it aside for him, she remembered the empty tin she'd seen by his cooled fire the morning after their first night on the trail. He had told her he'd already eaten and wasn't hungry, but apparently he'd changed his mind during the night. Either that or thrown the food aside. Stubborn man.

They each went about their duties in silence. Matthew finally grabbed his tin, snapped a hasty thank-you, and walked to where the animals were tethered. He had yet to ask her about where she'd gone last night in Denver. It would seem that the pledge he'd made to Pastor Carlson about seeing her safely to Idaho only covered their time on the trail itself. If she got harmed, maimed, or killed while in town on her "own" time, apparently that was her own misfortune. She couldn't help but smile at the thought, knowing the comment would have coaxed a grin from Hannah as well.

When the horses were hitched again and they were ready to move out, Annabelle walked on ahead, leaving Matthew to follow behind her in the wagon. She pulled her bonnet farther over her forehead to help shield her face from the noonday sun. It felt good to walk for a while and even better to put some distance between her and Matthew Taylor.

That afternoon and into the next day, miles of vacuous plains accumulated behind them until Annabelle started to feel as though they were the last two people on earth. A frightening thought at best. She wanted to believe that some of the terrain seemed vaguely familiar from having passed this way before with Jonathan and Jack Brennan's group, but she honestly couldn't say she recognized it. The endless subtle rise and fall of barren land all looked the same, until late that afternoon. . . .

Sitting beside Matthew on the buckboard, she saw something in the distance, standing alone and abandoned on the plains, like a forgotten memorial. Realization set in and a quick rush of air left her lungs.

She leaned forward as the wagon drew closer. "Matthew! Stop the wagon, please."

He made no indication of heeding her request. "It's just a pile of stuff someone left behind. Nothing we need."

"I asked you to stop the wagon, Mr. Taylor." She looked over at him, impatience warring with her joy. "Please," she added again, more firmly this time.

Giving her a dark look, Matthew obliged and abruptly pulled back on the reins. His sudden obedience jolted her back on the bench seat, and she sensed his satisfaction.

Too overjoyed to let his mood tarnish the moment, Annabelle climbed down from the wagon and went to stand before the familiar pinewood dresser. How had it slipped her mind to watch for it along the way? She ran a hand across the top, hardly believing it was still there. The trail of her hand left a smear of dirt in its path, caking her fingers with it. She smiled and brushed the dirt away.

"We don't have room for anything else. We're full enough as it is."

Ignoring his voice behind her, she took in the condition of the dresser. The second drawer was missing, but other than being in need of a good scrubbing—and the same could be said for her—it was in good shape. She glanced at the few crates she'd been forced to leave behind and discovered them empty. Remnants of a campfire nearby provided answer as to the whereabouts of the missing drawer, and a smattering of paw prints dotted the area.

Already anticipating Matthew's reaction, Annabelle began removing the empty drawers. "Would you climb down and help me with this please?"

"You're not serious. . . ."

"Do I sound like I'm joking, Mr. Taylor?" She hefted one of the solidly built drawers and deposited it near the back of the wagon, mindful not to overdo it with the child growing inside her. Walking back, she noticed Matthew hadn't budged. "You're wasting time, Mr. Taylor." She tried for a lighter tone. "And like they say, time is a valuable commodity."

"You'd definitely know about that, wouldn't you, ma'am?"

Annabelle stopped in her tracks, her back to him. So that's what this stony silence from him was still about—what she used to do in her former life. She turned. Matthew's eyes, the set of his jaw . . . everything about him said he was itching for a fight. But she knew just what to say to take it right out of him, and she would manage it without uttering a single hateful word.

"My husband . . . *your* brother, Jonathan . . ." She paused as a sudden hush fell around her at the mention of Jonathan's name. Even the wind seemed to linger for a moment, waiting to hear what she would say. Her heart beat faster, yet her voice held steady. "He fashioned this dresser for me as a wedding gift, and I'm not leaving it behind. Not for a second time."

Matthew opened his mouth to say something, then apparently thought better of it. His gaze moved to the piece of furniture behind her, and gradually all anger drained from his expression. She could almost read his thoughts by the varying shadows playing across his face—this was the place where his older brother had finally grown so ill and weak that he had taken to bed in the wagon and died. That's why these items had been left behind.

Moments passed. Neither of them spoke.

Matthew lifted his eyes to the western horizon, where the mountains were bathed in purple gray and the sun was slowly wedging itself behind their highest snowy peaks. Perhaps he too was sensing whatever it was that she'd felt moments before.

He set the brake and climbed down. "We'll camp here for the night." His voice had grown quiet. He set about unhitching the team. "Leave it," he said softly when she started to lift another drawer. "You get dinner on. I'll see to that."

Nothing in his voice hinted at command. Quite the contrary, so Annabelle did as he requested.

Throughout the evening, she watched as he went about his tasks with the efficiency she'd quickly grown accustomed to seeing from him. He worked with a thoroughness that bespoke pride in seeing a job well done. But there was a certain solitude about him now that kept drawing her attention back, especially when he took such care in wiping down the dresser before loading it into the back of the wagon. She had planned on cleaning it herself but held back when she saw him.

By the time she laid her head on the pallet that night, Annabelle thought she'd figured out what he had been doing. Across the camp, Matthew lay by his own fire, facing away from her. She rolled onto her back and stared up into the night sky, letting her eyes wander from star to star, and finding that there were so many she could scarcely focus on one without another sneaking into her view.

Perhaps in some odd way, in Matthew's wiping away the dust

and dirt from that dresser, in having his hands follow the same smooth lines that his older brother had cut and planed, he had been laying Jonathan to rest. And perhaps the common love they both still held for one man—this tenuous tender thread that had so far caused them such discord—would prove to be the very thing that might one day bring them both peace.

CHAPTER TWENTY

GATHERING HER WITS ABOUT HER, Annabelle walked through the open doors of the saloon, breathing a silent prayer. *God, please guide my steps tonight. If Sadie is here, let me find her.*

Dusk had descended by the time she and Matthew made camp on the outskirts of Parkston, a tiny trail town tucked along the northern border of the Colorado Territory. For some reason she couldn't explain, she hadn't wanted to tell him where she was going that evening, or even that she was going into town. So this time, unlike Denver, she purposefully waited until he was asleep before slipping away. The passing of the last two days had birthed an increasingly comfortable truce between them. Though she wouldn't go so far as to label Matthew chatty, they had begun to talk some, and she hated to do anything to upset that delicate balance. Besides, she very much doubted that Matthew would approve of or lend his support to what she was doing.

Dissonant chords from an out-of-tune piano compounded the noise in the smoke-filled saloon. A barkeep pounded the assemblage of ivories mercilessly, mangling the bawdy tune Annabelle knew only too well. She counted about twenty tables, every one of them full. Patrons not playing cards either watched from afar or stood hunched over their drinks at the bar.

She scanned the room for women. Five worked the tables and a sixth was headed up the side staircase, a man in tow. Annabelle's gaze connected with the bartender. He was already watching her.

She smiled. He didn't.

Burly and baldheaded, he went back to his work, but she knew full well that his attention was focused on her as she wove her way through the tables toward him. If Sadie was here, or had been in the past, this man would know.

She'd brought her money with her, all of it, secured in a pouch and tied around her upper thigh, where it couldn't be easily taken, and certainly not without her knowledge. She wished now that she'd left some coins out for a drink. Not that she drank. That vice had lost its appeal years ago, after she had seen time and time again the price it extracted. Like she'd read in one of Patrick's sermons . . . alcohol gave with one hand while thieving with two.

She edged her way between two men at the bar, creating a space close to where the bartender stood. The men moved but gave her the once-over—that scrutiny men gave women when they were imagining what they looked like uncovered. At least that's how Sadie said it. Annabelle remembered the night Sadie first used the phrase, soft and low with that accent of hers, and how all the other girls had laughed. The memory deepened her determination to find the child.

The man to Annabelle's right wore a confident expression she recognized. He smiled and opened his mouth to say something, but when met with her glare, his hope withered. He moved away.

"Who're you lookin' for?" The bartender's muscular arms were spread wide on the counter before her.

Annabelle resisted the urge to back up, knowing any sign of weakness would cost her. This man wasn't just burly, he was massive. His right hand dwarfed the bottle of whiskey he cradled, his thick fingers overlapping the lower half. She could only imagine what those hands would look like fisted. He wouldn't appreciate being toyed with, and she had no intention of trying.

"A young girl. She might've come through here within the last five or six months, give or take."

"A lot of young girls come through here." He reached for a glass, poured a shot, and set it in front of her.

She shook her head. "You'd remember this one. Long dark hair, olive skin, almond-shaped eyes. Exotic looking."

"When you say young . . ."

"Fifteen. But she looks older."

His focus shifted to somewhere behind her, then back. "You came here alone."

Her pulse missed a beat at the look in his eyes. She didn't need to respond; he hadn't asked a question. She mentally retraced her steps to the door, knowing full well she would not leave the saloon without this man's consent. She thought of Matthew back at the camp and wished she had confided in him about where she was going. Not that he would've agreed once he'd discovered her purpose. He wouldn't be caught dead in a place like this.

"Who sent you?"

He knows something. She answered quickly. "I came alone." Hesitating would give the wrong impression. "The girl's name is Sadie. She's just a child. And she's also my friend," she added, hoping honesty might entice his openness.

His gaze wandered over her face, her neck, her bodice. Annabelle stiffened.

"Meet me in the back room. Five minutes."

She shook her head. "You misun—"

"I said five minutes." In one fluid motion he drained the shot glass in front of her and thunked it down hard beside her hand. "That part's not open for discussion."

With a quick jerk of his head, he motioned to the door off to the side behind him, and Annabelle felt a lead weight drop into the pit of her stomach. He made a show of looking down at the bar. She traced his focus to her hand resting on the rail. She was trembling.

"Wait for me inside." A dark gleam lit his eyes. As he reached for the shot glass, his hand brushed across hers, gave it the slightest squeeze. He then turned away, but not before she caught a subtle change in his features. At least she thought she saw something. It happened so fast she couldn't be certain.

Heart racing, she scanned the crowded room. The din of noise pressed in around her, mingling with the cigar smoke, making it difficult to breathe. Was she reading the man right? If so, she was one step closer to finding Sadie. If not . . . *Oh, God, if not . . .*

She glanced back at the bar. From the same bottle, he poured himself another drink. He tossed it back and looked straight at her. She couldn't do this. Her love for Sadie went deep, but what this man was asking for was impossible now. And once she went through that door, there would be no going back.

Anger suddenly welled up inside her. God had given her so much in these past months, but she'd also done some giving of her own. Making changes in her life, in herself, that would be more to His liking. And this is what He did for her in return? Purposefully, she'd been careful not to ask Him for too much. Because she knew what it was like for someone to take and take and take—and never give anything in return.

Still, she had expected more from God than this. Tears burned her eyes.

Clenching her jaw, she turned to leave. She took two steps, then felt herself being lifted from the floor.

"I said five minutes. But I'm startin' to think I won't need that long."

Raucous laughter rang out from the crowd.

The room turned upside down as the bartender threw her over his shoulder. The blood rushed to her head. The air left her lungs. He strode toward the door.

Unable to scream, Annabelle did what came naturally from years of living with the goal of survival. She sank her teeth into the tender flesh of his back. His shirt tasted of sweat and smoke. Gagging, she bit down harder.

The bartender let out a low growl and grabbed her hair. Searing pain spread across her scalp. The muscles in her jaw went slack, and her head pounded like it might split open. Her upside-down world spun.

More laughter from the crowd. "She's a spunky one!" "Teach that woman a lesson!" "You might need more than five minutes, after all!"

He carried her through the door and down a dark corridor. Annabelle screamed and dug her nails into his upper arm until his flesh gave. He kicked open a door at the end, and tall as he was, she braced herself for the doorframe to catch her backside on the way through. But he ducked just in time.

He slammed the door behind them. "You shouldn't have come here alone, asking questions like that."

Hanging over his back, Annabelle frantically reached above and behind her for his face. Found it and went for his eyes.

Swearing loudly, he upended her and set her down hard on her feet. "You're a spirited little thing—I'll say that for you."

She dragged in air, trying to right the room's spin, then lunged for the door.

He easily blocked her and warded off her blows. "Calm down and listen to me for a minute."

She scanned the room for a weapon. A straw mattress lay on the floor in the corner, obviously well used. A desk strewn with paper was pushed against the wall. Above the desk, a board cluttered with charcoal portraits of men's faces stared back. She bolted for the desk and jerked open a drawer.

The man came from behind, pulled her hand free, and slammed the drawer shut. He pressed her against the desk, trapping her. "I won't hurt you. I promise."

His breath was warm against her hair. A tremor started deep inside her. She thought of her child and of the damage this man could inflict with a single blow. Annabelle bit the inside of her cheek until she tasted blood. To cry or beg would only make it worse.

After a moment, as though giving her time to calm, he moved away, placing himself again between her and the door.

"You will not touch me." She spoke the words slowly, already knowing it was futile. She was no match for him.

"Listen to me." He stepped toward her.

She moved back and met the wall behind her. The tremor inside her fanned out. Her legs went weak. She shook her head. "I can't do this. Not again," she whispered, more to herself than to him.

"I'm not gonna do anything to you, ma'am. But I had to get you out of there. Those questions you asked drew attention. And that's not something you wanna do around here."

"But I thought . . ."

"I know what you thought. But I give you my word—I won't lay a hand on you. Harsh or otherwise. You would've known I was tryin' to help you if you'd just taken the drink. It's sarsaparilla—a special bottle I keep under the counter. Comes in handy at times."

She hiccupped a breath, still watching, not quite trusting.

"The owner of this place spotted you. More than that, his man at the bar heard you asking about the girl. She was through here all right, about four months ago, I'd guess. They stayed awhile, then left."

"They?" she asked, using the wall behind her for support. Relief spread warm through her arms and legs.

"Two men were with her. They worked a deal out with the owner—I don't know what it was. I only know that business was good for the next few days."

Annabelle massaged the top of her head, her scalp still tingling.

"Sorry about that," he said, following her motions. "But the man who owns this place, and the men he works for, they don't like bein' questioned. Not about the business that goes on here, and especially not by some slip of a woman. No offense intended, ma'am."

She huffed a laugh. "None taken."

"A man came lookin' for the girl while she was still around." He shook his head. "He started asking questions and the men here worked him over somethin' awful."

Gallagher, Betsy's man in Willow Springs, immediately came to mind. "Was he tall? Bearded, with a head full of dark hair?" At his nod, right or wrong, Annabelle felt satisfaction at knowing Gallagher had experienced some payback. "Thank you for your help, Mr. . . ."

"Probably best we don't swap names, ma'am. I don't know which way they headed when they left, only that they took the girl and set out in a hurry one mornin'. But if you do decide to keep lookin' for her, be careful. Those men'll think nothing of doin' to you what they did to that fella. Or worse."

Knowing she was far from invincible, Annabelle nodded. "I've known men like that all my life. And I've already seen their worst."

His hard face softened. "I already reckoned that, ma'am," he said quietly. "I just figured you got out somehow."

Realizing what he was saying, she swallowed. Would there ever come a day when she wouldn't wear her old life so plainly for all to see? She briefly looked down at her hands, then back at him. "How did you know?"

He gave a shrug. "I've been around this for a long time. When you walked through the doors tonight, you didn't flinch. A . . . normal woman . . . well, she would've been shocked. She would've turned and left. But you didn't. In a glance, you worked the room and found your best mark." He grinned. "Me."

Seeing his smile drew one from her. Her experience had nearly cost her in this instance. "Thank you again, for your help." She started toward the door.

He held up a hand. "I'm afraid it's not gonna be that easy."

She paused beside him.

"If you walk back into that room without me and try to leave here, you're gonna be stopped. They already know you're here about the girl. We'll walk back in together. I'll give a nod, tellin' 'em I've taken care of things, and then you'll be allowed to leave."

Reluctant, she agreed.

"One more thing. . . ." His eyes swept her up and down. "If you leave this room like that they're gonna know this wasn't what it looked like, and then my boss'll pull us both in to talk. And I make it a point to talk to that man as little as possible."

With sick understanding, Annabelle nodded and looked down at his hands.

Sighing, he gently tipped her chin. "I'm not gonna hit you, ma'am. Here . . ." He wiped some of the blood from the scratches on his arm and streaked it across her cheek and jaw.

She wished she could take back how she'd questioned God's provision moments ago. "Thank you," she whispered. "For doing this."

"Does your husband know you're here?"

She frowned, then saw him looking at her left hand. "Oh, no . . . he doesn't."

A commotion sounded in the hallway.

"There's no lock on the door, so you best hurry." Untucking his shirt with one hand, he pointed at her bodice with the other. "I'll get you outta here safe, I promise."

Annabelle pulled the pins from her hair and riffled her fingers through it. She hesitated for a split second, but as the footsteps in the hall grew closer, she pulled the hem of her shirtwaist from her skirt and began unbuttoning the top buttons. As she did so, something caught her eye. A name . . . on one of the charcoal pictures hanging above the desk. The face bore only the slightest resemblance to the man.

Her hands froze. She took a step closer and reached out, certain she was misreading it. Then the door crashed open, and she spun around.

Matthew Taylor stood in the doorway.

CHAPTER TWENTY-ONE

AT FIRST, MATTHEW COULDN'T REACT. All he could do was stare.

Annabelle's shirtwaist was unbuttoned and revealing, her hair disheveled, and a giant of a man stood beside her. Matthew reached inside his jacket for his gun.

Annabelle started toward him, clutching the fabric of her bodice. "Matthew, you don't understand. This isn't what—"

"Don't." He shook his head, knots tightening his stomach. "Don't try to explain this away." From the blood streaked on her face, he could tell the man had gotten rough with her. It was her own fault, but still, the sick feeling inside him worsened. It didn't make any sense. It was like a dog returning to its vomit. Why would she come back to this life when she'd been given a way out?

He'd followed her into town, aware of when she'd left and guessing where she was going. Leaving their camp unguarded for so long wasn't his first choice, but he'd purposefully chosen a spot close to an outlying homestead, and once and for all, he wanted tangible proof about Annabelle Grayson. He'd watched her enter the establishment, had waited, then followed her in, firmly set on catching her in the act this time and hoping he was still one step ahead of the bounty hunter he'd seen in Willow Springs.

But when he'd kicked the door open and had seen her standing there, getting dressed again, he'd felt none of the satisfaction he thought would come at having been proven right.

He leveled the gun at the man, who appeared much more perturbed than frightened. "I'm leaving here with this woman, and I don't want you trying to follow us out."

"Mister, I don't know how you got back here, but if I don't follow you out the front door, you won't be leavin' here at all. I give you my word."

Matthew took hold of Annabelle's arm and pulled her through the doorway. "We'll just see about that."

The man acted like he might follow them until Matthew leveled his aim again. Then he stopped and raised his hands in truce. "Ma'am," he said, giving Annabelle a pointed look, "you'd better talk some sense into him, and make it fast."

Matthew slammed the door behind them, shutting the other man inside, and pulled Annabelle down the darkened corridor.

She resisted, slowing their pace. "You don't know what you're doing, Matthew. That man was the bartender. I approached him earlier. He was helping—"

"I saw what he was helpin' himself to, Annabelle. I'm not blind." He continued down the hall, dragging her with him. For once, she had no smart reply. He got to the door and leaned down close to her face. "Why would you come back to a place like this and . . . *do* what you just did when—" His voice broke, which only fed his anger. He tightened his grip on her arm. "When Johnny bought your way out? My brother loved you, for whatever reason, God help him. He cared about you . . . and this is what you do?"

She stared, unblinking.

When Matthew reached to open the door, she put a hand against it.

"Stop and listen to me, Matthew. I made a mistake coming here by myself. I realize that now. But that man can help get us out of here. He said if I tried to leave here on my own, the owner would stop me. He'll stop you too. You don't understand what—"

"I didn't have a problem walking into this place, and we'll walk out the same way."

Pulse racing, he opened the door and stepped through, immediately spotting the woman who had told him where to find

Annabelle. Her expression held warning. He glanced back behind them down the darkened hallway. Empty.

But the door to the back room stood open.

"Matthew! Look ou—"

The blow to his lower back sent him to his knees. His gun fell to the floor. Before he could reach it, a booted foot kicked it away.

"I think you're takin' something that belongs to me, mister. For a few more minutes, anyway. So the way I see it, if you plan on taking her outta here, you owe me."

Matthew struggled to his feet, the rush of pain making his head swim. He blinked to clear his vision and saw Annabelle struggling against two men holding her fast. Then he looked up at the bartender towering over him. This was the man she said was helping her? The woman had a strange definition of a hero.

Disoriented, Matthew didn't move fast enough.

The blow to his jaw sent him staggering back, but it didn't lay him flat out. Not like it should have if the bear of a man had put his full weight behind it. Through a blur, he saw the bartender coming at him again. For being so huge, the man moved with amazing agility.

He grabbed Matthew's shirt, hauled him off his feet, and slammed him into the wall. Everything went black for a minute, although Matthew could still hear the faint roar of cheering from the crowd. Johnny had always told him that the most important part of fighting was knowing when to fight and when to walk away. It scalded his pride, especially in front of Annabelle, but there was no way he could win this one. He'd be lucky to walk out in one piece, and he wouldn't risk her further hurt, not with the pledge he'd made to Pastor Carlson. He felt the giant's hand come around his throat and expected him to squeeze tight. But he didn't.

Instead the man brought his face close. "If you want to walk out of here alive with that woman," he spoke through clenched teeth, "you'll do exactly as I say."

From across the room, Matthew detected the worry in Annabelle's eyes. Her attention honed on him, she no longer struggled against the men who held her. The grip around his throat suddenly cinched tighter, and Matthew focused back on the bartender, deciding it might be best to listen.

When the bartender finished and finally let him go, he turned, and Matthew struck him from behind. The man spun and hit him hard in the face. Again, with force unworthy of the muscles banding his thick arms, but Matthew went down anyway. Getting to his feet, he landed a punch below the man's rib cage and stepped back, clenching and unclenching his right hand to work out the sting. It felt like he'd just tried to put his fist through a brick wall.

He tasted blood and wiped his mouth. "I don't owe you a thing. And neither does she."

"Is that so?" The bartender smiled and scanned the crowd that had grown quiet around them. "How many people here think he owes me?"

Cheers went up.

"How many people think *she* owes me?"

More cheers, laughter.

He looked back at Matthew. "I guess you're wrong about that, son. I can understand you bein' protective of your whore, and that's fine by me. But you need to pay me for time wasted." The bartender stepped closer. "I'll let her go for . . . five dollars. That'll about cover it."

Matthew glared at him . . . then pulled the bills from his pocket and counted them out into the man's hand.

The bartender smiled. "Nice doin' business with you." Then he nodded to the men holding Annabelle. But they didn't let her go. He glanced back at Matthew, guarded surprise on his face.

Matthew heard footsteps behind him. The man walking toward him was well dressed, roughly twenty years his senior. With his dark hair slicked back and not a hint of mercy in his features, he reminded Matthew of Antonio Sedillos. Thinking of Sedillos and the price he'd placed on his head back in Texas sent a chill scuttling up Matthew's spine.

The man stopped a few feet away. In his dark eyes shone a will not to be questioned. "Do you always have this much problem with your woman? That she would seek company here instead of at home, with you?"

That drew laughs from some of the men.

Matthew fought the urge to look at the bartender, knowing better. "No, sir, I don't. This was her first time. I thought she'd changed." He coerced a smile. "But once a whore, always a whore, I guess."

Murmured agreement trickled through the room.

The man's eyes narrowed. "Pardon if this offends," he said, his expression saying just the opposite. "But I look at you and I don't see a man who knows how to handle a woman. Especially a woman like this." He nodded to the men holding Annabelle, and they brought her before him.

Her hair flowed free over her shoulders. Her expression was hardened in defiance.

Matthew started to move, but when he saw a flash of warning in her eyes, he stilled.

The man lifted a dark curl from her chest and rubbed it between his fingers. "Don't tell me. You bought her from a place like this, thinking that taking her out of here would change who she is." He shook his head and made a *tsk*ing sound. "Only a fool believes that someone can change a person's destiny. Let me give you some advice, man to man." He gave Matthew a fatherly look, then ran a finger along Annabelle's jawline and slowly down her throat, stopping short of where her unbuttoned shirtwaist lay open.

Only the quick rise and fall of her chest hinted at her fear.

Matthew stiffened, itching to retaliate. Knowing he couldn't.

"Deep down a woman wants to know that her man is strong and has the power to protect her." Absurd sincerity lined the man's expression. "Would you agree?"

"Absolutely," Matthew answered, wanting to deck him.

"Then I would suggest that tonight you teach her a lesson in that kind of protection."

Knowing exactly what the man was referring to, he tried to imagine what Annabelle's life must have been like dealing with men like this. Her head was bowed, arms limp at her sides. Disgust twisted his stomach as he answered. "I'll do that. Thank you for the advice."

"You're most welcome." He gave his men another nod, and they immediately granted Annabelle her release.

She came to stand beside Matthew, her head still bowed. Matthew gently took hold of her arm to leave.

"Ah, just one more thing."

Hearing false gentility in the man's voice, Matthew turned. And found himself staring down the barrel of his own gun. Instinctively, he moved in front of Annabelle.

A slow smile spread across the man's face. "You forgot something." Switching the gun to his other hand, he held it out, handle first.

Matthew reached for it only to have it pulled back.

"To make sure you understand exactly what kind of lesson I'm talking about, I'd like to demonstrate, if you don't mind."

Matthew took a step forward. "I do mind." From the corner of his eye, he saw the bartender and noted the almost imperceptible shake of his head. "This woman belongs to me, and if there's any lesson she needs to be taught, I'll be doing the teaching."

The man's features hardened in challenge. "By all means, then, please."

Hating what he had to do, Matthew faced Annabelle again. Her head was still bowed. "Look at me."

She didn't.

Grabbing her chin, he forced her face up. "I said look at me." A fleeting light in her eyes told him she knew what he was doing. Still, he could hardly bring himself to follow through.

He struck her once across the face. She stared back, defiant. His chest ached.

He struck her again and prayed she would keep her head down. Slowly, she lifted her chin as if to say, "That's all you've got?"

He struck her again, as hard as he dared, and this time she kept her face lowered.

"I promise," she whispered after a moment. "I won't do it again."

Matthew sorely wanted to cover the marks on her cheek but instead shoved her toward the door. He waited until she was safely outside before turning back. "She won't be back here again."

The man handed him his gun. "And neither, I trust, will you."

CHAPTER TWENTY-TWO

ANNABELLE MADE IT OUT THE door and onto the darkened boardwalk, then pressed back against the building. Waiting. Listening.

"She won't be back here again." Matthew's deep voice carried to her.

She touched her left cheek, still feeling the sting from his hand. Judging from the tortured look she'd glimpsed in his eyes, his blows had hurt him a great deal more than they had hurt her.

"And neither, I trust, will you."

She closed her eyes. *Don't say anything else, Matthew. Leave. Just leave.*

Seconds later, he walked out the door, gun in hand, his face like stone. When he turned and saw her, a portion of the hardness melted away. Annabelle sensed the words building up inside of him, ready to spill out, but she shook her head. As though understanding, he threw a last glance behind them and gently took hold of her arm. He led her down the empty street to the corner and pulled her with him into an alley.

Her name left him in a rough whisper. "I'm sorry . . . what I did back there, what I said . . ." He reached up as though to touch the side of her face, then hesitated. "I didn't mean it. I—"

"I know, Matthew. I know."

TAMERA ALEXANDER

In the dim light of the coal-burning streetlamp, all she could see was his tender regret. "Are you sure you're all right?" He searched her face.

His earnestness made her smile. She had anticipated an apology, but nothing like this. She gave a quick laugh, attempting to lighten the moment. "Matthew, that was nothing. I've been through a lot worse, believe me." She had meant for the words to ease his conscience. They had the opposite effect.

Sighing, he slowly leaned forward until his forehead rested against hers. His hands moved up her arms and came to rest on her shoulders. His breath was warm on her face. He closed his eyes, but Annabelle didn't dare close hers. Nor did she move an inch. Their bodies weren't touching, but they were too close. Nothing about this was inappropriate on his part. He meant nothing by it, she knew. Yet she'd never been so fully aware of another person's nearness in her entire life.

Unnerved by her reaction, she gently pulled back.

A frown eased across his brow. "Wait here." He disappeared around the corner and returned a minute later, a handkerchief dripping in his hand. He wrung out the cloth and tilted her chin.

Only then did she remember the blood the bartender had smeared on her face. As he worked to wipe away the stains, a picture flashed in her mind—of his reaction at having found her in the back room.

"About what you saw tonight, I want to explain. When you walked in . . . it wasn't what it—"

"I know," he whispered.

"But the look on your—"

He held up a hand. "I said I know. The bartender explained what you were doing there . . . when he had me by the throat against the wall." A sheepish smile crept over his face. "He was a very persuasive man."

Annabelle couldn't help but giggle. "If I hadn't known he was on our side, I might've been a bit more worried about you."

Matthew feigned an injured expression, then grew serious again. "I followed you into town tonight fully expecting to catch you in a compromising situation." He briefly looked away. "Part of me even *hoped* I would so I could prove once and for all that you hadn't changed. That the Carlsons, Kathryn . . . everyone had been wrong about you. And that I had been right."

It was obvious that this was one apology that, though sincerely offered this time, wasn't coming easily. Doubt still lingered in the subtle lines of his face, telling her he wasn't fully convinced about her in the long run. Not yet, anyway.

She nodded in response, not surprised by his honesty—he'd been painfully honest with her before—but completely taken aback by his humility. This was a side of Matthew Taylor she had not seen.

He went back to gently wiping her cheek. "I end up fighting my way out of there, assuring your safety—" he shook his head, a telling tip of his mouth drawing her attention—"and this is the thanks I get."

She delicately fingered her jaw. "A most unconventional way of assuring a woman's safety too, I might add."

His hand stilled, and she immediately regretted having brought it up again. Her face grew warm.

"I've never hit a woman before, Annabelle."

"I know, Matthew . . . I could tell." She meant it in all seriousness, but when he grinned, she did too. Matthew had held back with her, much like the bartender had done with him. His arms and shoulders, muscled from years of hard work, were capable of dealing a far greater blow.

"I promise," he whispered. "I won't do it again." A gleam lit his eyes as he parroted back what she'd said to him moments ago in the saloon.

"I'll hold you to that."

He took a step back, and his gaze dropped to her bodice. It happened so fast. He blinked and averted his eyes. His jaw tensed. Then, as though against his will, he looked back again.

Annabelle's face burned. She clutched her shirtwaist and presented her back to him, already fumbling with the buttons. She had a chemise beneath that covered her, but she knew men well enough to know it didn't take much to distract their thoughts. Her hands shook badly, and the exasperating buttons were so tiny, she couldn't manage to—

"I'll just wait over here, until you're . . . finished."

"Yes, thank you. I'll only be a minute."

She shut her eyes and took several deep breaths, seeing only the look on his face. She had spent her entire adult life enticing men. Wearing what would attract their attention. Using words in such a way that they too became part of the game. Touching men in seemingly innocent ways, when innocence was the furthest thing from either of their minds. She cringed inside at the possibility that Matthew might think she had tried to use those tactics on him.

After a moment, she calmed enough to coerce the buttons through the narrow holes, then joined him where he stood waiting on the street.

She fell into step beside him, and they walked back to camp, unexpected ease embracing their silence. Thankful to be leaving the tiny town of Parkston, she used the moments to sift her thoughts. Repeatedly, they returned to this difference between men and women—how drawn a man was to look at a woman's body. And how a woman was drawn by such very different things. Knowing the Creator must have had a purpose in it—and not questioning His wisdom—she still didn't understand why God had created men and women so differently in that respect. The design seemed hopelessly fraught with confusion and strife.

She considered the man beside her and all that she knew about him—unaware though he may be. And she vowed to be more careful around him, purposing in her heart not to dress or act in a way that would knowingly bring about that struggle she'd seen on his face moments before.

The moon's pale pewter light rippled off something in the distance, and she realized it was the white tarp of the wagon. A most welcome sight. Uncertain how and when it had happened exactly, she acknowledged with some reservation the unexpected affection she had for him. Like his brother, Matthew Taylor was good and decent—even if he was stubborn as the day was long and overly critical at times. Remembering the shy, boyish look that had swept his face when he referred to the bartender having him by the throat, encouraged a chuckle.

"What's so funny?"

She shook her head. "I was just thinking of you back there, with the bartender."

Matthew drew in a quick breath. "Given more time, I think I could've taken him."

She laughed. "I have no doubt in my mind." A cool breeze billowed the wagon canopy, and she rubbed her arms, just now realizing how tired and hungry she was. Dinner hadn't appealed to her much before, but now she could think of nothing else. She had banked her fire before going into town, and she noticed that Matthew had done the same. "Well, I best get my fire going."

"Mind if I do it for you?" He looked up as though gauging the position of the moon. "Sunrise isn't that far off, and I'm afraid it might take you that long to get it started again."

"I'll have you know it only took me thirty-nine tries tonight. However, I'll gladly accept your help."

He had her fire built and blazing in no time, then stood and made as if to leave.

"I didn't eat much before and was going to warm up something." She glanced away briefly. "I didn't know if you might be hungry?"

Minutes later they sat, on opposite sides, enjoying the fire's warmth and the quiet prairie, eating warmed salt pork and beans and washing it down with water. Despite the meal's simplicity, Annabelle relished it, and the company.

"Why didn't you tell me what you were doing? Going into town like that."

She looked up to find him staring at her. His tanned face appeared almost bronze in the yellow-orange glow. She laid her tin plate aside. "Because I didn't think you would approve and thought you might even try to stop me."

He shook his head slowly. "Heaven help the man who tries to stop you from doing anything, Annabelle."

She smiled, knowing how true that once was, but also knowing how Jonathan McCutchens had changed all that. If only Jonathan had known how much he'd done for her, how much he'd taught her in such a short time. But maybe he did.

"Who is she? This woman the bartender said you're looking for."

Matthew's question drew her back, and she prayed for the right words to come. "She's someone who used to work at the brothel in

Willow Springs." She could feel the tension rise in him from where she sat. "She was taken this past January, in the middle of the night. They found blood on her pillow." Staring into the fire, she told him everything the bartender had said. "I'm determined to find her," she added, intentionally softening her tone.

That got his attention. "At what cost?"

Knowing he wouldn't like her answer, and anticipating the conclusion he would draw, she couched it as gently as possible. "My plan is to buy her out of whatever contract or . . . situation she's in."

It took him a minute, but he finally nodded, his expression a clear denial that the gesture indicated agreement. "Using whose money?"

Unwilling to play this game with him, she kept her tone subdued. "You and I both know whose money I'll use, Matthew."

"Do you think that's what Johnny would have wanted?"

His question struck her as needless because within it was the very answer he sought. She watched him for a moment, waiting, and gradually saw understanding move into his expression.

He looked away. "What if you don't find her?"

"I believe I will."

"But what if you don't?"

She lifted her shoulders, then let them fall. Tears rose in her throat as she imagined where Sadie might be at that moment. "Then I think . . . for every day of the rest of my life—" Her voice cracked. She couldn't stem the emotion tightening her chest. She breathed in and out, her head down. "I'll regret not being able to do for Sadie what Jonathan did for me." Feeling a tear trail down her cheek, she forced her gaze up. "And what you did for me . . . tonight."

From the swift stab of comprehension knitting her brow, she knew he got her meaning. This time he didn't look away, and she admired him for it. "How long have you known this woman?"

"I met Sadie when she first came to the brothel in Willow Springs four years ago." She hesitated, knowing this would be especially hard for him. "She was eleven years old."

His frown deepened, his expression saying he thought he'd misunderstood. He shook his head. "Eleven? But . . . that's the same age as . . ."

"Lilly." She finished the sentence he could not.

Disbelief. Revulsion. Pity. Anger. All flashed across his face, one after the other.

"Sadie's parents came here from China in order to give their children a better life." She sighed. "I don't know what happened exactly. Sadie never has talked much about it. She doesn't talk much about anything, really. But I do know her parents died and she was left alone out here." She shook her head. "Not a good thing to happen to a young girl in this territory."

Matthew lowered his head to his hands, and Annabelle could almost hear the inaudible groan coming from deep inside him. She drew up her knees and rested her forehead against them, praying for Sadie, praying to find her, praying for Matthew as he got yet another glimpse into the kind of life she'd led.

The crackle of the fire ate up the silence.

After a few moments, he rose. The sound drew her head up. Emotion shone in his eyes.

"We'll be crossing into Wyoming Territory tomorrow. There're a handful of places along the Union Pacific line running between Cheyenne and Laramie." He paused. "Do you know of any town in particular where they might've taken her? That might be known for . . . having a place like that?"

Annabelle shook her head. "They could've taken her anywhere. Pretty much every town, no matter how small, has *places like that.*"

He didn't answer for a moment. "We'll find her," he whispered, and he turned and walked past the wagon into the darkness.

Annabelle waited until she couldn't see him anymore, then reached for her blanket and curled onto her side—weary, thankful, and strangely hopeful. She waited several moments—hearing Matthew's movements across the camp, the whinny of the horses, followed by the low murmur of his voice as he spoke to them—until the noises ceased. Then she pulled the parchment she'd taken from the back room of the saloon from the pantalets beneath her skirt.

She studied the likeness of Matthew Taylor, seeing only vague similarities mirrored in the crudely drawn features. The connection might've been lost on her altogether if not for the name. She read the charges laid against him. She wouldn't have figured Matthew for a gambler. But then again, judging from the wanted poster in her hand, he apparently wasn't one. Or at least hadn't been a very good one.

A rueful smile accompanied that thought—not at his quandary, but at their discovered similarities. They were both running from a past. This would explain his air of desperation when applying for this job, and possibly his eagerness to leave Willow Springs . . . if someone had discovered him. Or was close to it.

She curled the parchment and shoved it into the heart of the flames. As the edges charred and the paper withered to ash, a bittersweet realization moved over her. She'd misjudged him, in many ways. But in one opinion specifically she was especially thankful to have been proven wrong.

Matthew Taylor did, indeed, bear a striking resemblance to his older brother after all.

CHAPTER TWENTY-THREE

S HIFTING HIS WEIGHT, Matthew peered down at her from across the fire. "What do you mean you don't know how to ride?"

When she didn't answer, he tilted his head in hopes of getting her attention. But she continued to add ingredients to the bowl cradled in her lap, apparently unwilling to look up, which was odd given the ease that had developed between them during the past week.

He never would have guessed it could happen based on the sparks that flew during their first few conversations in Willow Springs, but they were actually getting along pretty well now. He was glimpsing a side of her he hadn't seen before, and though he wasn't ready to hand over complete trust, he'd begun to look forward to the evenings when they ate dinner and talked.

"Annabelle?" he prompted softly.

She pushed a strand of hair from her forehead with the back of her hand, continuing to focus on her task. "I said I just don't know how, that's all." Her tone was light, but she shrugged in a way that said she didn't want to talk about it further.

Which made it all the more inviting to him. She'd already driven the wagon twice in the last few days as they'd begun following the Platte River, shadowing Jack Brennan's scheduled route.

TAMERA ALEXANDER

She'd handled the team of horses over the bumpy and often deeply rutted Wyoming plains better than he'd anticipated. Still, that wasn't the same as riding. "Have you ever tried before?"

"I rode when I was a girl." She sighed, shaking her head. "But that's been a few years ago."

"I could teach you. I bet you'd pick it back up real quick."

She pursed her lips, her focus still pinned to the mixing bowl. "I appreciate that, Matthew, really. But I'm fine with driving the team or walking when I need a respite from the wagon."

He watched her add a bit more flour to the dough. Patrick Carlson had been right about her biscuits, and Matthew had come to look forward to them. Especially when they were hot and fresh, like tonight. His gaze went involuntarily to her left cheek. Not once had she mentioned again what he'd done to her in the saloon that night, but the memory was never far from his thoughts.

He studied her for a moment, unable to account for the certainty inside him but somehow knowing that she wasn't telling him the whole truth. There was something else behind her reasons for not knowing how to ride a horse. He just didn't know what it was. Was she afraid? Not likely. Not with everything she'd been through in her life.

Ever since Annabelle had told him about the girl, Sadie, one question kept resurfacing in his mind—how young had Annabelle been when she started working at the brothel? He prayed her story wasn't similar to Sadie's, and whenever he considered that possibility, an ache rose up inside him.

He studied the delicate features of her face. One thing he was sure of now—if given a choice, Annabelle would never have chosen such a life. And it shamed him to think he once thought she had. He'd seen the proof in her eyes that night in the saloon, and again when she'd spoken of Sadie, and also in the sparkle she gained with every mile that distanced them from Willow Springs.

"You'd love riding, I'm sure of it. If you'd just give it another try." With her fierce independence, she would savor the sense of freedom. He could already picture her astride the powerful gelding, giving him the lead. "Let me teach you, please."

She shook her head. "Thank you for offering, Matthew, but I'm simply not interested."

Determined to discover the reason behind her pat refusal, an idea came to him. He crouched down where he could see her expression more easily. When she suddenly took a deeper interest in the biscuit dough, her forehead crinkling in concentration, he could tell she knew what he was up to. And he enjoyed the anticipation.

Resting his forearms on his knees, he heaved an exaggerated sigh. "Well, I didn't want it to come to this, Mrs. McCutchens, but . . . we each have to pull our own weight on the trail, ma'am. I made that real clear with you before we started out. And I'm afraid your not being able to ride is hindering our progress."

Not looking up from the bowl, she began to knead the lump of dough. "Is that so, Mr. Taylor?"

Annabelle was masterful at hiding her smile at times like these, much better than he was. But her voice had taken on that uppity tone, which was far more rewarding than a smile at this stage of the game.

"It is, Mrs. McCutchens, and I'm afraid that if you don't live up to your end of the bargain, I'm going to have to give you notice, effective immediately. You'll have to find another trail guide. I'd hate to do it, of course, but—"

"Oh, of course," she said, then rewarded the dough with a swift punch, no doubt pretending it was his face.

"But . . ." He feigned a sigh. "Sometimes a man has to make tough choices."

"Yes, a man does. However, a woman does as well." She pinched off an ample portion of dough, rolled it in her palms to form a ball, flattened it to about an inch thick, and placed it in the Dutch oven warming over the fire. The biscuit dough sizzled in the melted bacon fat drizzled over the bottom.

The aroma caused his stomach to growl, and Matthew cleared his throat in hopes of covering it.

Annabelle leaned over the pot and breathed in, closing her eyes. "Mmmm, doesn't that smell good?" She finally looked at him then, her expression going forlorn. "Oh . . . but I'm sorry. Biscuits are only for the hired help."

The woman could be cruel. And he loved it. "Well, I might could be persuaded to stay. For a day or two longer at most." He reached for a piece of dough from the bowl.

She yanked it away and held up a hand. "I fear I've not been satisfied with your work as of late, Mr. Taylor. And I've been meaning to talk to you about it. There's too much dust and wind, and it's far too dry here for my taste. I believe you promised me rain before we left Willow Springs. Sang me some sad tune about not being able to wait another day because of the threat of it." She made a show of searching the canopy of cloudless dark blue skies overhead and over Laramie's Peak to the west.

She sighed. "So . . . I'm afraid I'm going to have to dismiss you after all. And I feel just terrible about it."

Her serious expression, coupled with the close-to-genuine sincerity in her voice, almost made him chuckle. "How do you do that?"

"Beg your pardon?" The barest hint of humor warmed her voice.

"How do you manage to act so sincere when I know you're anything but?"

She placed the last biscuit in the Dutch oven and covered it with the lid. "Simple. You have to enjoy the anticipation of making someone else laugh as much as you enjoy laughing yourself." Her smile turned mischievous. "And it helps if you're a really good liar."

He laughed, noting how her eyes sparkled the moment she allowed the pretense to fall away, like the vibrant blue of an unclouded sky. "Now that, Annabelle McCutchens, is one of the most honest things I've heard you say." He ignored the smart look she gave him and leaned over the fire to inhale the aroma. "How long 'til the biscuits'll be done?"

"The same as every other time you ask me. About fifteen minutes or so." She held out her hand, and in it was a piece of biscuit dough she'd somehow managed to save back.

He popped it into his mouth and stood, then held out his hand for the bowl. "I'll go wash it for you."

Surprise shone on her face. "Why, thank you, kind sir," she said, her tone becoming playfully formal.

"You're most welcome, ma'am." His fingers brushed against hers in the exchange, and he paused, keenly aware of how alone they were and of the blush deepening her cheeks. He told himself it was due to the fire's warmth, but he wondered.

After a second, he cleared his throat. "I don't mind doing it. Your biscuits are well worth it. And besides, this way we'll have more time after dinner for your first lesson."

He walked away, imagining the daggers she was shooting at his back.

"How will Manasseh know what I want him to do?"

"Same as any other male. You tell him."

Her anxious expression disappeared for a split second.

Seeing her death grip on the reins, Matthew took hold of her hand and pried open her fingers. "Loosen up a bit. Here . . . face your hand palm down with your fingers pointing toward his neck. Good, now put your little finger under the rein and your other fingers over it." She was good at following instructions, when she wanted to. "Now turn your hand a mite so your thumb is on top and your knuckles are facing forward."

"This isn't as comfortable. I'd rather hold it like I was."

"It'll become second nature—don't worry. Manasseh's as gentle as they come, Annabelle. He won't hurt you."

"I've seen the way he runs. You two fly across the prairie."

"That's only because I give him the lead."

She shot a glance at Matthew and then back to the horse. "What if he thinks I'm giving him the lead?"

Ducking his head to hide his grin, Matthew busied himself with checking the girth he'd already adjusted. "He won't take off with you, I promise."

Manasseh chose that moment to snort and toss his head, and Annabelle tensed up again.

"He's just sensing your nervousness. You'll both be fine."

"I still don't see why I have to do this."

Matthew stroked the horse's flank. "You don't have to. But I'm proud of you for giving it a try."

She sat up a bit straighter. "Why can't I ride like all the other women I've seen?"

"First off, not all women ride sidesaddle. Not in these parts, anyway. You'll have more control riding this way, and you'll feel safer. Besides, no one's out here to see you, and you can always learn to ride sidesaddle later, if you want."

"I suppose you'll teach me that too?"

He detected the snip in her voice but chose to let it pass. "Remember, keep your weight balanced in the saddle. Don't lean too far to the left or right. Move forward a bit." Without touching her leg, he gestured for her to scoot forward. "You always want to sit in the lowest part of the saddle. Let your legs lie gentle around the horse. Don't squeeze too tight." He took hold of her foot. "The heel of your boot should line up with the stirrups, and the balls of your feet should rest right over the stirrup iron. Keep your toes pointing forward and your heels pointing down."

Her stoic expression said she doubted she could remember to do all that at once. But having seen how well she handled the grays, Matthew figured she would be a natural at this—once she got past her fear.

"Keep your upper body straight but not stiff. And face forward."

She took a deep breath and did as he asked.

"Relax."

"I am relaxed."

"Just let your arms rest by your sides."

"They are resting!"

He nodded slowly. "I can see that." He softened his voice. "Just imagine that your forearms are an extension of the reins."

She gave a quick laugh. "I'd rather imagine the reins wrapped around your neck."

He ran his tongue along the inside of his cheek. "If that helps you."

"It does." After a second, she looked down and he caught that spark in her eyes.

He hesitated, wanting to ask but not wanting to pry. "You said you hadn't ridden since you were a little girl. You didn't say, but I'm guessing something happened . . . that scared you."

Her jaw tensed. She looked down on her hand holding the rein. "I've only told this to one other person." She gave a harsh laugh that held a trace of embarrassment. "I was thrown. Stupid horse just took off for no reason. Jumped the corral and bucked me at the same time."

"Were you hurt?"

"I broke my arm. My father made me get back on later that afternoon. He led the horse around to make sure I was safe, but I promised myself then that I'd never ride again."

A fleeting frown crossed her face, and it occurred to him that she'd never mentioned anything about her childhood or her parents before. Judging from her shadowed expression, she was wishing she still hadn't.

"The stupid horse . . . did he have a name?" Matthew asked, changing the subject.

She frowned in his direction, a bit of humor in the gesture. "Cocoa!"

He grinned. "And I'm betting you haven't had any of that to drink since then either."

"As a matter of fact . . . no, I haven't. I used to love it but somehow lost my taste for it after that." Manasseh shifted beneath her, and Annabelle let out a gasp. All humor vanished. "Can we please get this lesson over with?"

Matthew quickly reviewed the instructions they'd already gone over, then took a step back.

Annabelle barely touched her heels to the horse's flank, then sat, waiting. Manasseh tossed his head, snorted, and turned his head to look at her, as though wondering what to do.

"Do it again, Annabelle. Firmer this time, and make a kissing noise." He demonstrated.

She parroted the sound, and Manasseh responded. Holding the reins with one hand, she gripped the pommel with the other, jouncing up and down in the saddle.

Matthew walked alongside them. "Relax your legs. Let them hug his sides. And don't be scared of him. That's it." He was impressed with her efforts and told her so. "Now, tell him where you want him to go."

"Don't tempt me," she said beneath her breath.

He grinned and shook his head, then watched as she laid the reins against the left side of Manasseh's neck. The horse turned right and headed for the wagon, slowing when he came to it.

She huffed. "Why did he go this way?"

"Because you told him to."

"I thought I said to go left."

"If you want him to go left, lay the reins against the right side of his neck."

She did as he said, then sighed. "He's not listening. I told you this was a bad idea."

Hearing the irritation in her voice, Matthew got a glimpse of the impatient young girl in the woman before him. "Remember how I told you to get him to back up?"

She pulled back on the reins. Manasseh edged backward.

Matthew watched for the next few minutes, saying nothing, and witnessing her confidence level build as she gave commands and Manasseh did as she bade. "Take him a bit farther out now. Down to that clump of sagebrush and back." Halfway back, she surprised him by nudging the horse into a canter and maintaining her seating perfectly.

When she returned, she was short of breath, her face flush with pleasure.

He took hold of the horse's bridle and rubbed the white tuft between Manasseh's eyes. "How was it?" As if he had to ask.

"Can I take him around again?"

"Be my guest. From the look of things, he likes you."

She grinned and reached down to stroke his neck. "Really? How can you tell?"

He shrugged and, remembering her advice from earlier, managed to completely mask his humor this time. "Because he hasn't thrown you yet—which is what he usually does when he doesn't like somebody."

Her eyes widened, then gradually narrowed as Matthew showed his hand. "Matthew Taylor, there's going to come a day when you'll need me to teach *you* something, and I can hardly wait for that opportunity."

"That makes two of us, ma'am."

She smiled and took off at a canter.

CHAPTER TWENTY-FOUR

YOU CAN GO FIRST." Matthew tilted his head toward the creek, knowing she could hardly wait.

She squinted as though hesitant. "Are you sure you don't mind?" At his nod, her face lit. "I won't be long, I promise."

"Take your time."

"But it'll be dark soon, and I want you to have time."

He reached for two more biscuits from the Dutch oven and leaned back in front of the fire. "It's not like I've never bathed in a creek at night before, Annabelle. Besides, I want another cup of coffee . . . and these." Holding up the biscuits, he wriggled his brow.

"All right, then, if you insist." She walked to the wagon and rummaged in the back for a few minutes, then started for the creek, her arms laden.

He stopped chewing. "What do you plan on doing down there? Settin' up house?"

"I haven't had a real bath since we left Willow Springs a week and a half ago, and I'm wearing a layer of dust and dirt for every mile of prairie we've crossed. My hair, my clothes, my skin all feel like—"

He held up a hand and glanced down at his own clothes. "Believe me, I understand. I just think I'm more accustomed to this life than you are."

"While that may be . . ." She cleared her throat, a gleam in her eyes. "Let's just say I want you to have equal time to bathe."

Ignoring her droll expression, he motioned again toward the creek. "There's a deep enough pool a ways upstream. Not much privacy on the other side of that ridge, but unless you're shy of an occasional prairie dog or salamander, you should be fine."

Unable to miss the perk in her step as she walked away, he watched her until she crested the shallow ridge, about a stone's throw from where he sat. He scanned the horizon from west to east. The sun had claimed recent safe refuge behind the snow-capped peaks, leaving behind a wide swath of burnished blue. And back to the east, a slivered half moon was just beginning its nightly journey across the sky.

Movement caught his eye.

He spotted the top of Annabelle's head. Her left arm came up, then her right, then a piece of clothing appeared. Realizing what she was doing—and what *he* was doing—he looked away. But he could still see the image in his mind. Deciding he needed more of a deterrent, he got up and moved to the opposite side of the fire, where his back would be to her. The view this way wasn't nearly as nice, but it was far less tempting.

He finished another biscuit, downed the last of his coffee, and poured another cup. Then slowly, begrudgingly, a truth began to unfold inside him. One that, until that moment, had only loitered at the edge of his thoughts. He understood now how Johnny could have grown to care for this woman.

He lowered his head. *Johnny . . .*

Not a day went by that he didn't miss his brother and wonder what things would be like if he were still here. Matthew winced, remembering the last time he'd seen him. That night in the shack. The heat—and regret—of their argument crept back into his chest.

"She doesn't love you, Johnny. She's only using you. You know that, right?" He had glanced at the closed door of the back room where Annabelle had disappeared, unconcerned about her overhearing.

Johnny, normally swift to retaliate, smiled instead. "I know that, Matthew."

Matthew raised his hands in disbelief. "So, are you just having some fun here? Is that what this is about? Not having to pay for it this time?" Johnny's expression darkened, and Matthew knew he'd touched an old nerve.

"Be careful, Matthew." He spoke the words quietly. "I love Annabelle. She's my wife, and I won't tolerate anyone disgracing her. Even you."

"Disgracing her!" He barely managed to stifle a curse. "She's a whore, for—"

The next thing Matthew knew he was flat on his back, sprawled on the dirt floor. Johnny towered over him. The left side of Matthew's face throbbed. He tasted blood. Johnny held out a hand, but Matthew shoved it aside and struggled to his feet, still unsteady.

"I won't stand for you talkin' that way about my wife." Johnny shook his head and rubbed his fist. "I'm sorry, Matthew. My temper still gets the best of me from time to time."

Unable to ignore the sincerity in his brother's voice, Matthew worked his jaw. "Nice to know some things haven't changed in the past eight years." Blinking to clear the fog from his head, he retrieved his hat from where it had landed and knocked it against his thigh.

He could try and take his best shot right now, and he figured Johnny might even let him. He'd grown up being thankful for his brother's size—the same brute strength that had just laid him out flat had also saved his life, more than once.

Matthew shifted his weight. "If you knew the only reason she married you was to get out of the brothel, why'd you do it?"

Johnny lifted a brow. "I never said that was the only reason she married me. I was agreein' to the part about her not loving me." Johnny's gaze trailed to the closed door as he crossed the small space in four long strides. He added another log to the flames and watched the sparks shoot up the crumbling chimney as he eased his tall frame into the rocking chair. The wooden joints creaked in complaint, as though at any moment they might admit defeat and surrender. "I know Annabelle doesn't love me, Matthew." His voice grew soft. "Not yet, anyway—not like that. But she will, given time. I'm trustin' she'll learn to love me."

"Trusting she'll learn to—" Matthew gave a sharp exhale. "Do you really think a—"

Johnny's eyes flickered with warning.

This time, Matthew heeded it. "That a *woman* like her can learn to love a man? After all she's done? After what she's *been*?"

"That's exactly what I believe. People can't give what they haven't got, Matthew. But I think people can change, if given a chance. With the right strength in them." He shrugged. "Look at me. I've changed."

Matthew fingered his jaw again, nodding. "I can see that."

Johnny began a slow, methodical rocking, evidently choosing to ignore the sarcasm. "You remember the filly that found her way out to our farm when we were kids? She'd been all beat up. She had those scars crisscrossin' her withers?"

Matthew fought the urge to roll his eyes, already seeing where this was headed.

"She wouldn't come to anybody. She was scared and hurt and hungry. Everybody else said to put her down." With his thumb and forefinger, Johnny made an imaginary gun and pulled the trigger. "They couldn't see what I saw." He shook his head and leaned forward, forearms resting on his thighs, long legs spread wide. "She would've eaten the entire bag of oats that first afternoon if I'd let her. Took me all winter just to calm her enough where I could get close . . . where she trusted me enough to let me touch her. Remember how she'd come when I whistled for her?" A deep chuckle rumbled in his chest. "And you used to try and whistle for her all the time, and she wouldn't even look at you."

Matthew remembered the horse. She was an ugly thing—even fleshed out and fully grown. All scarred up with that mangy coat growing back in uneven patches. Running his tongue along the edge of his bloody lip, he decided to keep those thoughts to himself.

"Some people are like that, Matthew. They've been hurt." Johnny's whisper grew more hushed, the creak of the rocker competing with his voice. "They're broken inside, thinkin' they're not worth much." He took a cup from the table by his leg and slowly poured its contents on the dirt floor beside him. "They think their lives are like this water here—all spilled on the ground, it can't be gathered up again." A small puddle formed at first, then fanned out in tiny rivulets. In a sweeping motion, Johnny brushed his hand across the dirt floor until the thirsty ground had consumed all traces of moisture. "But I've come to believe that God doesn't just sweep away the lives of people who feel that way about themselves. And I don't think we should either. We need to give each other second chances, whether we deserve them or not." He resumed his rocking, slow and steady.

Matthew looked at the dark spot of dirt by Johnny's chair and caught the sheen in his brother's eyes. He was unmoved. Johnny had always possessed a soft spot for lost things, whether they were stray critters or wounded animals. But to think that Johnny had been duped, that somehow this woman had gotten him to think he was on some mission of mercy . . .

That was more than Matthew could stomach.

Even with their frequent disagreements, Matthew had always admired his brother. How could he not? Johnny's shirt hid the scars, but Matthew knew the faint stripes from his father's thick leather strap were still there, across Johnny's broad back and shoulders.

Johnny had always been weak when it came to women, and apparently Annabelle Grayson had found a way to use his weakness—and her expertise—to her own advantage. But he wouldn't stand by and let Johnny take another beating, or pay the price for someone else's mistakes. Not again.

"You're being duped, Johnny. Can't you see that? She'll leave you as soon as she gets what she's after."

"And just what do you think it is she's after?" Johnny suddenly stopped rocking. "Or do you just figure that no woman could ever care for a big, clumsy oaf like me."

Matthew refused to be sidetracked by this old wound, though he remembered it well. "She's after whatever money you've got. And no doubt she knows how to get it too."

Emotions had flashed across Johnny's face so rapidly that Matthew hadn't been able to settle on what his brother's next reaction would be. But he'd readied himself for another one of Johnny's punches, just in case.

Matthew stared into his empty coffee mug and grimaced, remembering how that night had ended. He looked back at the eastern horizon now cloaked in darkness, and a high-pitched whinny jerked him fully back to the moment.

Then a sixth sense brought him slowly to his feet.

Night blanketed the prairie outside the circle of firelight, and he found himself blind to what lay beyond the soft glow. He searched the direction where he'd tethered the horses, roughly twenty feet from where he stood, then focused in the opposite direction, where Annabelle had gone.

"Annabelle, are you all right?"

He waited, listening, then called her name again. From the short distance the moon had traveled, he estimated no more than half an hour had passed since she'd left.

Another high-pitched whinny. The horses snorted.

Matthew felt down beside him for his rifle, and his hand closed around it. He stepped into the shadows, impatient for his vision to adjust. The prairie, indiscernible to him seconds before, slowly became a shaded world of varying grays.

To his right, the horses suddenly reared back, fighting the restraints. A low growl sounded off to his left, and an icy finger of dread trailed up his spine. The horses pawed the ground, their frantic neighs splitting the night.

Matthew whirled and cocked his rifle, ready to take aim.

Snarling. The scurry of paws. Then a pair of reddish eyes emerged through the gray. Head slung low, the animal loped toward him on spindly legs. In his peripheral vision, Matthew sensed movement to his right, near the horses, but kept his finger on the trigger, taking dead aim on the wolf's skull.

He squeezed tight, and the animal dropped. Heart pounding, he spun in time to see two more wolves lunge at one of the grays. The horse reared up, kicking, and let loose a frenzied scream. Matthew squeezed off another round. The larger wolf yelped, veered to one side, and retreated into the night. The other followed on his heels.

Matthew quickly reloaded. He circled, searching the darkness and the livestock, fighting to hear above the pounding in his ears. Then he ran toward the creek, slowing only once he neared the ridge.

"Annabelle?" His breath came hard. When she didn't answer, he feared the worst.

A splash sounded downstream. He raised his rifle, cocking it and taking aim in one fluid motion.

"Matthew . . ."

He exhaled, then saw a shadow peek up over the hill. He lowered the gun and stepped forward. "Are you all right?"

"Yes, but stop! And turn around . . . please."

He did. He couldn't see much in the dark, but still he looked away.

"Are they gone?" The quaver in her voice gave away her fear.

He uncocked the rifle. "Yes . . . for now. I killed one, wounded another, and then they ran. Not sure how many there were."

"Are the horses safe?"

He shook his head at that, smiling. "Yes, I think so. And I'm fine too. Thanks for asking."

He heard a soft chuckle.

"You're the one standing there with the gun, so I figured you were fine. Now . . ."

He heard a rustling of grasses on the bank where her voice was coming from.

"Would you mind heading back to camp so I can get dressed?"

"Yes, ma'am, I do mind. I'm not leaving you out here alone." He took a few steps away from the ridge, keeping his back to her. "I promise you, I won't look."

No movement sounded behind him, then he heard her mumble something indistinguishable, which made him smile all the more. A few minutes later, she climbed up over the embankment, a bundle in her arms. Her wet hair hung in dark strands over her shoulders and down her back, and as she walked—wordless but watchful—beside him back to camp, he caught the scent of lilacs.

Matthew gave the livestock a thorough check. He cooed in low tones to the horse the wolves had tried to get at, calming her until she would let him run a hand over her legs. She wasn't favoring any of them, so that was a good sign. He made a sweep around the camp perimeter before returning.

Annabelle was sitting by the fire, her back to him. Her hair was freshly combed, and she held something up to her face. As Matthew came closer, he realized it was a mirror. She held it at different angles, turning it this way and that, then stopped and brought it closer to one side of her face. She lifted a hand to her right temple and seemed to trace a path there.

Feeling as though he were intruding, Matthew purposefully scuffed his boot in the dirt.

She instantly lowered the mirror and tucked it down beside her. "Are they gone?"

"All's clear. None of the horses were hurt, and the cow's fine."

"That's good." She looked up at him, then back down again. "Matthew . . . would you mind if we were to share the same fire tonight? Under the circumstances."

He didn't answer immediately, letting his silence coax her attention back. He still detected traces of fear, though he knew she'd be hard-pressed to admit to it. "I think that'd be fine."

Smiling her thanks, she spread her bedroll out on the opposite side of the fire from his and lay down, staring into the flames.

He stretched out, rifle close at hand, and searched the night sky.

"Thank you, Matthew."

In the softness of her voice, he sensed something deeper than a simple expression of gratitude, and it touched a place inside him.

"Just doin' my job, ma'am. After all, I am the hired help," he whispered back.

His body was tired but his mind raced with unspent energy. After a few minutes, he heard Annabelle's even breathing and rose up on one elbow. One of her arms was cradled beneath her head and a hand was tucked beneath her chin. She had a peaceful look about her. He stared at her for a long moment, then lay back down, knowing sleep was far off for him.

What on earth was he doing out here with her? He sighed, knowing what his original reason had been—the land waiting in Idaho.

"Come with us, Matthew," Johnny had said to him that night in the shack. His brother's voice was so clear in his memory. "Come with us to Idaho. I've got some property there, like we used to talk about having when we were kids. There's enough for the both of us." Johnny leaned forward in the rocker as he described the meadows and streams clustered in the foothills of the mountains. His face nearly glowed as he talked about it.

Matthew managed to hide his surprise at the offer, while his gut told him that Johnny was exaggerating. Wouldn't be the first time. "Where'd you get money for land like that?"

"I sold the homestead in Missouri. So half of that land's rightfully yours."

Matthew laughed. "Our old farm wouldn't bring the kind of money you'd need for acreage like that."

Johnny shrugged. "I managed to get things turned around in the last few years, plus picked up some extra jobs here and there and made enough to lay some aside. The homestead sold for more than you might—"

"No thanks, big brother." Matthew held up a hand, shaking his head. "I've got a chance for a real ranch of my own down near San Antonio. Got a man down there who says he's willing to back me." He surveyed the shack with its sagging roof and slumped walls, and slowly crooked one side of his mouth. "Besides, if this is any proof of how well things have worked out for you, I think I'll stick with Texas."

Hurt showed in Johnny's expression, and though Matthew wasn't glad about it, he saw an opportunity. He never could beat his brother physically, but he'd always been able to best him in an argument. Johnny had muscles, Matthew had words. They had always been his advantage with his older brother, and he would use them again if it would get Johnny to see what a mistake he'd made. Even if it meant hurting him in the process.

Johnny clasped his hands between his knees. "Why don't you come home, Matthew? I think it's time."

His brother's question caught Matthew off guard. "Home." He scoffed. "Do you think Idaho would be home to me?"

"It could be," Johnny said, his voice soft. "I think you'd find what you've been searching for out there for all these years."

"And just what do you think it is I've been searching for? Both of us are talkin' about the same thing—starting up a ranch. 'Cept I'll start mine down in Texas. On my own."

"On my own . . ." Johnny laughed softly. "Those can be dangerous words for a man to pin his hopes on."

"Since when did you get to be such a philosopher, Johnny?"

A slow smile came. "I've done some changing in the past few years." Just as quickly, the smile disappeared. "You won't find what you're searchin' for down in Texas. It's not there, Matthew. And running from the memory of Haymen Taylor—what he did to you, to me—won't lead you any closer to where you want to be. Believe me on that."

Matthew's frustration mounted. "And you won't find what you're searching for between the sheets with that woman in there either. I've known women like her, and I can tell you exactly what they're aft—"

"You've known women like her?" Johnny's eyes narrowed.

In that instant, reading his brother's expression and realizing what he was implying, Matthew steeled himself. Not for another punch. No, Johnny saved that for when he was good and angry and couldn't think of a quick enough reply. This particular topic was well trod between them, and wearisome to Matthew. But Johnny wouldn't dare let it pass. Not when another chance at poking fun at his little brother had just been handed to him.

"You know what I meant."

"No, I'm not sure I do. You said you've *known* women. Is that true?"

Heat poured into Matthew's face. "I didn't mean it like that. What I meant was that I know something about *this* woman. I know she's worked in a brothel in town for years. I know things about her that will change your mind. I've heard stories from other ranch hands, Johnny. Things she's done with them."

Johnny stood and took a step toward him. "How old are you now, Matthew?"

Matthew held his ground. His brother had never been quick-witted, but he could be demeaning. And seeing Johnny's expression—watchful, sober—Matthew realized he was going to drag this out by pretending to be none the wiser.

"You must be what . . . thirty-two now?"

Matthew's fists curled tight around the rim of his hat as the implication of the question resonated in the silence. Blood surged through his veins, bringing instant heat. He had nothing to be ashamed of. Johnny was the one who should be ashamed—him and that whore in the next room. So why was *his* face burning?

"Thirty-two . . . and you've never been with a woman." Slowly, Johnny shook his head, surprise in his expression.

It wasn't a question. It was a statement, and every muscle within

Matthew tensed. Once, just once, he'd like to punch his brother hard enough to take him down.

Johnny shrugged his massive shoulders. "That's okay, Matthew. It's good, really. Our mama would be real proud of you for—"

That was all the patronizing Matthew could take. He hauled back and put his full weight into a right punch. Straight to Johnny's jaw.

Johnny staggered back a step but maintained his footing. His eyes went wide with shock.

Pain exploded through Matthew's fist, only fueling his anger. He wanted to take his brother down. And he knew how to do it. "You know what, Johnny? Mama wouldn't be proud of you. She wouldn't be proud of what you've done or who you're with right now." Matthew threw a scathing glance at the bedroom door. "She'd be ashamed of you and what you've done with your life. For what you're doing in there with that whore."

"Matthew, you got me wrong. I was tryin' to—"

"I got you just fine. I always looked up to you, and now I don't know why I ever did." He gave a humorless laugh. "You're weak, Johnny. You're weak and you're foolish, and I'm glad our mother isn't here to see just how much like Haymen Taylor you turned out to be."

Johnny's face contorted, and Matthew braced himself, knowing this time the blow would knock him out cold. But nothing happened. As the haze of his anger thinned, Johnny's face came into clearer view again, and a sick sensation knotted the pit of Matthew's stomach.

"You're right, Matthew. Most of my life I've lived in a way I'm not proud of." Johnny's deep voice sounded small. "I've made a lot of mistakes, and I'm sorry for those. Growing up . . ." He shook his head. "I could've done better by you in a lot of ways. I know that now. But I've changed, Matthew. I'm tryin' to be a better man, and . . . I'm not as foolish as I used to be." He held out his hand. "If you're willin', I'd like another chance at being brothers again."

Matthew's emotions warred inside him. He was ashamed for having said those things. None of them were true. He'd said them from injured pride and from wanting Johnny to see what a mistake he was making with Annabelle Grayson.

Then something caught his eye. The bedroom door opened

slightly. Had that woman heard their argument? Heat poured through him at that possibility and at imagining the mocking a harlot like Annabelle Grayson would no doubt give him upon learning about his inexperience. Especially at his age.

"Matthew?"

Something moved beside him and yanked him back to the present. Matthew jumped, half rising from his pallet.

Annabelle knelt beside him, firelight accentuating the shadowed concern on her face. Matthew knew it was her, but still ... the injured look on Johnny's face was all he could see. Shame and regret poured through him remembering the last thing he'd ever said to his brother, and especially in knowing that Annabelle had no doubt overheard every word.

"Matthew, are you all right?"

Her eyes, a deeper blue in the firelight, searched his, and the awareness in them unnerved him.

"I'm fine." He sat up. "Why are you awake?"

"I thought I heard something a minute ago." She lifted a shoulder and let it fall.

He ran a hand over his face and reached for his rifle. "I'll check things out. Go back to sleep."

He made a loop around the camp twice, finding everything quiet. Stopping by the wagon, he stared up into the dark night sky, swallowing hard as the stars began to blur. No matter how he tried, he couldn't block out the words that kept replaying, over and over, in his mind. Words he regretted more now than when he'd said them in anger last autumn. *"I'm ashamed of you, Johnny. I wish I'd never had a brother."*

CHAPTER TWENTY-FIVE

T HE FOLLOWING NIGHT, Matthew paused just outside a gaming
hall in western Wyoming. Rowdy noise from the crowd within
carried through the open doors, and a buggy passed behind
him on the street. He was thankful Annabelle wasn't with him, but
that didn't lessen his concern for her since they had parted ways in
town moments ago. It had been his idea to handle it this way. At
first, she'd put up an argument, but after their experience in Parkston nearly two weeks ago, he'd insisted that he visit the saloons
and gaming halls in the towns they passed—despite the risk to
him—and that she visit the brothels. He honestly believed she'd be
safer since she knew that side of things far better than he did. But
more importantly, he didn't want to risk her discovering the truth
about him and what he was running from.

Back in Willow Springs it had bothered him that she might find
out and use the knowledge of his gambling debts against him. Now
he was concerned she would learn the truth and discover he wasn't
the man she thought he was. Somehow that possibility hurt even
more.

That morning, as the sun roused itself from slumber, he had
gone to the creek, bathed and washed his clothes, and returned to
camp before Annabelle awoke. He'd paused and watched her as she
slept, remembering what she'd said about him having equal time to

bathe. He'd never met a woman who handed out opinions so freely while still managing to hold other things so close to her vest.

Taking a deep breath, he walked through the open doors of the gaming hall. His goal tonight was simple. He'd order a drink that he would barely touch, ask a few questions, then leave.

"What'll ya have?" A wiry little man with a head too large for his body awaited his response opposite the bar.

"Whiskey, straight up."

The bartender poured him a drink, and Matthew couldn't help but contrast this man's slight stature to that bear of a bartender back in Parkston. Just his luck . . .

He cleared his throat. "Where can a man get some entertainment around here?"

"One street over. Gray clapboard building on the south side. Tell 'em I sent you." The barkeep leaned forward. His eyes grew larger—if that were possible. "They're good about keepin' tally of the clients I send their way, if you know what I mean."

Matthew nodded, circling the top of the glass with a forefinger. "They got all kinds?" He took a slow sip.

The man smiled and reached beneath the counter. With the same ease he might use when dealing a hand of draw poker, he laid out five photographs on the bar.

Matthew nearly choked.

The man chuckled. "They're somethin' aren't they? 'Specially this one." He tapped the corner of a picture with a tobacco-stained forefinger.

Matthew had heard ranch hands talking about photographs like this, but he'd never seen one himself. He scanned the women's faces, though the pictures had clearly not been taken to showcase those specific features. None of the women appeared to be Chinese, but Annabelle had told him there were ways of making a girl look altogether different, like a woman before her time. Still, he didn't think any of them could be Sadie, as Annabelle had described her.

With effort, he focused on his drink and cleared his throat. "How young do they go?"

The bartender grunted. "I'm followin' ya, friend, but you're about a month late on that one. Had a young one through here around then. Didn't ever get upstairs to see her, but I heard about her. Far away lookin' gal, from what I was told. Black hair clear past her waist."

Matthew's heart pounded against his ribs. He could already imagine Annabelle's reaction at hearing the news. He forced a disappointed sigh. "But that girl's not here anymore."

"'Fraid not."

Matthew hesitated, not wanting to appear overeager, but needing to know. "Any idea where she might be now?"

The man shook his head, then tapped the picture again. "But hear me out—this one right here, she'll for sure . . ."

Matthew left his drink on the counter with the man prattling on. When he reached the corner where he and Annabelle were supposed to meet and she wasn't there, he continued in the direction of the brothel and spotted her walking toward him.

"Nothing," she whispered when she got closer, her head bowed. "I could only talk to the madam, and she wouldn't tell me a thing."

He gently tilted her chin upward. "Sadie was through here—about a month ago. We're getting closer, Annabelle. We're going to find her."

Her breath left in a rush. Her eyes misted. She stepped forward like she might hug him, then stopped and clasped his hand between hers instead. "Thank you, Matthew," she whispered, and gave his hand a brief squeeze before letting go.

Silently, they walked on down the street to where they'd left Manasseh tethered. Matthew snuck a few glances at Annabelle along the way, at a loss to explain the unexpected disappointment dogging his steps.

He yanked the reins free from the post and led the horse around. "You ride forward this time."

"I don't mind riding in back again." She gestured for him to mount first, as though the matter were settled.

Annoyance quickly replaced Matthew's disappointment. "I nearly lost you on the way into town tonight. Twice. And as I recall"—he tipped one side of his mouth to show it wasn't that big of a deal, while wondering why he was making it into one—"I told you to hold on."

She lifted her chin. "I did hold on."

"To the back of the saddle, yes! But not to me." The response came out gruffer than he intended.

She held his stare for a moment, then shrugged and looked away.

From the way she was acting, a person might get the notion she was shy of touching him, which seemed highly unlikely given her experience. He quickly reviewed the time they'd been on the trail together so far and tried to recall the last time he could remember her purposefully touching him. And couldn't. Even more frustrating, he didn't know why that would bother him so much—but it did.

Aware of how harsh his voice had sounded moments before, he intentionally softened it. "I just don't want to get back to camp and find you're not with me, that's all."

She peeked up at him, then smiled and slid a boot into the stirrup. She swung her leg over, quickly situating her skirt. "Uh-oh . . ."

Her foot was dangling, still several inches from reaching the stirrup irons. "I'll fix it," he said, brushing aside the folds of fabric from her skirt. He searched for the stirrup leather in order to shorten the strap.

She leaned forward and cooed to the horse, whispering in a soft, low voice. The folds of her skirt shifted again and lifted to reveal a shapely calf.

Matthew averted his eyes, trying to focus on his task, but suddenly all he could see were those photographs. It was as if the images were burned into his mind. Without warning, a question jumped to the forefront of his thoughts. "Did you ever let anyone take pictures of you?"

She stilled at the query, then turned. For a moment all she did was stare. "No," she finally whispered, "I did not."

Matthew was partly ashamed for having asked, but mostly relieved at her response. She moved her leg as he reached again to shorten the strap, pressing her skirt to her ankle with one hand this time. She did the same when he came around to the other side.

He slid his boot into the stirrup iron, gripped the cantle, and swung up behind her.

She turned her head slightly. "You saw some photographs. . . ."

Heat flooded his face. Her statement came out soft, not accusing, yet he felt an accusation anyway. "I didn't ask to see them. The bartender just . . . showed them to me."

Saying nothing, she faced forward and gave Manasseh a firm prod.

As they rode back to camp, Matthew found himself studying her—the resolute set of her shoulders, slender though they were, and the way her nearly black hair fell across them to hang down her back. He realized then that she wore it done up most of the time. Either that or twisted tight in one long braid that trailed down the center of her back. Still, how had he been with her all this time and missed how long it was? Or how it curled that way at the bottom?

With care, and certain she'd be none the wiser, given the plodding rhythm of the horse, he lifted a strand and rubbed it between his finger and thumb. Silky to the touch, a single curl wound itself around his forefinger with no prompting. He liked her hair better this way. He liked *her* better this way.

As that thought took firmer hold inside him, he didn't resist when the gentle curve of her waistline begged for his attention. Unbidden, the pictures he'd seen earlier that night crept back into his vision. Annabelle told him she'd never posed for pictures like that, and he believed her. But countless men had seen her that way. Had been with her . . . *that way.*

He had gotten a glimpse of what her life had been like, and he wanted to do everything in his power to help her distance herself from it. To give her a fresh start. She wasn't that woman anymore. Somewhere along the way he'd become convinced of that and had grown to like her in the process. But would he ever be able to truly see her as different? He recognized the good in her, her kindness and compassion. But would he ever be able to look at her, as a man looks at a woman, and not remember what she had been? What she had done?

Matthew stared at the dark curl still encircling his finger, then slowly inched his hand away until the curl's spiral thinned, could no longer hold, and finally slipped free.

Even if he wanted to care more deeply for Annabelle, her past— and his—would never allow it.

Her hand trembling, Annabelle stared at the spots of blood darkening the white cloth. She glanced over her shoulder to make sure Matthew wasn't back from his scouting ride with Manasseh, then checked a second time. And a third. Each time, the cloth came away with fresh stains.

Moving a hand over her abdomen, she leaned against the wagon for support. It didn't make sense. She hadn't experienced any cramping in recent days, she hadn't been working too hard, and she'd gotten plenty of rest, just like Doc Hadley instructed. He had said bleeding wasn't wholly uncommon during pregnancy, so her baby was probably still fine. And it wasn't much blood. Only spotting.

She tried to deny the next thought entrance, but it bullied its way past her defenses. And her stomach went cold at its dark whisper. What if she was losing Jonathan's child? She closed her eyes as a fragile moan rose in her throat.

She took a quick breath and felt wetness on her cheeks. When she heard the distant sound of horse hooves pounding the dry, hard prairie, she repositioned her skirts and hid the cloth. After pouring water over her hands and drying them on her apron, she walked out from behind the wagon.

Matthew was still some distance away, and she watched him ride into camp from the northwest. He and the gelding moved like one as they sailed across the Wyoming prairie, leaving clouds of dust in their wake. Seems the horse liked these early morning rides as much as Matthew did.

They were making good time on their journey and had passed Independence Rock and Devil's Gate in the past three days. The landmarks were breathtaking in their beauty and encouraged a sense of community within her for the thousands of sojourners who had passed this way before them, some of whom had carved their names into the granite face of Independence Rock.

Annabelle bent to check the coffee, then lifted the lid on the cast-iron skillet. The corn bread was golden brown and crusty, the way she liked it. But her earlier craving for it was gone.

She handed Matthew a cup of coffee when he strode up. "Be careful—it's hot."

He shook his head, a grin ghosting his features. "Every morning you tell me that. Like I haven't just seen you take the pot directly from the coals." He took a cautious sip. "Mmmm ... you make good coffee. Thank you."

She managed a smile. "You're welcome."

He quickly glanced at her and away again, then confined his attention to his cup. Clearly, he had something on his mind.

She recalled the night the wolves had attacked and the anguish she'd seen on his face when she roused him. She'd known then that he was wrestling with something—bad dreams, haunting memories, regrets—something that had sunk its talons in and wouldn't let go. She was familiar with stories from Matthew's childhood and knew there was plenty of each to choose from.

The look on his face when he'd shared the news about Sadie earlier in the week had also been telling. She had started to hug him—which honestly surprised her as much as it seemed to have him—but then she'd held back ... and had sensed his annoyance over it.

She poured herself a mug of coffee and sat on an upturned crate. "Find anything on your ride this morning?"

"It's clear until about two miles out, then there's a dried-up creek bed that might give us a headache or two." He claimed a seat opposite her. "I rode up and down a ways each direction, trying to find a better path to cross on but had no luck." He hesitated. "A couple of days ago, on a fella's advice in that last town, I chose a route a few miles farther north than the one Brennan indicated on the map you gave me. I was thinking we could meet up with them faster this way, and there weren't any towns in between where they might have stopped. But seeing that creek bed, I have a better idea now of why Brennan swung to the south."

Regret lined his expression. Hearing the same in his tone, she offered a conciliatory nod. "But if it's dried up, what does it matter?"

"It's rutted with some deep gullies in spots, and there're plenty of rocks and boulders, and a steep grade on the north slope. We'll need to clear a path before we can cross, but I can do that easy. It'll just take me a while. I'll probably have you ride buckboard when we cross, holding the reins just in case, while I go in front and lead the team. I can watch the wheels better that way too. Together, we can get the wagon across, no problem."

She nodded in agreement, her mind drifting back to her earlier discovery that morning. Part of her wanted to confide in him about her fears for the child inside her, while a greater part of her remembered how he'd reacted when he'd first learned about it. He'd not mentioned the baby since leaving Willow Springs, and she wondered if he ever thought about it or if he even believed there *was* a baby. Knowing there was nothing he could do, she decided to keep it to herself. Besides, God already knew, and maybe His knowing would be enough.

Matthew sliced a piece of corn bread, slathered it with butter, and took a bite. "Mmmm . . ." He held up the remainder, acknowledging his approval.

Annabelle smiled her thanks, her thoughts turning to what awaited them. "Any idea of how far we are from Idaho? Or when we might meet up with Jack Brennan's group?"

He drained his mug. "We've made good progress so far. If we can keep up this pace and fair weather holds, we should meet up with them in about two weeks' time. By the fourth of July for sure."

"Brennan told Jonathan when we set out from Denver that if he's on schedule, he doesn't have the wagons travel that day. They have a celebration that evening with fiddle playing, dancing, games, and lots of food. Even fireworks, from what I remember Jonathan saying." With her being so recently widowed, she knew no one would ask her to dance, but she looked forward to the festivities just the same.

Despite the topic, a somber shadow darkened Matthew's expression. He refilled his cup and took a slow drink. "There's something on my mind. Something I've been wanting to say to you."

Annabelle thought she knew what was coming, but this man had surprised her before. She kept silent, giving him room to arrange his thoughts.

"That night . . . in the shack." He cleared his throat. "The one last fall . . ." His voice held a gentle inflection, almost like he was asking a question.

As if there could be another night in question. "Yes, I know what night you're talking about," she answered softly.

He chewed the inside of his lower lip, hesitating again. "I said some things to Johnny that I wish I could have taken back before he . . ." His jaw clenched briefly. "Before it was too late. I don't know why I said them." He sighed. "No . . . that's not true. I know exactly why I said them. I was angry and hurt, and saying those things was my way of getting back at him. It always was." He shook his head. "Since I couldn't ever hit him hard enough to take him down—"

"You used words to injure him instead. You're good at it too." She tempered the truth with a smile. "But then again . . . so am I."

He watched her for a moment, understanding in his gaze. "Yes, ma'am. That's something we definitely have in common." He rubbed a hand along his bristled jaw. "It's too late for me to tell Johnny I'm sorry, no matter how many times I've wished I could, but . . . I can still tell you." It seemed to take all of his concentration to get the next words out. "I'm sorry, Annabelle. I said some hurtful things about you to my brother that night, knowing you could probably hear every one of them." He paused. "Am I right to assume that you heard *everything* Johnny and I said to each other that night?"

For a moment, time seemed to pause.

His apology was real. She didn't doubt that. She also knew what else he was fishing for—the question he didn't want to ask.

Since that night in the shack, she'd known that Matthew had never been with a woman in a physical sense. She'd seen his embarrassment when she had opened the door, full well knowing what he had been thinking at the time. That she would make fun of him, which she had almost done back in Willow Springs. But thankfully God had stayed her spiteful tongue.

She saw penitence in his eyes now, coupled with timidity, and wished she could tell him how much more of a man his choice made him in her estimation. But she couldn't find the words to answer his unspoken question and was fairly sure he wouldn't want to discuss the matter with her anyway.

Finally, she nodded. But by then, the lengthy pause had answered for her.

Matthew leaned forward, his arms resting on his thighs. He laid his cup aside, then pushed to standing. "Well, it's time we moved out."

She rose and went to stand before him. So many times in her

life she'd used words to hurt people, to put them in their place, to get revenge. And though she knew the next words out of her mouth would hurt, she also prayed they would heal.

She reached out and took hold of his hand. "Matthew, look at me." When he finally did, she saw evidence of the silent battle inside him. "Jonathan knew you didn't mean those things you said. He told me as much before he died." Matthew clenched his jaw tight, and her throat threatened to close at seeing his reaction. "He loved you to the very last, and I'm sure he's still loving you even now. Just like he promised to keep on loving me."

Matthew took in a deep breath and wrapped both of her hands between his. Annabelle closed her eyes at the tenderness of the gesture. His thumb traced lazy circles on the top of her hand, and a tremble moved through her. She felt a tear land on the side of her wrist but wasn't sure if it was hers . . . or his.

L ATER THAT DAY, Annabelle wiped the moisture from her brow, drank deeply from the canteen, and dabbed the water on her face and neck. The cool, dry air of morning had long since been chased away by the midafternoon sun, and heat rose in thick waves across the arid plains. The prairie offered no shade other than the cluttered confines of the wagon, which was stifling hot. She much preferred being outside, where she could enjoy the occasional breeze that was gradually picking up as the day grew long. Same as the bank of dark clouds building in the north.

She cringed as Matthew hoisted another of the larger rocks from their path. His shirt was drenched with sweat from having carved out a path for them to cross the dry creek bed. He sank down on the edge of the south bank, and she took his freshly filled canteen to him.

He tipped it up and took a long drink, then poured the remainder of it over his head, face, and neck. He combed his hair back with his hands. "Thank you." His breath came heavy. "I didn't think it would take me this long."

She heard the frustration in his tone and followed his gaze to the thunderhead rising like an ominous tower in the sky. Neither of them had voiced their concern, but they'd both watched it build throughout the day.

"Can I do anything else?" Other than leading the gelding, two of the grays, and the cow across earlier, and tethering them on the other side, he hadn't allowed her to lift more than a few small rocks. Which she was secretly grateful for, under the circumstances. She'd managed to seek the privacy of the wagon and had checked twice during the day, relieved to find no fresh spotting. Seems God had been faithful to hear her prayers.

Matthew shook his head. "I just need to clear out those last few rocks. Then we'll try crossing." He glanced again to the north. "We need to get across before that storm breaks. If we don't, we might be stuck on this side for a day or two. Or more."

She frowned at the creek bed. "Do you really think that much rain could fall?"

He rolled his shoulders. "If that thunderhead breaks like I think it will, this ravine will fill in a matter of minutes. The ground is dry, but it's also sunbaked. It won't be able to soak up the water fast enough." He pointed to the north bank. "It's a mite steeper on that side too. Not bad, but if it starts to rain heavy, it'll turn to mud pretty quick."

"So let's pray it doesn't rain until we get across."

"Believe me, I already have been." He pushed himself up, weariness weighing his expression.

She reached for his empty canteen. "I'll make sure everything in the wagon is secured."

He smiled. "You've done better out here than I thought you would."

"So have you," she added without hesitation, enjoying his grin. "I'm thinking of giving you a raise."

He laughed. "I just might take it after today. Either that or some of your biscuits."

"It's a deal. And with gravy this time."

A look of pleasure came over his face as though he were tasting them right then. "Now, that's something a man can work for." Tossing her a wink, he turned back to his work.

Unable to move, Annabelle watched him as he hefted a sizeable rock. Matthew Taylor was simply too handsome for his own good. And when he'd winked at her . . . Safe from his watchful eye, she playfully fanned herself.

A strong breeze kicked up just then, plastering her skirt against her legs. She looked north to the thunderhead, scanned the vast open plains to the southeast, and suddenly felt very small in comparison.

An hour later, she sat on the buckboard, reins in hand. A cool, raw wind whipped down from the northwest across the prairie, bringing the scent of rain and kicking up swirls of dust. Tumbleweeds scurried across the plains as though trying to outrace the storm. Charcoal-tufted clouds layered the skies overhead, blocking the sun and casting a veil of gray over the distant mountains.

Matthew stood gripping the harness at the front of the team. "Just hold the reins," he instructed. "Don't do anything unless I signal you." He gave her a half-hearted smile. "You ready?"

"Ready," she called with more confidence than she felt. She braced her legs for balance as he'd shown her. At his gesture, she flicked the reins and the wagon bumped and jolted as the wheels sought placement among the uneven gullies ribboning the dry gulch. Without warning, the wagon dipped to the left. The wheels groaned in protest, and crates and boxes in the back all shifted to that side.

Matthew held up a hand, and she pulled back on the reins as he had instructed.

She leaned over to see what the problem might be. "What happened?"

He came alongside and bent down. He ran a hand over the wheels. "They're holding up fine. We just slipped into a gully, that's all."

His tone might have been even, but Annabelle noted the firm set of his mouth. She peered down to see the wagon wheel partially obscured by the deep rut of earth, then felt the splat of a raindrop on her arm.

She looked up to see Matthew gauging the darkening skies. "We'll go ahead and follow this one as far as we can across, then we'll cut back over." He jogged back to the front.

It sounded like an easy enough plan—not that they had much choice. Annabelle leaned over and followed the line of the rut ahead. She saw how deep it went. How far could a wagon tilt without tipping? Especially with this wind. Trusting Matthew, she waited for his signal, then gave the reins a snap. She braced herself as the wagon lurched forward.

They managed to cover only a few arduous feet before the skies opened.

She was quickly drenched, as was the once-dry creek bed. She thought again about how right Matthew had been. Within the space of five minutes, the creek bed was covered. Gauging from the shoreline, the water was no more than a couple of inches deep at most.

A crack of lightning jagged across the sky. She counted to three before hearing the thunder rumble overhead. Canopying a hand over her eyes, she had trouble making out Matthew's form as he struggled in the rain to coax the four horses forward. The team seemed tentative to follow, whether from the load they pulled or the rain or the thunder, she wasn't sure.

She glanced at the reins in her hands, wondering if she should help by urging their progress on this end. Matthew had said not to do anything until he signaled her.

She waited.

Sheets of blowing rain blurred her vision. She squinted. Did his arm just go up? That meant for her to stop the team. But they seemed to be moving pretty well. What if he was in trouble? Or had fallen . . .

Unable to see much of anything in front of her now, she pulled back on the reins and brought the wagon to a halt. "Matthew!"

Then the wagon moved beneath her. Not really a jolt. More of a sway. Gripping the reins with one hand, she held on with her other and peered over the left side. Water reached halfway up the wheel.

She called his name again, then saw him striding toward her through the water.

"What are you doing?" he yelled.

"I thought you told me to stop!"

He shook his head and bent to check the wheel, water swirling around his thighs. He shoved a hand through his hair. The wagon moved again, and Annabelle gripped the buckboard, certain it would tip any minute.

"I'm going back up front," he shouted. He held up both hands, fingers spread wide. "Count to ten. Then give the reins a good whip. The horses are spooked. Make it hard and firm so they feel it."

He disappeared into the gray murk, and she started counting, frantically wondering if he meant for her to count fast or slow. She reached ten before she thought she should have and prayed he was ready. She brought the reins down hard across the horses' backs. They whinnied. But the wagon didn't budge.

Gritting her teeth, she whipped the reins again, so hard her shoulders burned. And this time she sensed forward progress. Not a sway this time, but a definite pulling motion. The wagon rocked beneath her, and she knew the horses were struggling to pull the wagon out of the deep, muddy rut. She gave the reins another firm whip and nearly slipped from the buckboard when the wagon surged forward and suddenly righted itself. Wind splayed strands of hair across her face. She brushed them back with her forearm, the leather straps cutting into her palms.

She caught a glimpse of land ahead and blinked to clear her vision. The slope appeared and reappeared before her in the driving rain. In the failing light, it looked more formidable than it had a couple of hours ago.

She heard her name and turned to see Matthew climbing up beside her.

He leaned close. "The bank is slick, but we don't have a choice. If we don't get up now . . ." He grabbed the reins, not finishing his sentence.

She turned to look behind them and her jaw went slack. Torrents of water swelled the sides of the once-dry gulch.

"Hold on," he yelled.

She did.

The reins made a sharp crack against the horses' flanks, and the animals surged forward, pulling the wagon with them. They faltered and slid back. The creek's swell crested the rim of the wagon bed. Annabelle thought of the flour, the cornmeal . . . then realized how foolish a concern that was in comparison to what they faced.

Matthew whipped the reins feverishly, and finally the first two horses crested the top of the bank. But the other two struggled, their hooves unable to gain footing.

He stood and shoved the reins at her.

She took them but grabbed his arm. "Where are you going?"

"They're not gonna make it. Either that or the tongue's gonna snap." Without further explanation, he leapt from the buckboard and landed on the muddy embankment. He grabbed for the harness of the nearest horse but slipped in the mud. Annabelle's breath caught when a hoof came dangerously close to his arm. She waited, then breathed again when he reached out and took hold of the harness. The animal pounded the muddy banks for footing but somehow Matthew managed to climb onto the horse.

Then she realized what he was doing. Foolish, brave man . . .

He dug the heels of his boots into the horse's flank. It tried to rear up, finding itself encumbered by the harness. But the crescendo of power seemed infectious, and the other horses responded. The first two grays surged over the ridge, clearing the bank and spurring the second pair on behind them.

The wagon angled and tipped as it climbed. For a moment, Annabelle could see nothing but the angry gray of sky. Lightning streaked overhead. She half waited to hear the harness snap and to feel the wagon plunging beneath her back into the water. The blunt board of the seatback cut into her lower spine as she braced herself against the footrest and held on. Her legs ached from fatigue. Just when she thought she couldn't hold on any longer, the sky took its rightful place again and land fanned out on either side of her.

The wagon kept moving so she held on until it came to a stop. Then she set the brake and called for Matthew.

He didn't come. She called again.

Her voice was lost on the wind, and suddenly she was twelve years old once more—alone, frightened, and searching for her parents' faces in a sea of chaos. Men and women screaming. People running across the camp with nothing but their nightclothes on. She could feel the low rumble that had awakened her in the darkness so long ago. Like thunder, except that it moved through the earth that night, instead of the sky. The ground shook and the roar grew louder, as though the Kansas prairie was angry at having been awakened from a deep slumber. The patch of earth shuddered beneath her thin legs and she crawled to the edge to peer out from beneath the wagon.

"Stay under the wagon, Annie!" Her father's voice was harsh, but his expression wasn't.

Obeying, Annabelle scooted behind a wheel and peered up at him through the spokes. "Where's Mama?"

"She's gone to find Alice."

Annabelle looked behind her and discovered her younger sister's pallet empty. A sour pocket formed in the pit of her belly. It was *her* job to watch Alice.

The roar became deafening. Dust choked the air.

"Whatever happens, Annie, you stay beneath this wagon. You hear me?"

Her stomach went cold at the look on her father's face. "Yes, Papa!" She nodded, hot tears sliding down her cheeks.

He started to leave but then reached back and touched the tip of her nose like he always did. "I love you, Annie girl."

Her chin had quivered. "I love you too, Papa."

Not until Annabelle heard her own sobs did she realize she was crying. She closed her eyes in hopes of persuading her memory, but no matter how she tried, she couldn't recall the exact features of her parents' faces anymore. Nor those of sweet young Alice. Then she felt a touch to her arm, and the tide of emotion crested inside her.

She opened her eyes to see Matthew motioning for her to climb down. She breathed in short bursts, trying to keep the tears at bay.

He took hold of her arm as she stepped down, then brushed wet strands of hair back from her face. "Are you hurt?"

She shook her head as childhood memories, long since buried, clawed the back of her throat.

He framed her cheeks with his hands. "Annabelle, are you okay?"

"Where did you go?!" she screamed, the haunting image of her father disappearing into the night still filling her head—the last time she'd ever seen him.

Matthew stared. "I had to check the horses and the wagon." His tone clearly said she should have known that.

Annabelle nodded and tried to turn her face away, but he guided it back. "Are you sure you're okay?" He briefly looked down at her midsection, then back up.

So he was finally acknowledging there was a child, or at least the possibility. "I'm fine," she said, both thankful and weary. Before she could pull away from his hold, he lowered his head.

Sensing what was coming, Annabelle panicked—then stilled when his lips brushed her forehead.

Once, twice.

Warmth melted down through her chest and into her arms and legs, and she did what she'd wanted to do the other day but hadn't. She laced her arms around his waist and laid her head against his chest. His arms came around her and drew her closer, and she was certain she'd never felt so safe in all her life.

Matthew chanced a look at her across the camp while still working the flint and steel to get a fire going. Not an easy task since all the kindling was soaked clean through from the storm, just as they were. There'd been a moment this afternoon when he had feared the swollen rain waters would sweep the wagon away, taking them with it. He'd seen the stark fear in Annabelle too, and that had spurred him on.

The temperature had dropped when the storm hit and then a second time once the sun dipped behind the mountains. His fingers were stiff and cold, and he rubbed his hands together to make them more agile. Gathering a tuft of damp tinder about the size of an egg, he rubbed it between his fingers and blew on it until the moisture lessened and it finally separated. Balancing the tinder in his left hand, he went back to work with the flint and steel. After several failed attempts, the memory of their first night on the trail came to mind, and he smiled recalling how long it had taken Annabelle to get her fire started. But she hadn't given up.

A spark flew.

He dropped the flint and steel to cradle the fledgling flame and gently breathe life into it. It crackled and glowed in his palms. He quickly transferred it to the stack of wood and, kneeling, blew on it again until the flame took hold.

He felt warmth seeping through his damp shirt as he rubbed his right arm. It hadn't hurt much until now.

"You're bleeding!" Annabelle came and knelt beside him.

"Only a little." Her hair was still damp and hung in a tangled mass down her back. Mud streaked her face. "You did good back there. Real good."

She huffed. "I could've gotten us killed." Remorse shadowed her eyes. "Now take your shirt off."

He caught her hand. "You couldn't see, Annabelle. I couldn't either. You thought I'd told you to stop. You did nothing wrong."

She frowned and gave him a begrudging nod, then lifted her chin. "If you want those biscuits tonight, Mr. Taylor, you'd best be taking off that shirt."

Obeying, he smiled at the smartness in her tone, still hearing lingering traces of guilt. "Have you checked the supplies yet?"

"We lost most of the cornmeal, and half the flour and salt. But I figure those are things that can be replaced."

"And we didn't lose any of the horses." Pulling his right arm through the shirtsleeve, he grimaced.

"Oh, Matthew . . ."

Worry furrowed her brow, and he craned his neck to see the back of his arm, unable to make out much more than blood and bruising. But he sure felt it. "What's it like?"

"Did the horse do this?"

"Um-hmm. I'm just lucky he didn't get the bone."

"I thought you were hurt, but then when you kept going . . ."

He shrugged. "Didn't have much choice at the time."

"I'm going to need to clean it, and it's going to hurt like blazes."

"Thanks for putting it so delicately. That helps."

She smiled and shook her head. "Wait here. I'll be back." She returned minutes later, her arms full. She spread a blanket down on the ground and gestured for him to lie down.

He shook his head. "I'll be fine."

She gave him a look that said otherwise. "All right, turn your arm toward the fire so I can see it better." She rubbed a damp cloth over the injury.

Her touch was light, but Matthew's head swam at the mixture of pain and having eaten nothing since lunch. He clenched his jaw and turned to watch her, trying to gauge from her expression how serious the wound was. When she grimaced and swallowed, he decided to focus elsewhere.

Her clothes were still wet, and he knew she had to be chilled.

His thoughts went to the child she carried, and he wondered at what point along the way he'd become convinced of that reality. He couldn't say exactly. He only knew that the more he got to know her, the less he believed she'd make up something like that. "You need to get those clothes off and get warm."

"Soon," she whispered, intent on her task. After several minutes, she paused. "I'm going to have to stitch this up, Matthew. The gash is deep."

He'd already figured as much. "Have you done this before?"

She sighed, nodding reluctantly. "But I can't promise it's going to be pretty when I'm done."

He wished now that he had some of that whiskey he hadn't drunk in the gaming hall.

She reached for something behind her. "Here." She held a bottle to his lips. "Take a few swigs of this. It'll help with the pain."

He caught a whiff and wanted to hug her all over again.

"Okay . . ." she said, finally pulling the bottle away. "I think that's enough."

The back of his throat burned as warmth slid down his chest and cratered in his belly. He closed his eyes. He'd had his fair share of injuries but had never been stitched. He hoped she knew what she was doing. From the way she threaded the needle, he guessed she did.

"This will hold it until we can get you to a doctor. How far are we from making the next town?"

He winced, feeling the needle going in and out of his flesh. "About a day or so."

"When we get there we'll find a doctor and go to the mercantile for supplies. We'll get some more cornmeal and salt, and I'll also look for some honey. You've all but finished that off."

"It's good with your corn bread and biscuits." His voice echoed in his head, sounding farther away than it had before, and he wished now that he was lying down.

"I didn't realize you had such a sweet tooth or I would've brought more along with us." Her voice was low and soft. "It'll be good to get to a town again. I might even see if I can post a letter to Kathryn and Hannah, just to tell them how we are—and to let them know we haven't killed each other yet. They'll be happy to hear that."

Annabelle wasn't a woman who prattled on and on, and he was aware that she was trying to distract him. He liked the sound of her voice.

"I've thought of sweet Lilly several times too. I bet she's wearing that hair ribbon you gave her and thinking about you every day. Though for the life of me, I don't know why."

He detected the humor in her tone. "I think I want to lie down now, Annabelle."

As though she'd already anticipated his request, her arm came around his back. Her touch felt good.

She helped him down to the blanket and eased him onto his left side. "Now lean your weight against me." She scooted close against his back. "There . . . just like that. Good."

He felt a slight tug on his arm again, then heard her humming. He couldn't remember having heard her hum before. "Do you always do that when you're sewing?"

A soft chuckle. "Hush, and get some rest. I'll be through here in a minute."

He closed his eyes, vaguely aware that he was drifting. "Remind me to hug you again. Later . . ." His last moment of awareness was of a feather-soft kiss to his brow and then wondering if she was still going to make her biscuits.

CHAPTER TWENTY-SEVEN

M ATTHEW BLINKED REPEATEDLY. It took him a minute to realize where he was. The dusky purple sky dotted with fading stars told him sunup wasn't far off. The cool morning air, unusually moist, carried traces of the former rains, along with bacon frying and freshly brewed coffee. He breathed in the smells of comfort and felt the emptiness in his stomach expand.

He moved to stretch, then inhaled sharply and fell back on the blanket. Pain shot up his right arm and across his shoulder, dispelling his hunger. He squeezed his eyes tight and breathed through clenched teeth until the rhythmic march of pain finally eased back to a steady thrum.

Blessed cool touched his brow. He peered up to see Annabelle kneeling over him, her hand on his forehead.

"Don't try to move. You've had a rough night."

Wanting to moan, he tried to mask it with a laugh and failed miserably. "What did you do to me last night, woman?"

She smiled and cradled his face. He closed his eyes again at the coolness of her hands and gentleness of her touch, feeling as though he'd lived this moment before, yet knowing it was impossible. Still, something about the way she touched him evoked a memory, a sense of well-being and trust.

"You're warm," she whispered.

He heard the splash of water and felt a damp cloth moving over his face. Looking up at her, he knew with a certainty that, whatever Annabelle had been, she was someone else now. He studied her features, trying to read who she was, as though he were seeing her for the first time in his life.

She reached over him for a blanket and her hair fell across his chest.

He couldn't help but breathe in her scent and found momentary distraction from the pain. "Mmmm . . . you smell good. Like . . ."

She paused, her face close to his.

His attention went to her mouth, to the way her lips slowly parted, and he suddenly forgot what he'd been saying. He swallowed involuntarily as another hunger awakened within him. "Like . . . biscuits," he finally whispered.

She stared at him for a second, then sat back. "I smell like biscuits?" Laughing softly, she rolled up the blanket and propped it beneath his head. "You mumbled something about biscuits last night in your sleep. Is that all you ever think about?"

Right now, food was the furthest thing from his mind, and if he'd been able, he would have moved away from her in hopes of redirecting his thoughts. As it was, Matthew did what came second nature to him, working to keep his expression serious. "No, ma'am. On occasion I think about other things." Watching the silent question move into her eyes and discovering that it answered one of his own about her, he gave her a slow smile. "Sometimes I think about your corn bread."

She briefly tucked her bottom lip behind her teeth. "Well, thank you, Mr. Taylor. A woman likes to know she's appreciated. Now, here, drink this."

Helping him lift his head, she held a tin cup to his lips. Water washed down his throat and chest, sloshing into his empty stomach and renewing his hunger.

But this time, it was a hunger Matthew could welcome.

———

"I don't care. This just doesn't seem right." He frowned up at her, then at the reins in her hands.

She situated herself on the left side of the wagon seat and peered down. "Why doesn't it seem right? Because you're a man?" She motioned to his arm. "You already ripped some of your stitches this morning when you harnessed the grays. Do you want me to have to sew that wound a second time?"

Matthew enjoyed the way her eyes flashed when she was riled, like lightning in a cloudless sky of blue. They'd lost a day of travel due to his injury, and though he wouldn't admit it, he felt weak as a newborn pup and sore to the bone. But their tarrying hadn't been in vain. Most of the wet patches of earth that were mud yesterday had dried to hard cake by this morning.

"Give me a minute to think about that." He tilted his head. "Any chance you might do some more of that humming?"

She tucked her chin and glared.

Matthew hid his grin and walked around to the other side of the wagon, knowing she was right. He climbed up beside her, feeling the slow throb beneath the makeshift bandage. He leaned back, showing evidence of his surrender. "No, ma'am, I don't guess I'd welcome that experience again."

A smile played at the corners of her mouth. "Well, I'm glad to hear it. Because I nearly fainted that night right after you did."

He saw color rising to her cheeks. "Don't tell me that was the first time you'd ever sewn up a person?"

She shrugged. "There's always a first time. . . ." She slapped the reins and the team responded. The wagon lurched forward.

Holding his right arm close as the wagon bumped along, Matthew watched her as often as he thought he could get away with it. Pieces of hair curled around her face. She'd worn it loose again, and he was glad for it. He noticed again the scar edging her right temple, and a fierce protectiveness rose within him imagining how she might've gotten it. He'd wanted to ask her about it before but somehow didn't feel he'd earned the right to.

They stopped briefly at midday to water and rest the animals. Before starting out again, he insisted that she curl up in the back of the wagon. She looked overtired, and he hoped she could get some rest, despite the constant jostling.

By late afternoon, they reached the town of Rutherford, Wyoming. Whether from his wound or from the heat, or perhaps both, his head ached and he felt as though he could sleep two days straight through.

He helped Annabelle down from the back of the wagon. "Do you want to head on to the mercantile or go with me to make sure the doc sews me up right?"

At first she smiled, then her expression grew somber. "I think I'll go to the doctor with you. I'd . . . like to see him too, actually."

He thought she'd been acting weary, but she didn't appear to be ill. "Is something wrong?"

"I'm fine. I just want to make sure that . . . everything is okay."

He thought of the child. "Have you been feeling poorly?"

"No, not exactly. I'd just . . . I just want to talk with him, that's all."

She started walking toward town and he followed, not having to guess this time. He knew for sure something was wrong.

When the doctor opened the door, Matthew wondered if the man was really old enough to be hanging a shingle outside his door. With rust-colored hair and metal-rimmed spectacles, he looked more like some grade-school boy who had borrowed his father's coat and trousers.

"I'll see whoever would like to go first." The doctor pushed his spectacles farther up his nose and waited.

Matthew encouraged Annabelle to go, and surprisingly, she didn't put up a fuss.

Half an hour later, she emerged from the examination room, leaving the door ajar. From her strained expression, Matthew could tell she was on the verge of tears. He rose. "What's wrong? What did he say?"

She shook her head and looked down. "He said I'm fine. I was worrying for nothing."

"Then why are you—"

She shook her head again, and Matthew followed her glance to a man seated on a neighboring bench.

"Not here, Matthew. I'll tell you, but later . . . please." She wiped her eyes.

He caught the doctor watching him from inside the room, and the expression on the man's face suddenly made him appear much older than moments before.

Annabelle wiped her cheeks. "He said for you to go on in. I think I'll run across to the mercantile and—"

"No. You sit here and rest, and wait for me. I won't be long." He lowered his voice. "The woman who sewed me did a fine job, so I don't think it'll take this fella long."

That drew a weak smile from her, and she agreed.

Matthew walked into the patient room and closed the door behind him.

"She did a pretty fair job, considering," the doctor commented minutes later, examining Annabelle's handiwork up close. He adjusted his glasses. "And probably saved your arm in the process. I'm going to clean the wound first. You have a lot of bruising around the tissue, but that will heal with time. How did this happen?"

Matthew told him, giving him only the essentials.

"I'll need to suture it again, so why don't you go ahead and lie down on the table."

His mind occupied with Annabelle, Matthew did as the young doctor requested and laid back. It took him a minute to gather his nerve. Then he cleared his throat. "I was wondering if I might ask you a question, Doc." He glanced at the door. "It's about . . . ah . . ."

The doctor followed his line of vision. "I understand," he said before returning to his task. "Wives are sometimes quite shy about discussing such topics, even with their husbands."

Matthew started to correct the man, then caught himself. Realizing his opportunity, he was also aware that he'd have to apologize to Annabelle later, but at the moment his concern for her outweighed his guilty conscience.

He nodded, hoping his face wasn't as red as it felt. "She's always been real shy that way with me."

Compassion shone in the doctor's expression. "She told me everything that's happened. . . ." He paused, needle in hand. "This will be uncomfortable. I can give you something that will make you drowsy if you'd like. You won't remember a thing."

Not missing the irony of the situation, Matthew shook his head. "No thanks. I think I can handle it," he said, absently wondering if the doctor hummed while he sewed. Feeling the needle slide in, he gritted his teeth.

"She told me about the bleeding she's been experiencing. . . ."

It was all Matthew could do not to react.

"But she said it has stopped now." The doctor paused as he stitched, leaning close to check his work. "And she hasn't had any more pain in recent days either—which is a good sign. She still fears she might lose this baby, and while I understand her concern, I assured her that I saw no indications of that happening at this stage."

Matthew thought of Annabelle sitting on the other side of the door. "Then why did she look like she was about to cry?"

"A woman's emotions can be very fragile when she's with child. Your wife is worried, especially considering what happened with her first pregnancy."

Matthew's stomach knotted tight, a fresh wave of guilt layering his concern.

"I assured your wife that how she lost your first child has no bearing on this pregnancy. Those were extreme circumstances, and after all this time, her internal injuries should be completely mended. Of course, there's no sure way of knowing"—the doctor's voice grew softer, more tentative—"if the inside of her body is as healed as we'd like to think."

Matthew wanted to ask what those injuries were but knew he couldn't. "But you think she'll be able to carry this baby . . . until it's time."

"Again, from all current indications, I'd say yes. She needs to get plenty of rest, eat nourishing foods. . . . Fresh air will do her good as well."

"Rest, nourishing food . . . fresh air." Matthew's mind raced in a thousand different directions, all paths leading back to questions he had no right to be asking—and couldn't—seeing as how he was "her husband" and should already know the answers. "Did she tell you that we're traveling?"

"Yes, she did. And I'll tell you the same thing I told her—she's a strong, healthy woman, and women have been giving birth since creation. As long as you're careful and she doesn't overdo, I honestly see no reason for concern. Besides, you'll be settled in Idaho long before your little one arrives." He stood. "Now, let me bandage this up again. Then I'll get you a sling and you two can be on your way."

Matthew sat up slowly, his head fuzzy. "Is there anything else I should do . . . for her?"

The young physician paused and once again gained an air that bespoke wisdom beyond his years. "Be gentle with her, and understanding. And even when you don't understand, which will be most of the time, let her know you love her and that you're proud she said 'I do.'"

Matthew sensed there was more coming.

"At least I think I'm quoting my father correctly," the doc added, a dry smile edging up the corners of his mouth.

Still considering the young physician's parting advice, Matthew took hold of Annabelle's arm as they left the office and he escorted her across the street to the mercantile. She didn't seem close to tears anymore. In fact, he never would have guessed she'd been upset earlier. But he knew better than to question her about anything now. Patience was a virtue he seemed destined to learn with this woman.

"I made us each a list while you were seeing the doctor," she said once they were inside the mercantile. She handed him a slip of paper, then leaned close, lightly touching the sling cradling his arm. "Are you feeling all right?"

"Fine," he lied. "Why?"

"You look a little pale."

"I'm just tired. And hungry."

"I'm ready for dinner too. When we finish up here, I need to post a letter. Then I'll be ready to go."

"Telling Hannah and Kathryn we haven't killed each other yet?"

Her brow rose. "So you *were* paying attention."

He read her list. "Sure you don't want your hired help to do all this?"

"I would if my hired help weren't on his last leg." A gleam deepened in her eyes before she turned and walked down the aisle.

He read down through the items she had assigned him. "Honey's not on my list, so I hope it's on yours."

She glanced back at him. "It is. Right after corn bread and biscuits."

Matthew let her have the last word. He was busy mentally adding another item to his list. He gathered what he could find from the shelves, then approached a silver-haired woman behind the counter.

"Can I help you with something, sir?" Her round face and deep dimples gave her a kindly appearance.

"I'd appreciate that, ma'am. I'm having trouble finding a few things, and . . ." Checking over his shoulder, he spotted Annabelle on the far side of the store. "I need to ask a favor of you." He spoke softly to the clerk.

When he finished she whispered, "I think I can handle that," and disappeared into the back.

He noticed a calendar on the wall and scanned the rows of boxes marked with an X leading up to the twenty-seventh of June. Then he recalled the excitement in Annabelle's voice when she had told him about the special Fourth of July celebration Jack Brennan arranged for his travelers. Brought all the fireworks and such along with him. By Matthew's calculation, he and Annabelle were still pretty much on schedule to meet up with them in time, at least according to Brennan's original timetable, though the day lost to his injury would make it tight. They still had a week.

When the woman returned, she tossed him a wink and hastily wrapped one of the items in paper. As she boxed up the goods, she made a show of nestling it in the bottom.

"Thank you, ma'am," he whispered, then inquired after Brennan's group.

"Oh my, yes, I know exactly who you're asking about. Mr. Brennan has been coming through Rutherford for years. When he has time, he and my husband enjoy a rousing game of chess there in the back room." She gestured, smiling. "We so enjoy seeing that man."

A picture rose in Matthew's mind of a man whose stature and experience was akin to that of Bertram Colby's. He looked forward to meeting Brennan.

"In fact, it wasn't that long ago that they passed this way. They were here last Sunday, a week ago. I remember because my husband opened the store up special, just for them. Seems they'd had some trouble along the way. Maybe some weather slowed them. . . . I don't quite remember now."

Matthew was already picturing Annabelle's reaction. They

would easily catch up to Brennan within a week. "Thank you, ma'am. For everything."

Careful of his arm, he loaded the crates of food and supplies into the wagon. As they walked the short distance to the post office he shared the good news.

"This calls for a celebration!" Annabelle pulled a tin from her reticule, removed the lid, and held it out. "For your sweet tooth."

He peered inside, grinned, and took a stick of the striped candy. He swirled it between his lips, feeling like a kid again. "Peppermint was always one of Johnny's favorites."

Annabelle paused on the steps leading up to the boardwalk. "I know," she said quietly. "He said it was one of yours too."

Matthew opened the door to the post office and let her precede him. As she went through the entrance, he spotted a man striding toward them. An unsettling sense of familiarity struck Matthew first. He looked again, connected with the man's gaze, and went stone cold inside.

CHAPTER TWENTY-EIGHT

HIS EYES WERE THE first thing Annabelle noticed.

Then as the man got closer, she realized it wasn't his eyes that made her wary so much as it was the manner in which he looked at her. She got the impression he was absorbing every detail about her, storing away the information for quick recall.

He touched the brim of his hat, slowing. "Good day, ma'am."

"Good afternoon." She heard the post office door close behind her and glanced back to see Matthew standing outside on the boardwalk, his back to her. She'd assumed he would accompany her inside the post office, but . . . apparently not.

"Excuse me, ma'am. I think you dropped something."

Annabelle was only now aware that the letter she'd brought in to mail wasn't in her hand.

The man bent to retrieve it, and as he straightened, he scanned the front of the envelope. She frowned at his choice of action, then quickly smoothed her expression.

Taking the letter from him, she forced a smile. "Thank you."

"You're most welcome." He removed his hat and combed a hand through jet black hair.

From the road dust that layered it and the dirt coating his trousers and long jacket, she figured he'd been riding for days. And with that drawl, she easily guessed where he hailed from.

"Seems you're a long way from home, ma'am."

"Yes, I am." She tilted her head. "But how did you know that?"

He shrugged. "Lucky guess, I suppose." His dimples slowly deepened his stubbled cheeks. "And it helped that I read the address on your envelope. But then"—a dark brow rose over hazel eyes—"you already knew that, didn't you, Mrs. . . ."

Surprised by his truthful admission but not by his attention to detail, Annabelle fingered her wedding band. "McCutchens . . . Mrs. Jonathan McCutchens. And yes, I did see you read it." She matched his raised brow. "I thought it was in poor taste."

His smile became sheepish. The transformation was unexpected and softened Annabelle's first impression of the man. "My apologies, Mrs. McCutchens. It's a bad habit I've picked up through the years."

She sensed genuineness in the response, and in him. "What? Of reading others' mail?"

He actually laughed. "Of being overly curious. Comes with the territory, I'm afraid."

"And what territory might that be?"

He looked at her more closely. "Do we know each other, ma'am? I've been through the town of Willow Springs several times in recent years, and again not too long ago. For some reason, I get the feeling we've talked before."

Annabelle's mouth went dry considering that possibility. If she'd met this man in Willow Springs, chances were good it hadn't been to talk. She snuck a glance back through the window and caught Matthew watching her. His strained expression told her his arm must be hurting, and she already knew he wasn't feeling well. She needed to cut this short.

"I'm sorry, sir, but I don't recall ever having met you. You must be confusing me with someone else."

His slow nod told her he considered that last part doubtful.

Her attention was drawn to an employee hanging posters on a bulletin board on the far wall. When the woman stepped to one side, Annabelle honed in on one in particular. A weight dropped into the pit of her stomach.

She heard the man laugh softly.

"Don't tell me one of those faces looks familiar to you, ma'am?"

Her heart leapt to her throat at the question. What were the odds. . . ?

All at once, details flashed through her mind. Matthew's expression, his reluctance to come inside with her just now. This man's attention to detail and recent trip to Willow Springs. In that instant, all the disjointed pieces of the picture jarred painfully into place.

It wasn't pain she had seen in Matthew's seconds ago. It was *fear.*

Detecting humor in the man's question from seconds before, she decided to play along with it. "Actually, a few do look familiar. I was thinking I saw them at church this past Sunday."

He laughed, but it seemed to lack the convincing quality it had before.

She cleared the tickle in her throat. "I'm sorry, but I need to ask you to excuse me. I'm in a bit of a hurry."

The man glanced out the window Annabelle had checked minutes ago. Thankfully Matthew's back was to them.

"I'm sorry for having kept you, Mrs. McCutchens." He put his hat back on. "I hope you and your husband have a safe journey on to Idaho."

She paused, staring.

He shrugged again, dimples framing his mouth. "The return address."

Her world was growing smaller by the minute. "You really need to work on those bad habits, Mr. . . ."

"Caldwell. Rigdon Caldwell." He touched the rim of his hat. "Can't promise anything there, ma'am. Some habits are hard to break, but I'll try." His hand was on the door latch when he turned back to the mail clerk. "Polly, if you get anything for me tonight, I'll be at the hotel." He opened the door. "I'm pushing north myself, Mrs. McCutchens, so maybe I'll see you and your husband along the way." He paused. "It's a small world, isn't it, ma'am?"

More than you know. "Good afternoon, Mr. Caldwell."

Annabelle waited, watching him close the door and nod to Matthew as he passed on the boardwalk. She went to the counter, where the clerk stamped the letter and counted back her change.

As she was leaving, Annabelle took another peek at the poster in the second row, third from the left, and wished she could snatch it off the wall like she'd done with the one in the saloon. But she knew better. Then another charcoal-sketched face caught her eye. She slowed and huffed a soft laugh, not feeling the least bit humored.

The sizeable reward amount at the top of the page drew her attention, and she studied the rendering of the man's face. The artist had done a very good job at capturing his likeness. Thankfully, the person who had drawn Matthew's had failed to do the same.

Matthew said nothing when she came out, but his unease was palpable. Knowing that anything she said would be revealing, for them both, she decided to keep quiet unless he asked.

They passed a diner on their way back to the wagon, and through the front window she spotted Rigdon Caldwell seated inside. As though following a beacon, he lifted his head at the precise moment they passed. Annabelle caught his almost imperceptible nod and was certain they hadn't seen the last of him.

On their way out of town to make camp for the night, Annabelle and Matthew made a few more stops —visiting the brothel and two saloons—but they found no evidence of Sadie having been there. Near the outskirts of Rutherford, they passed a church, and Annabelle wished tomorrow were Sunday so she could visit. The building reminded her of the church back in Willow Springs. She imagined what it would be like to walk through those white double doors and have people smile and greet her, maybe even have the minister take her hand like Patrick often did when he spoke with people before and after the service.

She felt Matthew watching her and realized she had been staring. He looked from her to the church, then back again, and she perceived a silent question in the gesture.

When he chose not to voice it, she decided to ask one of her own. "Did you ever go to church in Willow Springs?"

The plod of hooves filled the interim void.

"Yes . . . a couple of times."

She massaged her lower back, overweary of this wagon seat. "What did you think?"

"What do you mean?" Matthew secured the reins in his left hand and held his right arm close to his side.

The set of his shoulders communicated a weariness that went far deeper than needing food and rest. She would have offered to guide the team but had sensed that he needed to have control over something at the moment.

"I mean . . . what did you think about the service? The hymns? About Patrick's sermon?"

"I don't remember much about the hymns, but I remember what Patrick preached about. Or more rightly, *how* he preached."

He stared out across the prairie, and Annabelle got the sense he was recalling something farther back than Patrick's sermons.

"I remember he talked about forgiveness. But he did it in a way that made you think that forgiving people was part of God's plan all along, not an afterthought once we'd messed things up."

Annabelle didn't miss how he'd phrased his response. *"Once we'd messed things up."* Not after *people* messed things up, but *we.* He had included himself in that.

She nodded. "A lot of Patrick's sermons were about forgiveness."

His head whipped around. *"You* went to church there?"

The shock in his voice drew a laugh. "No. I haven't been to church like that since I was a girl. But Patrick used to practice his sermons on me when Hannah was busy or just got tired of listening." She giggled. "I bet that woman's missing me about now."

They drove on in silence for another couple of miles. Matthew was choosing to make camp farther from town than he normally did, she noted.

Finally, he tugged on the reins with his good arm. "This should be a good place to stop for the night." He set the brake and maneuvered his way off the buckboard, favoring his right arm. "Hannah will be glad to get that letter you mailed today."

Annabelle climbed down on her side, wondering if he was laying the groundwork to question her about the man in the post office. "Yes, she will. I'm glad the town had a post office."

He began unharnessing the grays. "That man . . . did you know him?"

"No, I didn't."

"You've never seen him before?"

Disbelief weighted his tone. Maybe it would be best to get it over with right now, just admit to knowing about Matthew's past.

Then she imagined his reaction at discovering she knew. He already carried enough guilt for them both.

"No, I haven't."

"Just thought you might've . . . by the way you were talking to him."

She came around to his side and bent to help him. "I dropped my letter and he handed it back to me. We exchanged pleasantries, that's all." She stole a glance at him.

He unbuckled a strap and pulled it through. Even at this simple task, his breath came heavy. Perspiration glistened on his brow.

"Matthew, let me do this." She reached to help. "With your arm, you're in no shape to—"

He yanked the strap from her. "I can do it. You go start dinner."

She moved to the next horse, ignoring his stubbornness. Maybe if they worked together for a while they could finally talk things through. "At least let me help you—then I'll start dinner."

"I don't need any help." He reached over her and took hold of the buckle in her grip.

Trying to lighten the mood, she held on tight and smiled over her shoulder. "Stop being so stubborn, for goodness' sake, and let me—"

"I said I don't need your help, Annabelle!"

She stilled at the sharpness in his voice—then took a step back.

A muscle jerked in his jaw. "I prefer to do this on my own."

On my own. A familiar phrase coming from him. And dangerous words for a man to pin his hopes on, she'd overheard Jonathan say.

It was on the tip of her tongue to tell Matthew that he could go ahead and unharness the grays by himself, and rip out every stitch in the process. But his thinly veiled anger stayed her tongue. Because she saw through his anger, to what lurked beneath.

Through the years she'd learned that, like women, men wore masks too. Except theirs were all the same. Men weren't supposed to cry—so they became angry instead of showing sadness. Men weren't allowed to be scared—so they became angry instead of showing fear. She knew what Matthew was going through because she'd lived in that grip of fear for as long as she could remember. But no more. She'd been freed.

And she wanted him to experience that same freedom as well.

———————

Clouds on the distant horizon lit up for a split second before going dark again, as though the sun had risen and set behind them in the blink of an eye. No thunder. No rain. Only voiceless lightning embracing the vast night sky. Matthew studied Annabelle's profile as she watched the display, envious of the wonderment in her expression, while trying to stave off the hopelessness inside himself.

Since spotting the bounty hunter five days ago, Matthew had spent every day waiting for the man to catch up with them. His imaginings were getting the best of him, but part of him had actually begun to wonder if Annabelle had somehow learned about his past and was planning on turning him over to the bounty hunter for the reward. It was foolish, he knew. She'd never given him any indication that she even knew about the gambling debts, much less that she would ever betray him. But what if she'd seen a poster along the way and had never said anything?

"Our first night in the Idaho Territory, and it's like God's putting on a show just for us." She spoke softly over her shoulder, as if speaking any other way might somehow cause the display to cease.

He leaned forward and tore another piece of roasted meat from the skewer. He chewed slowly, watching the patchy tufts of clouds appear in the night sky, then quickly vanish again. He couldn't help but remember how well she could play a role.

She turned to him and smiled, tucking her hair behind her ear. She held his gaze for a moment longer than necessary before returning her attention to the celestial performance. Matthew knew then that fear was driving him down this path. Annabelle would never betray him that way. Not after what they'd been through. Besides, she would've come to him immediately if she'd found out about his gambling debts. She would've never let him live it down either, not with the way he'd treated her at first, bringing her past up at every opportunity. No, he was convinced she didn't know.

A warm breeze rustled the prairie grass, leaving the faintest hint of moisture in its wake. He would miss nights like this—with her, out here, alone. Three days prior, they'd traversed South Pass, a gap in the Rockies that enabled travel farther west. No narrow gorge, South Pass was a valley measuring almost twenty miles wide. He expected they would meet up with Brennan's group within the next couple of days—well in time for the July fourth celebration two nights hence.

"Does your arm hurt?" she whispered.

"Not too bad today. It's getting better." He matched the softness of her voice. Why, he didn't know.

She looked pointedly at the meat roasting over the fire. "You could've waited, you know. Given the wound a chance to heal more."

"We haven't seen antelope in a week. No guarantee when we'll see them again. Besides, I wanted fresh meat." And she hadn't had any in days. The doctor had said she should get plenty of rest, nourishing foods, and fresh air. Fresh air abounded, and he'd been doing all the work he could. Rising earlier to get a head start and encouraging her toward less demanding tasks, but that took some doing. The woman wasn't easily redirected once she set her hand to something.

"Do you think we'll find her, Matthew?"

Thoughts of Sadie never seemed far from her mind. While he still held out hope that they would find her, the farther north they went, the more doubt set in. "Yes, I think we will."

"Thank you for not hesitating when you answered. Hesitation shows uncertainty, you know." She gave him a look worthy of an old schoolmarm before lying down on her pallet. "Either that, or it means you're lying."

"I'll try to remember that." Smiling to himself, Matthew banked the fire and stretched out on his bedroll, his mind and body equally exhausted. Ever since the night the wolves attacked, he and Annabelle had shared a campfire, and they had settled into a routine. He didn't mind it. Truth be told, he enjoyed it now. Closing his eyes, he drew his blanket across his chest and began the silent count, betting she wouldn't make it past five minutes tonight before asking the first question.

The chirrup of crickets, the crackle of the fire, and a full stomach competed with his task, tempting him toward slumber.

"Do you think God makes us pay for our sins, Matthew? Even after we're forgiven?"

Three minutes, twenty-one seconds. He wished his hunches at

the gaming table had been this good. He couldn't remember exactly what night the questions had started, only that he was growing to enjoy lying in the dark under the stars, talking with her. Reminded him of when he and Johnny were boys.

Matthew considered her question, knowing that the One who could answer her question perfectly was most likely listening at that very moment. "Yes . . . and no," he answered quietly.

He heard her soft laughter. Her questions were never easy. Not that he had all the answers, or that she thought he did. He used to think he had things pretty well figured out, but now . . . So much of what he'd once been sure of, he was now sure he'd been wrong about.

He locked his hands behind his head. "I think we're given room in this life to make choices, and that includes making bad ones from time to time. No matter how sorry we may be, we still have to pay the cost." He stared at one constellation until the seven stars blurred, then merged into one. *Lord, if you can hear me, if you're listening . . . I'm sorry for what I've done.* He swallowed. "I don't think that means God hasn't forgiven us. It just means that we're responsible for the choices we make. Both the good . . . and the bad."

"Do you think He ever hurts us on purpose?" she whispered after a moment, her voice sounding smaller than before.

Verses Matthew had been compelled to put to memory as a young boy came back to him, but they would be of little comfort to her. Same as they'd been to him. *"Many will say to me in that day, Lord, Lord . . . And then will I profess unto them, I never knew you: depart from me, ye that work iniquity."* And *"for by thy words thou shalt be justified, and by thy words thou shalt be condemned."* His throat tightened as he recalled hearing those words preached week after week from the pulpit. With his father standing behind it. *"For all have sinned, and come short of the glory of God."*

He heard a sound and rose up on one elbow. Annabelle was lying on her side, blanket pulled beneath her chin. Even from across the fire, he could see the glistening on her cheeks, and the guilt lining her face sliced through him. She must have thought he had been talking about *her* bad choices. . . .

"Annabelle, I was talking about me just now, not you."

She inhaled a ragged breath. "It's just that I . . . I read a story about a man and woman who slept together when they shouldn't have, and . . ." She pressed her lips together.

Matthew remembered seeing her off by herself earlier that evening, reading, but he hadn't known what.

She sniffed. "The woman became pregnant with a child from . . . their union, and God wasn't pleased. He forgave the man and woman and said that they wouldn't die for their sin." She paused, her composure slipping, her voice barely audible. "But that their baby *would*."

Matthew got up from his pallet and went to kneel beside her. "Are you having problems? More pain like you had in Willow Springs?"

She shook her head. "But don't you see . . .? If God took *that* child, Matthew . . . he might see fit to take mine and Jonathan's too."

At the mention of his brother's name, Matthew thought of Johnny and Annabelle, together, as man and wife. And for the first time, he looked upon the child she carried inside her womb as a part of Johnny. How could he not have made that connection before?

He sat beside her. "Annabelle, the story you read, was it about a man named David?"

She nodded, her eyes closing. Tears pushed out from beneath her lids.

He reached out and touched her shoulder, giving it a gentle squeeze.

A shiver stole through her.

He leaned in to tuck her blanket closer around her body. But when their eyes met, he began to question the wisdom of his gesture. Not long ago this woman had been wholly unattractive to him. How had she changed so much in such a short time? He concentrated again on the answer he'd been giving. "What that couple did was wrong—there's no arguing that. But there was a lot more involved in that situation than just their sleeping together."

She finally managed an unconvincing nod.

He noticed her hair then, spilled loose and dark across her pallet. He fingered a strand, wishing he could remove her doubt. He cradled one side of her face, and she released a soft breath.

"You and Johnny . . . you were married. It was completely different between you."

The wrinkle in her brow voiced her skepticism, while hinting at a vulnerability he'd not yet glimpsed in her.

He traced the curve of her cheek and inched downward to the softness of her neck, struck again by how alone they were. His gaze swept the length of her body, lingering before returning to her face again. For a moment, they simply stared at each other. Desire moved through him. Not only physical desire for her, but a deep yearning to *know* her. His hand trembled. His thoughts went where they had no right to go, and vivid images filled his mind. He had no doubt she knew exactly what paths his thoughts were taking. But then again, of course she would.

She didn't move. Her expression neither invited more nor did it condemn him for the liberties he'd taken so far.

Not wanting to, Matthew slowly drew his hand away.

He took a steadying breath, and surprisingly, another thought surfaced through his tension. One he hoped would help them both. "I grew up thinking that God was waiting to punish me, Annabelle, for all I'd done wrong—that He was just trying to find a reason to send me straight to hell. But I don't believe that anymore, and I don't think that's what the Bible teaches either."

He chanced another look at her but saw only the softness in her eyes and the curve of her mouth, and he turned away again in order to continue his thought. "I think that as a person grows closer to God, maybe it's not so much the consequences of our wrongdoing that are most painful . . . Even though those are hard enough to face sometimes." He paused, thinking of San Antonio, of Johnny. "Maybe the most painful part is when we finally realize that—in spite of all Christ has done, all He's given—we end up hurting Him, and ourselves in the long run by wanting what *we* want . . . more than what *He* wants." He shrugged his shoulders. "If that makes a lick of sense."

For the longest moment, she didn't answer. "More than you know," she finally whispered.

Matthew walked to his bedroll and lay back down. He scrubbed a hand over his face and rolled onto his side, away from her—as if that would help any. He'd never get to sleep now. Not with his heart

TAMERA ALEXANDER

pounding like he'd just run a five-mile race.

Minutes passed.

He listened for the evenness of her breathing that would confirm she'd fallen asleep. And didn't hear it. Stopping himself with her just now had been one of the hardest things he'd ever done. But thinking of the men who had used Annabelle, taking what did not belong to them, selfishly meeting their own needs without a thought of what was right or wrong or of what was best for her had helped him restrain his own desire.

He wouldn't do that to her. He wouldn't be another one of them. Not now. Not ever.

CHAPTER | TWENTY-NINE ❧

NNABELLE SQUINTED UP AT him in the morning light. Matthew was already dressed and . . . was that coffee she smelled? Or maybe his attempt at it. She pushed to sitting and stretched to loosen the soreness in her back, then raked a hand through her hair. "I overslept. I'm sorry." But little wonder with what he'd done to her last night.

She had lain there for no telling how long before finally managing to find sleep. And she knew from his shifting and the occasional sigh that he'd done the same. Regardless of her past experiences with men, she found herself in uncharted territory with this one.

"You didn't oversleep. I'm just up early."

"And already have the coffee made?" She stood and smoothed her skirt.

"Not as good as yours, but I tried." He handed her a tin cup. "Careful, it's hot," he warned.

She detected the telltale gleam in his eyes. Raising a brow, she took the cup by the handle and tried to imitate his voice. "Every morning you tell me that. Like I haven't just seen you take the pot directly from the coals."

His mouth slowly curved as he stared at her, arms crossed.

Emotions brewed behind those brown eyes of his, and she

would have baked biscuits by the dozens to know his thoughts at the moment. Then again, remembering last night, probably best she didn't. She brought the cup closer and blew across the top. Certainly didn't smell like coffee. Or look like it. She took a cautious sip.

The second the warmth touched her tongue, she knew.

She peered up at him over the cup, not sure which was sweeter—the smooth chocolate filling her mouth or the adorable expression on his handsome face. She swished the warm cocoa over her tongue, savoring its sweetness before swallowing.

"Delicious," she whispered. On impulse, she stood on tiptoe and kissed his smooth cheek, balancing the cocoa in her left hand, then quickly stepped back before he had time to consider anything further. "Thank you . . . for this." She raised the cup. "But even more, for remembering."

She'd seen desire in men's eyes before. The desire in Jonathan's eyes, softened with devotion, had been unlike that of any other man before him. And Matthew's eyes had held a similar passion last night. But the way Matthew looked at her now sent a wave of emotion through her like nothing Annabelle could remember. If the chocolate in her mouth hadn't already been melted, it would've done so on the spot.

He held her focus, not turning away after a moment as he normally did. She hadn't moved an inch but would've sworn they were closer to each other. She needed to defuse the moment and knew a thousand different ways to do that—but right now couldn't recall a single one of them.

As though aware of her need for rescue, he feigned touching the rim of a hat he wasn't wearing. "Pleasure's all mine."

Relieved, Annabelle looked away, only then noticing. "You're wearing fresh clothes."

"Yes, ma'am. And I cleaned up too."

"I can see that." He'd shaved, and damp curls clung to his collar at the base of his neck. A piece of hair—not a curl exactly, more a wayward strand—fell across his forehead. And though she liked it right where it was, she still had to resist the urge to reach up and brush it from his face. "What's the special occasion?"

"It's Sunday."

She shrugged and took more sips of the cocoa. It had cooled some and was no longer hot—just right. "You said yesterday that we had plenty of time to catch up with Brennan's group. What's the rush?"

"There's a town about a mile or two up the road, and I'm betting they have a church."

As she swallowed his meaning became clear. "Really?"

"If Idaho churches are anything like the ones back in Colorado, I'm figuring we can still make it there in time for the singing, if a certain young woman will stop dallyin' around, drinking cocoa, and get ready."

Annabelle finished the cocoa in three gulps and shoved the empty cup into his hands. "I could kiss you again, Matthew Taylor."

"Best not do that, ma'am. I'm gonna have trouble enough listening to the sermon as it is."

She laughed and hurried to get ready, catching his soft chuckle behind her.

Annabelle could hear the singing as soon as Matthew brought the wagon to a halt beside the others in the field. Even after he climbed down, she sat absolutely still, listening to the blended voices and wanting to memorize the moment.

The simple white building, adorned with a matching white steeple, sat atop a small rise of land on a side road jutting off the town's main street. Bursts of pink and yellow flowers blossomed by the stairs leading up to the open doors, and Annabelle wondered if the woman who had planted them was part of the chorus of voices floating toward her.

In that moment, something Jonathan had said to her on the banks of Fountain Creek over a year ago took on new meaning. She truly did feel like a new person now, changed inside. While she might be able to pinpoint a moment in time when salvation had come to her, Annabelle had the feeling that growing to understand that gift of grace, and surrendering to it like she wanted to, would take her a lifetime.

"I actually meant for us to go inside, Annabelle. Not just sit in the wagon and listen."

She glanced down to see Matthew standing by the wagon,

smiling. "It's called *savoring the moment,* Mr. Taylor. Have you heard of it?" She grinned at the way he ran his tongue along the inside of his cheek, fair warning to her that sarcasm was to follow.

"That's all good and fine, but any chance of doin' some savoring as we walk?"

Hand tucked in his arm, she carried the Bible Kathryn had given her in the crook of her arm and accompanied Matthew to the door. He stood aside and waved her to precede him. Suddenly nervous, she shook her head and nodded for him to go first. He gently took her arm and led her alongside him.

He gestured toward a pew in the back. She scooted between the rows and sat down on the hard wooden bench. It instantly reminded her of the wagon seat, but she didn't mind. She moved back until her spine was flush against the pew, then surveyed the gathering of forty or so people. The tune of the song they were singing was familiar to her, but the words, thankfully, had been changed. As she took in her surroundings and considered where she was, a smile tickled her mouth. She couldn't help but feel as if she'd managed to get by with something sneaky.

She watched Matthew lean forward and pull a book from beneath his seat. Cheating a glance at the man's book in front of him, he flipped to the page and held it so Annabelle could see.

He didn't sing loudly, but the voice she heard coming from him caused her throat to tighten. She leaned back slightly to sneak a glimpse at him. Not only did Matthew know the words without having to look at the page, he also knew the tune. She riffled through her memory for what Jonathan had told her about their church-going days as boys, but he'd always spoken about the Lord in a more present tense. The only good things she remembered Jonathan sharing about his childhood had been about his mother— and the man sitting beside her now.

They remained seated for the prayer that followed as well as the next two songs. Then an older gentleman walked to the front and took a place behind the pulpit. "Our reading today will be from the fourth chapter of the book of Second Corinthians."

Without being told, everyone stood, Matthew included, and she felt his hand drawing her up with him as he rose.

The gentleman at the front read the verses, unhurried, pausing, giving the words time to sink in. Somewhere deep inside her, Annabelle remembered having experienced this as a girl. Open windows on either side of the building ushered in a breeze, spreading the scent of lilacs and sunshine. And newness.

Jonathan had said that a person couldn't love someone else until they'd first learned to love themselves, and he'd been right. She knew that now. For the first time in her life, she could look inside herself, at who she was, and not cringe at what she saw.

Standing there among all these fine people, she couldn't help but wonder what kind of woman she might have been if her life had taken a different turn. But then excitement swept through her at imagining what God was going to make of her life now. Now that He had set her on a new course.

Matthew kept his attention on the menu. "Order anything you like. My boss pays me well."

Annabelle responded with a telling tilt of her head and that droll look of hers that only egged him on. "In that case . . ." She turned to the young woman waiting beside them. "I'll have the roast beef with potatoes and green beans, please. And a piece of apple pie for dessert."

Matthew handed back his menu. "I'll have the same."

After their waitress left, Annabelle leaned forward. "She was looking at you, you know."

He shook his head at her smirk. If he said he hadn't noticed the woman's attention, that would be a lie. But to say his interests were wholly engaged elsewhere was far too revealing. "You look very nice this morning, Annabelle. I was proud to be with you at church."

Her smirk faded as she gently eased back against her seat, apparently at a loss for words. He enjoyed the rare moment and the attentiveness in her expression as she studied him.

The young woman returned shortly with their meals. She placed Annabelle's before her first, and then set Matthew's in front of him. "I checked on what you asked me about earlier, sir. That wagon train passed by here day before last."

Matthew voiced his thanks as the woman left, then tossed Annabelle a wink. "We'll be with them tomorrow for sure—I promise. Well in time for that celebration."

Conversation came easily between them as they ate lunch, and an hour later they headed back toward the wagon. The businesses they passed on the boardwalk were closed, but a fair amount of traffic still busied the streets.

He had a hard time imagining finally reaching Johnny's land, only to have to leave Annabelle there. But several things had become clear to him in recent days. He didn't want to spend the rest of his life running, checking over his shoulder, afraid of who might be there. He also wanted to honor his brother's last wish, in the truest sense. Johnny had set out to give Annabelle a new life. He had started this journey, and Matthew would see it to completion. Johnny had been right that night in the shack. Matthew had spent the better half of his life running, and it was high time he saw something through to the end. First, in seeing Annabelle settled. Then, in facing what he'd done in San Antonio.

Though the second reckoning would prove far more difficult, and costly, than the first.

"Matthew . . ."

He felt her grip on his arm and turned.

Annabelle's face had gone pale. She couldn't seem to gain her breath.

He put an arm around her waist, his first thought going to the child inside her. "Is it the baby?"

She shook her head in quick, short movements, her focus glued to some faraway point.

"Tell me what to do, Annabelle!"

She shook her head again and took hold of his hand, squeezing it tight. "Very slowly, turn and look across the street."

He stared at her for a moment, not understanding, then finally did as she asked. He searched the boulevard, scanned wagons and buggies and their occupants, passersby strolling the boardwalk, and people crossing the street.

He shrugged, still not seeing anything.

She squeezed his hand tighter. "There! Passing in front of the livery."

He finally spotted her.

A small dark-haired woman walking close beside a man. Too

close. The man had a grip on her arm. She stumbled. The man held her fast, but there was no concern, no tenderness, in the act. She was so small, but she carried herself with a quiet dignity, her black hair falling smooth and straight past her waist.

Matthew's pulse jumped. He stepped forward. Annabelle stopped him with a hand to his arm, and he heard her shuddered sigh. Together they watched the man and woman disappear into a single-story gray clapboard building at the far end of the street.

ANNABELLE STOOD IN THE darkened alley and peered across the street to the gray clapboard building, thankful for Matthew's presence close beside her. The crowd inside the gaming hall had swelled as evening stretched past the midnight hour, and the laughter, coupled with drunken voices crooning bawdy tunes, could be heard two streets over. To an unsuspecting soul, the warm lights and sounds coming from the hall might have seemed like a welcome invitation. But she knew better.

Unable to make out Matthew's face in the shadows, she sensed his unease. "Are you sure you don't have any more questions?"

"Only about a hundred of them." He laughed softly. "Main one being . . . is there another huge bartender inside who's waiting to have a little chat with me?"

She laid a hand on his arm. He covered it. "Thank you for doing this, Matthew. Both for me . . . and for Sadie."

"If only Johnny were here to see me now. After all the grief I gave him about going to these places." His laugh was hushed. "Somehow I know he'd see the humor in it."

At the mention of Jonathan, they both grew quiet. They talked about Jonathan often, but there were things she wanted to say to Matthew about how she'd felt about his brother, about what Jonathan had done for her, how he'd planted the seed for change in her life. She hadn't shared that with him yet, but she would, one day, when the time was right.

She went over in her mind the plan they had concocted that afternoon. "Once you get inside, be sure and ask for—"

"I remember," he said softly.

"And whatever you do, don't use Sadie's name. That'll give you away for—"

"Annabelle! I can do this."

She went quiet at his sharp whisper. Though she couldn't see his eyes, she imagined they held gentle rebuke, but also determination. The same determination she'd seen in him when they first spotted Sadie earlier that day.

He gently touched her cheek. "We've been through all this. I know exactly what to do."

Trusting him, she blew out a breath and nodded.

Matthew was halfway across the street when she remembered she'd forgotten to tell him something. She kept her voice hushed. "Matthew!"

He turned and slowly walked backward a few paces.

"I'm praying for you."

"And I'm depending on it."

Once he crossed the threshold of the open doors, she lost him in the crowd and the smoky haze of cigars and oil lamps.

As the minutes passed, her pulse evened out. With every beat of her heart, she thanked God again for guiding them to this place and asked Him to protect Matthew and help him get Sadie out safely. After weeks of searching every town they'd passed, she had simply glanced across the street and seen that precious child. She'd recognized Sadie instantly—as well as the man dragging her along with him.

Mason Boyd was one obstacle Annabelle had not anticipated.

Boyd's face came to mind, and she marveled again at how closely the artist had come to capturing the meanness in the man's eyes. The list of crimes printed on the bottom of the parchment she'd seen tacked to the post office wall hadn't included most of what she'd heard attributed to him, and she believed every charge. She ached inside when thinking that Sadie had been in the company of that foul man all those months.

And she had hated having to tell Matthew earlier that afternoon that she knew the man who was with Sadie. As she waited for him to process the information, she had easily predicted the one question his thoughts would lead him to—the one question she didn't want to answer.

"How do you know him, Annabelle?" His hushed tone revealed the heart of his fear.

She opened her mouth but words wouldn't come. "I knew him . . . from before," she finally whispered. At his wordless stare, she nodded.

A sickened look clouded his face.

"I'm sorry, Matthew."

He took a step back, shaking his head. "You don't need to apologize to me."

"But I feel like I need to."

His hands went up in a defensive posture. "Well, you don't!" He turned away from her, his tone abrupt. "That part of your life is over!"

She knew that part of her life was over, but he sounded as though he was still trying to convince himself.

"Matthew," she said softly to his back, wishing he would let her see his face. "I can't do this alone. I need your help."

He bowed his head. "I'm sorry, Annabelle. I just—"

She heard his deep sigh, and her breath caught when he took another step away from her. Surely he wouldn't bring her this far only to desert her now. She took a step toward him, unaccustomed pleading filling her voice. "Matthew, please . . ." She briefly clenched her jaw at her next admission. "I don't have anyone else."

When he turned back, a frown shadowed his face. Then, slowly, understanding softened his features. "I'm not going to leave you, Annabelle." His voice was unexpectedly tender. "It's just that . . . when I think about . . . what men have done to you . . ." He studied the boardwalk beneath his feet, then gradually looked back at her. "Whatever you need me to do . . . all you have to do is ask, and I'll do it."

Annabelle had sensed hidden meaning in his words earlier that afternoon but hadn't pursued it. And neither had he.

She kept watch on the building, as though Matthew might walk out with Sadie at any moment. But she knew better. It would be much longer than a few minutes, and he wouldn't be leaving by the front door, if their plan worked at all. She prayed he would remember everything she'd told him and that God would whisper the rest in his ear as he had need.

She had a hard time standing still and finally decided to head back to the wagon just so she'd be ready. She started across the street, resisting the urge to get close enough to peek through the front window of the gaming hall.

"Mrs. McCutchens."

Annabelle jumped at the voice and spun around. All she saw was his shadow, but the man stood no more than ten paces from where she'd just been standing. She squinted, as though that would help her see him in the darkness. "Who's there?"

As he came closer, she took steps back, maintaining her distance.

"I won't hurt you, ma'am. I've been waiting to talk to you."

Hearing the drawl in his voice, her throat went dry. "Mr. Caldwell?"

"Yes, ma'am. You've got a good memory." He walked closer.

Her back was to the gaming hall, so she knew her face was hidden in the shadows. His face, however, was softly lit by the light coming through the open doors.

"I'm here to talk to you about the man you're traveling with."

She nodded slowly, her mind racing. "You mean . . . my husband." She hated to lie. "What business do you have with Jonathan?"

"I don't have any business with him, ma'am." Caldwell's gaze was unflinching. "Jonathan McCutchens is buried back in Willow Springs, Colorado Territory. I'm here to talk to you about Matthew Taylor."

Suddenly her lungs wouldn't draw air. "I don't know who you're talking about." Even to her, the response sounded strained and unconvincing.

Rigdon Caldwell's eyes narrowed.

Clearly he didn't believe her. And she couldn't blame him.

She prayed, not knowing what to ask for. She only knew that she was more aware of being in God's presence in that instant than she had been seconds before. Shame filled her at having tried to lie her way through, but—*dear God, please forgive me*—she would do it again if it meant keeping Matthew and Sadie safe. What other choice did she have? What else could she—

Only what we do for God will last.

She blinked at the force of the memory, wondering how long it had been since she'd thought of it.

"Mrs. McCutchens . . . Annabelle." Caldwell's voice held sincerity. "I know the man you're traveling with is not your husband. His name is Matthew Haymen Taylor, and as I believe you already know, he's wanted for gambling debts. I've been hired to bring him back to San Antonio, where he'll be given the opportunity to face his accuser and stand trial if deemed necessary."

Hearing the charges against Matthew laid out that way somehow brought them into clearer focus. "Mr. Caldwell, did you know about us that day back in Rutherford?"

"No, ma'am, I didn't. But your reaction at those posters didn't help you much."

Heat rose from her chest into her face as she relived that moment. She shook her head. "He's a good man, Mr. Caldwell. He's just made some mistakes."

"I understand that, ma'am. But I still have a job to do."

She considered that. "Who do you work for?"

He paused. "I work for hire, ma'am."

She nodded, taking that in, her thoughts a blur. What was Matthew doing inside? Had he gotten to Sadie yet? Was she cooperating with him? And what did it matter if Matthew couldn't get past Mason Boyd, and now this man.

With little notice, her thoughts slowed. They took a turn, and she looked back at Caldwell. "Who hired you to find Matthew?"

He didn't answer.

"A moment ago, you mentioned his accuser, Mr. Caldwell. Who hired you?"

"A man you don't want to deal with, Mrs. McCutchens. And a man I try never to disappoint."

His answer wasn't surprising, and it was one she understood. "How much are you being paid?"

"More than you could possibly afford."

She knew he was right. Then something struck her. "Why did you come to me first, Mr. Caldwell? Why not approach Mr. Taylor directly?"

"Because every time I've seen him, he's been armed. And he's also been with you."

She frowned, not remembering Matthew carrying his rifle with him into a town.

As though reading her thoughts, Caldwell tugged back his duster. "He carries his revolver here." He pointed to the one tucked inside his belt, then around to his back. "Or here."

Annabelle remembered Matthew having a gun that night in Parkston, but she hadn't been aware of him routinely carrying it.

"You may not think much of me or what I do, ma'am, but my fight isn't with you. It's with him." He looked beyond her to the gaming hall.

She acknowledged that bit of decency in him and wondered if within that decency she might find an edge. "Mr. Caldwell, what if you didn't have to disappoint your employer? What if we could come to some sort of . . . mutual agreement?"

"Well, that depends. What exactly did you have in mind, Mrs. McCutchens?" He smiled, his expression telling her that such an agreement did not exist.

MATTHEW STOOD IN A HALLWAY toward the back of the building, trying to act as if he'd been in this kind of place and done this kind of thing before. He shifted his weight, leaned against the wall, and shifted again, all under the watchful eye of a man whose arms resembled the thick pine beams running the length of the ceiling above them. He'd only gotten this far due to Annabelle's regrettable know-how—and sincere prayers. She had proven to be a thorough teacher, and so far, he'd passed every test.

But the hardest was yet to come.

He figured nearly two hours had passed since he had first walked into the gaming hall. He'd waited at the bar for almost an hour before being taken back to meet Mason Boyd. That had been an experience Matthew wouldn't soon wipe from his memory, though he already wished he could. *Foul* best described the man in every sense.

The creak of a door he couldn't see brought Matthew's head up.

The man gestured to him. "You're in. Double knock means your time's done."

Matthew walked past him and around the corner, committing details to memory as he went. Only two doors opened from this hallway. One on his right, which stood slightly ajar. The other clear at the end, which he'd already confirmed led out the back of the building, and which was, presumably, why a man stood guarding it. Hoping Annabelle was right about this, and having no reason to doubt her so far, Matthew chose the open door and closed it behind him.

Her back was to him, and he waited for Sadie to turn at the sound of the door latching.

She didn't.

Light from a single oil lamp on a table illumined the windowless room, leaving shadows to crouch in four barren corners. The only other pieces of furniture were a closed trunk by which Sadie stood and the bed.

"What will be your pleasure, sir?"

Her voice surprised him. It sounded cultured, feminine, not at all young. Lilly Carlson came to mind. Sadie had been about Lilly's age when she'd first come to the brothel in Willow Springs. Contrasting Lilly's sweetness and purity with the oppressive darkness cloying this room, he suddenly felt sick.

He kept his voice low, repeating word for word what Annabelle had told him to say. "I'm not here for pleasure. I won't touch you. I won't hurt you. I give you my word."

Slowly, the girl turned. Her movements were so restrained, so measured, the red gown she wore barely shifted about her ankles. "Then why do you pay money to come in here?"

Matthew took a step forward. Sadie didn't move, but he felt her loathing. It emanated from her, like the distrust mirrored in her dark eyes. The eyes of a woman in the face of a child. His chest ached. "I'm going to tell you something, and I need you to trust me . . . Sadie."

He waited for her reaction, but her expression remained detached.

"Annabelle sent me to you. She's here in town with me."

Sadie's gaze flitted over his shoulder and back again.

Annabelle had warned him she wouldn't believe him. It was likely the men who had taken her from Willow Springs had used a similar ploy. He forged ahead, knowing his time was measured. "We've learned that sometime tonight, Boyd will be moving you again, and we might have an opportunity to get you away from him. We have a wagon waiting, just out back. You can have a new life, Sadie. You can start over again, just like Annabelle did. She'll be with you, to help you."

Sadie tilted her head, one brow raised. The gesture seemed vaguely familiar. "I do not know you, and I have no reason to believe your words. In my eyes, you are no different a man from Boyd."

Matthew didn't care for her comparison. "But I am, Sadie. I'm a very different kind of man. I won't do the things to you that he has done."

She responded in a language he'd never heard before.

The words might have been lost on him, but her coolness toward him wasn't. At least he'd managed to get a reaction.

He held up a hand. "I can prove to you that Annabelle sent me."

"I do not—"

"You met Annabelle back in Willow Springs. She told me how you ended up at the brothel. You were eleven years old at the time. You were scared the first few days you were there, so you slept in her bed with her. You became good friends. She looked out for you as much as she could, but she couldn't be there all the time. Like that night when you got hurt out at the ranch, at Casaroja. She felt responsible for those times like that, Sadie. She still does."

She nodded toward the door. "Your time is up, mister."

No knock had sounded. That was a contrived move on her part to get him to leave, and Matthew knew it. He took a step closer. "You were at Larson and Kathryn's wedding. You held little William that day. He cried a lot. You said he had his father's eyes, and Annabelle said yes but he had his mother's stubbornness."

Sadie walked to the door and opened it.

On impulse, Matthew reached behind him and slammed it shut, then kept his hand against it. This wasn't working—not like Annabelle had said it would. But he couldn't leave this child here. Not and face Annabelle again. He was struck by how small Sadie was and how much damage a grown man could inflict on her with very little effort. Then he thought of the many who had already done just that.

He took a deep breath. "Sadie, I'm telling you things that only Annabelle and you would know. Don't you see that?"

She slowly lifted her head, a fierceness in her eyes. "I do not believe the words you say are from my friend. She would come herself."

"She wanted to come but was afraid Boyd would recognize her. So she sent me instead."

"Annabelle has never been afraid!"

"Annabelle isn't afraid for herself, Sadie. But when it comes to someone she loves, she can be very much afraid."

A double knock sounded on the door.

He racked his brain for anything else he could say or do to convince her.

"I will ask you a certain thing, and we will see if you can answer." The youthful features of her face were uncompromising.

Sensing his opportunity slipping away, Matthew nodded. "Fair enough."

She phrased her question to him, hesitating in a couple of places as though trying to recall how to pronounce a word.

He listened, then slowly shook his head. The odds of this working had been stacked against them from the start. Beginning with how long they'd been searching for this girl, only to look up one day and see her standing there. He should have known it would turn out this way.

Sadie finished, her face defiant in challenge.

But Matthew also detected a spark of hope there too. "Cocoa," he whispered, unable to suppress a grin. "That stupid horse's name was Cocoa."

Gradual light spilled into the girl's fathomless eyes. She softened. "Is Annabelle close?"

He was struck by the sudden transformation. "Outside, around the back. She's waiting for us. I just haven't quite figured out how we're going to get—"

Shouts sounded in the hallway beyond the closed door. Two muted pops followed. Matthew reached for the latch just as the lock clicked into place. He tried to open it. It wouldn't budge. He shook harder.

Sadie reached out. "That will not work. It locks only from the other side."

He gestured for her to step back, then rammed his left shoulder into the door. A dull thud rewarded the effort. He tried again and heard wood splinter, but the door held fast.

He exhaled and rubbed his left arm, feeling the pain shoot across to his right. A quick check of the hinges found them rusted and set. It would take time and tools to pry them loose—and he had neither. He'd brought his gun, but Boyd had confiscated it at the bar before granting him entrance to the back.

"I know this is a silly question, Sadie, but . . . there's no other way out of this room. Right?"

The tilt of her head, the way she peered up at him through half closed lids, was answer enough.

He nodded. Quiet or not, she knew how to get her point across. Like someone else he knew.

A faint clinking brought his attention back to the door. Like metal against metal. He jiggled the latch.

"Matthew?"

Hearing the voice on the other side brought both relief and concern. He leaned closer. "What are you doing in here? If Boyd sees you, he'll—"

Only then did he notice Sadie close beside him, her focus fixed on the latch.

The clink of metal against metal again. Then a clicking noise. The lock tumbled. The latch lifted and the door opened. Matthew stared in disbelief. Was there no end to this woman's ingenuity?

In an instant, Sadie was in Annabelle's arms, pressing close, her arms wrapped about Annabelle's waist.

Matthew stepped past them into the hallway as Annabelle whispered something indistinguishable to the girl. Sadie nodded and hugged her tighter.

The corridor was empty. The guard that had been seated by the door at the far end was gone. Matthew walked to the corner and peered around. When he saw the man slumped on the floor, he turned, slack-jawed, back to Annabelle. "Woman, what on earth did you do?"

They traveled through the night, stopping only long enough to rest and water the livestock. Progress was slow, but Matthew wanted to put as much distance between them and Mason Boyd as possible. He glanced back occasionally in search of pursuers, but the half moon's silvered light illuminating the Idaho plains behind them revealed none. He also checked to see if he could make out Annabelle and Sadie in the wagon bed, but they were lost in the shadows beneath the canopy. When they'd first set out, he'd heard their chatter, their voices sometimes talking over one another. But it had been quiet for the past three or four hours now. While his body was dog-tired, his mind couldn't rest.

He thought back over the sequence of events from the night before and grew more eager to question Annabelle about it. How she managed to get past Mason Boyd and his men was still a mystery to him. But even greater than his curiosity about that was his thankfulness to have finally found Sadie and to have her with them. Watching Annabelle with the girl was like watching a mother with her child. Though she'd never actually said it aloud, he had sensed Annabelle's apprehension about becoming a mother. Having observed her tenderness and concern for Sadie, he had no worries that Jonathan's child would be well loved.

Jonathan's child.

He looked up at the last dwindling star in the east and wondered if something Bertram Colby had said that day back at the Carlsons' home was true—if people who had gone on could somehow see how folks here were faring. True or not, it sure made a man feel more accountable for his actions.

Around noon, they stopped to eat a hasty lunch of cold beans and corn bread. Matthew wished for some of Annabelle's coffee to revive him but preferred to put the time it would take to make it toward travel instead. Sadie stuck close to Annabelle every minute, making it impossible for him to speak privately with Annabelle.

He noticed Sadie didn't speak to him unless he spoke to her first, and then all he got were one-word answers. He didn't think she much cared for him. Or maybe it was men in general she didn't like. Considering what the young girl had been through, he wouldn't blame her if that was the case.

Rifle in hand, he made a quick check of the grays before they headed out again.

"Sadie and I were just talking, Matthew," Annabelle said as he was about to get into the wagon. "How 'bout if we drive for a while? You didn't get any sleep last night, and we did."

He'd already considered that over lunch but hated to ask it of her.

She smiled as though reading his thoughts. "Honestly, Matthew, you must be worn to the bone. You gave us a chance to rest last night. Now let Sadie and me return the kindness. We'll wake you at the first sign of trouble."

Hesitating, he saw Sadie's almost imperceptible nod. "I'd appreciate that, ladies. Thank you."

Sadie laid a hand to Annabelle's arm and whispered in her native tongue. Annabelle gave a hasty answer back.

Matthew's mouth fell open. "You speak Chinese?"

Annabelle smiled and Sadie followed suit. "Only a little. Sadie's taught me a few phrases that come in handy on occasion. Don't worry. We weren't talking about you."

He looked between the two of them, then shook his head, feeling as though he was outnumbered. He massaged the soreness in his right arm.

Annabelle frowned. "Is your arm hurting again?"

"Not much. I'm fine," he lied, growing more tired by the minute. "Gettin' some rest will do me good." He handed her the rifle.

Annabelle took it, an odd look coming over her face.

"Don't tell me—you know how to shoot like you know how to sew someone up."

"Actually, I *have* shot a rifle before. I'm just not sure I'd be able to hit anything if it really counted. But"—she held up her free hand—"I'll take it, if you insist." She gestured for Sadie to climb up to the wagon seat.

Matthew took the weapon back from her. "First horses, and now this. Seems there's one more thing I need to teach you before we part ways, Mrs. McCutchens."

A look of surprise flashed across her face, then hurt, before she quickly disguised it. He'd meant for his comment to be humorous and hadn't intended for it to come out that way.

She briefly glanced away. "So once you get me to the ranch"— her tone became more guarded—"you're not planning on staying?"

This wasn't a conversation he was ready to have. "I haven't really thought much about it." Seeing her expression fall, he winced at how that sounded, especially knowing it wasn't true. "What I meant to say was—"

"I think I know what you meant . . . Matthew." She turned to climb into the wagon.

Sighing, he gently took hold of her arm, aware that Sadie was watching them from the buckboard. He waited for Annabelle to look back at him. "With all due respect . . . Annabelle, I'm sure you don't."

They stared at each other for a moment. Then she gave a slight nod, which he took as an agreement that they would discuss this later.

"Wake me the minute you see anything suspicious."

Again, she nodded.

He helped Annabelle up to the bench beside Sadie and then went around to the back of the wagon and climbed in. He sat facing out the back, propped against blankets Annabelle and Sadie must have used during the night. The wheels bumped and jarred beneath him. The space inside the wagon was hot, and he loosened the ties on the canopy to allow a breeze. After making sure the safety latch was on, he cradled his rifle against his chest and was asleep in minutes.

"Matthew!"

He heard his name being called from far away and struggled to respond, but he kept feeling himself being pulled back down by a suffocating force.

A distant explosion sounded. Like what he'd heard in the gaming hall last night.

The fog cleared. Remembering where he was, he bolted upright, his breath coming heavy. Annabelle's was the first face he saw, then Sadie's peering from around the corner of the wagon canopy.

He blinked, trying to come fully awake. "Is it Boyd?"

Annabelle smiled softly. "Lower the rifle, Matthew. It's not Boyd. We're safe."

"But I heard a gunshot."

She reached out and laid a hand atop his on the weapon, urging him to lower it. "It wasn't gunfire."

Her deliberate touch, coupled with the earnestness in her eyes, brought him more fully awake. She motioned for him to climb out of the wagon, then pointed northwest across the Idaho plains to something far in the distance.

→ C H A P T E R | T H I R T Y - T W O

E
MOTION TIGHTENED ANNABELLE'S THROAT as she regarded the scene before them. Matthew guided the wagon up and over the slight crest of land and then gently tugged on the reins. The team of grays slowed to a halt, snorting as if begrudging the brief delay. Sadie—who had chosen to walk for a while—also paused up ahead.

No more than a half mile away, clustered in three circles in the middle of the vast plains, a group of fifty or so wagons sat huddled, their canopies once gleaming white now dingy gray against the barren prairie. At this distance, the convoy more closely resembled a fleet of sealess ships moored for the night rather than a group of lumbering farm wagons plodding west.

Unexpectedly, Jonathan's memory pressed close, and Annabelle recalled having viewed a similar scene with him last May, the morning they'd congregated with the others outside Denver. Jonathan had paused the grays at the crest of a rise, much as Matthew was doing now, and for several moments she'd sat silent beside her husband, amazed at the gathering. A sense of pride had washed over her at seeing the number of men, women, and children united and working together for a common purpose—to make a better life for themselves. Unexpectedly, that same sense of pride moved through her again.

Matthew gently nudged her. "Looks like we made it in time for that celebration."

She smiled up at him, imagining what it would be like to dance with him. Assuming he knew how. Not that she planned on dancing tonight, it still being so close to Jonathan's passing. But if Matthew didn't know how to dance, that was certainly one thing she could teach *him* someday. And she'd enjoy having the upper hand.

He gave the reins a flick and the wagon lurched forward. After a brief glance behind her, Sadie also regained her stride. Annabelle had sensed the girl's need for solitude earlier, and understood it.

Matthew leaned close. "You and I need to talk about something."

Seeing the seriousness in his eyes, she began to imagine what that "something" might be. Her emotions were still tender as she recalled what he'd said earlier that day about them parting ways once he got her to the ranch. Then, after questioning him, hearing him admit he hadn't even given the idea much thought had hurt her even more. They'd never spoken about what would happen once they arrived, but somehow she had begun to consider—even to hope—that he might actually want to stay, and she took it as a good sign that he wanted to discuss it now.

She gave a slight shrug, not wishing to appear overly eager. "We can talk about it now, if you like."

He stared at her for a beat. "All right."

The look in his eyes told her she'd guessed the topic correctly.

He focused on the horses for a moment, and then a smile started to emerge. "Just how *did* you manage to get rid of the guard at the door last night? And then knock that other man senseless?"

Realizing she'd misguessed his intent, Annabelle forced a laugh to cover her disappointment. She wasn't at all prepared to talk to him about that. Not yet.

Buying time, she gave him a sideways glance. "I come to your rescue, and you show your gratitude by questioning how I did it?"

"I'm grateful, believe me. But I'm also curious." His tone said he wasn't going to let this drop so easily.

She quickly laid out her response in her mind, working ahead to anticipate possible questions. "I waited for you and Sadie outside the gaming hall just like we agreed, but when neither of you came out after so long, I got concerned. So I walked as far as the front door, and then there was some sort of commotion inside." She added what she hoped was an innocent-looking shrug for effect. "I used that chance to sneak back. I saw only the one man, and he was on the floor when I got there." Having stayed within the boundaries of truth, however stretched, she tried to gauge whether he was convinced.

Suspicion tinged his expression. "How did you unlock the door?"

"Oh, that was the easiest part," she answered with a sigh. And it really had been. "My father was a locksmith. I learned how to pick a lock almost before I learned how to read." She waited, hoping she'd satisfied his curiosity, at least for now, yet knowing she'd have to tell him the truth. Soon.

"How is she?" he asked after a pause, looking ahead.

Sadie was walking back toward them.

"She's hurt, and tired, and scared. But despite what people think when they first meet her, she's a fighter. I think she'll be all right, in time."

Matthew stopped the wagon, and Annabelle scooted over to make room for Sadie on the bench seat. She took the girl's hand in hers, warming when Sadie moved closer. She wasn't surprised that the child rejoined them, not with the cluster of wagons looming ahead.

Huddled together on the edge of the encampment, a group of boys bent over a collective task. A series of cracks and pops suddenly sounded, and with whoops and hollers the boys set out in different directions. One in particular was headed straight for them. Looking up, he skidded to a halt when he noticed them, sending clouds of dust puffing about his heels. He yelled something to the others, and they all took off running back to camp. As the boys neared the wagons, men and women ceased their doings and turned. One man in particular stood out among them.

Annabelle recognized him immediately as he strode toward their wagon.

Lean and well-muscled, Jack Brennan stood a head taller than every other man around him. She guessed him to be roughly Matthew's age, maybe a few years older. People fell in behind him as he passed, and it struck her again that she'd never before seen a man lead with so little effort.

He approached Matthew's side of the wagon. "Mrs. McCutchens. It's good to see you again."

She'd forgotten the kindness in his voice and the gentle strength that emanated from him. No wonder men followed him without question and women with marriageable daughters fell in tow. "Mr. Brennan. It's good to see you again as well."

She caught Matthew's hasty glance from Brennan to her and back again, and wondered at his reaction.

Brennan took a step closer. "I've thought about you often in recent weeks, ma'am." His voice softened. "And about your husband as you laid him to rest near Fountain Creek."

She hesitated a split second. "Thank you," she whispered, pretty sure she hadn't shared that detail of her plans regarding Jonathan's burial before they parted ways.

"Jonathan was a good man, God rest his soul." Brennan extended his hand to Matthew and introduced himself. "My personal thanks to you for escorting Mrs. McCutchens safely back to us."

Reaching down, Matthew shook his hand soundly. "Matthew Taylor, and it was my pleasure to do it."

Annabelle waited for Matthew to mention his connection to Jonathan, but surprisingly, he didn't. He remained oddly silent.

Brennan's glance encompassed the three of them, and she wondered what conclusions he might be drawing about Sadie. The girl's silky black hair and delicate features made looking past her impossible. But to his credit, Brennan didn't ask, nor did his gaze linger overlong.

"Well, we're glad you're all here. You're just in time for the celebration!" He motioned. "Bring your wagon on around, and we'll help you get settled for the night." He looked back at Annabelle. "There's someone else here who'll be happy to see you again too, ma'am. I'll make sure you find each other over dinner."

Annabelle knew the minute Bertram Colby spotted the three of them sitting on a blanket. His friendly countenance brightened as he wove a path through the crowd, balancing his overfull plate. Perhaps he'd secured another position as a trail guide, which would account for his presence here. "Mr. Colby, what a pleasant surprise."

"Oh, it's so good to see you again, Mrs. McCutchens. Taylor here's been guidin' you well, I've no doubt." He clapped Matthew on the shoulder as Matthew stood to shake his hand.

Matthew winced slightly, it being his injured arm. "Good to see you again, Mr. Colby."

"Yes, Mr. Taylor has done an excellent job of guiding us." Annabelle noted Colby's attention swing to Sadie. "Mr. Colby, this is Sadie, a friend of ours from Willow Springs who joined us."

Colby lifted his hat. "How'dya do, miss?"

Sadie gave the slightest of nods, then confined her gaze to her lap.

Annabelle motioned for Colby to join them. "What brings you out here, Mr. Colby?"

"Well believe it or not, there's a story behind that, ma'am." He shoveled in a bite of apple pie and chewed.

"Is that so?" Annabelle raised a brow and grinned, aware of Matthew's close attention and having sensed a growing unrest in him since they'd arrived.

The past two hours hadn't afforded them time to talk. Not with men from neighboring wagons surrounding him to ask about their journey, and women coming to offer condolences on Jonathan's passing and to see if they could help with anything. With effort, Annabelle drew her focus back. "I'm sure we'd all love to hear that story, Mr. Colby."

As Colby spoke, she found her gaze returning to Matthew, then Sadie. Sadie had hardly touched her food. She sat poised, erect, and completely withdrawn. From Matthew's occasional glances, Annabelle knew he'd noticed Sadie's behavior too.

Once Colby finished his tale, Annabelle seized the pause in conversation. "It's amazing how God works in people's lives, Mr. Colby. I'm so glad our paths have crossed, and I hope we get the chance to visit again. Now, if you'll please excuse us . . ." She rose and discreetly indicated for Sadie to follow her lead. "I think Sadie and I will retire for the evening."

Colby and Matthew stood as well.

"Retire? But there's dancin' to be done, ma'am." Colby's expression went sober and he looked down briefly. " 'Course, with you still bein' in mourning and all . . . There's still the fireworks and music. Surely you fine ladies don't wanna be missin' that."

"Yes, Mrs. McCutchens, please stay. I think you'll enjoy the festivities we have planned for the evening."

Annabelle turned at the sound of Jack Brennan's voice.

"The fiddlers are just getting warmed up, and . . . I'd appreciate the chance to speak with you later."

"I'd like that, but—"

Matthew stepped forward. "I'll take Sadie back since she's not feeling well. You go ahead and enjoy the festivities, Mrs. McCutchens. I know you've been looking forward to this, and . . . no doubt you'd enjoy time to talk with your friends."

"*Talk with your friends.*" Annabelle detected a stiffness in his voice. She tried to catch his eye, but he wouldn't look at her. Even more surprising was Sadie moving closer to Matthew, silently accepting his offer.

Colby held out his arm and grinned. "Well, I guess that settles it, ma'am. Let's you and me head over and get us some cider."

Seeing no way out of it, Annabelle accompanied Mr. Colby while Matthew escorted Sadie back to the wagon.

After nearly an hour of listening to Bertram Colby's stories while watching others dance, Annabelle finished her cup of spiced cider and managed to excuse herself. She made her way back through the crowd toward the wagon. Numerous people had approached her, offering condolences on Jonathan's passing, treating her with respect and kindness, which still felt foreign. These were good people, and a sense of community existed among them that made her long to be a part of it. But while pleasant enough, this evening simply hadn't turned out as she'd imagined.

She felt a touch on her arm and turned. "Oh, hello, Mr. Brennan. . . ."

"You're not trying to sneak away before the fireworks, are you?"

She feigned a look of surprise at having been caught. "Actually, I was. I'm sorry. I need to head back and check on Sadie."

"Mind if I walk in that direction with you?"

"Not at all." She picked her way around the various campfires, smiling at the couples and families seated on blankets, enjoying the activities. Several people stopped Jack Brennan on the way, and he took the time to speak with each of them.

Once clear of the crowd, Annabelle glanced back over her shoulder. "You've been busy this evening, Mr. Brennan. I think the line of young women waiting to be your dance partner wrapped halfway around the camp!" She laughed. "I daresay you've acquired several admirers on this trip."

A shy look crossed his face. "It's only because there are so few of us single men along this time."

Though knowing that wasn't the case, she let the comment pass. Fires dotted the outer rim of camp and helped to illuminate the dark path. They could still hear sweet harmonies from the fiddles as they neared the westernmost circle of wagons. The music's earlier fast pace had calmed, no doubt due to people tiring, and Annabelle imagined couples dancing slowly, and maybe a trace closer, to the tunes being played now.

"Did you and Mr. Taylor, and the young lady, have any problems on your journey?"

"A few mishaps, but we made it fine." As they walked, she told Brennan about the flash flood and the wolves, not bothering to correct his misassumption that Sadie had been with them from the start. Then something else came to mind. "Mr. Brennan, something I think you need to know, not that it makes any difference, but . . ." She briefly told him about Matthew being Jonathan's younger brother and how he'd shown up to apply for the position.

Brennan's expression reflected surprise—then regret. "Having to find out about his brother that way must have been hard on him."

Annabelle thought back to their time in Willow Springs. "Yes, it was especially difficult for a while."

His steps slowed. "Mrs. McCutchens, there's something I need to tell you as well. I'm not certain, ma'am, whether this is of huge importance or not. But I feel I should mention it in light of Jonathan's passing."

She paused, and he stopped beside her. "I must admit, Mr. Brennan, you have my curiosity piqued."

"The day before we left you, Jonathan gave me a letter and asked that I post it for him."

"A letter . . ."

"I don't know what it contained, Mrs. McCutchens. Jonathan didn't volunteer that information, and I didn't see it as my place to ask." His voice grew soft. "All I knew at the time was that he was dying and that he asked me to do this for him."

"And it was kind of you to agree to do it. Whatever it was, it must have been important to Jonathan or he wouldn't have asked it of you."

"Those were my thoughts as well."

She hesitated. "By chance, Mr. Brennan, do you remember who the envelope was addressed to?"

"Yes, ma'am. It was addressed to the Bank of Idaho in Sandy Creek. I mailed it at the next town we came to. A few days after we had to leave you." He shook his head. "Which was one of the hardest things I've ever had to do, ma'am."

"Mr. Brennan, we all understood the possibilities of what could happen on the journey. You were very clear on that from the outset."

"I appreciate your understanding, Mrs. McCutchens, but . . . reciting what might be done and then following through with it once something happens are two very different things."

"How true that is." They continued on down the path.

When their wagon came into sight, she spotted Matthew seated on an upturned barrel. The campfire he'd built was burning low and steady, offering dim light to the area. His head came up at that moment, and even though they were still some distance away, she got the feeling he was staring straight at her.

"I can walk from here, thank you," she said to Brennan. "I want you to know how much I appreciate what you did for Jonathan, and for telling me about it now." After they'd bid each other goodnight and he started to leave, she remembered her earlier question. "Mr. Brennan . . ."

He turned.

"You mentioned something earlier about my having laid Jonathan to rest near Fountain Creek. How did you know about that?"

A sad smile crossed his face. "Jonathan told me something when he gave me that letter. He said he needed to take care of two final things. One was the letter, and the other was about being buried by Fountain Creek, where the two of you courted." He paused as though trying to remember the exact wording. "Jonathan said he entrusted me with the first and knew he could entrust you with the last."

Annabelle briefly closed her eyes, almost able to hear the deep resonance of Jonathan's voice as he would have made that request of Brennan. "Thank you . . ."

Walking the rest of the way alone, she laid a hand over her abdomen. Still weeks away from showing, she thanked God for having brought Jonathan, and this precious baby, into her life. Looking up, she slowed her steps, swallowing against the knot in her throat. *And thank you, Lord, for also bringing* this *man into my life.*

Two brothers, so very different, yet so similar. Just like her feelings for them both.

Matthew rose at her approach and moved toward her, his back to the fire, his face cast in shadows.

She realized then what it was she'd been looking forward to about tonight. What it was she'd been anticipating. It wasn't the music or the fireworks or the food. It had been about being with *him,* and enjoying those things together.

"How's Sadie feeling?"

He glanced back at the wagon. "She's fine. She's inside, asleep."

"Have you just been sitting here all this time, by yourself?"

He nodded. "Feeling guilty?"

His voice held a smile and prompted one from her. "Maybe a little," she admitted.

"Sadie and I talked for a while. Then once she went to sleep I settled in here, enjoying the quiet and waiting for you."

Annabelle held up a hand, not sure she'd heard correctly. "You and Sadie *talked?*"

"For a while."

"Really?"

He nodded again. "Did you have a nice time at the dance?"

She didn't want to complain, especially since he'd missed it. "Yes, it was very nice."

He tilted his head in the direction where Brennan had just walked. "I should probably go talk with him about Sadie. Let him know who might be following us, just in case. I won't be long." He started in that direction.

As he passed her, Annabelle touched his arm and he stopped.

"I already told Mr. Brennan about all that, just now, as he walked me back." Guilt trickled through her at the lie, and she wished *her* face was shadowed instead of his. "I thought it would be best if he knew . . . just in case something happened, like you said."

Matthew nodded as though he understood the situation, which she knew he didn't. She needed to tell him the truth. She wanted to. She just didn't know how to go about it yet.

"Thank you for taking care of that."

"You're welcome," she whispered, surprised when he stepped closer. And even more so when he reached for her hand.

Caught off guard, she watched, speechless, as he lifted her hand to his lips and kissed her open palm. Once, twice.

A tremble moved through her.

He shifted, and the glow of firelight fell across his face. "You don't have to be nervous around me, Annabelle."

"I . . . I'm not nervous." She just couldn't breathe, that's all.

His slow smile said he begged to differ. "You're trembling."

She shook her head. "I'm . . . just chilled."

"Really?" With his other hand he touched her cheek. "You feel a mite warm to me."

She attempted a laugh, but it came out strangled-sounding. She would have thought her previous experiences with men would have dulled her to the shiver working its way up from somewhere deep inside her. She'd always been in control. Shielded. Detached. As though watching from a distance. But now . . .

She gently pulled her hand away and took a step back.

"What's wrong?"

"Nothing's wrong, Matthew. I just . . ." How could she explain this hesitance inside her? For anyone familiar with her past, it would be laughable. Yet humor was the furthest thing from her mind.

"Just what?" he asked after a moment, his smile gradually reaching his eyes.

If she didn't know better, she would've thought he was toying with her. But she *did* know better. She knew *him*. And yet she also knew that if Matthew hadn't made up his mind by now to stay in Idaho, then he hadn't grown to care for her as much as she'd hoped. And she already cared for him far too deeply.

He moved toward her. "Annabelle, I—"

Again she put distance between them.

"Why do you keep moving away from me?" His quiet voice held only question—not accusation.

She looked everywhere but at him. "I'm not moving away. I'm . . . giving us space."

"What if I said I don't want that much space between us? Not anymore." He took a step closer. "And what if I were to say I don't think you want that either?"

Her mouth slipped open. She promptly closed it, wondering what had gotten into this man. Whatever it was, she needed to stop it before it went any further. "Then I'd say I think you've been into the whiskey again, Matthew Taylor. And with no wound to blame it on this time."

He laughed, and the sound of it suddenly allowed her to breathe again.

A resounding boom echoed from the opposite side of camp, and seconds later, the night sky lit with bursts of red and white. Another pop sounded and a streak of blue shot straight up into the darkness, exploding into a thousand specks of color. The specks rained down toward the plains, never quite completing their trek.

Cheers could be heard from across the camp.

Annabelle watched the fireworks, while also keeping an eye on Matthew. He hadn't moved. Neither had she.

A final burst of color filled the sky, followed by more cheers, and then the night fell quiet around them once more.

"Did you enjoy the dancing tonight?"

She looked over at him, thankful for the momentary reprieve in which to gather her wits. "You asked me that earlier."

"No. Before, I asked you if you had a nice time *at* the dance."

She laughed softly, both confused and curious. "Surely you don't think I actually danced with anyone, Matthew."

"Just answer the question, Annabelle. Please," he added more softly.

She bowed her head for a moment. "No, I didn't really enjoy it. The music was nice, people spoke to me. . . . They were all very pleasant, but . . . the dancing wasn't my favorite part." She gave a slight shrug. "This evening just didn't turn out like I'd hoped."

A moment passed.

He extended a hand. "Would you give me a chance to change that?"

She looked at his outstretched hand, then at him as his question became clearer.

"If it helps, you know we would've danced with each other at your wedding, Mrs. McCutchens. *If* we'd been on speaking terms at the time."

That coaxed the tiniest laugh from her, but still, she knew she probably shouldn't. She looked around to see who might be watching or if others were walking back from the celebration. But she and Matthew were quite alone.

He cleared his throat. "Annabelle, I'm asking you to dance, not marry me."

The subtle sarcasm in his voice set her at ease. This was the Matthew she knew and was comfortable with. "Do you even know how to dance?"

"Can't say that I do." He brushed a finger across the top of her hands clasped at her waist and winked. "I'll make you a deal. . . . If I miss a step, I'll let you teach me."

Her mouth went dry at the look in his eyes.

She slipped her hand into his, and Annabelle quickly discovered this man didn't need any lessons. He might not have been the smoothest dancer, but Matthew Taylor knew exactly what he was doing.

Swaying in rhythm to a nonexistent tune, she followed his lead, her hand on his shoulder, his hand pressed against the small of her back.

After a while—she wasn't sure how long—he stopped, and she drew back slightly so she could see him. He seemed to want to say something, but no words came. Instead, he slowly traced his thumb along the curve of her lower lip. Then his gaze dropped to her mouth, and his silent question was unmistakable. He was asking for her permission.

She wanted to answer, but the hesitance inside her wouldn't allow it.

Apparently, he interpreted her lack of response as her answer and drew her close to dance once again. He didn't loosen his hold from before or distance himself. And when he looked down at her again, the intensity in his eyes hadn't faded. Quite the contrary.

"I can wait," he whispered.

Searching his face, she knew with calming certainty that he meant it. He pulled her closer, and with the crackle of the fire as the only accompaniment, they danced.

What was it about Matthew that touched a place inside her that no other man ever had? Not even Jonathan. And how could she be standing here now, feeling for Matthew what she should have felt for his brother? She half expected a sense of betrayal to accompany the thought. But it didn't.

She remembered telling Jonathan, just before he died, that if given the opportunity, she would have spent the rest of her life learning to love him the way she wished she could have. And she'd meant it.

"A person can't give what they haven't got."

Tears rose to her eyes as she remembered what he'd said. She'd given Jonathan all she had to give, at the time. For any other man that wouldn't have been enough. But it had been for him. And though he never saw the fruit of it, he'd planted within her heart the very thing she lacked in order to love him. Through his unconditional acceptance of her, through his loving her despite her weaknesses and brokenness, he'd taught her how to love.

She stopped dancing and drew back to look at Matthew again. She laid a tentative hand to his chest. "Is there any way you'd consider asking me that question again?"

Matthew's expression clouded. "I wish I could, but . . ." Barely above a whisper, his voice convinced her she'd missed her chance. "I just can't remember the question."

She watched a smile inch its way across his mouth. She should have known better than to have left herself open like that. A look of anticipation moved over his face that warmed her, head to toe.

He traced another path—similar to his first, feather light—across her lips. And this time, she answered without hesitation.

He kissed her, gently at first. After a moment, she couldn't help but smile, and she felt him do the same.

He pulled back slightly. "Did I miss a step somewhere?"

"Not at all," she answered softly. "I'd just like to change my

answer to your earlier question. You asked me if I enjoyed the dancing tonight, and I said it wasn't my favorite part. . . . I was wrong."

Satisfaction slipped into his eyes, leaving no doubt he knew
what she meant.

"It *has* been my favorite part." She pursed her lips. "Next to the
spiced cider, of course."

His arms tightened around her. "Well, that's real good to know,
ma'am. I've always been partial to a good cup of cider myself."

Then he cradled the back of her neck and kissed her again, more
thoroughly.

MATTHEW WATCHED AS JACK BRENNAN made his way through the crowd and toward the wagon that would serve as a makeshift platform. The distant outskirts of Boise City made a welcome backdrop. Nearly two weeks had passed since they'd met up with Brennan's group, and together, the close-knit community had endured their share of struggles along the way. The steep ascent and even more difficult descent of Big Hill had been a challenge. They'd lost two wagons when the rigging gave way and the ropes snapped, sending two wagons plunging downhill. Thankfully, no one had been seriously hurt in the accident. Though they'd still had time to travel a couple more miles that day, Brennan had insisted they camp there for the night.

Matthew saw several men stop Brennan as he approached the platform, shaking his hand or clapping him on the back. Women reached out and touched his arm, conveying their thanks.

His esteem for Brennan had steadily grown over the past couple of weeks, despite his hasty opinion formed on their first meeting. It had caught him off guard to discover that he and Brennan were so close in age. He'd expected a man with Brennan's trail experience to be a person of greater years. Someone more like Bertram Colby. And he'd have been embarrassed to admit it to anyone, but having misconstrued Brennan's initial concern for Annabelle hadn't helped his opinion of the man either. But even from that, something good had come. It had spurred him to act when he might not have.

"And just what is that smirk for?" Annabelle asked, standing beside him.

"I'm not smirking. I was . . . contemplating."

"You were too smirking." She turned to Sadie. "Wasn't he smirking?"

The barest hint of a smile touched Sadie's mouth. "Yes, Mr. Taylor, you were."

Annabelle grinned at him, giving Sadie a sideways hug. "See, I told you!"

Matthew scoffed playfully. "Ganging up on me again."

He and Annabelle had spent a lot of time together over the past few days but none of it alone. Not like the night of the dance. He remembered every detail of their kiss that night. Some days he could think of little else.

Cheers went up as Jack Brennan gained the platform. He raised his hands to quiet the crowd. But instead of growing hushed, the people cheered and clapped all the more. Brennan shook his head and laughed. He waited a moment and tried again. This time, the crowd complied with his wishes.

"Several of our number will be leaving us tomorrow, so this being our last night with all of us together, I thought I'd share a few words."

"Only a few, Jack?" came a voice from somewhere near the back.

Laughter rippled through the crowd.

"Watch out, Harley. It's not too late for me to lose you somewhere across Oregon."

That drew even more laughter, and Matthew was again impressed by the sense of community that had developed among these people and how easily Brennan fostered it. In a way, he would miss the camaraderie once they branched off tomorrow and headed farther north toward Johnny's ranch. His anticipation at seeing the land was both exciting and painfully bittersweet.

Brennan started speaking, and the quiet chatter ceased. "I appreciate each one of the families represented in this gathering tonight. You men and women . . . and children," he added, winking at someone in the front, "have done well in this journey. You've got iron in your souls and determination in your hearts." His deep voice carried over the hushed crowd. He spoke for several minutes, recalling humorous incidents that had happened along the way, reliving memorable moments, and good-naturedly ribbing a few men who tried to heckle him.

Then he paused, and his expression grew somber. "Since departing Denver that first morning, we've become more like a family and less like strangers. But we've also left behind some of those we love most dearly in this world."

Matthew experienced a tightening in his chest as he sensed what was coming.

Brennan pulled a piece of paper from his shirt pocket. "If you'll bear with me, I'd like to read the names of those we've had to say good-bye to. I'll read them in the order in which we laid them to rest."

Matthew saw Annabelle bow her head, and he did likewise. He reached for her hand and laced his fingers with hers.

"Jonathan Wesley McCutchens . . . Jewel Eloise Young . . . Imogene Elizabeth Anderson . . . Ben Everette Mullins . . ." Brennan paused between names as he read.

Matthew sensed a common thread being woven through him, Annabelle, Sadie, and everyone around them. He chanced a peek at Annabelle beside him. Her eyes were closed, her head still bowed. Tears trailed Sadie's cheeks, yet she didn't make a sound. She didn't move.

"Virginia Mae Dickey . . . Onice Dale Whitehead . . . Rayford Denton Whitehead . . . Agnes Preston Gattis . . . Charles Wilson Gattis . . ."

He'd never imagined so many had been claimed from their number. No doubt over the past few days, he'd spoken to mothers, fathers, sisters, brothers, and grandparents who were still mourning their loved one, trying to let go and move on inside even as they continued to push westward.

Brennan read the final name, folded the list, and bowed his head. Everyone did likewise. "Dearest Jesus, you know our hearts. Every pain we feel, you feel. Nothing happens to us that doesn't first filter through your loving hands. We sorely miss these loved ones we've laid to rest, and we ask, please, Lord, that you bring peace to the hearts that are hurting and guide our path to bring us Home to you."

———————

Matthew looked past Sadie, quiet on the wagon seat beside him, to Annabelle, keeping pace with them on the gelding. He peered over to check how she was holding the reins. They were looped through her fingers, just as he'd taught her. He'd been right about this becoming second nature to her.

Since parting from Brennan's group three days ago at the Snake River, the mood among the three of them had taken a more somber tone. Matthew knew where *his* tension stemmed from—having to leave soon. And he had almost convinced himself that Annabelle's reticence was rooted in the same thing, at least in part.

Twice in the last couple of days, he'd come close to confessing everything to her. Telling her about San Antonio, his debts, the bounty hunter—everything. But the lack of privacy, and mainly his lack of nerve, kept him from it. He would do it before leaving. He just needed to find the right moment.

"How much farther do you think, Matthew?" Annabelle asked.

"No more than a day. You'll be *home* sometime tomorrow." The smile he mustered felt stiff and unconvincing.

They drove longer into the day, his desire being that they'd be able to arrive at the ranch before dark the following day. As Annabelle and Sadie set about preparing dinner that night, he unharnessed the grays, led them to a nearby stream, and set them to grazing until after dinner.

When he returned, he caught the familiar aroma of Annabelle's biscuits. She and Sadie were working side by side, laughing about something. He paused by the wagon to watch Annabelle, following her movements as she bent over the fire and lifted the lid from the kettle using the hem of her apron. He rarely gave any heed to Annabelle's clothes, but he'd long noticed the curves beneath them.

At that moment, she turned. When their eyes connected, she stilled.

A slow smile curved her mouth and Matthew returned it, feeling all the while like a child having been caught with his hand in the cookie jar. Yet her manner bore no reproach over having caught him staring, and he was thankful for her understanding. He didn't see her only in *that way,* after all. He saw all of who she was. But desiring her was part of that *all.* Kathryn Jennings had challenged him to try and find some common ground with Annabelle. Considering the outcome of that request, he let out a sigh. He'd found so much more than common ground with this woman. The transformation that had taken place in her had him dazed.

"Do I have time for a quick bath in the stream?" he asked.

"If you make it fast. Then Sadie and I'll take our turns after dinner."

He grabbed the wash bucket from the wagon, along with a fresh change of clothes, and set out down the path. After he'd walked a ways downstream, he peeled off his clothes and sank into the cool water. He soaped up his hair, then dunked his head several times, noticing how long his hair had gotten since that last cut in Willow Springs. He finished bathing, shaved, dressed again, and made his way back to camp.

When he rounded the bend, he found Annabelle and Sadie waiting. Their simultaneous smiles had an unexpected effect on him, but it was the glimmer of mischief in Annabelle's expression that triggered suspicion.

His steps slowed. "What's wrong?"

"Nothing's wrong." Annabelle shrugged. "We're just glad you're back."

Sadie held out a tin pan piled high with crisp bacon, boiled potatoes, and biscuits already split and slathered with butter.

With a thank-you, he took the plate and shot a glance at Annabelle. He then looked back at Sadie, not trusting these two—especially together—in the slightest. He knew better. He studied the food, then seeing nothing unusual, lifted the tin over his head and peered beneath it.

That drew a soft chuckle from Sadie.

Annabelle giggled. "I promise you, Matthew. We didn't do anything."

"Right . . . and I'm supposed to believe you."

Annabelle's mouth dropped open. "I'm hurt. Truly." But her tone said otherwise.

He turned to Sadie. "If *you* tell me there's nothing wrong with my food, Miss Sadie, then I'll believe it."

The sweetest look of sincerity came over the girl's face. "There is nothing wrong with your food, Mr. Taylor. I give you my word."

Without hesitation, Matthew tore into a biscuit, noting the way Sadie's face lit up. "You, I trust," he said between bites. "But her"—he motioned toward Annabelle—"not a chance."

Sadie laughed full at that before getting her own plate. The sound of the girl's laughter was almost musical, and Matthew couldn't help but steal another look at her. Still baffled by their initial reaction at his arrival back to camp moments ago, he sat down to eat—and worked to hide his surprise when Sadie claimed the spot of ground next to him.

He chose not to comment, deciding to let her set whatever pace she wanted in their relationship.

They ate in silence for a while. Then Sadie set her plate aside. "We were speaking of you upon your return, Mr. Taylor. That was the reason behind our smiles." She bowed her head, her hushed voice growing even softer. "I thank you for what you did for me. You do not know me, and yet you did this. I owe you much for your kindness."

Not knowing how to respond, Matthew looked at Annabelle for direction and saw the tears in her eyes. Sadie reached out a hand toward him, stopping well shy of touching him.

Following her lead, he offered his hand to her, but palm up, letting her make the final decision.

She placed her hand in his and gave the tiniest squeeze. "I am glad you are here, Mr. Taylor."

It took a moment before Matthew could respond. "Not half as glad as I am, Miss Sadie," he whispered. "And I give you *both* my word on that."

Annabelle awakened during the night. Unable to sleep, she rolled onto her back and let her gaze wander lazily from star to star overhead. Resting her hand on her stomach, she imagined who the baby nestled inside her might favor once it was born and whether it was a boy or a girl. She hadn't experienced any other problems recently and offered up a silent prayer of thanks.

The end of December still felt like such a long way off, but she wasn't at all eager to wish away the coming months. Doubt tugged at her resolve every time she thought about being a mother to this child. Yet from continued experience with God, she was learning to trust that He would provide what she needed, when she needed it.

She heard a stirring and rose up on one elbow. Sadie lay nestled in a blanket nearby, her eyes closed. Annabelle looked across the fire at Matthew, unable to see his face, but the telling rise and fall of his chest told her he was still asleep. She stoked the waning fire and watched the flames flicker and draw new breath.

A tide of emotion swept through her that she could only describe as profound gratitude. Her breath caught in her throat as she thought back on the afternoon when she and Matthew had "just happened" to see Sadie walking down the street in the company of Mason Boyd. The odds of finding the precious girl had been stacked against them. Apparently stacked odds didn't intimidate the Almighty—and neither had the events of her past life.

The night air trembled around her. She lay back down and closed her eyes. Tears crept from their corners. None of the men she'd been with had ever apologized to her—not that she would have expected them to. Even though she'd left that life behind, she realized in that moment what a burden of unforgiveness she'd been carrying around inside her—both for them and for herself.

Emptying her lungs of air, she breathed in deeply again, filling them until she could hold no more. Her chest tingled with cool, and she felt a touch of lightheadedness. Wiping her tears, she pulled the blanket up closer around her chin.

If God could forgive someone like her of so much, surely she could do the same.

Annabelle awakened refreshed, and following breakfast she repacked the crates. A ticklish sensation flitted inside her stomach every time she imagined seeing Jonathan's land later that day. She was certain Matthew shared her eagerness. He'd been up before the sun and had worked quickly to harness the grays.

She spotted him across camp. Remembering how he and Manasseh used to sail across the range most mornings early on in their journey, she figured Matthew might welcome the chance to ride again. Especially today. When she asked him as much, he admitted that he would, so she and Sadie climbed up into the wagon and followed his lead.

Images of the ranch that Jonathan had planted in her memory kept springing to mind, and Annabelle shared them with Sadie as the morning drew on. Jonathan had been right—Idaho resembled Colorado in many ways. The mountains spanning the plains and valleys, along with the sprinkling of evergreen and pine, made her feel as though she hadn't traveled that far from home. Yet the closer they got to the town of Sandy Creek, and to her new home, the more tightly wound her nerves became.

They made Sandy Creek by noon, but as she and Matthew had previously agreed, they bypassed the town in favor of locating the ranch before nightfall.

She called to Matthew riding just ahead. "How much farther, Matthew?"

She could tell he was smiling by the curve of his cheek.

"If I had a dollar for every time you've asked me that on this trip, I'd be a much richer man."

"Just get me and Sadie to that ranch and you *will be* a much richer man."

He turned in the saddle and looked back at her. "You know, I'd almost forgotten about that."

She knew by the tone of his voice that he hadn't but decided to test him anyway. She gently nudged Sadie with her leg. "As soon as we arrive, Mr. Taylor, I'll pay you the remaining third of the money you're due."

She heard his deep chuckle.

"Yes, ma'am. You do that. And I'll take the other third in gold."

She laughed at his response, but even more at Sadie's chuckle beside her.

After they'd ridden a good hour north of Sandy Creek, Matthew stopped and motioned to his left across a narrow valley cleaved by foothills. Annabelle spotted the road veering off. She followed its path to where it disappeared in a curve shadowed by a stand of towering evergreens. She pulled the wagon beside him and reined in. The mountains rose in the distance, breathtakingly beautiful.

"Is this it?"

He surveyed their surroundings. "We've come about the right distance. According to Johnny's directions, this is it. But I don't see much. I'm tempted to ride on ahead and see what's down this road before taking the wagon."

Annabelle shook her head. "No. I want us to go together."

He tipped his hat. "Yes, ma'am. I guess that's the way I'd prefer to do it too." He winked at Sadie, then prodded the gelding forward.

Annabelle slapped the reins. The road dipped and curved, but the path was wide and gave ample room for her to maneuver the rig.

When Matthew reached the bend in the road, he moved to the right and waited for her to catch up with him before prodding Manasseh forward again. "You said you wanted to do this together."

Annabelle glimpsed her own anticipation, and nervousness, in his face.

The air beneath the canopy of evergreens was noticeably cooler and sweetened with a pungent scent. Annabelle found her hands shaking as she guided the wagon beneath the tunnel of branches.

"Just in case I haven't told you, Mr. Taylor, thank you for everything you've done for me, and for seeing me safely here." She was unable to imagine what it would be like to not see him every day, to not share his laughter.

His smile came on gradually. "It's been my sincere pleasure, Mrs. McCutchens."

When they broke into the bright sunshine again, Annabelle raised a hand to shield her eyes from the brilliant light. As her sight adjusted, she could hardly comprehend what lay before her. Surely she and Matthew had made a mistake.

CHAPTER THIRTY-FOUR

S O MUCH MORE . . . were the words that came to Annabelle's mind as she guided the wagon down the road into the sheltered valley. She regarded the scene, feeling as though she were studying a landscape from a picture book. A landscape amazingly similar to the one Jonathan had painted in her memory.

To the west, prairie grass gleamed golden brown in the slant of the afternoon sun. A breeze from the north blew across the valley, and the grasses bowed in its wake, as though a giant hand were skimming the tips of their blades. Cattle dotted the landscape. Maybe as many as three hundred head, but it was hard to tell at a glance. A barn with two corrals was positioned off to the east. Ranch hands milled about.

Then her attention was drawn to a cabin, set back into a cove of the valley, with two floors—if the dormer windows atop were real. Tears rose to her eyes. Jonathan should have been there. He should be sitting beside her right now, sharing this. He had built it all, and it didn't seem fair that he was gone while she, and their child, remained.

She felt a hand cover hers, and her eyes burned. Sadie's fingers were cool to the touch.

"All of this belonged to your Jonathan?"

"*Your Jonathan.*" She nodded, remembering when Patrick

Carlson had used that same phrase. She looked past Sadie to see Matthew astride the gelding. As though sensing her attention, he turned. Her own bundle of emotions was mirrored in the tight set of his jaw. She detected sadness, regret, and unmistakable yearning in his expression. And she couldn't help but wonder if part of his yearning was for *home*.

For what he couldn't recall of his mother. For what he'd missed with his brother. And for what he'd never known with Haymen Taylor.

With a simple nod, Matthew encouraged her to precede him down the road.

Even from a distance, Annabelle spotted an occasional ranch hand looking up. A worker would pause, then return to his task. But as they drew closer, the men stopped what they were doing and followed the wagon's progress toward the cabin. Annabelle nodded to them, feeling more than a little conspicuous. She brought the wagon to a halt in front of the cabin and set the brake. She moved to climb down, surprised to find Matthew already there, waiting to help her.

"Thank you," she whispered, wanting to say more about the moment but unable to find the words. She felt the same from him. Sadie climbed down behind her, and Matthew caught the girl's hand. Sadie moved to stand close beside them.

At the sound of a door opening, they all turned toward the cabin.

A young woman walked out onto the porch and to the edge of the stairs. "How might I help you fine people?"

Annabelle took in the woman's pleasing features and stepped forward. "Forgive me for asking like this, but is this Jonathan McCutchens' place?"

The woman studied the trio for a moment, and then her lips parted in a smile. "You must be Annabelle." Spoken like a statement, a question shone in her sun-kissed complexion.

"Yes, I am. I'm . . . Jonathan's widow."

The woman descended the stairs with the grace that Annabelle would have expected, even without knowing her. "Welcome," she said, taking both of Annabelle's hands in hers. "We've been waiting for you. My name is Shannon."

Annabelle detected a hint of an Irish heritage in the faint lilt of her voice, which perfectly companioned her thick red curls. Movement in the doorway caught her eye, and Annabelle spotted an older gentleman toddling toward them, his gaze trained on the porch steps as though they were a thing of delight.

Shannon turned and raced back up the stairs. But Matthew beat her to it. He gained hold of the elderly gentleman just before he took that first step, which, from the relief showing in Shannon's expression, would have been ill-fated at best.

"Oh . . ." Shannon sighed. "Thank you. I can't turn my back for a minute." She lovingly brushed the thinning gray hair from the man's temple. "I thought you were still napping."

"I was. But then I woke up and couldn't find you."

The old man's voice was distinctive, deeply resonating, and seemed inconsistent coming from such a frail body.

Annabelle heard a gasp.

Matthew took a half step back, his face paling.

"Matthew? What's wrong?" she asked.

But he didn't answer. He only stared at the elderly man still safe in his grip.

"Matthew? Matthew *Taylor*?" Shannon's eyes widened. "*You're* Mr. McCutchens' younger brother?"

"Yes, ma'am," he whispered, his voice hoarse.

The young woman's rosy complexion slowly lost a bit of its color as well.

Annabelle looked from Matthew to the man beside him and back again—and instinctively she knew. In Matthew's expression was a pain so deep she felt the blade of it in her own chest.

"This man . . ." he finally managed, his voice a harsh whisper, "is my father." The muscles in his jaw clenched tight. "This is Haymen Taylor."

M ATTHEW LOOKED DOWN AT THE frail man in his grip, unable to quell the anger rising inside him. Haymen Taylor was supposed to be dead. He had gladly buried his father's memory long ago—wishing he could have been there to bury the man physically.

Annabelle's face reflected both shock and compassion. Sadie's did too. But he only shared one of those emotions. He turned back to Shannon. "Johnny told me our father was gone."

"Johnny. Johnny . . ." His father mumbled the name as though trying to place who Johnny was.

Haymen Taylor's brown eyes were dimmer than Matthew remembered, and absent of their usual harshness. His father lifted his hand, and Matthew instinctively clenched his jaw. How many times had he cowered in fear when he'd seen this man's hand coming at him?

The man ran a trembling hand over Matthew's stubbled cheek. "Are you Johnny?"

Matthew briefly looked to Shannon for explanation, but she only shook her head, unshed tears rimming her eyes.

He cleared his throat, his own eyes watering. "No, sir, I'm not. I'm . . . I'm Matthew."

His father stared at him for the longest time, and Matthew

waited for recognition to move into the man's vague expression, dreading the moment it did, because he knew what he would see—familiar disappointment, and another reminder of what a failure he had been in his father's eyes.

Haymen Taylor's blank expression mellowed. He smiled pleasantly and patted Matthew's chest. "Well . . . you look like a good boy."

Stunned, Matthew couldn't think of a reply.

His father took a step back toward the door. At Shannon's nod, Matthew let go of the feeble old man.

"Why don't we all go inside and see what—" His father paused, a frown creasing his forehead.

"Shannon . . ." the woman supplied softly.

"Ah yes. And we'll see what Shannon is making for dinner."

He shuffled back inside, his steps slow and measured. He left the door standing wide open behind him.

Keeping close watch on his father as he went through the entryway, Shannon put her hand on Matthew's arm. "Whatever Mr. McCutchens told you, Mr. Taylor, he was right when he said that your father was gone. He didn't die, but he finally left us, just the same, about two years ago. And when he did, this kind gentleman came to live with us in his stead."

Matthew listened, still trying to comprehend that his father was alive. And so drastically altered.

Annabelle climbed the porch stairs, bringing Sadie with her. "When did all of this start?"

"I began coming here to help take care of your father-in-law about five years ago. He was already suffering from some memory loss. Mr. Taylor would repeat himself. Ask the same questions over and over again. He couldn't remember dates or people, and once he got lost on the property. Thankfully we found him down by the creek in the back, unharmed. Over time he became more agitated, suspicious. He started to see and hear things that weren't real." She checked on the man through the open doorway again. "He gradually worsened and could no longer feed or dress himself. Or take care of his other needs," she added quietly. "It got to be more than your brother could handle during the hours I wasn't here, so he asked that I move to the ranch and see to Mr. Taylor's needs full time."

Matthew moved to see his father standing in the hallway, gazing at a picture on the wall. He couldn't imagine Johnny having taken care of Haymen Taylor that way. Not after what the man had done to him. All they'd talked about as boys was the day they would take off and leave the old man behind.

But Johnny never had.

"Your brother was a fine man, Mr. Taylor. I've not met a more kind or generous soul." She paused. "Part of this . . . illness that your father has used to make him ramble. He'd talk for hours about the past, about your mother and both of you boys. Most of the time, none of it made much sense." She looked down briefly, then back to him. "But at other times, a great deal of it did."

Understanding softened her expression, and a sense of shame moved through him. Not that this woman knew about his childhood but that he hadn't been here to help Johnny bear this burden through the years. Johnny had suffered the greater abuse. He wasn't even Haymen Taylor's son, and yet he'd stayed. Matthew lowered his head, unable to bring himself to look at Annabelle, certain she was thinking the very same.

After dinner that evening, Matthew stood at the large window in the main room on the cabin's first floor and stared across the valley to the open plains. This was exactly the kind of ranch, and home, he and Johnny had talked about having when they were kids. It was as if his brother had traveled the West and finally found a setting that matched the wild-eyed dreams of those two young boys.

Why had Johnny not told him about all this when they saw each other last fall? He sighed. Thinking back over the conversation, he realized that Johnny had. He simply hadn't been willing to listen.

"Mind some company?" Annabelle asked, joining him at the window. For a moment, they said nothing. "It's so much more than I imagined."

He nodded, watching the sun as it raced toward the western horizon. "It's just like he described. I thought Johnny was exaggerating when he told me about this place, like he'd done with so many other things when we were kids." He focused on a spot miles out on the prairie. "He always had that way about him, seeing things, and people, as they could be, not like they were." And it was that very trait that had enabled Johnny and Annabelle to be together.

He heard Annabelle's soft sigh.

Johnny had seen in her what no other man had looked deep enough to find. Johnny had taught him so much in life, and it seemed that Matthew was still learning from his older brother, even now.

She moved closer. "How are you doing?"

He knew what she was asking and shrugged. "Just trying to make sense of it all. I can't believe my father is still alive. He's so different." He struggled, not knowing what to do with the years of anger stored up inside him. Anger at a man who no longer existed. How did a person begin to forgive someone who had done them so much wrong? Especially when that someone had never asked for forgiveness in the first place?

He recalled watching Shannon with his father during dinner that night. She looked at Haymen Taylor with an affection that Matthew had never felt for the man in his entire life, and it left him strangely bereft inside.

"What's on your mind, Matthew?"

Annabelle wove her fingers through his, and surprised by the gesture, Matthew tightened his hand around hers, thankful to have her beside him. He bowed his head, trying to put it into words. A part of him wished they were back on the prairie together, just the two of them, sitting by the fire with miles of nothing around them.

He looked down at her. "Would you like to take a walk?"

"I'd love to. Just let me tell Shannon and Sadie."

She returned a minute later. As they were leaving, Matthew reached for his rifle by the front door, and Annabelle gave him a pointed look.

"I just thought it might be wise, since we're not familiar with the countryside yet." Before she could say more, he took hold of her elbow. They descended the porch stairs, and he offered her his arm. She tucked her hand through. "What are Shannon and Sadie doing?"

"Shannon was reading your father a story, and Sadie looked like she was enjoying it as much as he was."

He was torn between gratefulness that Sadie was finding some happiness and the continued anger and regret that churned inside him. He chose a path that led them past the barn and corrals and toward the western foothills. The murmur of cattle in the fields carried to them, and the scents of hay and manure mingling with the cool evening air reminded him of being on the Jennings' ranch back in Colorado.

He estimated another half hour of daylight—and then a while longer before the low-hanging glow in the west would completely surrender to darkness. Not that he minded being in the dark with Annabelle. He was almost tempted to see if he could get them "lost" for a while just to spend more time with her.

"Are you going to remember how to get back?" A soft gleam lit her eyes as though she had read his thoughts.

He feigned hurt at the comment. "In the last nine hundred miles, have I gotten us lost once?"

She laughed. "No, you haven't. But I've learned to read you pretty well in the last few weeks."

Smiling, he slowed his steps and then stopped. "Okay, why don't you tell me what you read right now?"

She reached up and brushed back the hair from his right temple. "I see a man who's struggling with years of bitterness and hurt, who has unanswered questions that he knows might never be answered now. I see a man who's made mistakes in his life—no greater than anyone else's—and who wants to let go of all that far more than he wants to hold on to it. But he doesn't know how."

Matthew let out the breath he'd been holding for the past few seconds. He'd expected a far less serious answer. "Next time could you be a little more honest with me? Don't hold back so much."

Annabelle flashed him a knowing smile.

He motioned to a boulder jutting from the side of the mountain and jumped up first, then leaned down and pulled her up beside him.

She promptly sat down, stretched out her legs, arranging her skirt around her, and leaned back to enjoy the view. He joined her, and for several moments, they sat in silence.

She was right. He had years of questions stored up inside him, and he wanted answers. He wanted his father to apologize for what he'd done. For beating Johnny. For causing their mother such heartache. For being overly harsh and placing an unbearable weight of expectation on his youngest son's shoulders—a weight that had crippled him in many ways. And for not living in their home the tenets he had preached so ardently from the pulpit year after year after year.

"You know, Matthew, there's a question you've never asked me, and somehow I always thought you would." Annabelle hesitated, staring out across the plains, not looking at him.

He knew the question she meant, but somewhere along the way the answer to that question had grown less important to him. And the woman she'd become, far more. "How you came to be at the brothel."

She nodded.

"I wondered, especially at first. But then after that night in Parkston, in the saloon, I realized that however it had happened, you would never have chosen that life. Then when you told me about Sadie . . ." He paused, not wanting to speak the thought that was forming in his mind, for fear of what she would tell him next. "I was so angry . . . so sick inside, that I didn't ever want to imagine something like that having happened to you." And he prayed even now that it hadn't.

Though she didn't move an inch, he felt her withdrawal, and he knew the truth.

His throat tightened. She began to tell her story, and after a moment, he turned away in order to hide his reaction.

". . . And then the next morning, when the sun rose, there was a swath cut in the earth about a half-mile wide where the buffalo had churned up the ground. I wasn't ever allowed to see the bodies." Her voice had fallen to a whisper. She didn't speak for a moment. "They just told me that my parents and Alice were gone. Twelve people died in the stampede that night. Another family in the group took me in. I could tell right off the wife didn't like me, but the husband—" Her voice faltered. She blew out a breath. "He'd always been especially nice to me, along with some of the other girls."

The sick feeling in the pit of Matthew's stomach expanded. He wanted to stop her, to reach over and tell her it didn't matter. But he couldn't. Because it did.

"I traveled and lived with them until the wagons reached

Denver. They were headed to Oregon, and that's where I thought I was going too." She scoffed. "But one night the husband asked me to go into town with him." She took a breath and let it out slowly. "He said he needed me to help him carry back some supplies. By then, I already knew what kind of man he was and what he was capable of." Meaning weighted her words. "He had a foul temper, so I did what he said. We got to town that night and that's . . . that's when he told me he was leaving me there. He took me to a house and introduced me to a woman. I actually thought it was a school for girls at first." She paused again. "I know it's hard to imagine, but I really was naïve at one time."

Matthew heard the gentle sarcasm in her voice and turned back toward her. The sun had set, leaving only the faintest veil of gray light over the land. He couldn't see her expression and wondered if she was waiting for him to say something, but even if he could have thought of something to say, he couldn't push words past the knot in his throat.

"Before he left I asked him if I could follow him back and get some things from my parents' wagon. We hadn't brought any of my clothes or other things with us into town. I wanted something to remember my family by. The woman spoke up and said I wouldn't need any of those things there. But she was wrong." Her voice became weak, strangled. "I needed those things more then than I ever had before." She let out a held breath. "The man left me there, and I never saw him again."

Matthew stared at the halo of orange left by the sun's departure. "How ol—" He stumbled over the question, anger and disgust choking the words. Full well knowing this was in her past, the sudden desire to protect Annabelle was overwhelming. His heart felt as though it would pound straight through his chest. "How old were you?"

Silence lengthened and with every beat of his heart, he imagined her having been younger and younger.

"I was twelve the night my parents and little Alice were killed."

A pang tightened his gut. He'd never wanted to kill a person before. But in that moment, if given the chance, he knew without a doubt he could have killed that man for what he'd done to her, to her life.

She'd drawn her knees up to her chest. Her forehead rested against them, face hidden. Annabelle had endured far more pain and betrayal in her life than he ever had at his father's hand. Yet she didn't seem to carry a weight of bitterness inside her at the wrongs done to her—not like he did. How was that possible?

And how could there have ever been a time when he considered himself better than this woman?

"You were right, Annabelle, when you said I've made mistakes in my life." Remembering how he'd treated her when they'd first met two years ago, then again with Johnny, and at the Carlsons' home, shamed him. He'd treated her as if her life had been her choice, and he'd thrown it back in her face at every opportunity.

"If you want to talk about it, Matthew, I'm a pretty good listener. When I put my mind to it," she added with a soft laugh.

The sincerity of her voice tugged at Matthew's guilt, but not firmly enough. "Some things you have to work through on your own."

"On your own." She repeated the words back slowly, her tone gentle, yet he sensed a soft reproach in them. "There's something else I've needed, and wanted, to say to you, Matthew. Remember when you got Jonathan to admit that I didn't love him?"

Woundedness had slipped into her voice, and Matthew saw her turn toward him. He kept his focus ahead, wishing—as he had many times—that he could take back those words.

"You were right. I wished I could have loved Jonathan like a wife is supposed to love her husband. I tried, but—"

"Johnny knew how you felt about him. He said you were honest with him from the start, Annabelle. I said those things that day to hurt you." This time it was his turn to look at her. He studied her profile in the fading light, remembering what Johnny had said to him in the shack that night and wondering at the timeliness of his brother's words now. "People can't give what they haven't got. You gave him what you could, and . . . I can see now how Johnny would've loved you like he did."

She bowed her head.

He had honored Johnny's last desire in seeing her safely to this place where she could begin her new life. Johnny had started the journey, and Matthew was grateful to have been given the chance to finish it. He only wished he could stay and watch her life unfold, to be a part of it. But he couldn't offer her something he wasn't capable of giving. There was still something he had to do. A debt he had to pay.

And oddly enough, the one person who he couldn't bring himself to reveal his past to was the very woman who had given him the courage to face it.

———

On the way back to the cabin, Annabelle waited for him to say something. Anything. But as they passed by the barn, Matthew still hadn't so much as whispered a word. And since rising from the rock and briefly helping her down, he hadn't touched her either.

She had calculated the risk in telling him the details about her past, but she'd felt an inner prompting to share it and had convinced herself he wouldn't hold it against her. Not after everything they'd been through. And she honestly didn't think he held it against her now. It was more than that—something deeper. By the time they made it back to the cabin, she had decided what it was.

She remembered his sickened expression when she'd first told him about Sadie, and that same look had crossed his face tonight when he had helped her down from the rock. Matthew still cared for her, she was certain of that. He simply couldn't look at her the way a man looked at a woman—not with knowing what he knew.

He'd even said as much. *"I can see now how* Johnny *would've loved you like he did."* How *Johnny* had loved her . . . but not Matthew.

When he opened the front door of the cabin, their eyes connected for the briefest of seconds. Then he looked away and turned back inside himself. He motioned for her to precede him, and Annabelle felt the gap between them widen.

Shannon met them in the front hallway. "So you did manage to find your way back. I was beginning to wonder." A smile lit her face.

When Matthew didn't answer, Annabelle jumped in. "Yes, we did, thank you. We walked all the way down to the edge of the property, by the big rock."

Shannon opened her mouth, then closed it and nodded. "Well, good, I'm glad." She motioned down the hallway. "Mr. Taylor has retired for the night, and I'm going to do the same. Sadie's still up reading in the front room. Your beds are made and ready for you. You know where my bedroom is, so please knock if you need anything. And Mrs. McCutchens . . ."

Annabelle smiled at the formal address. Twice this afternoon she'd encouraged the young woman to call her by her given name, but apparently it hadn't swayed Shannon's determination.

"You've already had a caller this evening."

Annabelle managed a casual tone. "Really?"

"I didn't think you'd be this long, so I asked him to wait in the front parlor. He stayed for a while and then left. Said he'd be back tomorrow. His name was . . . Mr. Caldwell, I believe."

Annabelle's stomach went cold. She sensed Matthew's tension but didn't look at him.

"Did he say what he wanted?" Matthew asked. "Or who he was?"

Annabelle cringed inwardly at Matthew's questions, then remembered the rifle in his hand. Had he suspected something already? And worse, why would Rigdon Caldwell come to see her *here*? That wasn't part of their agreement.

"No, he didn't give any details. Just that he wanted to speak with Mrs. McCutchens."

Annabelle moved toward the stairs. "I bet he's from the bank in town. I think I'll head there first thing in the morning and see if I can catch him."

"I'll go into town with you." Matthew's tone said he wouldn't brook any argument, so Annabelle gave none.

Shannon said good-night and started down the hall. "I'll have breakfast ready for you by six-thirty."

Annabelle was halfway up the stairs when she remembered Sadie. She turned back to find Matthew still standing at the base of the stairs, watching her.

"I'm leaving tomorrow, Annabelle. After I see you safely into town and then back here."

She gripped the banister and slowly descended, stopping on the last step, standing at eye level with him. "Leaving? For where? Will you be back?"

He didn't answer for a moment, and she found herself praying he would tell her the truth. About his past, about his feelings for her . . . or lack thereof.

He shook his head. "I don't know."

She searched his eyes, looking for a clue as to what lay behind his carefully guarded expression, and hoping for one that would disprove her suspicion about his not seeing her the same way anymore. She had read him so easily before—why couldn't she now?

"Would you come back, Matthew . . . if you could?"

A frown shadowed his features. "I wish I could undo the past, Annabelle . . . but I can't." He lowered his head, then slowly looked back at her. "Thank you for sharing with me what you did tonight. I know that wasn't easy. And I'm—" He paused. "I'm sorry for what you've been through."

Biting the inside of her cheek, she nodded, his answer confirming her earlier suspicion. Loneliness swelled inside her. Stepping past him, she went to check on Sadie.

CHAPTER THIRTY-SIX

MATTHEW BOLTED UPRIGHT IN BED. Heart racing, senses alert, he gripped the rifle beside him, cocked it, and searched the shadowed corners of his room. Waiting. Listening. He heard it again.

A muted thump.

He pulled on his pants, grabbed the rifle, and opened the door. The hallway was dark. The door to Annabelle and Sadie's room was closed, and the crack beneath it was absent of any glow. He slowly opened the door. Seeing the prone outlines of their bodies on the bed, he pulled it closed again.

He peered down the staircase leading to the first floor, the set of stairs resembling a dark hole from where he stood. Pressing back against the wall, he began the descent, easing his weight on each stair in hopes of avoiding a creak. Halfway down, he saw a shadow cross at the base of the stairs. His heart beat double time.

Caldwell was the foremost suspect in his mind. Annabelle may have thought the man who'd visited that night was from the bank, but Matthew's gut told him different. He didn't know how the man had traced them here, but he was betting it was the bounty hunter he'd glimpsed first in Willow Springs and then again at the post office in Rutherford. Concern shuddered through him as he wondered how the man had learned Annabelle's name and why he was trying to contact her.

Matthew eased his weight onto the next to last step, stopping when a creak sounded beneath his bare foot. A single bead of sweat wove a path down his spine. When he heard movement in the main room off to his left, he bypassed the last step and padded silently to the front hallway.

He tightened his grip on the rifle. He didn't plan on shooting the man—that had never been his intent. He only hoped to buy some time to talk to him. Maybe persuade him to work out a deal, as if he had anything left to bargain with. Matthew pressed back against the wall behind him.

Taking a deep breath, he rounded the corner and saw the man standing in the threshold of the kitchen. He was staring straight at him.

"Pa?" The name was out of Matthew's mouth before he could fully process it.

"Who goes there?"

His father's deep voice sounded so authoritative that, if Matthew hadn't known better, he might have been intimidated. He gently released the hammer on the rifle, set the safety, and laid the gun aside.

"It's me, sir. It's Matthew." As if that would tell his father anything.

Sure enough, his father's expression remained a blank slate.

"I'm the man you met this afternoon." Matthew crossed to the woodstove, opened the side door, and stoked the warm embers. They flickered to life again.

"Ah ... you're the young one who wouldn't let me use the stairs!"

His father's voice gained a reprimanding tone Matthew had once been accustomed to hearing. Strange to hear it now and not feel that old sense of wariness. Using a piece of kindling, he lit the oil lamp on the kitchen table. Instantly, a warm glow blanketed the kitchen.

"What brings you down here in the middle of the night, sir?"

"Why do you keep calling me *sir*?"

"Does it bother you?" His father had always demanded it of both him and Johnny, and had threatened the leather strap when they forgot.

His father harrumphed. "I guess not too much."

An unexpected smile came at his father's response. "Are you hungry, sir?" He moved to the pantry and opened the door.

"No. I came looking for Laura. I woke up and she was gone again."

Matthew stilled at hearing his mother's name. "Laura is gone, sir."

"Well, I know she's gone!" Agitation sharpened Haymen Taylor's voice. "That's why I'm looking for her!"

Matthew shook his head. "No, sir, I don't mean gone like that. What I mean is she's deceased. Laura died over twenty-five years ago."

"Why that's the most fool thing I've ever—" Instantly, the frown on his father's face fell away, only to have sadness follow on its heels. He lowered his head; his frail shoulders began to shudder as he wept. "Is that why I can't find her?"

Afraid his father might crumple where he stood, Matthew helped him into a chair. He couldn't remember what his parents had been like together, but this outpouring of emotion wasn't at all consistent with the man he'd known before.

Matthew reached out to comfort his father, then stopped himself. Images of earlier years spent with this man passed before him, and none of them were pleasant. As his father's sobs shook his feeble body, they tore through those old memories, and Matthew bent down and put an arm around his father's shoulders.

His sobs gradually quieted. "I just wanted to tell her I'm sorry. I haven't been a very good husband to her of late."

Not knowing what else to do, Matthew nodded and listened.

After a moment, his father wiped his nose on the sleeve of his nightshirt and stood. "Do you need help getting something to eat? I just came down here for a bite myself."

Matthew was hardly able to keep up with the shift in conversations. "Yes, sir. I was thinking of making myself a sandwich from some of the roast left over from dinner. Interested?"

"Sounds mighty good to me."

Matthew made a sandwich, cut it into two pieces, and sat down at the table with his father. He picked up his half and started to take a bite when his father cleared his throat. Matthew looked up.

"Aren't you forgetting something?"

Immediately, Matthew felt all of six years old again. He bowed his head and, with effort, reached across the table for his father's hand. When his father didn't pray, he did. "Thank you, Lord, for this food and for this company. Bless us and keep us safe through the night." He paused. "And please let Laura know we miss her."

He finished praying and lifted his head only to find his father staring straight at him. Noting the marked changes that time and illness had left there, it struck Matthew that a different man dwelled behind those eyes now.

Haymen Taylor slowly nodded. "You did good."

It took Matthew a moment to answer. "Thank you, sir," he whispered, then sat and watched his father eat for a moment before starting himself.

After they finished, Matthew walked him back down the hallway to his room and helped him into bed. Waiting to make sure his father didn't decide to take another late-night jaunt, he stood outside the room, the door open, until he heard the man's gentle snoring.

"The mind is an amazing—and frightening—thing, isn't it?"

He turned to see Shannon standing in the doorway to her bedroom a short distance down the hall.

He nodded. "How do you know when he gets up during the night?"

She gestured toward the door beside him, where bells were affixed to the latch.

"Once you put the rifle down, you did a fine job, Mr. Taylor." Shannon smiled. "I didn't have the heart to interrupt."

He laughed softly. "My nerves are a little jumpy tonight, I guess."

Matthew felt a prick of guilt when remembering she'd been taking care of his father all this time. He imagined Johnny seeing to his father's needs all those years too—caring for the man who had inflicted the welts on his back.

"I've been fortunate to be able to take care of your father, Mr. Taylor."

Her comment caught him off guard. "Fortunate? How's that?"

"In caring for him, in watching his memory diminish, I've gotten a glimpse of what forgiveness must be like from God's perspective."

He didn't answer, not quite following.

"When God forgives, He wipes the slate clean, so to speak. Something you and I don't have the power to do. I'm not sure whether He really doesn't remember our sins anymore, or whether He just chooses not to hold them against us." She shrugged. "Either way, I've learned to appreciate that more in recent years." She paused, then nodded toward the door again. "If you'll close the door, I'd appreciate it. That way I'll hear him if it happens again." She went back to her room, leaving her door ajar.

Matthew retrieved the rifle on his way back to bed, but sleep didn't come quickly. For a long time, he lay awake dwelling on the words his father had spoken to him. Words he'd waited over thirty-two years to hear.

"You did good."

MATTHEW AWAKENED THE NEXT MORNING, surprised when he saw sunlight edging through a crack in the curtains. He pushed from bed, his head fuzzy from too little sleep. He dressed quickly and packed his saddlebags, thinking about what the day held. He was doing the right thing in returning to San Antonio, in choosing to face up to what he'd done. He only hoped he could convince Señor Antonio Sedillos to listen before meting out punishment. Mercy wasn't a trait the man was known for.

Matthew opened the bedroom door and spotted a note on the floor. He bent to pick it up, already recognizing the handwriting.

Dear Matthew,

I've left something for you on the table in the hallway. I found it late last night and thought you should have it. I've gone into Sandy Creek and will be back as soon as I can. Please don't leave before I return.

Warmly,
Annabelle

P.S. I borrowed Manasseh.

Don't leave before I return? Borrowed Manasseh? That fool woman! He'd told her last night he'd go into town with her. Warning stole through him knowing that Sedillos' man was somewhere close by and that Annabelle was alone in town. Sedillos was the type of man who would use whatever advantage was available.

Saddlebags in hand, he strode across the hall, grabbed what she'd left for him, and raced downstairs and out the front door.

"Good morning, Mr. Taylor," a ranch hand greeted as he entered the stable.

Matthew couldn't remember meeting the man. Word sure traveled fast around here. "I need a horse," he said, winded from the run.

"Yes, sir. Right away, sir. Mrs. McCutchens took the tan geld—"

Matthew raised a hand. "Yes, I'm aware of that. Do you know how long ago she left?"

The man pulled a saddle from the rack. "About an hour ago, I'd guess. Maybe a bit more."

Matthew exhaled through clenched teeth. He watched the man expertly saddle a black mare, willing him to work faster, yet knowing he couldn't have done it any faster himself. He glanced down at the worn leather book in his grip, then opened the front cover.

His brother's name was written on the inside, right below his mother's. He gathered the pages in his right hand and fanned them with his thumb. As they flipped by, he saw scribbles in the margins, and places where the text had been underlined. Twice. Apparently Johnny and their mother had given this Bible a great deal of use.

Matthew tucked it into his saddlebag, then slipped his left boot into the stirrup, vowing he would do the same. If he lived through this.

———

"I appreciate your coming in so soon following your arrival, Mrs. McCutchens." Mr. Hoxley waited by her chair until she was seated, then moved behind the massive pine desk that dominated the room.

"It's no trouble at all. I'm happy to make the time." Annabelle glanced at the clock on his bookshelf. Surely Matthew had found her note by now. She could well imagine his reaction at finding her—and his horse—gone. But taking the gelding had been the only way she could make certain he didn't leave before she completed her business in town.

For a moment last night, she'd thought he was finally going to tell her about the gambling debts, but then he hadn't. Stubborn, foolish man! Over the past weeks, Matthew had learned to extend grace, but he hadn't learned how to accept it yet.

"I brought the documents from the bank in Willow Springs with me." She laid them on Mr. Hoxley's desk.

The leather chair creaked as he leaned forward to take them. He skimmed the pages. "Your journey from Colorado to Idaho was pleasant, I trust?"

Though *pleasant* hardly began to describe the experience, Annabelle mentally cataloged the events of past weeks and nodded. "Yes, it was. Thank you, sir."

"A Pastor . . . um . . ." Mr. Hoxley traced his finger down a file that lay open on the side of his desk. "A Pastor Carlson confirmed your late husband's passing with the bank in Willow Springs, and also provided them with a letter Mr. McCutchens had addressed to him. That letter, along with one we received here at the bank, served as your late husband's last will and testament. Mr. McCutchens was thorough and straightforward in his wishes, ma'am."

Annabelle sat a bit straighter at mention of the second letter. "Mr. Hoxley, do you still have that letter, by chance?"

"Why, of course. We added it to your file. Here it is."

Jonathan's instructions had been brief. The letter simply stated that upon his death, all of his worldly possessions were to pass to her. In her entire life, she'd never owned anything, never had security of any kind, and now to have all this. She lifted the letter to read the document affixed to it.

Her focus immediately went to the second line on the page. *Annabelle Grayson McCutchens.*

Then just as quickly, she noted the entry preceding it. A heavy line had been drawn through Jonathan's name directly above hers. She followed the length of the row across the columns on the page, and something inside her gave way. She stared at his name and tears rose to her eyes. With one stroke of a pen, all that Jonathan had labored for, all that he and Matthew had dreamed about, became hers.

She wiped her cheek and held the documents out to the banker.

"Actually, I need you to sign right there by your name." He handed her a quill and moved the bottle of ink closer. "Your signature will complete the transfer of ownership."

After glancing again at the name above hers, Annabelle signed.

Mr. Hoxley gathered the documents and eased his chair back from the desk. "Is there anything else I can help you with today, Mrs. McCutchens?"

She glanced at the clock again, her pulse gaining momentum. "Yes, sir. There's one more item of business we need to discuss."

———————

Matthew reined in the black mare in front of the bank and dismounted. Inside, he scanned the room for her.

A woman approached from a side office. "May I help you, sir?"

Matthew forced a calm he didn't feel. "Yes, I'm looking for a woman . . . a Mrs. Jonathan McCutchens. She had business here this morning, and I'm hoping to catch her."

"I didn't meet with anyone by that name, but perhaps someone else did. I'll check for you."

"Thank you, ma'am, I'd appreciate that."

She walked away, and Matthew turned to look out the front window. As people passed on the boardwalk outside, he searched their faces, praying to see Annabelle's among them. Standing at the edge of the window afforded him a better view down the street. Someone at the far end of the boardwalk caught his eye. But just then a freight wagon rounded the corner, crowding the thoroughfare and making it impossible to see. He moved down a couple of feet and stepped closer to the window.

He went cold inside.

He strode outside to the mare and unsheathed his rifle. Opting for the road instead of the congested boardwalk, Matthew made his way past the freight wagon and other wagons caught behind it, past carts and livestock, to the corner.

He only thought he'd spotted Annabelle. But he was positive he'd seen the bounty hunter.

He peered through windows of businesses as he passed. A barbershop, a land and title company. His steps slowed outside Haddock's General Store, and he scanned the crowded aisles. Nothing. Standing on the corner, he searched down the street to his left, then to his right. On impulse, he headed west.

He passed a newspaper office, dress shop, and haberdashery. If anything happened to Annabelle because of this, he didn't know what he would do. *God, don't let her pay for my mistakes. Let me stand accountable. But please . . . not her.*

He started to head in the other direction, then stilled.

There she was, entering a hotel a ways down the street. Heart pounding, he crossed the avenue and peered through the side of the front window. The lobby was clear. He stepped inside. Her voice carried to him from a side hallway.

Another patron approached the front desk, and Matthew seized the opportunity to scoot across the lobby and around the corner. A door was closing at the far end of the hall. He slowly started toward it, checking behind him as he went. Reaching the room, he leaned close, listening. Then he gently tried the knob.

It turned without complaint.

Nerves taut, he drew a last prayerful breath and flung open the door.

ANNABELLE STOOD TO MATTHEW'S RIGHT, facing him.
She stared, unflinching, and the disturbing sense that she'd been expecting him skittered across his nerves. The click of a chamber loading registered a fraction before he felt the barrel against his left temple.

"Put down the gun, Mr. Taylor."

Annabelle winced, then nodded, as though telling him to do as he'd been asked. The lack of surprise in her expression confirmed his former suspicion. He turned slightly to see behind him, but a firm nudge from the steel shaft encouraged him to face forward again.

Rifle in his left hand, he raised his right. "Okay, I'm putting it down."

He bent forward slowly, scanning his surroundings as he laid the rifle on the floor. A bed, a table, a desk and chair in the corner. He stood up, watching Annabelle for a sign. A slight nod or a telling look—anything that would help him figure out what was going on.

Her eyes connected with his but revealed nothing.

If he had been alone, he might have tried something. But not with her here. His thoughts went to the child inside her. He heard the door latch behind him.

"Cross the room and stand beside Mrs. McCutchens."

He hesitated.

"Now!"

The blunt barrel pressing against his back was persuasive enough. Once beside her, Matthew slowly turned, and discovered he'd guessed correctly. "Please, let Mrs. McCutchens go. Your business is with me, not with her."

"Actually, my business used to be with you, Taylor." A slow smile pulled at the man's mouth. "Now it *is* with her."

Matthew's gut twisted remembering the story Annabelle had told him last night. Imagining the sick fear she must be experiencing at this moment, he reached over for her hand, then angled his body in front of hers. He would die before he let this man touch her.

His hand found hers. She took his gently, not gripping in fear. He turned and looked at her. She seemed more remorseful than frightened.

"Annabelle?" he whispered.

Tears rose to her eyes. "Matthew, this is Mr. Rigdon Caldwell." She indicated the man holding the gun. "He's been tracking you since you left Texas."

"I know," Matthew admitted, feeling the weight of guilt on his shoulders. "I never could bring myself to tell you before, Annabelle." The shame he felt at her knowing about him was nothing compared to his need to see her safe. He should have told her a long time ago. If anything happened to her ...

"This is all real nice, you two, but I've got to be in Boise City by nightfall."

Matthew took a step toward Caldwell. "I'll go with you, and I'll go without a fight. Just as long as Mrs. McCutchens can go free, and unharmed."

Caldwell's attention shifted between the two of them, finally settling on Annabelle. "Ma'am? I'm runnin' out of time. Not to mention patience."

Matthew trailed Caldwell's gaze back to Annabelle.

Her hand tightened around his. "Matthew, I don't know how to tell you this, so I'll just say it straight out. The night that you went into that gaming hall for Sadie ... as soon as you went inside, Mr. Caldwell approached me on the street. He didn't hurt me," she said quickly, as though aware of the rush of protectiveness filling him at that moment. "He just talked to me and—"

"And told you about what I'd done." Matthew tried to put a word to the emotion he saw moving into her eyes.

She winced slightly. "Actually . . . I've known about that since that night in Parkston. I saw your picture hanging on the wall in the back room with the bartender."

Unable to respond, Matthew stared as her meaning sank in. She'd known all along. . . .

"Mrs. McCutchens, Mr. Taylor."

In unison, they both looked back across the room, and let go of each other's hands.

"Ma'am, you strike a hard bargain, but it's been a pleasure to do business with you. Mr. Taylor, no need to keep checking over your shoulder anymore. Not for me, anyway. Consider your account with Señor Sedillos settled, and he sends his gratitude for turning in Mason Boyd." Caldwell moved toward the door, stopping to bend down and pick up Matthew's rifle. He released the hammer, unloaded and pocketed the cartridges, and put the gun on the bed. "Just in case you're the kind of man who carries a grudge." He closed the door behind him when he left.

Matthew was still sorting through all the details of what had just happened. "All this time, you knew," he whispered, both astonished and a bit irritated. "And you never said a thing. You let me go mile after mile after mile, looking over my shoulder, not sleeping at night, anxious every time we went into a town."

Her hands were knotted at her waist. "Yes," she answered softly.

Strangely, only now did she appear afraid, after all they'd been through. "Where did you get the money?" As though he needed to ask.

"I took a loan against the ranch." She reached for something on the desk behind her and held it out. Her hand trembled. "This belongs to you."

The struggle mirrored in her expression unnerved him. He took the piece of paper and unfolded it, curious. He read it, then looked back at her. "What do you think you're doing?"

"When I saw that document this morning, I realized that, from the start, Jonathan intended to share this with you. Not with me.

Why do you th—" She cleared her throat, a frown forming. "Why do you think there are two large bedrooms upstairs—identical to each other?"

"Annabelle . . ." He reached for her.

She pulled away, putting up a hand. "I saw the way you looked at me last night, Matthew. After I told you . . . about how I . . ." She blinked, and tears fell. "I know you can't look at me in that way anymore."

Matthew brushed away a tear, knowing how wrong she was. "Can't look at you in what way?" He moved closer. "Like I'm look-ing at you right now? Annabelle," he whispered, "if you sensed any-thing from me last night, it was me wishing that I could go back and change things for you, make them right."

"But that's just it. You can't change things, Matthew. What happened . . . happened. I can't erase any of it."

"And I'm not asking you—"

She pointed to the document in his hand. "If you'll just sign there on that line, that will make it official."

He scanned the sheet again, dwelling on the heavy mark striking through the first entry that contained Johnny's name . . . as well as his. His throat tightened. When Johnny originally filed the deed, he had listed Matthew as co-owner. All those dreams they'd had as boys, Johnny hadn't forgotten.

Annabelle's name and signature were on the next line and had also been crossed through. Underneath that, the name Matthew Haymen Taylor had been written in. He recognized Annabelle's handwriting.

She took a deep breath and let it out. "I took some money out for me and Sadie. Not much, but enough for the two of us to get settled. I think Jonathan would have wanted that, under the circumstances."

Matthew stared at the deed, taking in what she'd done. This foolish . . . good-hearted woman.

She motioned toward the quill and ink bottle on the desk.

"You're sure this will make the transfer of the ranch legal and binding? There's nothing else we'll need to do?" Waiting for her response, he watched the emotions play across her face. Any remaining doubt he had about the kind of woman Annabelle

Grayson McCutchens was fell away completely in that moment.

"Yes, I already spoke with the man at the bank this morning."

Satisfied, he leaned down to use the top of the desk, then returned the quill to its holder. Annabelle reached for the paper, but he pulled it back slightly, sighing as he did. "You knew about me but you never said a thing. You never gloated, you never threw it back in my face. You didn't remind me over and over about what I'd done wrong . . . even though that's exactly what I did to you."

A frown shadowed her lovely brow. He resisted the urge to smooth it away and held out the paper instead. She stared at him for a second, then lowered her eyes to the page. He knew the moment she understood what he'd done.

She gave a small gasp. "You're not serious. . . ."

He closed the distance between them. "Would I write it in ink if I wasn't serious, Mrs. McCutchens?"

A single arched brow said she knew what he was doing, and a hint of a smile said she had sufficiently recovered from her surprise.

"So . . . do I get an answer now?" He glanced back at the closed door. "Or do I have to sweep in and rescue you again?"

That drew a laugh, as he'd anticipated. "Oh, please, not that! I'm afraid if you keep trying to rescue me, you're going to get us both kill—"

He put a finger to her lips, remembering the incident at the saloon in Parkston. On impulse, he leaned down and kissed her right cheek, most leisurely, three times—then drew back. "Just give me your answer, Mrs. McCutchens. Please," he added softly.

Her eyes gained a sparkle. She held up the document and read from it. " 'Matthew Haymen Taylor and Annabelle Grayson McCutchens, equal partners.' I like the sound of that."

Matthew laid the deed aside and gently drew her against him, aware that she came without the least hesitation. "I'm making that offer on one condition."

"And what condition would that be?"

"That you'll be open to exploring future partnership opportunities of a more . . . personal nature." Already having seen the answer in her eyes, he traced the curve of her lips with his forefinger.

"Why, Mr. Taylor, are you asking me to dance?"

He smiled, remembering that night on the prairie. "In a manner of speaking . . ." He brushed the hair back from her right temple and slowly kissed the length of the scar there, willing whatever wounds were left inside her to be made whole and asking that God might somehow use him to help. "Yes, ma'am, I guess I am."

Once she opened her eyes, she searched his face. "And if I miss a step, will you teach me?"

Matthew cradled the back of her neck, hearing both the playfulness and seriousness of her request. "How 'bout we just take things slow and agree to learn together?"

"I'll match whatever pace you set, Mr. Taylor," she whispered, smiling. "I do believe we have ourselves a deal."

A C K N O W L E D G M E N T S ❧

One name may grace the cover of a book, but its contributors are many. To the following, I offer my sincerest thanks.

To Jesus, your endless grace and mercy sustain me. To Joe, your wonderful wit has made these past twenty-one years and counting such a joy. I look forward to many more! To Kelsey, your vibrant spirit is a reflection of Christ and a blessing to all who know you—your mom most of all. To Kurt, your tender heart reveals a man of God and makes this mother proud. To Doug and June Gattis, your enthusiasm inspires me. What a blessing to have parents who are also dear friends. To Dr. Fred Alexander, my father-in-law, you donned your editor's cap to read the final galleys, and your comments and catches were stellar, as expected. Thanks for being one of my greatest (and most humble) encouragers.

To Deborah Raney, you read all my words and make them, and me, so much better. I'm so glad you're always just a click away. To the *CdA Women*, your fingerprints of creativity and humor are all over this book. To Judy Hicks, your knowledge about horses is invaluable, as is your friendship. To Suzi Buggeln, you add such sparkle to my life. Thanks for brainstorming *Remembered* (Book 3) with me at Red Robin. To Virginia Rogers, your insightful comments helped to shape this story early on, and really encouraged me. To the women at Journey, your prayers and kind support continually renew my strength. To Karen Schurrer, your gift with words makes all the difference in my writing, and our shared laughter . . . well, all the difference in my day. To my Bethany House family, partnering with you is pleasure in the purest sense.

To my readers, your responses to *Rekindled* have encouraged me more than you can possibly know. I love our exchanges and look forward to meeting you face-to-face. And finally, for those who have lost their purity or had it taken from them as Annabelle and Sadie did, there *is* a place where innocence is restored—His name is Jesus.

———

TAMERA ALEXANDER is a bestselling novelist whose works have been awarded or nominated for numerous honors, including the Christy Award, the RITA Award, and the Carol Award. After seventeen years in Colorado, Tamera and her husband have returned to their native South and live in Tennessee, where they enjoy spending time with their two grown children.

Tamera invites you to visit her at:

Her Web site   www.tameraalexander.com
Her blog   www.tameraalexander.blogspot.com
Twitter   www.twitter.com/tameraalexander
Facebook   www.facebook.com/tamera.alexander

Or if you prefer snail mail, please write her at the following postal address:

Tamera Alexander
P.O. Box 871
Brentwood, TN 37024

More Historical Fiction From Bethany House

Lauraine Snelling Returns to Red River
After graduating in May of 1900, Andrew Bjorklund and Ellie Wold make plans to marry once the harvest is over and their new house is finished in Blessing, North Dakota. When tragedy strikes, will they be able to keep their faith when the life they looked forward to is now unraveling?

A Promise for Ellie DAUGHTERS OF BLESSING #1 by Lauraine Snelling

Laugh-Out-Loud Historical Fiction
Ruth Caldwell has always tried to live up to her mother's expectations of what a lady should be…often with less than impressive results. When she's forced to journey west to meet the father she's never seen, she hopes that this might be the place she'll finally fit in. But her arrival brings about more mayhem than even Ruth is used to.

Letter Perfect by Cathy Marie Hake

New From the Author of *A Bride Most Begrudging*
Rachel van Buren arrives in Gold Rush San Francisco with two wishes: to protect her younger siblings and to return east as soon as possible. However, both goals prove more difficult than she could imagine. But Rachel won't give up without a fight, and soon all will learn an eloquent and humorous lesson about what truly makes a lady.

Measure of a Lady by Deeanne Gist

In the Tradition of Janette Oke and Beverly Lewis
After losing her family to illness, Summer Steadman seeks employment in a small Mennonite community. Widower Peter Ollenburger hires her to teach his young son, believing she is the answer to his prayers. He soon discovers, however, that helping this outsider may have troublesome consequences.

Waiting for Summer's Return by Kim Vogel Sawyer

Be the first *to know*

Want to be the first to know
what's new from
your favorite authors?

Want to know all about
exciting new writers?
